A GOOD WOMAN

Lisa Appignanesi has been a university lecturer in European Studies and was Deputy Director of London's Institute of Contemporary Arts. Her works of non-fiction include *Freud's Women* (with John Forrester), a biographical portrait of Simone de Beauvoir, and a history of cabaret. She has edited *The Rushdie File* and a number of books on contemporary culture, as well as producing various films for television. Appignanesi is also the author of four works of fiction, including *The Dead of Winter*. *A Good Woman* is her third novel. Lisa Appignanesi lives in London with her two children.

LISA APPIGNANESI

A Good Woman

McArthur & Company

Toronto

For my mother, Hana
and my daughter, Katrina

Extracts from 'Law Like Love' by W.H. Auden
reprinted by kind permission of Faber and Faber Ltd

First published by HarperColins*Publishers* 1996
This edition published in 1999 by McArthur & Company
Copyright © Lisa Appignanesi 1996

Canadian Cataloguing in Publication Data
Appignanesi, Lisa
     A good woman
Canadian ed.
ISBN 1-55278-070-8
I. Title.
PR6051.P616G66 1999   823'.914   C98-933103-2

Set in Linotron Galliard by
Rowland Phototypesetting Limited,
Bury St Edmunds, Suffolk

Printed in Canada

McArthur & Company
322 King Street West, Suite #402,
Toronto, Ontario M5V 1J2

10 9 8 7 6 5 4 3 2 1

'One's real life is often the life
one does not lead'   OSCAR WILDE

For all their help with the days and ways of the law and of France, I am very grateful to John Forrester, Helena Kennedy QC, Hervé Landry, Elisa and Jean-François Rebérioux and Roger Salloch. Needless to say, they bear no responsibility for the uses their advice has been put to.

PART ONE

I would have liked this story to have a happy ending. You know the kind I mean: soft morning light, the couple arm-in-arm walking into a distance beckoning with future promise, the past eradicated. It's not like that. Though sometimes I think the future I'm in is that happiness. You'll have to judge. It's all finally a matter of perspective. And the perspective is what I'm trying to find.

It was when I realised that people were taking everything I said seriously that I knew I had to leave New York. I had entered the second minute of my fifteen minutes of fame and I could have mumbled the most bizarre nonsense – 'today I bought a pound of bananas' – and the sentence would have been scrutinised for its deeper significance and seen as a step on the road to a good life. And then something else happened which made leaving imperative.

I am not cut out to be a public figure. Quite the contrary. My talents, such as they are and I'm well acquainted with them, find their fullest expression behind the scenes. It was the purest accident that I had stumbled into the limelight where I didn't belong. And I ran from it. Ran fast and far. All the way to what some might have considered my home.

Home is where this story begins.

⚖ 1

Paris is all sky, a cold bright blueness which rinses stone white and attacks the eyes. Only the placid nymphs in the fountains of the Concorde seem immune to it. So they should be. They have sat watching weather and traffic, hurtling clouds and endless processions, for well over a century. I, on the other hand, need my dark glasses. For more reasons than I care to think of.

But I take them off in the plush gloom of the Hotel Intercontinental. From behind the reception counter, a man with impeccable hair and smile addresses me politely.

'*Bonjour, Madame. Vous avez reservé, Madame?*'

I nod, give him my name, or at least the name that came to my lips when I made this booking at the airport. 'Maria d'Esté'. It is my mother's name. Why have I chosen to use it?

I write the letters with an untried flourish in the hotel register. My nails against the white paper are a perfect, unchipped carmine. The body is oddly resilient.

It is my turn to smile politely as the man scans my passport, takes in the discrepancy between Maria Regnier and the name in the register, settles on the photograph with almost tangible relief. I can see the fantasies mounting behind his eyes, the illicit bodies taking shape on crumpled sheets, the irate husband or wife at the door, the divorce detective inspecting the register. Indeed, I catch him sneaking a glance at my hand, in pursuit of the telltale ring. I have not known so many men for nothing.

'*Vous restez combien de nuits?*' he asks me.

I balk at this. I have no idea how long I am staying. Two nights, three, six, seven . . . I point imperiously at my three overburdened cases. The remains of my life stuffed into worn leather. 'Have these taken up to my room,' I tell him. '*J'ai un rendez-vous.*' And though I have no one to meet, I know that I need to get out there into the

5

glaring blue of the streets, if only so that I can learn to be as unruffled as those stone nymphs.

As I turn on my heel, I give him the polite smile again. My mother taught it to me, I now remember – that quick arching of the lips, that *'Bonjour, Monsieur'* and *'Merci, Madame'*, that little nod, a short cut to a bow, endlessly repeated at the butcher's and the baker's, in all shops and public places large or small. At least once a day for the length of my childhood, she reiterated the value of social correctness.

☖ 2

This is my mother's city. I left it when I was eighteen and have not set foot in it for some fourteen years. I had never intended to return. Memories of it neither haunted me nor seduced me. Yet I have come here now.

I walk through the columned arcades which flank the Tuileries Gardens and stare desultorily into shop windows – useless bric-a-brac, cheap souvenirs side by side with expensive apparel for the richer tourist. Huddled on the ground beneath one of these columns is a supine woman, her head wrapped in a flowered shawl. Her eyes are closed in sleep or misery. In the folds of her tattered brown coat a small child kneels, its hands clasped, its eyes raised in a medieval supplicant's prayer. I stop.

I am not a good person. I would rather avert my gaze from distress than confront it. I would prefer all beggars to be shipped to some asylum far from my attention than to have to trip over them in the streets of our western cities. But there is something in this child's posture which makes me reach into my bag and, for lack of French change, take out a twenty-dollar bill, and place it in her tin.

There is no flicker of expression on the child's face. The frozen eyes still stare steadily towards heaven. I have a violent urge to shake her, wake her mother, rail at her for lying here instead of doing something with her life, her child's life. I want to steal the child away, wash her, send her off to school.

I walk away, turn quickly into a sidestreet. I am shaking, as if I had been accosted in a dark New York alley. But the taste of the fear is different. It is more subtle, like a premonition. Perhaps it was simply to assuage that superstitious fear that I opened my bag.

No, I am not a good person. Not even a good woman. I know because I learned the lessons of goodness young, though I haven't thought about them for some time. My mother was the teacher and she was a

7

fine one at home as well as professionally, from all accounts. No hypocritical catechism for her. What she said, she did. I was taught to share because she shared. There was always a jar of freshly made soup, a slice of tart, an errand to be run for the old woman across the landing. Our spare room must have been on some refugee organisation's list. Strangers would turn up sporadically from distant parts of the globe – Argentina, Chile, Africa, Vietnam – and stay a week, a month, two. Their eyes would look glazed as my mother tried to communicate the basics of life in Paris to them or filled out incomprehensible sheets of printed paper.

From the time that I could read, she would sit me down with her over the accounts, which now that I think of it could hardly have been ample, and I would see the proportion allotted to charities of every designation. When I started to get pocket money, I too was asked to consider whether a part might be given away. Asked, mind, not told.

I hated the giving. A bright bauble always seemed to dangle in my imagination, as I parted with the centimes. The spare room, larger than my own, took on palatial proportions. I coveted it, almost more than I coveted the ruffled party dresses in the shop windows or the shiny new bicycles other children rode in the Luxembourg Gardens. Everything I had was second-hand or second-best.

I have reached the Place du Palais-Royal. I hardly recognise it. This is not the Paris we came to much. Perhaps this is why I have chosen a hotel in this part of the city. The posters on the Comédie-Française advertise Molière's *L'Avare*. I am not miserly. I am greedy. And as if to prove to myself just how spendthrift I am, how different I am now to the little girl I was, I sit down at one of those cafés with burgundy awnings and gorge myself on flaky croissant and *café au lait* and then top it off with a glazed raspberry tart heaped with fruit. Sitting in cafés was not something my mother believed in.

The cloak of memory has wrapped itself over my shoulders. It weighs heavily. I stare at passers-by to shake it off. I have not come here to remember. I have come here to forget.

When I knew I had to leave New York, my first idea was London. All my thoughts in those last weeks while I was selling up my share in the agency, briefing partners about clients they would be taking over, were about London. Then I realised that I knew too many people there, and too many more were promising to visit.

It was Steve who put it into words for me.

'I think you really want to disappear,' he said.

For the first time in our long working lives together, I caught him feeling sorry for me. It was an emotion he rarely gave and I never sought. In the recognition of it, we were both intensely uncomfortable.

Then he rushed on. 'Chuck and I bought this little place in Paris last year. You could go there. Stay for a while. I won't pass on the address.'

Paris. I know no one here, though it is my native city. Even my lips as I ask the waiter for more coffee curl oddly round the distant words. But the polite smile, like a mechanism they instantly trigger, falls readily into place.

As I get into my coat, put money on the small round table, I see myself in the waiter's lingering glance. Have I told you yet that I am tall with long auburn hair and grey eyes? 'Rita', my first boss in New York used to call me, and it took me a few weeks to realise he meant Hayworth. I tell you now, because my reputedly striking looks play a not inconsequential part in this story.

I stroll through the galleries of the Palais-Royal, wily old Richelieu's one-time palace. It comes to me that it was in one of the shops here that Charlotte Corday, herself a revolutionary, bought the knife with which she stabbed Marat, that hero of some people and executioner of others.

Murder wears too many faces.

△△ 3

When I was six or seven my mother started sending me to England for the summers. There was a teacher at the local *école maternelle*, the little nursery school where I had gone for my first years, who had a sister in Kent. The sister had a boy a little older than me and agreed to take me in.

Madame Pichon, as I knew her then, brought me over that first summer herself. On the ferry crossing the Channel, I sat on the deck with her and stared at the receding coastline of France and the ever tinier figure of my mother, who had come with us as far as Calais. I was filled with apprehension but also strangely excited. I had never been on a boat before, never seen waves chopping beneath me. Nor had I had many rides in a car. We didn't have one at home. Stephanie, as she instantly introduced herself, waving aside any family names, came to collect us in one in Dover. The square-shaped Morris Minor, with its polished wood trimmings and its vast hairy dog in the back seat, seemed to have walked straight out of one of those English adventure stories my mother had started to read to me in preparation for my trip. I leaned into the dog, perversely called Small, and as we bumped towards the farm, all my apprehension was swallowed up in the comfort of his fur and the big brown eyes and drooling snout he poised on my lap. Small is still clearer to me than his mistress.

Had my mother seen the farm that first year, her tiny perfect nose would have curled involuntarily in disdain. My mother didn't like dirt. And dirt there was aplenty on Millhill Farm. Not only dirt, but mud and cat and dog hair and dust and flies and a wonderful ramshackle disorder, made even more manifest by the profusion of flowers in every available pot or bowl. I learned all their names that summer. There were delphiniums and hollyhocks, clematis and buddleia, irises, lilies, sweet peas, morning glory, dahlias, daisies, geraniums and roses of every description.

I was there to learn. My mother was an English teacher and speaking

English was one of the cardinal virtues. It was to be the only one I excelled in.

Stephanie took one look in my neatly packed case, picked out underwear and socks, the odd jersey, and promptly closed it. She left me for a moment in that tiny room beneath the eaves and when she came back she was carrying two pairs of worn dungarees.

'Here.' She gestured at me in that loose-boned way that was to become so familiar. 'These'll do you.'

With a twist or two at the cuff, they did. I lived out the summer in those dungarees. Robinson's dungarees. And in them, I was prepared to meet Robinson.

He was only a fraction taller than I was, a slender boy with a mop of ash-blond hair like his mother's and candid eyes. I think it was at some point during that first teatime in the kitchen with the huge fireplace that Stephanie announced, 'Robinson doesn't usually like girls.'

I had all but given up concentrating on the flow of English which sounded so different from my mother's, and was busy covertly stroking Small, who had placed himself at my feet, but I heard that. Robinson's face was all red when I glanced at him.

'But he's promised to make an exception in your case,' Stephanie went on. 'And now that Small seems to have taken to you, it should prove all the easier.'

Robinson scraped his chair back from the table and mumbled something I couldn't make out, before waving a distinct 'come on' at me. I had never been allowed to leave table before the grown-ups or without special permission and I looked hesitantly at Stephanie, who seemed to make nothing of it. She just smiled and shooed me away.

Some time during that first week or two at Millhill Farm I remember saying to Robinson that I would prefer being a dog to being a girl. But by then it didn't matter. Robinson and I had become friends without even noticing that it had happened. The fields did it, those fields in which we ran or crawled about, pretending to be intrepid explorers in a hostile land. And the little wood where we darted from tree to tree, climbed and tumbled, in endless hide-and-seeks. In the stream which curled round the back of the farm, I learned to paddle about and fish with an old stick of a rod. Sometimes we sailed leaves of boats, imagining pirate ships attacking the royal fleet, racing downstream to see whose ships would first reach shore. When it rained, we clambered round the barn, jumping up and down on the prickly hay, constructing elaborate traps for each other. Or we lay quietly, our eyes tightly shut, Small between us, and tried to see if we could identify a particular cow's moo.

There was a horse, too, a broad-backed brown mare, who trod lazily and reluctantly round a field when we perched ourselves on her. She must have been at the origin of the name Robinson gave me. 'Mare' I was and 'Mare' I would remain for the length of those summers.

Sometimes two friends of Robinson's would cycle over from a neighbouring farm. Two boys a little older than he was. When they came Robinson would instantly abandon me, pretend I didn't exist. I don't know whether I imagined the sheepish look on his face then. In any event, I was left to my own devices, to weave daisy chains or preferably invent complicated structures out of bits of twig and stone in the woods. Traps again. All the while I would fantasise intricate plots in which the boys ended up helpless in deep snake-filled pits, or drowning, and it was up to me to save them if I so chose. I always let the other two boys rot or drown, slowly, painfully, and just in the nick of time rescued an eternally grateful Robinson.

When the other boys had left, Robinson would come looking for me. I would pretend not to notice him and carry on with my game while he shuffled his feet or grunted and made himself increasingly obvious. Then I would say I was perfectly happy on my own and didn't want to play with anyone. He would go away and come back with ever more enticing proposals, begging really, until eventually I would disdainfully agree to play with him. By the end of the summer, I was allowed to join in the boys' games. But sometimes Robinson left me out again just, I think, so that we could re-enact our ritualised little power plays.

I had never known life could be so free of adults. We saw Stephanie at mealtimes and fed the chickens with her or picked berries. Once a week, we would all pack into the Morris Minor and go to town with her for a shopping expedition. On occasion, too, we would help Chris and the other men with odd tasks. But that apart, the world was our own.

Childhood. The formative years, they're called. They would better be known as the re-formative years. We reform them all the time.

4

Chris was Robinson's father. He was a burly man with a ruddy face and huge hands which always had grit around the nails. He didn't speak much, except to ask us at dinner what we had got up to that day or ask us at breakfast what our plans were. What I remember best about him were his hands. He would tussle my hair with one by way of greeting or lift me up onto the mare's back as if I were no heavier than a daisy chain. I remember his smell too. He smelled of hay and wind, sweet and salty all at the same time.

He was the first father I had any experience of. At home in Paris I didn't have a father. Oh, I had had one once, my mother had told me that, but I had no memory of him and since I had no memory, I think I felt no particular absence. After that summer in England, I became aware of the lack.

My mother, in her customary white blouse and neat blue skirt, had come to fetch me from the farm and though I was painfully aware of the critical eye she cast over the establishment, she seemed genuinely charmed by Stephanie and Chris. This first parting was a tearful one. Robinson even gave me four of his best marbles to take home – amongst them a big glossy blue and a cat's eye which changed colours as it rolled. It was arranged that I would come back the following summer, this time with my own dungarees.

On the eve of my first day back at school I confronted my mother. We were in my room with its narrow bed and small desk and its single picture of George Sand's native village of Nohant. My mother was putting out my school clothes, arranging my notebooks in my leather satchel, when I asked her.

'What happened to my father?'

She looked at me quietly for a moment, nothing moving in her face, only a little flicker at the corner of her lips. Then she urged me into the kitchen. She boiled some milk, asked me if I'd like some honey in it, and poured the concoction into one of those huge breakfast bowls. Only when she had sat down did she look me in the eyes.

'Your father left us,' she said. She smiled, but it didn't come out quite right and I could tell by the way she was arranging things on the table, moving the sugar bowl, folding a napkin, that that wasn't the whole story.

'You mean he died,' I leapt in. I suspected she thought I didn't know about death. Grown-ups always made such a fuss and a hush-hush about it that perhaps she was afraid to tell me. But in England I had seen plenty of mice dead in the fields, seen Small paw them and roll them about, their grey corpses all listless and somehow shrunken.

'No, he's not dead.' She paused. 'He simply left us, when you were about two.'

'You mean he was a bad man,' I said. I couldn't imagine Chris leaving Robinson and Stephanie.

'No, he wasn't a bad man. He was a good man.' Her hands were clenched in front of her and I knew that she didn't want to go on talking. But I knew that she would. My mother was always fair.

'Why did he leave us?' I persisted. 'Did he hate us?'

'No, he loved us, loved us very much. Particularly you.' She tried that smile again, but this time it came out even worse.

'So why did he go?'

'He felt he had to. And he was right.'

I didn't believe she believed that last. 'Did you want him to go?'

'Yes.' Her voice cracked a little as she said it, so she repeated it again more firmly.

'Where did he go?'

'He went East.'

That was so vague I couldn't think what she meant, but my next question was all important, so I rushed on.

'Will he come back and see us?'

She stroked my hair then. It was an act that was reserved for when I was ill and I knew what she would say before she said it. 'I don't think so. It's far away.' I must have looked tearful, for she quickly added, 'When you're a little older, I'll try and explain it to you better.'

I don't know why I remember that first scene more clearly than all the others, but I do. To give my mother credit, she did try and explain it all to me again and again over the years whenever I asked. Gradually I learned that my father was a doctor, that he had been a member of the resistance during the war, that he had felt propelled to carry on doing good, useful things, that he had been asked by people he knew to go to Vietnam where he had been brought up to work at the Hôpital Grall, the French hospital, that she hadn't felt able to go with him, that it would have been too dangerous for me. In any case, her life was here, in Paris. But he had needed to go, so they separated. And he had been right to go, she always claimed, and always with tightly pursed lips.

She started to tell me stories about him, little things, about how he loved sailing and had once had a boat, how he loathed cabbage but would eat it anyway with a slight frown on his face, how he was very efficient at changing nappies; and bigger things, how he had been decorated for his war work, what a fine doctor he was, how he had taken up a speciality in burns and skin grafting.

The trouble was that the more fine things she told me about him, the less I believed her and the more I started to despise him. It seemed to me that he had done something unpardonable, that each of her stories was a little act of cover-up and forgiving. I suspected that deep inside her she too considered him unpardonable and resented him with a barely controllable passion. You only had to see how her lips and eyes didn't match when she talked about him to realise that.

When I grew older and started to criticise him, she would defend him adamantly. Whatever I said, she was always on his side, like some high-powered attorney well paid to perform a whitewash. I secretly admired her for her implacability, but I was after something else. I think I was after the truth.

Having learned the word 'divorce', I used it on her and asked her quite casually one night whether she had one and was planning to remarry. We were doing the dishes, she drying, I washing, and I can still see how a glass hurtled out of her hands and smashed into a hundred pieces on the tile floor. Her face when I dared to look at it was frozen. It was only when she was bent over with pan and brush, sweeping up splinters, that she answered me in a voice which was calm, if strained, to my ears. She was too old to remarry now, she said.

In retrospect, I suspect she always hoped my father would return. She had met him when no longer in her first youth and the six or so years they had spent together had obviously marked her for life. At the time when I began my interrogations, she must have been in her late thirties, still a slender, pretty woman with thick hair which she always wore neatly coiled back. She used to let me brush it sometimes and I would wonder at the single white streak which started at her brow and worked its way dramatically through that sleek darkness.

She never told me of any letters she might have had from my father in those years. But I do remember that she would read all the news about Vietnam assiduously, perhaps in the hope of seeing his name. And during the long stretch of the war, she belonged to innumerable committees – medical aid committees, relief committees, peace in Vietnam committees . . .

She remained a one-man woman. Quite unlike her daughter. And whether out of love or hate, I'm still not sure.

⚖ 5

From my base at the Intercontinental, I explore the city. I talk to no one but waiters and hotel receptionists. Each day I set out on foot and head for a different arrondissement. Sometimes, if my destination is too distant, I pop into the metro and emerge from its cocoon to wander haphazardly through streets without venturing into museums or galleries. I have no plan except that which numbers the districts. I simply gaze at façades, lose myself in markets, or sit in cafés watching the endless spectacle of the streets.

On my first day I climbed to the top of the Eiffel Tower and spent hours trying to work out where each borough began and ended. Then I started making my way through the left bank, beginning with a Paris I didn't even know existed, past the Quai de Grenelle to a new city like a Chicago in better taste with modern structures of glass and steel, television and computer companies, a flat expanse of park composed of fountains and secret gardens, each on a theme, each with its own rectangular glass conservatory. Saturday, I headed into the Seventh, those long, bland, elegant streets behind the National Assembly. Life here is all hidden, lived within immaculate walls. One only glimpses it when heavy gates open to reveal sumptuous courtyards or one stumbles onto the Boulevard St-Germain.

But I am not ready for the more familiar precincts of the Sixth yet. I change course and concentrate on the west of the city, wander up the Champs Elysées, veer north to find myself at the flower stalls of the Place des Ternes and then in the Parc Monceau. I sit on a bench and watch the leafless trees, listen to the children calling out to soberly dressed nannies.

It is only gradually and with a slight shiver of apprehension that I consider venturing towards streets that I have known better. Like a reluctant bird of prey I am circling round the sites of memory before daring to pounce.

On my fifth day I decide for some obscure reason to have breakfast in the hotel dining room. No sooner have I placed myself at a table that looks out on the glazed courtyard, than a voice calls out to me, closely followed by its fur-swathed owner.

'Maria Regnier, well I never. Can we join you?'

Before I can answer, Sarah Martin manoeuvres her ample form into the chair in front of me and waves a decidedly uncomfortable youth into the one at her side. 'How brilliant to bump into you here,' Sarah enthuses and before I have had a chance to say more than, 'Hello,' she has placed her order for a continental breakfast with coffee plus a plate of two eggs sunny side up with bacon, very crisp, please, for the youth she beamingly and simultaneously introduces as her son, William.

William squirms, while Sarah talks. And talks. Sarah has always talked unstoppably since I have known her, which is for three or four years now. She even talks while she is eating. Given that she is a food writer, this is perhaps remarkable, though it has to be said that while chewing, her talk is usually about the ingredients in her mouth. Be that as it may, Sarah is a fine writer and her column in *New York Magazine* can make or break a restaurant's reputation faster than I can scuttle up to my room, which is what I would like to do right now. I don't, of course. I sit and listen while Sarah tells me about everything she and William have done and eaten in the last few days.

I met Sarah when her publishers asked my agency to do the public relations for her first book. Have I mentioned yet that in the United States of Advertising, I am a PR agent? Nichols, Regnier and Peele Associates. Yes, even the firm bears my name, even if second in line. I'm a partner, or was until I left. I am an expert in that elegant straining of the truth which is known as hype. I create events or images for people or corporations who need creating. I do this so that the media can be seduced into making the right news of them. Hey presto! Demand is fostered or disseminated.

With Sarah it wasn't difficult. She was already more than half way there. All I did was dream up a little party for her to which the passing and gossiping great could be invited. We asked three of her favourite chefs to concoct dishes named for her. They were more than pleased to comply. A newly slimmed and theatrically coiffed Sarah guessed ingredients and chefs blindfold – to great rounds of applause. And the event and book were off and running in countless columns. Since Sarah is a great little chatterer, the chat shows were not far behind. The book sold extremely well.

I am not cynical about any of this. It is simply that these days I am a little worn. Nor can I muster the necessary hyperboles to greet Sarah's announcement that she is in Paris doing research for her newest project – a book, complete with a check-list of sumptuous recipes, about the best of Paris restaurants at moderate prices.

'You will join us tonight, won't you, Maria? We're going to this little place just by Notre Dame. La Petite Table, it's called. Meant to be terrific. We'd love Maria to come with us, wouldn't we, William?'

William looks up at me with a decidedly suspicious glance before turning his gaze back to his plate and muttering something that sounds like confirmation.

I plead a previous appointment, then look at my watch and leap up before Sarah can issue any further invitations.

'I've got to go. Sorry, darling,' I lie.

'Tomorrow evening, then?' Sarah takes me at face value and when I fidget her face lights up. 'Oh, I see, another one already.' Her expression wrestles between bitchiness and compassion and settles for the latter. 'It's the best thing for you, I'm sure,' she says. I can hear her thinking that for all my sins, I'm valuable. I'm good at my job, the best, some think, and I might be useful at some future date. Then too, I know a great many people. Sarah gives me a consoling look.

I wave goodbye hurriedly. I cannot bear these people feeling they can feel sorry for me.

Back in my room, I throw my things into my cases and ring the number Steve has given me. I break into a sweat as I wait for someone to answer. When I hear a voice, I am so relieved that I have to sit down on the bed.

6

The apartment is on the Rue d'Oudinot, a short unremarkable street in the seventh arrondissement. But the space itself on the fifth floor is remarkable. One long room painted in some pale ochre tint makes up most of it. The right wall is punctuated by five sash windows which look out on an exquisite courtyard garden, complete with lawn, a tree I can't name until its tracery takes on leaf, and an oval fountain. Tapestry-covered chairs are arranged so as to give the room an assortment of small enclaves. The central one is marked by a fireplace. Above it on either side fly two plump, gilded angels bearing candelabra. One end of the room gives onto a separate small but well-appointed kitchen. At the other, a polished ladder leads up to a mezzanine with a desk and divan. Finally, at the far end of the apartment, there is a bedroom in which stands a delicate four-poster bed.

I am enchanted. Steve and Chuck have found an assortment of pictures and objects which surprise and hold the gaze. There is a finely filigreed cornice from some gothic edifice. A Doric half-column stands by one of the windows. Above the mantel, there is a small, exquisitely painted oil which shows only a woman's calves and feet, leather-sandalled, walking gracefully but firmly over some site that can only be antique.

I want to scan the shelves of books, but my eyes return of their own will to those lightly shod feet. Where can she be going? I curl into one of the arched chairs and sit staring at her until the waning of the light startles me from my reverie. I have no idea where the day has gone, but I feel strangely at peace. I see no need ever to venture from this room again.

Three days later, however, I do. I feel bold. I know exactly where I am going. It is what I have avoided ever since I arrived.

The air is crisp and clear. I walk quickly along the Seine, past Notre Dame and cross at the Pont de la Tournelle onto the Ile St-Louis. I stop neither to look at the miracle of the flying buttresses, nor to browse in the little shops which have flowered on the island. I am afraid that if I pause I will lose my nerve. Hastily I make my way across the Pont Marie, along the Quai des Celestins and into the Rue St-Paul.

Now that I am here, I take a deep breath. This is the square mile of my childhood. This is where I was born. It is the bridge I have just crossed which gave me my name. My mother used to walk over it daily and loved the serenity of its stone, the arches of irregular size, the bouquets of carved lime. No Virgin Mary is my namesake, but Henri IV's chief builder of bridges, one Christophe Marie. Marie's planned bridge took a long time to come to fruition though. The first stone wasn't laid until Henri had met his assassin and another Marie, this time the stubbornly enterprising Marie de' Medici, Henri IV's wife and designated regent, my second namesake, had begun to grapple with the building blocks of Paris. And even then, it took another twenty-six years of chequered history to complete. Perhaps I should take courage from my bridge, so slow to reach its destination, but unwavering for the centuries since.

I turn the corner into the narrow Rue des Lions-St-Paul and stop at number eleven. My mother's house; the house where I spent my first eighteen years. I push open the huge studded door and stand in the cobbled courtyard. The silence resonates with the clatter of my heels, as noisy as memory. At the far end of the yard, by the ramped staircase, a small girl desultorily skips rope. She could be me. I skipped here. I imagine the daughter of Madame de Sévigné, yet another Marie, as my mother never failed to tell me, skipped here as well three centuries ago. The daughter, made eternally famous by her mother's chattering letters, was born here. She knew her father until she was six, Madame *la mère* having been left a very merry widow at the age of twenty-six. Repetition and variation.

I look up to the top windows and wonder what the apartment is like now. When we lived there, the old ceiling beams in the living–dining area were partly uncovered. From one of them an ancient hook dangled and I used to fancy that some poor soul had hung himself from the beam rather than face the guillotine. Three rooms radiated out from this slightly darkened salon – one of them, my mother's bedroom, crammed into the low-ceilinged attic which was reached by a steep, rickety staircase.

The thought of the attic makes me quiver. I remember Olivier. I have no wish to think of him. That is not why I have come here. But he is suddenly there before me, as solid as his square frame. I walk hastily from the courtyard, break into a run. Despite the bustling crowd, he is still with me when I reach the Rue St-Antoine. At the corner café where I collapse, he sits down beside me.

When my mother died, I was seventeen. I had just entered the *classe terminale* at the lycée, that arduous final year which would see me through my Bac. Needless to say, I was studying languages. My English was so fluent that my teachers simply assumed I was bored and plied me with extra work. Spanish was slightly trickier. But my difficulties had nothing to do with school, where I dutifully excelled. My mother's death had plunged me into chaos and I don't mean simply the emotional kind. I had no idea how to go to the bank, let alone how to pay an electricity or phone bill. My mother had only a small sum of savings and her pension would take months to unravel. More importantly, since I was not yet legally an adult and had no guardian, I was destined to become a ward of state, to be thrown on the relentless mercy of a blind bureaucracy.

Olivier saved me from that. He appeared from the midst of the substantial crowd at the funeral – my mother had a lot of close colleagues, if no particular intimates that I could designate – and put his arm lightly across my shoulder, before turning me round and forcing me to look him squarely in the eyes through the mist of my stupor. 'Don't worry,' he said. 'I'll see to everything.'

I was more than ready to put my trust in him.

Olivier Bouccicault was the Head of the History Department at the lycée where my mother taught. I had met him on a number of occasions, but he was hardly a frequent visitor at our apartment. My mother's life focused around her work and her committees. At home, apart from the transients we housed and the usual run of my schoolmates, we were largely solitary, a tight little unit of two. At weekends, she took me to films or theatre or museums sometimes with other friends, and very occasionally there was a dinner party. It must have been at these that I had encountered Olivier.

I had never paid any particular attention to him. He was just another of those vague presences who belonged to my mother's world. Now that I think about it, he must have been about forty then, hardly past his prime, a man with a square jaw and slightly thinning sandy hair and a face that made one think more readily of a boxer than a schoolmaster.

In any case, Olivier saw me home from the funeral and proceeded to interrogate me. He wanted to know what I wanted. Did I want to be housed with a family or did I want to stay where I was, at least until the year was out? Was I afraid to be on my own? Did I want someone to come and live with me, a tenant, a housekeeper, perhaps? Did I know how to shop? To do the washing? Who were my friends? Did I feel able to carry on with my studies? Was I having nightmares? He was matter-of-fact, slightly rough and strangely consoling.

I had only been coming back to the apartment until then to change my clothes. I had been staying with a girlfriend and her family and I knew that I couldn't stay on in those cramped quarters. By the end of that first evening with Olivier, I realised that I did want to carry on living in my mother's apartment. I knew all the neighbours. They were kind. And I felt safe here. It was, after all, the only home I had ever known. But was any of it possible?

Olivier arranged it all. He negotiated with the authorities and landlords and bankers. He talked to my mother's weekly help and had her come in twice a week and bring in a basic supply of groceries. He organised a collection at my mother's lycée so that I had a sum of money to see me through until pensions and the estate could be cleared. He dropped in to see me two or three times a week to talk about studies and life and rang me every day.

Then, two months or so after my mother's death, Olivier arrived with a large gift-wrapped package.

'Open it,' he said to me. He slumped down on the worn sofa which creaked with his weight and I could feel him watching me as I carefully undid the package so as not to rip any of the glossy paper.

Inside, there were not one but two dresses, a brown-and-white chequered concoction of the lightest wool and another in deep bottle green.

'I thought you'd like something new for Christmas.' Olivier was smiling. 'Your wardrobe is hardly, I've noticed, extensive.' He coughed, waved me away. 'Go and try them on and then show me.'

It was true that my wardrobe was poor. I had the two requisite pairs of jeans, an assortment of jerseys and then my mother's choice, some trim skirts, and white shirts that needed endless washing. My mother had always been both frugal and uncaring about clothes. They were there neatly to cover the body, not to display it. The chequered dress which I pulled on first I could instantly tell was just the opposite. It had tapering lines, a tightly fitted bodice with tiny buttons at its centre which moulded their way right up to my neck. I hardly dared look in the small glass above my chest of drawers. In any event I could only see my head and shoulders in it. And my everyday boots felt all wrong, but I marched out in them nonetheless to display myself to Olivier.

He looked at me critically for a moment, then came over to pull the Alice band I always wore in good girlish fashion out of my hair, which had grown longer now that my mother was no longer around to clip it to shoulder length.

'There.' He eyed me again from the side, then casually pulled his fingers through my hair, forcing it over to one side.

I don't know whether I would have been aware, then, that it was the first time he had touched me, apart from the requisite handshake, since the funeral, but he cleared his throat in an odd way and the silence which followed that sound was strangely heavy and too long. To cover it, he ran his finger down my cheek and said lightly, '*Pas mal*, not bad. Even quite pretty.'

I met his eyes, but he waved me away again, 'Now go and try the other one on and you can decide which you're going to wear tonight, because I'm taking you out to dinner.'

The green frock fitted me even better and I brushed my hair into the shape he seemed to have suggested. When I came out to show him, he was sitting on the sofa and he murmured, '*Très jolie,*' before patting the space next to him and urging me over.

I sat down beside him and he kissed me lightly but firmly on the lips, then breathed in a peculiar way before springing to his feet and diving into talk.

It's hard for me now to imagine how innocent I was then. Those may have been the permissive seventies, but I had been brought up as a proper little bourgeoise under my mother's vigilant eye and I had never been kissed by a man. My close friends were not particularly different. When we saw boys, we shook hands, and at the very few mixed parties I had been to, sex was a matter only of hints and blushes. England, with its more liberal atmosphere, might have provided greater freedom, but perhaps for that very reason my mother had stopped sending me there when I reached the age of fifteen. I now spoke quite well enough, she told me.

So Olivier was the first man to kiss me.

He kissed me again later that night after a dinner during which I had chattered with unusual brightness, spurred perhaps by his eyes. They had a glint to them. That second kiss was different. He folded me in his arms and smoothed the small of my back, my hair, while his lips pressed into me and his tongue flickered into my mouth. I liked it, liked his hands on me perhaps as much as his lips. He left a little hastily after that and didn't come round again that week, though he did phone me with his customary regularity to check on my well-being.

The next time I saw him, he was very serious. He grilled me about my work, checked through all my notebooks to make sure I was keeping up and then rose with solemn formality. I urged him to stay. I had tried my hand at roasting a chicken in the hope that he might and I wanted him to share it. Everything would be ready in a few minutes. He stayed, after excusing himself to make a phone call first.

With the myopia of youth, I had never thought about Olivier's life outside his contact with me. It never occurred to me to question him. I think I vaguely knew that he had children, perhaps a wife, but they didn't seem to live with him. We only ever talked about me or about politics, the state of the world. I was good at that. I could name every single cabinet minister and tell you what he did and did wrong. I was not my mother's daughter for nothing. But after that phone call, I asked Olivier whether he had another commitment, whether he had to go home. He shook his head brusquely and I laughed and skipped off to set the table with the best tablecloth and napkins.

It was over dinner that he asked me what my plans were for Christmas. I had been dreading the holidays. Christmas Eve was all right. I had been invited over to my friend Annette's and I would go to midnight mass with her family and stay over until the next day. But after that, long empty days spread themselves before me, so long that I had even begun to make lists of what work to do each day to fill them. Olivier saved me. He asked me whether I might like to go south with him. He had a little house in Provence and he usually went there during the longer school breaks. I was so grateful that I bounded into his lap and flung my arms around him. He held me tightly for a moment, then gently urged me away.

'Crack of dawn on the twenty-sixth it is then.' He took my hand

and seemed to be about to say something else, but changed his mind, only adding at the door, 'Bring some warm clothes. It can get very cold.'

We drove down in his little Peugeot, the car radio pouring out Mozart symphonies all the way, through the flatlands around Orléans, past the hills and dips of Burgundy and into the naked vineyards of the Beaujolais. We stopped in a restaurant in the midst of one for lunch. After that everything was industrial congestion and giant container trucks and I must have dozed off. When we arrived I was so groggy that all I was aware of was the smell of pine and the crackling chill of the air. Olivier quickly lit a fire that was already laid. I stood there watching the flames leap up into the chimney. The hot chocolate he put into my hand revived me a little, but only so that I half-took in the room, the presence of two plump, striped sofas. I promptly curled into one.

The next thing I knew, light was spilling through a vast picture window, making a garden of the flowery duvet Olivier had wrapped round me. I looked out, saw an oak, a little dip of a valley and in the distance the misty purple of the Luberon hills. For the first time in months, I took a deep, unencumbered breath and didn't wait for the patter of my mother's slippers on parquet.

That day we tramped away from the sleepy cluster of stone houses which was the hamlet and made our way on crisp ground through little copses which bordered vineyards, then up onto jutting hills and down again through woods of fragrant pine. By the time we returned, the sun was setting pink against the hills. In its light the house looked as if it had grown out of the ground. From the dirt road at the back, it was merely an old wall, a converted wash house at the edge of the village. Olivier's parents, I learned, had built onto it to form this long rectangular structure. In the summers, when the picture windows were open, the vine-covered terrace and the old oak became part of the living quarters.

We prepared dinner together that night. Olivier concocted some pasta in a fragrant mushroom sauce while I tossed a salad. I remember that I drank what for me must have been a great deal of wine. In any case we were merry, and it was in the midst of that merriness that Olivier suddenly announced, 'Oh, I almost forgot. I've brought you a Christmas present.'

'Me too,' I laughed, and raced to my room which was at the far end of the salon.

He was sitting in front of the fire when I returned and I shyly handed him the carefully wrapped book I had purchased after much browsing in second-hand bookdealers. It was an architectural history of Paris and I had chosen it for its lovely line drawings. I waited for him to open it to see if he was pleased. It was the first time I had ever given a present to an adult apart from my mother.

'It's perfect,' Olivier smiled. 'Very fine.' He leafed through the pages while I stood over him. 'Thank you.' He turned towards me and ruffled my hair. 'Now, you open yours.'

There were two packages. I opened the heavier one first and found three books, a volume of Saint-Simon's *Mémoires*, Madame de Sévigné's letters to her daughter, and a biography of Madame de Pompadour.

'For your history course,' Olivier prompted.

'From my favourite history teacher,' I beamed at him and hastily opened the second package. At first, amidst the deep blue tissue paper, I wasn't sure what the pale silk garments were. Perhaps when I realised, I should have had at least a momentary puritan revulsion. But I didn't. I was thrilled. I had been so starved of beautiful useless things that these creamy bodices that one wore secretly next to the skin seemed to me the height of the desirable. I threw my arms around Olivier and with a sudden flush of daring, I asked him whether he would like me to try them on for him. I didn't wait for a reply. I simply dashed to my room, pulled off my jeans and reappeared in the first of the all-in-one bodices.

The look Olivier gave me was, I think, my first inkling of the meaning of female power. He was silent for a moment, then he beckoned me towards him. 'May I?' he said in a strange voice.

I stood very still as he ran his fingers along my neck and down over my bosom. It felt nice and I didn't stop him, didn't stop him either as he pulled me closer to him and caressed my back, my hips, the tops of my bare legs. Then he kissed me, long and hard, and groaned oddly. When I met his eyes again, there was a question in them which I didn't altogether understand and I let him pull me towards the sofa. He started to kiss me all over then and I liked that too, liked the slight roughness of his chin, the gentle pressure of his fingers, the heat of him. In fact, I think I liked everything that first night, except perhaps

27

the momentary pain, the splash of blood on the white sheets of his bed where we eventually found ourselves, and the sticky stain his sperm left on my new bodice.

Olivier taught me a great deal in that week we spent together in the house beneath the purple hills and I must have been a willing pupil. He taught me how to take a man's penis in my hands and in my mouth. He taught me how to clothe it in a sheath so that the very clothing brought moans to his lips. He taught me how to arch my back beneath him and how to sit astride him and press my knees against his buttocks. He taught me how to stop just before pleasure reached its peak so that when I moved again, it became more intense. He taught me how to take pleasure in myself while he watched with a rapt expression on his face. And perhaps, most importantly, he taught me I was beautiful. He was a good teacher and I have never forgotten any of his lessons.

When we got back to Paris, Olivier came to see me with the same regularity as before our departure. But now he stayed later and sometimes we would spend Saturday afternoons in my mother's bed in the attic, which I had all but taken over. My own was so small. Occasionally, we went to the cinema or the theatre. Every so often, he would bring me a new silky or frilly undergarment, or sometimes a dress. I would parade it before him and he would sit there silently, his hands in his pockets, touching himself, until I could read from his eyes that he wanted my help and I would go over to him and offer it.

You might think that all this harmed my studies. Not at all. I worked with even greater diligence, certain of the fact that Olivier would arrive at his appointed hours. My friends were hard at work too and when we met for an outing on a Sunday afternoon, we would talk about our studies or exchange our fears about the coming exams. I never felt any need to tell any of them, even the closest, about Olivier. We had never decided this in so many words between us, but somehow I wanted to keep it secret.

In April, for my eighteenth birthday, Olivier brought me eighteen white long-stemmed roses and a low-cut black dress, complete with one of those underwired black corselets and matching stockings. The dress was exquisite. We were going out to La Coupole for dinner, and I asked him whether he would like me to change into it. He nodded, so I quickly went into my room to shed what I was wearing and pull on my new things. I had hesitated before, but now I also carefully put on the dark red lipstick I had bought as my own present. And I brushed my hair afresh to a ruddy sheen.

When I came out, Olivier stared at me as if he had never seen me before.

'Don't you like it?' I asked him.

'Silly.' He lifted my hair back from my face and kissed me fiercely. 'It's just that I've never seen you in black.'

We were very late getting to La Coupole and I remember just before we left the house and he was holding my coat for me, he asked, 'Do you like me, just a little, Maria?'

The question had never occurred to me, blandly, like that and I think I must have smiled at him a little curiously, for he murmured, 'The enigmatic Maria.'

In the restaurant while we ate and chatted, I kept looking at him covertly to see what he had meant by his question. Olivier had kind eyes with creases round them, a charming smile and when he undressed he had nice slender legs and smooth skin. And he was wonderfully generous to me. Of course I liked him, but there seemed to be more to his question than that answered.

It was that night, too, that Olivier asked me what I wanted to do after my Bac. I had assumed that I would go to university. It was what my mother had wanted and all the necessary steps were in place. But the fact that Olivier had posed it as a question made it no longer seem a given and that discomfited me too.

After that evening, everything seemed to change, not dramatically, but subtly, as if there had been a minuscule shift in our relations which grew greater by the week. I don't know if it was because of the black dress, or because so many men in the restaurant seemed to have stared at me, as Olivier kept pointing out. Or simply because I was now eighteen. But the change was palpable. Olivier would look up at me in the midst of our love-making with that question in his eyes. Or he would shudder convulsively when I took his penis in my mouth and gaze at me beseechingly when it was all over. If we went out, he would grip me possessively any time another man so much as glanced in our direction. And he laughed less. Whenever I told him what I thought was a funny story, he would grill me about who, what, where. We went out together less and I began to tell him less.

Then, one morning, a few days after my finals were over and I was spring cleaning the flat and feeling a little sorry for myself since Olivier had said nothing about holiday plans, a strange woman came to the door. She had one of those pert little faces with liquid eyes beneath a dark fringe.

'So you're the little slut,' she said, after she had stared at me for a moment. Then she lifted her hand and slapped my face hard.

I was so taken aback I didn't even have the wherewithal to ask her who she was. I just looked at her receding figure and then burst into tears. It was the second time I had cried since my mother died and I couldn't seem to stop.

A grim, distraught Olivier arrived a few hours later. He took one look at me and buried his face in my bosom. 'I'm sorry you were subjected to that,' he murmured. It was only then, as he talked, not quite making sense, that I realised that all along he had been more or less living with another woman. That woman.

'I told her. Told her about you. Told her I was in love with you,' he mumbled and started to make love to me, savagely, fiercely. I was strangely inert in his arms. In the midst of it all, he said to me, 'I told her I want to marry you, Maria. Will you marry me?'

I think I laughed then or it felt as if I were laughing while I kissed him, and when we had finished I said to him, 'No, Olivier, I won't marry you. I'm going to America. Straight after my orals, I'm going to New York.' The idea had just come into my head and I remember looking at him calmly, but with compassion, because he was so wide-eyed with surprise.

Oh it didn't end there. For weeks Olivier begged and beseeched, and then, because he was really a good man, he helped me. He gave me the address of a friend of his in New York, who taught at Columbia University. He helped me sell the lease on the apartment. But by that time, I was getting quite good at doing things for myself.

For a year while I was in New York, he wrote ardent letters to me. Then they stopped. I suspect he married the woman with the fringe.

Amongst the many other things Olivier taught me was that the less you tell men you love them, the more they love you. Perhaps, too, he led me to understand the value of a clean break. It is not a lesson I have always been able to follow.

♎ 7

Last night I dreamt of Olivier. In the dream he was very large and had snow-white hair, whereas I was very small, just a child. My mother was there too and we were both thanking him for something, I don't know what. I woke up feeling very happy, even though the rain is still falling and the sky is a colourless grey.

Time has taken on a new texture. I no longer feel it in compartments like the hourly segments on the pages of my once-crowded diary. There is no compulsion to lop off the present and race into the future. Sometimes I don't even know where the present is, I float in and out of the past so freely.

On the bookshelves in Steve's apartment, I found exactly the same edition of the biography of Madame de Pompadour that Olivier gave me that Christmas. I dip into it erratically and the excitement of the life of the royal courtesan comes back to me with all its initial flavour. To survive, the King's Favourite had to become an adept at the management of cabals and intrigues. Basic prettiness, talents for music and singing and acting, had all to feed the overarching art of pleasing. Appearance was of singular importance, from the velvet beauty spot adroitly placed on the cheek to the creation of settings, interiors, new houses great and small. Then too, the king had to be entertained, *'distrait'*, as the French say, and witty conversation was a must, together with a flair for organising parties and drawing out or patronising artists, writers, intellectuals.

So fascinated was I by Madame de Pompadour, that I remember scouring our shelves for books of a similar ilk. I found a surprising number – the signal was always a Madame in the name – and it occurred to me that my mother, for all her insistence that appearances counted for nought, must have shared my interest in these women who lived by their wits and often beauty, and who cultivated the ability to please. One other thing struck me as I read: husbands for all these women were at best of secondary importance. Perhaps that was the real reason for my mother's interest.

Amongst these books, there was another which bore the seductive title of *Femmes Fatales*. It was old and the print was quite large, which meant, I had learned from my mother, that it was probably a cheap edition intended for popular consumption. I read through the book quickly, entranced by its sensationalist prose, its lurid tales of *La Dame aux Camélias* and Lola Montez, both of whom I learned were real women whose names I can't now recall, and Nana and Lulu, perhaps Carmen, too. The stories told of enticing young women who had risen from nowhere, who had danced their way to fame and enslaved men; they told of strings of passionate affairs with artists and bankers and kings, of men enraptured and dying for love. But the women all died too, tragically young and horribly. When I had finished, I couldn't decide whether these women were meant to be fatal to men or to themselves.

It comes back to me now that one night Olivier spied this book on my desk. 'Studying, are you?' he said to me, his mouth tight. I didn't know what he meant and I must have smiled, as I always did when words eluded me. Perhaps now I do.

The sun has suddenly emerged, brightening the room with watery light. I decide to run down to the boulangerie. I have reverted to subsisting on bread and cheese, as I did for much of that last year in Paris. But as I walk I change my mind. Or perhaps the sign I see in front of a photography shop changes it for me. *'Une identité qui vous ressemble,'* it proclaims. 'An identity which resembles you.' I wonder if the photographer does a brisk trade in suitable identities and wonder if he could find one for me. And then I find myself in the metro and the familiar names are unfurling before me – Rue du Bac, Solferino, Assemblée Nationale.

A young man and woman get onto the train and sardonically announce they have been sent to us courtesy of the Ministry of Culture to show us what culture is. They start to perform an operatic duet, the woman's face lighting up with stagy smiles and simpers so that one forgets her lank stringy hair and tattered skirt. I reach into my pocket for the loose change I always have to hand these days for the derelicts who crowd the streets and subways, but a man's shouting, louder than the couple's song, distracts me as the train pulls into

Concorde. A stream of curses and spitfire rage pours from him, though he looks quite ordinary in his tweed coat and well-soled shoes. Nor does he seem drunk.

'If I want music, I'll go to the opera,' he hollers. 'I'm not here for your cruddy songs.' He pushes through the doors and I follow him. He is still bellowing, charging towards the driver's cubicle. 'Can't one even read one's newspaper in peace in the metro any more?' He waves his fist at the driver. 'Take care of your train.'

I am fascinated by his rage, but I slip away through the arch marked 'Correspondence'. Only when I get on the next train do I realise where I am heading. Louvre, Châtelet, Hôtel de Ville, St-Paul. Have I ever felt anger as pure and as uncontrollable as that? I am here.

I come up into the air on one of the spokes of the vast wheel which is La Bastille. In the centre stands the bronze column Louis Philippe built to commemorate the abortive revolution of 1830. A winged Liberty may soar defiantly at its head, but at the base of the column the victims lie buried, together, someone once told me, with two Egyptian pharaohs a wily Louvre curator bundled into the collective grave. The mummies were decomposing and a perfect opportunity for illicit burial offered itself.

These morbid thoughts present themselves to me as I approach the spoke in the wheel where my mother was killed – flung to her death on her way home by an overly boisterous driver, so that her body landed at the entrance to the Rue de la Roquette, the very street the hearses take en route to the cemetery of Père Lachaise.

I last stood on this corner a day or two after her death. I was angry. I was so angry that I think I must have been screaming out loud, for a policeman came up to me and started to quieten me down. I was so angry that I remember feeling that I could kill my mother if she weren't already dead. I wanted to shake her, slap her. I wanted to ask her what was all her goodness for if it only came to this? Why had she bothered to be so blameless, so self-effacing, so kind, so selfless? Why had she always skimped on herself, forgiven? There was no justice.

I came home and marched up to her room, banging my head on the low slope of the attic roof. I opened her wardrobe and I started to heave out her clothes, ripping as I went, creating chaos. Exhausted, I flung myself on her bed and cried or screamed, I don't know which. All I remember is that I vowed to myself I would never be like her. I would be a winner, not a loser; I would be selfish, not selfless; I would never mourn for a man who had abandoned me.

At some point I know I must have tidied up the mess I had made, for when Olivier came over to look through her desk for official documents, the room was once again neat.

I didn't like rifling through her desk. Its order demanded to be left pristine. Olivier did the searching, not that there was much to be done, for everything was meticulously labelled and he found what he needed quickly enough. After that I left the room untouched until my return from Provence, when I decided I would make it mine. Olivier's and mine.

At the Marché aux Puces, I found one of those brightly coloured Indian bedspreads and some printed scatter cushions. I splurged on bizarre cloth flowers, outsize yellow marguerites with velvety centres whose textures I can still feel. To top it all off, I bought a poster in iridescent blue from Matisse's Jazz sequence. Armed with my purchases, I set out to transform my mother's room. It was while I was at last sorting through her things – putting clothes into jumble bags, lecture notes into boxes – that I came across the letters and the diary.

By the side of the bed, there was an old oak nighttable with five small drawers. Nothing of great interest here: odds and ends of newspaper clippings, a pair of reading glasses, a jar of night cream, a small jewellery case containing some simple gold earrings, a chain, ancient report cards of mine, a pack of untouched butterfly notepaper I had once given her for a birthday present, and then in the bottom drawer I saw a blue folder with those elastic grips that come up over each end. Next to it, tucked into the far corner of the drawer, a black notebook.

I don't know why, but as soon as I saw these two objects, I had the sense that here was what I had been searching for all my conscious life. With slightly shaky fingers, I carefully edged the elastic round the edges of the folder. Inside there was a small stack of letters on cheap yellowy paper.

'*Ma très chère Françoise,*' the first began. The writing was tiny, difficult to read. A doctor's writing, I thought, and my eyes raced to the bottom of the page. *Je te serre très fort, Guy.*' Guy, my father. I trembled. I had coached myself to despise my father for so long, but now I trembled, and my first thought was that I would write to him, go to him instantly. Did he know of my mother's death, his *'très chère Françoise'*? There was an address under the signature. A long, complicated address, but the city was clear. Saigon.

Then my eyes fell on the date: 9 December 1962. I think the tears came into my eyes. Too long ago. Over sixteen years. I quickly lifted the stack of letters from the folder and turned to the last. This one was written in stubby pencil and there was no date on it, only a month, July, and no address. I leafed back a sheet and now there was a date, November 1971, but still no address. Could there have been one on the envelope? I wanted to scream. There were no envelopes in the folder. I ransacked the letters and then, calming myself, began to read in what I knew, given my mother's habits, must be a sequence.

I read and reread into the small hours of the night. After the first letter, I grew hesitant, slightly shy. This was, after all, private material, and I could feel my mother's disapproval. So I skimmed to begin with, looking for my name, needing to know whether they talked about me, what he felt about me.

Each and every letter bore some reference to me. At first they were of the kind, 'Please give Maria a huge cuddle for me,' and then, as the years passed, there were questions, 'How does she look now? How is she doing at school?' Once there was a thank you for a picture sent, a comment about how pretty I was, how wonderful it would be if he could see me in the flesh, perhaps one day, he would. This must have been when I was about four.

The tone was always tender and solicitous, as it was towards my mother, but tinged with what I understood as sadness. On the whole, though, the letters were oddly impersonal, as if some of their feeling had been soaked up in the vast distance they had to cross to reach us. There weren't that many either, given the long passage of time. More in the first years and then fewer and fewer, though I worked out that these were at relatively regular intervals, my mother's birthday, holidays. How he could have bothered with these, in the midst of the growing horror of the war he was living, was in itself a marvel. For horror there was and it occasionally erupted on the page like a howl of pain, despite the terseness of the language. He would talk of the dearth of supplies, of severed limbs, of savage burns, of the bravery of children. These letters felt like messages in bottles flung into swirling seas, as if he knew they would be indecipherable by the time they reached us, but the gesture of writing them was a call towards another

35

world, of safety, of calm, where a light in the dark signalled the comfort of a home and not the flare of a gun.

Towards the bottom of the pile there was a letter which I couldn't understand at first. When I did, it made me so angry that I wanted to hit my mother again, tear her hair out. It seemed that my father had been in Paris. Had been in Paris and I hadn't seen him. From what I could make out, it must have been during one of my English summers: 1969. But the thought that the simple Channel crossing hadn't been made, that I hadn't been brought over or they come to see me, was so perverse I didn't know how to express my rage. And it was my mother's doing.

I read this letter so many times that it stayed imprinted on my mind. 'I am still saddened,' my father wrote, 'that you thought it best that I not see Maria. I understand your reasons, that it would have unbalanced her, that you get on perfectly well without me. But she may not. It consoles me a little that you say you speak well of me when the occasion arises, though that may not allow her to hate me the less. Still, I have no choice but to bow to your decisions. The blame is, there is no question of that, all mine. Despite all this, it was a comfort to me to see you and to find you so well . . .'

It was no comfort to me, however. I was devastated. I had the feeling that if only I had been allowed to see him, I would have kept him with us. I would never have allowed him to return to Vietnam. I would have had a real, a living father. And would have had someone to turn to now that my mother was dead. I despised my mother for taking this opportunity from me. Despised my father too, for not seizing it of his own accord.

I remember sobbing, thumping the pillow on her bed with my fists, thrusting it across the room so that the feathers spilled from it.

There was another thing about my father's letters which troubled me. To start with they always talked of 'we'. 'We arrived safely', 'We have found an apartment', and so on. My instant assumption was that my mother had lied to save face. There was another woman in the picture and my father had gone off with her. Beneath my pitying reflex of 'poor mother', another voice bubbled up in me and sneered, 'It serves her right. She should have dressed better, done something with herself.'

And then I was no longer sure that this 'we' did incorporate another woman. It was someone called P and P, it turned out, was a little confused, but quite happy. P sometimes joined in embracing my mother and myself at the end of letters. Then P disappeared from this one-sided correspondence and was not heard from again.

When at last I turned to the black notebook, I felt as if I were poised on the final threshold. To cross over meant never to come back again. My mother, I sensed, would be forever altered if I picked any further at the lock of her secrets and opened the door to the final chamber. So I hesitated. And then I leapt.

The writing was my mother's familiar schoolteacher hand, straight, orderly letters, not too crowded together. But the spacing was erratic, as if all of her despair was contained in the gulfs between words.

The first paragraph is etched in my mind.

> Today he left me. I am numb, as if all the parts of me he touched have been anaesthetised. I hold Maria to me, cling to her body in the hope that its warmth will warm the dying that I am. Hope. I have written it, so it must be there. But first there will be that second death.

After that, there was white space, nothing, until two pages later.

'The bloody deed is done,' she wrote. It took me a while to work out what the bloody deed was and then it came to me that she had had an abortion. My father had left her when she was carrying his child.

I read all this slowly, in spasms. It was all too painful and part of me didn't want to know. What child, for all its curiosity, wants really to know the secret turbulence of its parents' lives? But I did read and I learned that my mother had never told my father of this second pregnancy. She wanted him to say that he would stay with her of his own accord. No external pressures, no added weight of choice between her and that other life he so adamantly felt he had to engage in. She was an honourable woman, after all. A good woman. She wouldn't keep him from his greater commitments unless he wanted to stay of his own free will. She resented him nonetheless, and of course felt the resentment was wrong. And she hadn't wanted the abortion, but sensed she couldn't cope with two children on her own.

There were phrases in the midst of all this that I couldn't penetrate. One of them talked of unborn life being sacrificed for a life already begun. I thought she must mean that my father in his capacity as doctor would save lives in that distant embattled Vietnam. Then I toyed with a much more purple scenario in which my father had left her for another woman who was pining away for him in some rice paddy. I thought I remembered her telling me once that he had spent time in the East before meeting her and that would make sense of it all. But I never really got to the bottom of it. The diary was hardly explicit about such mundane things as facts.

What was explicit was my mother's pain and the gradual, dare I say, brave, way, she pieced her life together again. Not that her hold on life was weak. She could have gone with him, after all. The diary examined that possibility and came down firmly against it. The words were not so very different from those she used directly to my face. What was different was the sense that her decision not to accompany him had initially had something of defiance in it, like a bet with herself that if she stood firm, she would win him over; he would bend to her greater reason and stay in France. For her, for love, for me. He didn't and she lost: it was too late for her to climb down. The trouble was that she never really got over it.

There were no dates in the diary, just fits and starts of raw emotion. But time must have passed, years, for there was an entry which could only have dated from after my father's visit to Paris, the one he talked about in his letter. Here she reasserted her reasons for not allowing him to see me. I was hers, only hers now. It was an act of vengeance. A victim's vengeance. She still loved him, but love has never been altogether devoid of power plays.

The final entry is the one that I think shook me most. It was dated just a few days before her own death.

> The letter came today, the one I have been expecting for too long, yet hoped would never arrive. Guy is dead. Has apparently been dead for some time, but no one thought to tell me. I didn't realise I still had hope until now that I recognise it is gone.

My mother, the last romantic. I remember I was sitting in front of the fire when I read this passage for the nth time. I wondered for a moment whether she had deliberately walked in front of that car on the Bastille and then erased the thought and began to tear out the pages of the diary one by one. One by one I placed them on the flames and watched them burn.

It was when I was about half way through that I noticed one of the sheets was thicker than the rest, that it was in fact two stuck together. I prised them apart, thinking I had missed something. I had. Between the two pages was a black-and-white photograph, slightly damaged by the glue that had spread. It showed a man and a woman, their arms around each other but moving apart, as if the camera had surprised them in an embrace. Their bodies were still facing each other, but they were looking at the photographer. Laughing. I recognised the woman instantly as my mother, though she was young, pretty and I had never seen that look on her face. The man was big, broad-shouldered, with a clear gaze and an open smile. My father. It could only be him, though in my mother's valiant attempt to excise him from my life, I had never seen a photo of him before. I gazed at the picture for a while and then, when I had finished burning everything else, the letters as well, I threw that too into the fire.

I am not a good person. The story of my life is the story of not being my mother.

⚖ 8

Now that I have confronted the site of my mother's death, I feel I have the run of the city. I can go anywhere, criss cross, north, south, east, west. The weather has turned beautiful again after days of rain. Plump white clouds travel freely against moist blue sky. I follow them. Follow people too, just to see where they will go.

Today I find myself in the vicinity of the Cimetière Montparnasse. I walk through the gates into this city of the dead where flowers bloom from grey stone. It is a peaceful city. Its inhabitants rest more easily than their memories in visitors' minds. My mother is buried here in the twenty-seventh section off the Avenue de l'Est, not far from the monument to Baudelaire. While the poet sagely contemplates his own writhing form, my mother lies beneath a slab of black marble which carries on its side the words *Famille d'Esté*. On the top, her name appears as Françoise Regnier, beneath her mother's and her father's and her grandparents'. I never knew any of them, though I did know about the little medals imprinted in full colour which her grandfather won in the First World War and the words *Mort pour la France – Membre du Réseau Musée de l'Homme*, which follow her father's name. In death families lie together, though life may have torn them asunder. Even Baudelaire, who broke with his parents to pursue his flowers of evil, is now tucked safely under their wing, hidden under the name of his despised stepfather, Aupick. Perhaps one day I will come to rest here too, next to my mother, my prodigal life erased beneath the greater weight of the family stone.

The temptation to stay now is so great that I race away, my hurry unseemly in this motionless city. To prove to myself I am still alive, I walk into the nearest pâtisserie and buy one of those round two-tier pastries incongruously known as *religieuses*. I eat it quickly, letting the rich cream drip down my chin. On the Boulevard Montparnasse, I mingle with the busy crowds. Everyone seems to have a destination. I follow one person after another in the superstitious hope that a sense of destination may be contagious. But they elude me, disappearing down metro steps or behind shop doors.

A street sign announces Rue Falguière. It is a quiet street until children suddenly teem out of a school building. They laugh and shriek, jostle each other with all the frenzy of released captives. A well-groomed, slightly stocky woman with short blondish hair above a plain high-browed face steps out of the school and makes her way quickly through the crowd. The children's voices fall as she comes between them and then rise, like a wave. I follow the path she cuts, cross back over the boulevard in her determined wake, and trail her into the elegant Rue du Cherche-Midi. She stops to look into the window of an antique shop. I stop too, just in time, at its far end. When I raise my head, she is looking at me. Our eyes meet. I have a sudden sense that I know those eyes – still, mellow brown, expressionless. And the woman seems to be about to speak. I turn away abruptly and cross the street.

Those eyes pursue me. Whom do they belong to? The image won't quite coalesce, much as I prod it.

Closer to the apartment, I stop in front of a newsagent's and scan the papers. I haven't done this in weeks. In New York, I would read two or three papers a day, look through a stack of magazines and watch television. It was part of my job, but I was also addicted. I needed a fix of print and images in my veins to keep the mental motors turning. Now the hunger suddenly fills me again. I buy *Libération*, *Le Monde*, the *Herald Tribune* and for good measure, the *Guardian*. I take my horde back to my lair.

At the door of the lift I meet the man who I have already noticed is my downstairs neighbour. We exchange our customary polite murmurings, but this time he extends the conversation.

'*Vous vous plaisez à Paris?*' he asks me, probably taking me for a visiting American. My *Herald Tribune* is foremost amongst my papers.

'*Assez bien,*' well enough, I answer. His accent isn't French. It has a touch of something northern in it, Scandinavian perhaps, or German, but perhaps it is his size or his glacial eyes which make me think that.

'Well enough, like me,' he smiles, acknowledging his foreignness.

I know from the particular curve of the smile what is going to come next, and it does.

'Perhaps you'd like to come in for a neighbourly cup of coffee,' he says. 'I'm about to make some.'

Despite the expectation, my panic is instantaneous. 'No, no, no thank you,' I mumble. 'Not today.' I try to hide my panic.

Why am I so afraid of being alone with a man? An ordinary man. It used to be so easy not so very long ago. A chat, then another, a couple of drinks, and perhaps after that, if one wanted it, a little pleasure. There is nothing to be afraid of. Yet I am afraid. And perhaps more than that. It's as if without knowing it, I have made a decision.

'Another time then.' He has taken me at my word.

I nod as he leaves the lift.

And why not 'another time'? I cannot go on like this forever, using my lips only to utter inanities to shopkeepers. For almost a month now, since the chance meeting with Sarah Martin, I have had a conversation with no one except my ghosts.

The door of the apartment closes behind me and as always, when I come in, my eyes look towards the picture above the mantelpiece, as if for reassurance. The woman is still walking, her feet firm on the pale ochre earth. I sit down in front of her and spread my French newspapers out on the coffee table. The headlines make no sense. I am out of touch and their shorthand is mystifying. CEE, FIS, OLP, CNPF, TVA. The letters mean nothing to me. So short a time, and it is as if I have fallen out of the world.

I turn to the *Herald Tribune* for comfort and to reassert my kinship with my fellow beings. To know what acronyms and initials stand for is to have power, as well as a sense of community. UN, US, GB, IRA, PLO are hieroglyphs I can decipher. Peace talks are in the headlines, between Israel and the PLO, Bosnians, Croats, Serbs, IRA and Loyalists; but headlines about carnage between the same parties also blare. The state of the world makes my own difficulties piddling. Perhaps that was why my mother was a news junkie. What matter one small well-fed, if not altogether happy, lifetime in this quagmire of horrors?

Satiated with affliction, my eyes wander to the classified columns. Escort agencies abound. Belgravia Orchids, Chic of London, Ferrari International, Suzy of Tokyo, Frankfurt and Paris, Educated and Elegant. Perhaps I should offer my services. Get paid for what I do best.

I skim through language schools and apartments and am suddenly riveted by a little boxed announcement. 'Women who Kill', it says in bold and then beneath, 'Attorney seeks researcher for study of women murderers. Fluent English and French, at least, essential as well as ability to word process, type, interview, and travel at quick notice.'

I must have stared at the ad for some time for when I look up, it is dark outside and without realising it, I have already switched on the hearthside lamp. Restlessness seizes hold of me. I start to pace the length and breadth of the apartment. Even the sight of those gliding feet doesn't calm me. I stare into the mirror. It shows me a face no different from the one I saw before I left New York. The cheekbones are still there, the wave of a nose, the full lips, the grey eyes. Perhaps there are a few more lines round them. I crinkle them to check. But no, faces show nothing. My face shows nothing. I grub round in my capacious make-up bag and come up with a stick of mascara, some lipstick. I put it on for the first time in weeks. Savagely I brush my hair.

The street is deserted. I turn the corner and go into the local café. A few men are hunched over the bar. Some younger ones bend over a flipper machine showing a jean-clad woman with a large bosom and a cowboy hat. Lights come on in different parts of her anatomy as the racing ball clacks and zings its way down the machine. The noisy youths push and prod and slap the side and the glass surface. I sit at a corner table and order a glass of sauterne. It is too sweet, but I drink it anyway.

'May I?' The man from the apartment below mine is suddenly in front of me.

Before I have a chance to answer, he sits down and stretches out his hand. 'Bjorn Johannsen,' he introduces himself.

I hesitate and then place my hand in his. 'Maria d'Esté.' It is the first time I have said my name since I checked in at the hotel.

'Another glass?'

I shake my head, only to change my mind. After all, I have come out because I felt restive. A little conversation may help.

'A coffee, please. *Un petit crème.*'

He waves the waiter over and then examines me. 'You said that like a native.'

'I am.'

'Not American, then?

'No, mostly French.' I tell him the truth, though the temptation to lie is great.

'I see. I thought the apartment belonged to Americans.'

'It does. I'm only using it for a while.'

He gives me an open smile then, as if everything has been cleared up, and proceeds to tell me about himself. I learn that he is from Stockholm, that he works in Paris for IKEA, that he doesn't particularly like the French. He says the last with a little self-effacing grin, adding that at least the nights are shorter here.

I settle back into the hard chair. I can read the signs. There will be few demands made of me for the next half hour. I am in for a life-story, professional at first, and gradually, confessional.

Men always confess to me. I don't know why. Someone once told me it was because of the way I tilt my head, so that I look as if I'm fascinated by every word uttered. And apparently I 'mmm' in a particular way, a sound which serves every purpose from question to comment and also acts as a provocation to more speech. Someone else told me, but that was when things were getting a little ropey between us, that it was because I was just a mirror and reflected whatever any pompous little arse wanted to see of himself.

It's not that I don't speak. It's just that I take a little while to warm to it. When needed, I can hold my own with the best of them. But it's not needed now. Bjorn Johannsen is off and away. He has finished giving me his impressions of Paris, he has told me about his work, and now that he's onto his second glass of beer, he's beginning to tell me about how his girlfriend didn't take to Paris.

I glance at my watch and in a great flurry start to rise. 'I must go,' I say. 'There's some work I have to finish tonight.'

'Oh.' His blue eyes narrow into a seductive look. 'I'd hoped you'd join me for dinner.' He puts a staying hand on my wrist.

I look into his eyes. They are undressing me. I find myself imagining the logical end of that undressing. I see his lips moving towards my bare skin. I feel their touch and as I feel it a dark head overlays his blond one. My stomach heaves with a violence I can barely control.

'Can't,' I mumble. 'Another time. Thanks for the coffee.'

As I turn the corner into a darkened street, the retching catches up with me and I spew the contents of my stomach and my life into the gutter. I wipe my mouth with a crumpled tissue and lean against a wall and shudder. Then I head homewards, resolutely placing one foot in front of the other.

No sooner am I in the apartment than the show of resolution becomes real.

At the corner of the desk in the mezzanine, there is a small old-fashioned portable. I take a piece of paper and off the top of my head begin to type.

> Dear Sir/Madam,
>
> Your classified ad in the *Herald Tribune* intrigues me. I could tell you a great deal about myself, but prefer in the interests of your time and mine to tell you just a little. I have all the qualifications you mention. I also have a reading and speaking knowledge of Spanish, though my ability to write in it is limited.

I then switch to French and note that I have held a responsible job for some years but would now welcome a change. References, if needed, can be had, though I prefer not to trouble anyone, until I have a clearer notion of the project at hand.

As I write, the idea of death curls round me like a serpent, clutches at my throat. Before I lose my nerve I address the letter and rush downstairs to post it. While I press the lid of the yellow box, I shut my eyes, screw up my face, and make a wordless wish. The gesture is involuntary. This is how I have always done it. This is how I used to do it in my early days in New York.

When I first arrived in Manhattan the city both excited and frightened me and the more it frightened me, the more excited I grew. I was avid for life, hungry for sights and smells and sounds. Sleaze or glamour, it didn't matter which, as long as impressions and experience crowded upon each other at breakneck speed. It was the careless avidity of youth, impatient only with constraint.

The run-down yellow cab which bumped me from the bus terminal to the hotel I had randomly chosen for its cheapness seemed to have served as a getaway car for some sleazy shoot-out amidst the yawning canyons of the city. Its corpulent, shirt-sleeved driver chewed gum, intermittently took slugs from a Coke can and when he abruptly turned towards me, it was to bellow out words I could barely understand. Amongst them was, 'English'. I nodded at this, and when he lifted my bags from the boot of the car, he looked me up and down slowly and smiled with approval. 'London, ya?'

I agreed, since it seemed to make him happy. It seemed to make everyone I met in New York happy. So half the time I simply let people think I was English. My being mistaken for an English person was the one thing about my life in America that would probably have made my mother proud.

The hotel was a nondescript building tucked in beside Lincoln Center. It smelled vaguely of urine mingled with disinfectant and had nothing to recommend it except that it was in New York and far from home. Outside, police and ambulance sirens blared, obliterating the sounds of the television where earnest men and women with bright teeth held up packages, bottles, tubes.

I think it was the sight of the tenth cockroach crawling out from behind the murky sink that made me decide that I would after all, as Olivier had insisted, ring his friend. I hung on for seven days – days replete with forays down Broadway and into the Village and up the Empire State Building and into museums – and then phoned.

Charles Delahaye, when he picked up the receiver, sounded as if he had been waiting for my call ever since he had received Olivier's letter. He urged me to pack my bags and come over straightaway. Dinner would be waiting and the spare room. He omitted to mention anything else.

The apartment was in the Nineties, just off Riverside Drive, a squat stone building with a lurching elevator which bumped its way to the fourteenth floor. When he opened the door, Charles Delahaye was all French charm, exaggerated as it can only be after years of living abroad. Dark hair, flashing eyes, a silk ascot round his neck, he embraced me a little too firmly and kissed me on both cheeks, before introducing me to his wife and children. I hadn't been aware of the existence of either and it would probably have been better for everyone if that condition had persisted.

The children, a boy of eight and a girl of six, grudgingly said 'Hi', and then returned to an argument which entailed chasing round the large sitting room to the loud but unheeded reprimands of their mother. It was evident from the first that after an initial survey of my appearance, Edith Rosen Delahaye was hardly overjoyed to see me.

Dinner was a bizarre affair, with Charles preening and chatting away to me in French, while Edith occasionally interrupted resentfully or rebuked him for not tending to the children. As the evening progressed in fits and starts, which the liberal addition of wine couldn't quite lubricate, it became clear to me that my hopes of instantly registering for a degree at Columbia University had been grounded in crass naivety. Even if Charles pulled strings to overcome lateness, there was the hurdle of what to my French eyes were astronomical tuition fees; nor as a non-resident could I immediately qualify for one of the state colleges.

By the time the children had been tucked into bed and we were sitting sipping coffee on gargantuan sofas in the sprawling sitting room, the solution which to everyone but me had obviously been evident from the start, was voiced. Until I found my feet, perhaps even a scholarship – Charles dangled this like a juicy carrot – I would live with the Delahayes as their au pair, do a little cleaning, pick the children up from school, speak to them in French, baby-sit, and of course, audit as many courses as could be arranged for. And *voilà*, Charles clapped his hands like some circuit magician whose hat has finally produced a rabbit, my life in New York would be taken care of for the time being at least.

My first instinct was to run from the house, abandon my bags for greater ease and go. Just go. But I sat there, paralysed by the sense that Olivier and Charles had planned this out between them, aware that everything that was being said made sense. I even nodded politely when Edith asked with exemplary curtness, 'You do know how to clean, I presume?'

And so, like a victim of one of Louis XV's *lettres de cachets*, my fate was sealed. My prison may not have had bars, but Edith, whom I thought of as my keeper, encircled me with so many rules and chores, that it may as well have had. Her dislike of me was not even particularly personal, I later realised. She simply hated me for being young, pretty, unmarried and childless. Which of those counts was the most serious, I don't know, but together they constituted a major felony. I was put to clean three hours a day, given a few hours to attend courses, and then the children were all mine. The excuse was that she was busy writing her thesis, but I suspect she liked the little terrors even less than I did.

None of this in retrospect would have been so dreadful, except that I could do nothing right in Edith's eyes. My dresses and clothes were wrong, my hair was wrong, my sorting through of a thousand toys was wrong, my vacuuming was wrong. Her every contact with me was a rebuke – to the point where my dreams took on a persecutory flavour. I would wake gasping for air in the middle of the night, not certain of who it was who had clasped my throat, or put gags in my mouth, or locked the bathroom from the outside.

Edith's rebukes only stopped when they merged into lectures. These had one theme with many variations and I suppose they were parts of that thesis I could never hear her typing. The theme was oppression, to be more precise men's oppression of women through the ages: the sins of patriarchy. Much of this was interesting. The problem was that while Edith talked about the wrongs of men and the rights of women, I had the sense that I alone was the target of her bile. A woman like her, I was nonetheless at fault. I was to blame. So that I would emerge from these lectures feeling not so much wronged, as that I was contemptible, at once object of hatred and self-hatred.

It was not so different from the seminar in women's studies, led by a friend of hers, she had fixed up for me to audit at Columbia. Here too, a long sequence of victimised, embattled women and heroines paraded before me, crushing me under their very weight as the injustices of patriarchy had crushed them. Once when I was elicited to speak, I said I found it hard to think about these stifled Victorian women. I had been brought up with strong, competent characters, women like Shakespeare's Portia or Lady Macbeth or Madame de Pompadour or Madame de Staël, who had saved lovers and friends from the revolutionary guillotine. A thick silence followed my words and for once I wished that my mother were here to explain things more lucidly. For of course, she had marched, once even alongside Simone de Beauvoir, for women's rights. But as I remembered it, her emphasis had always been on what was to be gained, not on the male enemy whose victim one was and from whom any gain had to be wrested.

Anyhow, in that silence which followed my one classroom intervention, I realised they didn't like my dresses either.

Charles's lectures on eighteenth-century France, which I attended as well, were better. They made me feel neither powerless nor despised, and I made some friends amongst my fellow students. But the material was largely what I had already studied, and when he invited me to his office to discuss my plans and possible scholarship applications, it became clear that *he* liked my dresses a little too much. He would smooth my collars, or straighten a shoulder, or find a button I had apparently missed. Gradually, too, it dawned on me that he always managed to be at the door when I emerged from the shower in the morning, or in the hall when I passed so that he could brush against me. Perhaps none of this would have bothered me quite so much if I had felt the least attraction for him. I was not, after all, a prude. The problem was that where I saw Charles, I also saw Edith, as if they had melted into one monstrous being.

Towards the end of my second month in New York, Charles asked me to meet him in his office, so that we could have lunch together and discuss my future in a more relaxed way. But there was nothing relaxed in the atmosphere that greeted me when I opened the door to Charles's office. His hair was dishevelled as if he had spent hours passing his hands through it. His eyes were intent, too bright, and as he ushered me in I heard the turn of the lock in the door behind me. Before I could sit down, he put his arms around me and tried to place a moist kiss on my lips. It landed on my cheek and as I wriggled away, he coiled me in language, wreaths of words telling me how beautiful I was, how he couldn't resist me, how he had fallen hopelessly in love with me, how he had the afternoon free, how there was a little hotel downtown he knew.

I still remember the sense of suffocation I had, the struggle to break through it and then the words which came to me in icy French. *'Tu es fou.'* You're raving.

They must have been accompanied by a glare, for Charles abruptly stopped his barrage and in the sudden silence, I unlocked the door and walked from the room, walked straight back to the apartment, packed my bags, and only then confronted Edith who was tucked away in her study at the far end of the hall.

'I've told you not to bother me in the middle of the day,' she glowered at me.

'I thought you'd want to know that I won't be bothering you at all any more. Say goodbye to the kids.'

I was rude, I know, and I savoured the rudeness. I didn't stop to answer her spluttering why's and what's. I gave no explanations. But I think in another minute I wouldn't have been able to resist betraying her husband's little misdemeanour, particularly when she hurled words like 'ungrateful' at me.

It wasn't that I thought that Charles had behaved immorally. I don't think I reflected on his behaviour very much at all. I simply knew that I wanted nothing to do with him. With either of them. One thing about me: I don't remember ever having gone to bed with a man I didn't want to go to bed with. I know these days received wisdom has it that men are beasts and incapable of taking 'no' for an answer. That hasn't been my experience. Perhaps my no's always sound definitive. Or perhaps men are simply afraid of beautiful women. It's the plain ones they think they can do what they like with.

In any case, I found a cab and on the spur of the moment asked to be taken to the Gramercy Park Hotel. It was the only address on the other side of Manhattan that came to me. I stayed there for two nights and then, thinking of my limited finances, moved into a cheaper rooming house on the other side of the square. Within two weeks, I had found a grimy studio in the East Village. I had also danced away nights in clubs, smoked a few joints, chatted to people. And sent off some seventy letters in response to job ads in the papers.

Each time I put a batch of these letters into the mail box, I shut my eyes tight, screwed up my face and made a wordless wish.

⚖ 9

I cannot sleep. I lie in the four-poster bed and stare up at its canopy of tiny golden stars. I am thirty-three years old, that *'mezzo del cammin di nostra vita'*, as Dante defined it. What shall I do with the rest of the road? I have already buried two lives and now meet only their shadows. And beyond the shadows, what then?

When I left my first life, I didn't think about the 'then'. I merely plunged. Now I think, but the thoughts take me round in circles, like the spiralling circles of hell.

I leap out of bed to rout the self-pity which has taken hold of me. These elegant rooms in this city of dazzling spectacle are no papered-over hell. I am simply hungry, I tell myself. I have forgotten to eat.

The misty green fridge reveals the remains of a chicken I bought yesterday, ready-grilled. I place it on the old pine table and pick at it, straight from the bag. I gnaw at legs, dismember the carcass, nibble the wishbone clean. The wishbone. I twine my little finger round one of its prongs and stare at the upside-down V. Suddenly those quiet, mellow brown eyes I encountered in the street are opposite me, but they are lodged in the face of a little girl. Two thick blonde plaits fall over her shoulders. She stares at me, stares at the wishbone, then closes her eyes so tightly that her whole face is creased with the intensity of it. She is wishing. She is wishing so well that I know her wish will come true.

My mother stands on the other side of the kitchen table.

'That's right, Beatrice,' she says softly. 'Now you make your wish and tug. You, too, Maria.'

I look at Beatrice and imitate her gesture, but I know there is no point. I cannot mimic the frenzy of desire Beatrice has put into her wish.

There is a little crack as the bone splits and then the sound of my mother clapping. 'Beatrice has it. You will have your wish, Beatrice. But you musn't tell what it was.'

'Thank you, Madame.' Beatrice's face has resumed its more customary expression, which is one of calm bordering on resignation. Her eyes, which have huge liquid dark centres, rarely seem to move or blink. She looks like one of those saints a book on my mother's shelves depicts. A knife may be digging into the folds of her dress, but her face, her gestures, betray only a serene gratitude.

I am fascinated by Beatrice the very first day I see her at school. I am coming up to nine and it is the beginning of the winter term. She is new to the class and she sits at the end of the front row. As the teacher introduces her to us, Beatrice sits precariously near the edge of her chair, tipping it forward. Her hands are tightly clenched on the desk, but her face is tranquil. There is a stillness to her which bears no resemblance to anyone else's in the class. Her face is not a particularly pretty face, rather plain really, but there is something about it which I have never seen before.

The other children feel it too. In the playground, they shun her for days on end. Even the most raucous boys don't pull her plaits. She stands at the edge of the courtyard and simply stares into space. But she doesn't look wistful. It is as if she is oblivious to the rowdy tumbles and shouts which make up recess. She doesn't seem to want to play. She is self-contained.

On Friday, I leave my noisy little group and walk over to her. I stand beside her for a while without saying anything, then I ask, 'Would you like to play?'

Beatrice looks at me as if my words have come across a distance of oceans and are muffled by waves. Then her lips curl slowly into a smile. The smile has a purity about it, like a single ray of early spring sunlight.

I put up my hands and motion for her to do the same. I begin one of the pat-a-cakes that has been making the rounds.

> 'My father runs a grocery
> My mother bakes the bread
> Come the summer holidays
> They'll both go to bed, bed, bed . . .'

With laborious seriousness, Beatrice learns the words.

Within two weeks, Beatrice and I are fast friends. We sit in the canteen together and I slip her all the bits of food I don't like. She eats everything dutifully. She doesn't talk much, but my patter makes up for two. At playtime, I make certain she is part of my group, though my last term's best friend makes fun of her, laughs at the patches on her clothes. So do the others. I like the fact that Beatrice's clothes are even more tawdry than mine and I stick up for her. Since the other girls are a little afraid of me, since I already tower over both girls and boys, they gradually accept her.

I bring Beatrice home with me after school. She is shy. She looks at my mother with astonishment when she sits down to have hot chocolate with us and talks to us about our school day.

'And what about homework?' my mother asks. 'Why not get it over with and then you'll have lots of time to play?'

The table is scrubbed clean and we bring out our plastic-bound notebooks. My mother looks over Beatrice's shoulder for a few moments and then she says to me, 'You might give Beatrice a hand, Maria. I think she has a little catching up to do.'

I help Beatrice with her long division, but I grow impatient. She is slow, doesn't understand. My mother takes over while I go off to my room and dig out cards, set up an elaborate game of spit. Beatrice, when she finally joins me, is not too quick to grasp this either. It occurs to me that she may never have played cards and I explain the sets to her and sequences of kings and queens and jacks.

'I'm glad you've made a friend of Beatrice,' my mother says to me when she comes to tuck me in for the night. She pauses. 'She's a sweet girl.'

I bridle a little at this. My mother has never told me that I am a sweet girl. But then she adds, 'And you're so clever. You can help her. Her last school couldn't have been much good.'

I like this better. I help Beatrice. She comes home with me after school two or three times a week, occasionally with another friend, and sometimes comes round on weekends as well. My mother takes us to see movies or we go to the Louvre and look at pictures of people with a lot of clothes on or women with none at all.

One week I have flu and am away from school for some days. When I get back, I notice that Beatrice has a huge bruise on her cheek. I ask her how she got it.

'Oh, it's nothing.' She raises her hand to her face. 'I fell.'

At playtime, my other best friend, Rachel, asks me, 'Have you noticed how Beatrice smells?'

'Don't be silly.' I am angry with her.

'It's true. Natalie says so. And Simon. And they sit next to her.'

'How did Beatrice fall?' I change the subject.

Rachel shrugs, then giggles. 'Ask Simon.'

I don't need to ask Simon. I know his tricks. He has a leg that mysteriously finds itself entangled in other people's feet.

I realise that the magic which initially kept Beatrice apart from the classroom fray has faded. Without my protection, she is prey to all and sundry.

'We'll get even with them,' I tell her after school.

But Beatrice demurs. 'It doesn't matter, it's nothing.' Then she asks me how my mother is.

'Fine,' I mumble and then somehow manage to put the question, 'Would you like a bath when we get back to my place?'

'Oh no,' she says, but I convince her, I tell her I want one too.

That evening I mention to my mother that it seems a little odd that Beatrice has never invited me home to her house.

My mother looks at me with her especially patient expression which signals a comment on life in general. 'Not everyone is as fortunate as we are,' she says. 'I think Beatrice is probably quite poor. She may not want to show you where she lives. People are like that sometimes. And she probably doesn't have a room of her own. She has a little sister, she tells me, and a brother.'

She hadn't told me, but I let it pass.

My mother rushes on. 'I am glad you've become such fast friends. Beatrice is a good person.'

The way she says this loads it with importance. I begin to see just how good Beatrice is. When she stays for dinner, she leaps up with alacrity rather than hanging back when it's time for the washing up. She listens to every word my mother says, then nods and smiles. She says please and thank you and *'Oui, Madame'* a lot. Her notebooks are of a tidiness mine can never hope to match. She can plait her own hair neatly in two minutes flat and it never spills out of its bands the way mine does. Then, too, she never gets angry and never talks back. And she never wants revenge, even when the other children are horrid to her. Beatrice is a good person.

Summer arrives and I am packed off to Kent for madcap games in English with Robinson. The golden fields, the expanse of the horizon, bleach out Paris. When I come back to school, everyone seems a little hazy to me, a little unreal. Even Beatrice. But she greets me with a beatific smile and assumes she is coming home with me. It is on the way home that I realise she has seen my mother far more over the summer than I have.

It is only some months later that this rankling develops into something I recognise as anger. For my mother's birthday, Beatrice brings her a large and expensive bottle of Chanel No. 5. My mother is overwhelmed. She hugs Beatrice to her and mumbles, 'How good of you. You really shouldn't have.'

'I wanted to,' Beatrice says.

As my mother showers us all with her new scent, I think of the two teacloths I have chosen for her in obedience to her rule of usefulness and feel like hiding the package. I know that the hug and peck she gives me are as nothing compared to Beatrice's.

The next day I ask Beatrice how she could afford to give my mother such an expensive present.

'I did lots of errands over the summer.' She turns her patient smile on me and then waves the matter away. 'By the way, your mother asked if I'd like to stay over this weekend. Won't that be fun!'

I nod but I am not happy.

Over the next months, Beatrice seems almost to be living with us. When the spare room isn't otherwise engaged, she is always there. She comes to us for Christmas. She makes herself useful, sets the table, takes the rubbish down without being asked, is thrilled to stand at the metro station with a box in her hand and collect money for my mother's charities. And my mother has been helping her with her work as much as I used to, so that now we are neck-and-neck for first place in class.

One day we are sitting together at the large table doing our homework when I spill a bottle of ink over Beatrice's notebook. I snatch the bottle upright and watch the circle of blue widen and spread and sink down through the pages.

'I'm so sorry,' I say, feeling blissfully happy.

Beatrice looks up at me with her mellow eyes. 'It doesn't matter.' She finds a page towards the end of the book which is untainted and dutifully starts her work again.

An imp of the perverse takes me over. I break plates and pretend that Beatrice has done it. I hide her notebooks so that she will be late delivering homework and find them for her miraculously the next day somewhere around the house. I take my mother's best pen and imply that Beatrice has perhaps stolen it. I begin to invite other friends home after school, avoid Beatrice when the bell rings, so that she is forced to ask whether she can tag along with us. I never stop her, but she becomes more and more like someone we treat as a mangy dog. The trouble is, she is happy with her scraps. Even when we whisper horrible things about her behind her back, so that she can hear; even when one day our game entails putting her in the large green rubbish bin in the square by the school and covering her over. Beatrice never complains. And my mother continues to sing her praises.

Beatrice, I say to myself, is my mother's better daughter.

No sooner do I acknowledge this, than Beatrice is suddenly living with us. How it happens I don't quite know, but it has to do with the fact that she has broken her leg. She is away from school for a few days and when she reappears, she is on crutches. A grubby white plaster cast sticks out from beneath her desk.

'I fell down the stairs,' she tells me without meeting my eyes and I imagine that someone has pushed her, perhaps her brother or sister.

'Did it hurt?' I ask.

She nods.

'So you won't be able to play for a while,' I say. 'You won't be able to come home with me after school.' It is a statement, not a question.

Beatrice looks away. 'No.' Her voice is funny. I can barely hear it.

That evening I tell my mother, 'Beatrice has broken her leg. She won't be able to come here any more.'

'Oh?' A deep crease appears in my mother's brow. She looks worried, even a little frightened. With a distracted air, she asks me to tell her how it happened.

'She fell down the stairs,' I reply and add, 'Her sister or brother probably pushed her. They were fed up with her being such a goody-goody.'

'Don't be silly,' my mother frowns.

On Saturday, when I come home at lunchtime after school, Beatrice is installed in our spare room. I had noticed her absence that morning, but thought little of it. My mother tells me nothing about how she convinced Beatrice's parents to let her go, nor what they are like. She simply says, 'Beatrice is going to stay with us until her leg is healed. Won't that be nice? And so much better for her to be closer to school.'

I grunt in the way my mother hates, but she lets it pass.

Every time we have chicken for dinner and my mother hands us the wishbone, I imitate Beatrice's gestures and wish with all my heart that Beatrice will soon be better and disappear. Forever, I feel, though I don't put that into the words of the wish. But Beatrice wishes better than I do and I am always left holding the short end of the bone. Until one evening, just before the summer holidays, when the top of the upside-down V remains in my hand. I stare at it in amazement, feel a miracle has taken place.

Sure enough, Beatrice's cast comes off two days later and after the summer break, she has disappeared. She is no longer in our class, no longer in the school. I hardly dare tell my mother, but she speaks to me about it herself.

'Beatrice and her family have moved to the country. She'll write to us when they have a permanent address.'

I feign sadness. Then in order to explain the smile which tugs at my lips, I add, 'She'll like the country. She always said she'd like to go to the country.'

'Yes.' My mother looks at me dubiously.

Beatrice writes, not frequently, but there are separate letters for my mother and myself. I answer the first two or three and then stop. I am not interested. My mother, I know, carries on, for occasionally she gives me news of Beatrice.

Then one Saturday, I must be about sixteen, I come home mid-afternoon and find a young woman sitting with my mother. It is not until I see her eyes that I realise this must be Beatrice. She doesn't look well. Her skin is blotchy, her face puffy. Her skirt is thick and shapeless. She seems years older than the rest of my friends. But the eyes are the same, mellow, benign, somehow more saintly than ever.

Conversation is difficult. We have nothing in common any more. She has really come to see my mother, ostensibly to ask for a job reference. But she asks me questions about school, about friends. She flatters me. And I feel guilt spreading through me as if I were somehow responsible for the way Beatrice has turned out. It is my fault. I escape as soon as I can. I have friends to see, an appointment at the cinema. All of this is true, but I am still escaping.

My mother tells me no more about Beatrice. I don't know whether she sees her any more or not. I certainly never hear from her again.

⚖ 10

The idea that the woman I trailed from the school on the Rue Falguière down to the Rue du Cherche-Midi is Beatrice obsesses me. I have gone back to the school twice and waited as the children spilled through the gates. But she didn't appear.

This morning, as I gaze down from the window into the courtyard garden, the sight of the sprouting crocuses and fat daffodil shoots makes me long for the country. I pull on my boots and jacket and head for the Luxembourg Gardens. Hardly the country, but at least there will be those flowers I am so good at naming.

On the way I pause at a travel agent's and look at posters. A cheetah lopes through long grass. A lion yawns regally, balancing himself on a tree-trunk. Masai-Mara, the pictures announce. Sunsets in Siam, reads the script above a group of men raking rice as white as snow in a peaceful paddy field. Golden beaches. Martinique, Ile de la Réunion, Guadeloupe. Places I never heard of in America but which my school books had carefully taught me were departments of France.

My first job in New York was in a travel agency. From the hundreds of letters I sent out after I had left the Delahayes, the third response was from something called French Affair. I was summoned to an interview. Since it was my third, I prepared myself a little better and reminded myself over and over that I had to impress my prospective bosses with my eagerness and talents, minimal as they were, before the crucial question came up.

The office was on the sixth floor of a block on Madison and 50th. It consisted of one largish room where French exhibition posters had pride of place: the Carnavalet, the Louvre, Matisse at the Musée d'Art Moderne. There were also two desks, shelves neatly ranked with brochures and a few chairs; plus a nether room. A woman who was visibly in the final stages of pregnancy showed me in to this back room where Mr Carruthers was waiting for me.

He was a gangling man with a shining pate and a wry turn to his lips, and he had a dapper air about him. His bow tie was a bright canary yellow, his shirt forest green and when he stood up to shake my hand, his trousers sported a perfect crease. He addressed and put his first questions to me in French and when I started to babble away at top speed, he lifted his knobbly hands to his ears and shouted, 'Whoaaa.'

I stopped in mid-sentence and he started to laugh. 'I was just checking that you had a command of the language,' he grinned. From then on he spoke to me in English. He explained that the agency worked with private individuals as well as other agencies to set up select trips for people who wanted to explore France, not just the usual tourist trajectories, but journeys that would cater to particular tastes and interests.

I dug out some history and asked him, 'You mean things like Louis XIV's France, or Napoleon's, or eighteenth-century architectural highlights?'

'Yes, all that.' He looked at me oddly. 'Not bad ideas, those.'

We chatted for quite a long time about this and that, and about why I had come to the States. He told me that my job would consist of liaising with clients to draw up itineraries, then with the French side, hotels, train schedules, car hire firms. He told me that some clients would require discretion, that others would be difficult. And then he asked me the hard questions.

No I had no experience, I told him, but I would work hard and my school results were good. I could type pretty well, I lied, and then hurriedly added that I would practise all day every day until the job started and every night after that. No, I had no references, but he could write to my teachers. My desperation was growing by the second and when he asked me the crucial question about working papers, I think I must visibly have stifled a sob.

'That's just what I thought,' he murmured. He gave me a long hard look and then grinned his grin again. 'Well, we can try. I know someone who knows someone who may be able to help. In the meantime, you can come in and learn the trade for pocket money.'

If he hadn't been sitting at the other side of the desk, I would have flung my arms around him.

And so I became a travel agent. It was Mr Carruthers who used to call me Rita when he wanted to tease me. I stayed with him for over a year, before the next thing came along and he agreed, not altogether happily, to let me go.

The beds of the Luxembourg Gardens are afire with the molten reds, rich purples and fuchsia pinks of pansies and primulas. I walk past the Italianate palace my royal namesake constructed for herself when the Louvre began to bore her, and head towards the central fountain. Children are sailing their little boats across the carps' heads, prodding boats and fish at once with their wooden sticks. 'L'amiral des voiliers', admiral of the sailing boats, we used to call the old woman who rented the ships to us by the hour. We each had our favourite number. Mine was ninety-five and it won many a race to the centre of the fountain.

From the presence of the children, I realise today must be Wednesday – a full free day for some, half free for others. My mother, I remember, used to rant about this free day set up to appease the clerics: if state schools were secular, there would nonetheless be time set aside when, if so wished, children could pursue a religious education. 'Half-measures,' she grumbled, 'calculated to drive working mothers mad.'

Past the wooded area where a few lone enthusiasts act out a ballet of Tai Chi, past the children's playground, I sit down on a bench. In the midst of the moist lawn before me stands Bartholdi's original for the Statue of Liberty. Was it here that my dreams of going to America were nurtured? Or was it simply the latest spate of Hollywood films?

The peace of the spot is suddenly broken by piping young voices. A flock of small schoolchildren appear. Two women are with them, ordering them into double files, hushing their clamour. One of the women begins to speak. I stare at her from the distance of my bench. It is her. I am certain of it. Beatrice. She may look far better than she did at sixteen, but the quiet gestures are the same. And the stillness is there like an invisible wall around her.

The Statue of Liberty explained, the group turns down the lane at my left. The woman I am sure is Beatrice doesn't look in my direction. I cannot but get up and follow. It is as if the piper has begun to play and her flute controls my limbs. I trail the group to the southern tip of the gardens and watch them congregate at a bus stop in front of the Closerie des Lilas. I hesitate. Have I gone mad? Why am I so certain this woman is Beatrice? Is it simply because she turned up unexpectedly in the Luxembourg today? But I hurry on. I may not have the courage to get onto the same bus, I may not have the courage to pronounce her name, but I know her destination. I catch up with the children on the Rue Falguière and watch the gates of the school swallow them. It won't be long now. It is almost noon. I am so tense with anticipation that perspiration wets my arms. I take off my jacket and wait.

On the dot of twelve the doors open and I cluster behind the waiting mums until I see Beatrice emerge. She walks quickly, her slightly heavy hips moving with a precise, efficient swing. Her suit is good, her legs a little thick but shapely in clear stockings and pump shoes. For a moment, seeing her like this, I am uncertain about her again, but I hasten after her nonetheless.

She pauses at the window of the same antique shop. I am about to speak. A little speech has crystallised in my mind: 'It's strange, I know, but you remind me so much of an old schoolfriend . . .'

Our eyes meet in the reflection of the shop window. And suddenly she turns towards me and says, her voice faltering, 'Maria Regnier?'

'Beatrice?' I respond hoarsely.

We stare at each other for a moment and then she touches my hand, squeezes it. 'How extraordinary. How utterly extraordinary. After all these years . . . I saw you here the other day, didn't I? I thought it was you, but then you walked away.'

Her voice has the same soft, slow inflection and the radiant smile she gives me makes me feel she has forgiven me or forgotten. I prefer to think it is the former.

'You look so wonderful,' she breathes.

'And you.' It is true. But what fills me with wonder is how her quiet plainness is still irradiated by something I cannot quite grasp. We gaze at each other for another moment and then I say, 'Shall we have a coffee? Catch up . . .'

She glances at her watch, nods. 'But I won't have very long today. I'm sorry. But now that we've found each other . . . I've thought about you on and off over the years.'

We sit in a café in the Carrefour de Croix-Rouge, gaze at each other. Conversation isn't easy. It is she who takes the lead. 'So tell me what you've been up to. What do you do?'

I laugh brittly. 'For the moment, I do nothing. I've been living in New York. I only came back recently.'

'I always thought you would be a teacher, like your mother.' She hesitates on the last word, gives it a breathing space of its own.

I shake my head. 'It's you, instead.'

She smiles that slow smile. 'Yes,' she acknowledges. 'But not half so good.'

'She would have been proud of you.'

'I would have liked that.' She stirs her coffee deliberately, then raises her eyes to mine. 'I wrote to her once after that last time I saw you both. But the letter came back.' Her face clouds over. For a moment, as she stares out of the window, it grows ugly, contorted, as if she can't forgive me for chasing her away from my mother. Or perhaps I imagine it, for as soon as she looks at me again, there is the same soft light. 'It was only when I came to Paris, some years later, that I learned she had died. I'm so sorry. She was so kind. So good.'

The way she says it brings an unaccustomed lump to my throat. For the first time, I, too, seem to feel sorry for my mother. But I say with an inappropriate laugh, 'She was still relatively young.'

'Yes.'

Beatrice is lost in some thought of her own, then she glances at her watch again.

'You were her better daughter,' I say, to keep her there, also because I need to say it.

'What a strange idea.' She reaches for her bag. 'I must go. But we'll meet soon. You'll tell me all about yourself.' She takes a pen from her bag and writes her phone number for me on a napkin. 'Please ring.'

'I'll walk with you.'

'If you like. It's not far.'

We turn left into the Rue de Grenelle. At the next corner, she pauses, gestures along a narrow street. 'We're just up there.' I am so much taller than her that she stands on her toes to kiss the air on either side of my face. 'You are all right, aren't you?' She looks at me with momentary concern.

'Yes.' The syllable doesn't sound quite emphatic enough, so I repeat it. 'Yes, of course.'

'I'm sorry I can't invite you up, but Marie-Françoise's English lesson begins in just five minutes, and then there's one of my SOS-Racisme meetings.'

'Marie-Françoise?'

'My youngest.' She waves, hurries along the street.

I watch her stop at a building on the right, tap out a code, push open a heavy wooden door. I wait a moment and then I walk slowly past the building. Beatrice has children, I think. Beatrice is married. Beatrice is a teacher. Beatrice lives in an apartment in one of the city's most desirable areas. Beatrice belongs to committees. Beatrice has come from nowhere and made a life for herself. She has named her daughter Marie-Françoise. Is it a coincidence that the name contains both myself and my mother? Surely not. Beatrice bears no rancour. She is good. She has not changed. There is a peace about her.

I realise that I feel the same fascination with Beatrice's goodness as I felt as a child. But now it comes to me that I would like to imitate it. Is it something one can learn?

Now that Beatrice has disappeared, I cross over to her side of the street and walk up and down its length, as if tracing and retracing her footsteps. I look up at the façades of the houses with their clear, simple lines, their symmetrical stonework, the clusters of grapes and leaves which punctuate the surface. Near the top of the building opposite, huge letters half-obscure the windows. '*A Louer*', I read. For rent. And a phone number. Without thinking, I quickly jot the number down.

I am suddenly supremely happy.

⚖ 11

Two days later a fast-talking estate agent drowns me in details about the apartment. Vaguely I take in square-metreage, two-year lease, new wiring, *taxe d'habitation*, but I am not listening. The apartment is perfect. One large airy double-fronted room in brilliant white, with windows which give on to the building opposite. Perpendicular to it, a smaller room – a bedroom – and next to that, bathroom and kitchen. All of it, one half of a square, along which runs a glazed hall over-looking a small courtyard. I take out my chequebook on the spot, but he slows me down, suspicious perhaps, tells me he will have to take references, account numbers, I will have to come back to the office with him.

He feels cheated in his work, I realise. I am not fulfilling the client's part of the bargain. He would have liked to show me two other apart-ments, a little larger, not much more expensive, and a third, on a lovely street, closer to the Seine.

I give him my most dazzling smile, gesture expansively. *'Mais celui-là me convient parfaitement.* It couldn't be better. And I would be so grateful if you could speed up the formalities.'

By the end of the day when I come back to Steve's place, I know that in two weeks' time, bar any hitches, I will be ensconced in an apartment from which I can see and learn from Beatrice's life.

The first apartment I thought of as properly my own was the one I moved into a little while after I left French Affair. My new job provided the cash, my new boss the impetus.

Grant Rutherford was his name and I met him when he came into the office late one wet and wintry afternoon when I had been with Mr Carruthers for some two months. He was a big man with a shock of ash-brown hair, a square jaw and eyes of a cold crystalline blue. The rimless specs which he perched at the edge of his nose did nothing to dispel the impression that he belonged outdoors. The space was too small for him.

'You're new.' He looked down at me through the specs and studied the clutter on my desk.

'Not that new.' I met him on it.

He made a noise which had something of a disdainful growl in it and said, 'Where's Carruthers? Or Myra?'

'I'll get Mr Carruthers for you.' I rose from my desk and walked a little stiffly across the room. I could feel his eyes on me and I turned to look back at him before I opened Mr Carruthers's door. He winked at me.

'You're an improvement on Myra. A big improvement. English?'

I shrugged and closed the door behind me.

Mr Carruthers and the man whom I now knew was Grant Rutherford sat in his office for a while, before Mr Carruthers ushered him back to me.

'You look after Grant, Maria. He wants a week in France, half of it in Paris and then something quiet – intimate, but interesting.'

Intimate was Mr Carruthers's code for a lovers' hideaway, I had quickly learned, so I dutifully brought out my intimacy files, two for Paris, half a dozen for the rest of the country, each of them containing photos, descriptions. I started taking Grant Rutherford through them.

He stopped me after only a few moments. 'Okay, okay, I don't need you to sell them to me. Just look at me for a whole fifteen seconds and then choose for me.'

I looked at him for what felt like a very long fifteen seconds until he said, 'Go,' and then I rifled through my files and brought out the brochure of a little artfully renovated hotel in the Ile St-Louis; and another establishment on the banks of the Yonne, a three-rosette restaurant which also offered a very few suites, all discreetly but sumptuously run, as reports had it, by a retired movie star.

He barely glanced at them before saying, 'Phone.'

'Now?' It would be after ten in France.

'Now. Please,' he added. He scribbled the dates down for me on a scrap of paper.

'This is next week,' I said, incredulous.

'This is New York. And that is a telephone.' He put the receiver into my hand.

I was lucky with the Paris call, less so with the second. He watched me as I tried to soft-soap, wheedle, encourage a room into existence, but it was no go.

'Good French,' he said.

'Bad luck,' I answered.

He grinned. It warmed his eyes a little. 'Never mind, try the next one. And I want an evening at the opera. One set of tickets for that Paris-Moscow exhibition. Two of this month's better restaurants. A list of clubs and a car that moves. All on one nicely typed sheet of paper by Friday afternoon this time. And while you ring your second country choice, I'll just go and see old Carruthers for a moment. All clear?'

'As clear as an alp on a bright winter day,' I muttered.

'Better start climbing.'

I started, reached another country hideaway, managed a reservation, and then realised that if I didn't hurry, I'd be late again for my computer class at the college. I had graduated from typing and now, on Mr Carruthers's advice, I was busy with computing and business management three evenings a week, plus a literature course for my own pleasure.

Just as I was gathering my books and pads together, Rutherford came back into the front office.

'Done already? We do work fast around here.'

'Don't worry, Mr Rutherford.' I raised my professional smile. 'Everything will be ready for you by Friday.'

'Maria's never let me down.' Mr Carruthers was right behind him. 'She's always as good as her word.'

'I'm glad to hear it.' Rutherford held the door open. 'Uptown? Downtown?'

'Down,' I murmured.

'In that case, you can share my cab.'

I accepted, perhaps a little too hastily. At the end of the day, the sheer density of the New York crowds, particularly as they surged up from the subway, sometimes overwhelmed me. I was used to crowds. But Paris crowds were different from New York crowds. In the chanting and placard-waving demonstrations I would bump into in front of embassies or along the avenues, there was a sense of barely contained violence, a reek of grievance far more palpable than anything I had ever experienced. I learned to lower my eyes, to look into a middle distance free of strangers, uninhabited by the homeless and the beggars.

In France, the meeting of eyes was part of the free-floating play of the streets. Here, to look directly at a passer-by was an act of provocation and the response was often aggressive. Some days, the adventure of it thrilled me. On others I was relieved to do without.

Grant Rutherford was apparently so pleased with the itinerary I had arranged for him that I had the mixed fortune of arranging two more in the course of that year. I learned from Mr Carruthers's discreet but suggestive cough that when Grant Rutherford came into the office himself, the trips were not with his wife. Rutherford was a cautious man, who didn't trust secretaries and liked seeing to details himself. He was a partner in an advertising firm which went by the name of Rutherford, Owen and Marks, someone to be reckoned with, and an important client.

By the time of his third jaunt across the Atlantic, we were on first-name terms. It was just after that that he rang me up and asked if I'd meet him for lunch, in the Grill Room at The Four Seasons. I was excited, despite myself. The American men I had met so far were mostly boys and after a couple of Italian dinners and fumbling episodes in cockroach-ridden bedrooms, I thought it was far better to pay for my own movie tickets and keep conversation strictly to books or business management.

I dressed carefully that day: a cream-coloured light woollen suit I had brought with me from Paris and only wore on special occasions; a silk shirt Olivier had given me, a scarf that brought out the copper in my hair. As I crossed the rosewood-panelled stage of the Grill Room, I had the sense that all the bright lights were on me. This was my debut performance and a hundred eyes followed my movements, conjectured whether I was a potential lead, or a permanent understudy; found their answer partly in the status of the man who greeted me.

Grant patted the banquette beside him. 'Good walk.' He looked at me speculatively. 'Have you modelled?'

I shook my head.

'You could.'

'Not my thing. In any case, I'm too old now. Not a minor, you know.'

He chuckled. 'Not too old for the more expensive mags. You have an expensive look.'

'Simply foreign.' I steered the subject away from myself, asked him about his most recent trip.

He waved the question away impatiently. 'Fine, well devised, as always.'

'If you don't give me more feedback than that, how am I to keep my files up to date?'

'You may not want to for much longer. I have a proposition to put to you.'

I almost choked on the Bloody Mary he had ordered for me. Not only was I not used to drinking spirits, but it seemed a little soon for propositions.

'And here I thought you were taking a downtrodden office wretch out for her lunch of the month,' I mumbled.

'That too, of course.' He grinned then gave me a hard, assessing look.

The proposition Grant Rutherford put to me over lobster and crisp leafy salad and proceeded to outline over nougat ice and a first then second cup of coffee was not at all what I had half-imagined. He was offering me a job. His firm now had three important French clients who sometimes proved a little tricky to deal with. Communication was too often a series of misunderstandings. There were tastes to be considered, cultural differences to be explained and manoeuvred. Not only did I have France in my bones, he told me, but I had a nose and tact. And I was efficient. Then, too, I was discreet and he thought I could be trusted to work to him and smooth relations with those clients. On the way I would learn about advertising, though the post itself was in his PR department.

Needless to say, I was thrilled, though I hesitated. I owed so much to Mr Carruthers. Grant told me he would sort out all that side.

He did. Three weeks later I was ensconced in my own little office, complete with sleek black desk, framed photographs from one of the fashion houses that Rutherford, Owen and Marks handled, and a swivel chair. If I turned it round, I had a sumptuous view of the East River.

I worked hard and I began to play hard. Often the two were indistinguishable. It was my job, Grant told me, to know who did what and get them to do it for me when whatever it was, was needed. I had to listen as assiduously to gossip as I listened to him. I had to know journalists and their specialisations, editors and photographers, restaurateurs and gallery owners, producers, artists and writers. I had to know clients' tastes and desires and learn to stretch them in our direction. And since almost everyone was a potential client, there was a lot of knowing to do.

Grant helped, as did others on the team. Invitations were put my way. I went to parties and exhibition openings and book launches and charity dinners. I scoured the fashion magazines and *Women's Wear Daily*, so that I could identify a designer's look at a glance, with no recourse to labels. I learned which restaurants specialised in which professions and how to see who was lunching with whom without losing the gist of my associates' or partners' conversation. On the way, I went to bed with a few people, and learned a little about American men.

I was dutiful. I kept notebooks as assiduously as Madame de Sévigné wrote letters, though perhaps not in quite so impeccable a style. The blue notebook was for office and clients and contained portraits, little character sketches of the people I worked with. Two blank pages followed each first entry, so that the pictures could grow fuller as I learned more about tastes and weaknesses. The red notebook was labelled media and contained everything I could garner from press and gossip about people in the field and their recurring interests. In the green notebook, I kept details of campaign strategies. At first there were more underscored questions here than anything else, but gradually, as I began to understand the nature of the work better, the green notebook grew into a series of elaborate diagrams. Finally, there was a black notebook in which everything that didn't fit anywhere else found a place. This was really the diary of my working life.

At first I kept the notebooks in French, since they were only for my eyes and part of me didn't want anyone to know how hard I was working to map the terrain of my new world. But soon, I don't quite remember when the change came, French went into abeyance and all but the blue notebook turned into English. The colour coding remained the same, though: year after year, blue, red, green and black, succeeded their predecessors. Sometimes, late at night, when I made my entries, a sense of power would zing through me. I would have the sudden certainty that I could orchestrate campaigns and intrigues with the best of them.

There are moments when I think that it was the continuing existence of these notebooks that kept me from being utterly overwhelmed, until the end, by life in New York's fast track. A tiny part of me remained detached, didn't need to sniff the coke twice, didn't need to feel implicated when the syringes came out in the marble bathrooms of gala gatherings on the Upper East Side. I would simply make a mental note, keep my cool and write it all down later for future reference in my notebooks. The buzz I got came from work. 'Not work,' my mother would have said in her best judging voice, 'but scheming. Did you ever help anyone?' I didn't, much. Not in her sense. But then, my mother's voice didn't speak to me very often in those days.

It was Grant who was my mentor. It was Grant who explained the ways of New York to me and who debriefed me after meetings and parties. It was Grant who told me where to have my hair cut, where to buy my clothes and accessories, and to make sure that whenever I might be seen by any of our fashion clients, I was to be seen in their gear. The firm would advance me a sum to that end.

Soon after that, it must have been some five or six months after I started at Rutherford, Owen and Marks, Grant mentioned that he'd heard from his secretary that I only had a small studio apartment, not in the most salubrious part of town. 'Are you interested in finding something else?'

I nodded. 'But I never seem to have the time to look.'

It was true. Now that I had a little more money, work was so all-encompassing, that even the idea of flat-hunting was more than I could entertain. I simply filled the studio with flowers – flowers I had always coveted and my mother had always refrained from buying – and concentrated my gaze on those.

Grant gave me a stern look. Sternness had been his mode with me ever since I had begun to work for him, as if I were on trial and any levity would detract from my attention to the hurdles that demanded to be leapt, and perhaps remind both of us about the questionable arrangements I had made for him in the past. I didn't mind. He was perfectly civil, if distant, in a way I had learned to identify as pedigree Yale, and the very coolness made whatever he imparted to me seem doubly significant.

But that day, I think I had hoped for a smile and a metaphorical pat on the back. Earlier in the week, I had managed, by a combination of wit and charm, to woo a French client back into the fold. He was the head of the Normandy Cheese Marketing Board and he loathed the humorous campaign our creative department had come up with for launching the cheeses. It worked on the negative stereotype principle:

'smelly but . . .' So we had 'smelly but succulent', 'smelly but sumptuous', 'smelly but substantial', 'smelly but sublime' – all complete with a beret-clad cartoon Frenchman, holding his baguette in one hand and his nose with the other in image one and then ecstatically biting into the cheese, now on the baguette, in image two. Jacques Perrault hated it. Only by dint of a great deal of manoeuvring and persuading and playing of the French card, did I manage to convince him to give us another week to come up with something that he wanted – which was high chic, good taste, and glamour.

Grant, however, said nothing about cheese. Instead he handed me a piece of paper. 'Ring Gerry Hynes tonight, about eight thirty. He's off to the coast for a couple of years and he wants to sublet on a semi-formal basis. Far cheaper than the going rate, but with the option that he may change his mind and be back here in six months' time. He's an old friend and I'll vouch for you.'

'Sounds wonderful.' I glanced at the number and address on the sheet of paper. 'The problem is that I'm dining with Jacques Perrault tonight.'

'Mmm. I see.' Blue eyes glinted at me with a trace of mockery. 'Well, if you're interested in the apartment, you'll just have to excuse yourself and scuttle off to the powder room at eight thirty.'

'I don't scuttle.'

He laughed. 'No, I guess you don't. Glide, then. But do it.'

I'm not sure if I managed a smile as I turned to the door.

'And, Maria, keep Perrault sweet. Keep up the good work.'

If that was the pat, it made very little impact on my back.

The apartment, nonetheless, was wonderful, two spacious rooms and a kitchen, overlooking Central Park at West 73rd. Four weeks later, I moved in. I inherited Gerry's bed and a kitchen table and a television set, but at the last minute he decided he couldn't part from his other possessions and he shipped everything else west. It took only a single taxi-load to bring the trinkets I had collected since I had arrived in the city over to the West Side. I had vases and bowls, plates and clothes and some books and that was it. The following Saturday, I bought a vast overstuffed white sofa, a glass coffee table and, at the Metropolitan Museum, a framed overblown poster of Bonnard's 'The Terrace at Vernon'. I don't quite know why I chose that one, except that it had three women in the foreground and a great many flowers.

*   *   *

It was not long after I moved that the party which was to prove so decisive for my future took place. The invite came from a certain Angelika van Helden who ran a SoHo gallery but whose husband ran everything else. Nor did it come to me, but to Wayne Masters, head of the PR section, who asked – though he was usually a little remote since I seemed to work for Grant rather than for him – if I'd like to come along. I was pleased to accept. I had begun to think that if I didn't pay more attention to Wayne, my life at Rutherford, Owen and Marks might in the middle-term prove difficult. So I tagged along with Wayne, who was a gentleman of the old school, probably in his mid-fifties, always in a trim pin-striped suit. And I behaved respectfully, listening to his every word, staying close to his side as he met old friends and acquaintances.

The party was in honour of a much-lauded British actor who was starring in a Noël Coward comedy which had just opened on Broadway. Everyone I could recognise in New York was there and many others I couldn't. Perfumes and labels thicker than the pages of *Vogue* battled for recognition against the old and new masters which lined the walls. From one side of the vast van Helden mansion music boomed. I identified some Coward songs and then forgot to listen in the mêlée of faces and voices. At some point in the evening, when I had had a few too many of the lethal cocktails that were making the rounds, I found myself dragged away from Wayne and towards the music by a young writer I vaguely knew.

William Sykes, in honour of the van Heldens, was wearing his best torn jeans and a partially tucked-out shirt. But he had a lanky grace to him and a lop-sided smile which could charm the creases out of any forehead and before I knew it, we were wrapped arm-in-arm and cruising round the dance floor. A little later, though time was none too clear, he was pressing me against some darkened column and was kissing me vigorously. I guess I must have been responding, for it took a little while for me to recognise the voice at my side.

'I think it's time to go, don't you?'

'She doesn't.' William Sykes answered for me.

'I do.' I slipped away from William and looked into the forbidding set of Grant Rutherford's features. 'I came with Wayne,' I said inanely.

'So he told me before he left.'

'Give me a ring.' William Sykes squeezed my arm.

I didn't answer. Grant was manoeuvring me towards the door. He didn't exactly hold me or press my shoulder but he manoeuvred me just the same, all the way to his car.

'I'll take you home.'

I didn't protest. I was too busy trying to work out whether he expected me to apologise and then thinking that he didn't own me twenty-four hours a day so I wouldn't, whether he expected it or not. And by the time I had worked this out, we had crossed town and he had parked at a stone's throw from my door.

'Are you inviting me up?' he asked, though it didn't sound like a question.

'Yes, of course, if you'd like to.' I was mumbling.

'Good, because we have some talking to do.'

I tried to delay the inevitable lecture.

'I love the apartment,' I said to him as I switched on the lights. 'I have thanked you for finding it for me, haven't I?'

He grunted, looked around. 'A little bare, I'd say.'

'It suits me that way. Can I get you a drink?' As I said it, I wondered whether I had anything in the house, then remembered a bottle of whisky someone had brought me. 'Whisky, coffee? I'm afraid that's all I have.'

'Both.' His tone was still relentless.

I retreated into the kitchen and tried to collect myself as I made coffee, chipped ice out of a reluctant container.

When I got back, he was slouched into the sofa and staring into space. On the table in front of him were my four notebooks laid out in a row, and I quickly piled them away as I put the tray down.

'What are those?' he asked.

'Notes. For work.' I met his eyes. 'There's so much to remember.'

He almost smiled. 'Then you'd better make a note of this.' He stood as I handed him the whisky glass, and started to pace.

'If I asked you to come and work for me, Maria,' he began drily, 'it's not simply because you're clever, but because you're a beautiful woman, with a good chance of growing even more so in the coming few years.'

He studied me for a moment as I shifted uncomfortably on the sofa. 'You flatter me.' I matched his tone, though I wasn't quite in control of the irony.

'No, I don't flatter you. I assess. Now, as I see it, beauty is not

73

there simply to assuage male desire. That's too easy. Beauty is there to be used tactically, to attract that desire and divert it to another end. Beauty, like language, like a catchy tune, is a tool for persuasion. You understand me?'

'You're telling me I'm the woman in the margarine ad. Look at me and think you're eating butter.'

He chuckled at this. 'Almost like that, but not quite so crude. Your beauty is there to oil the great social machine and make sure it runs smoothly in the direction of Rutherford, Owen and Marks.'

'And when do I get to stop being a mechanic?'

'Only in private.'

I had a sudden attack of giggles. 'You remind me of a story I once read about a priest in the seventeenth century. At morning mass, he preaches against frivolity and finery and the sins of the body. For evening mass, he asks the most beautiful woman in the village to stand at the church door in the hope that her charms will seduce alms from the miserly locals.'

'They teach you crazy things in French schools.'

'No crazier than what I'm learning here this evening.'

We stared at each other in thickening silence. Then he moved abruptly towards me and pulled me up so that we were standing face to face.

'I guess if any desire is to be assuaged tonight, I would rather it were mine.' His voice was a little hoarse as he said it and I drew away from him just a fraction so that I could see his eyes.

'Is that a question?'

He didn't answer. He kissed me instead. It was a long, slow, serious kiss and I only realised how much I liked it when I realised that perhaps I shouldn't.

'Did Will Sykes phrase a question?' he asked when he let me go.

I laughed. 'To tell you the truth, I don't remember.'

'Well, perhaps you won't remember this in the morning.'

He kissed me again, with more urgency this time, so that I could feel the imprint of his body against every inch of mine. You know how you sometimes have a rare sense that bodies fit one another, something about the texture of skin, the shape and location of all the separate parts, a fluidity of motion? Well, I had it then, with Grant.

The last thing I remember saying to him before limbs and lips took over completely, was, 'You mean, you don't want me to remember?'

He gave me that hard glint of his, then eased the zipper of my dress slowly down my back, so that the slip of a garment slid to the floor. After that his eyes only warmed me.

Grant Rutherford was a surprising lover, quite unlike any of the other New Yorkers I had known. Not that the others hadn't performed well. They had all read the manuals after all, and had mostly been round the block several times. But it was a performance they were engaged in and they all seemed to want intermittent reports on their prowess and a score out of ten at the end, as if we were acrobats in some competition for an athletic trophy. Having to admire their dicks seemed to be *de rigueur* and though I hadn't quite grown used to that, I had grown used to commenting on how this was nice and that was wonderful.

Grant wasn't like that. He didn't ask questions and he didn't fish for compliments. Best of all he didn't make me feel watched and waited for. He was sure, certain, silent. Maybe it was just that we fitted each other so well, there was no need for words. When we lay back to savour each other or to fill our glasses, the phrases that passed between us were like little bits of ourselves, childhood moments, secret flights of fancy.

I never thought about his wife, though I had glimpsed her twice in the office, a lean, leathery woman with tanned skin and a full-length mink coat. Maybe she was away that weekend, because he must have stayed very late. Though in the morning when I woke, he was gone. I watched the sunlight creep round the budding trees in Central Park and then dozed again. The next thing I heard was the sound of the bell. A youth with a baseball hat appeared at the door bearing a large deli bag. There were bagels and smoked salmon and cream cheese and freshly ground coffee. While I was gorging myself, the bell rang again. It wasn't Grant, as I had momentarily suspected, but another man, this time bearing a sumptuous bouquet of flowers. I laughed at the message: 'For desires assuaged. At least partially.' There was no need of a signature.

In the office on Monday, nothing had changed. At the staff meeting, there was no word or glance that betrayed what had passed between us. He still looked at me in the same stern way, from above his specs. He didn't avoid me, but he didn't search out moments to be alone with me. Perhaps he was waiting to see how I would behave and perhaps because of that I behaved no differently. In any event, during the days there was always so much to get on with, that there was little time for behaviour. Then, too, I think I relished the secrecy. Late in that week, I was in his office with a French prospective client, when something about the way Grant leaned back in his chair reminded me of how he had leaned lazily into the pillows of my bed, a big, satisfied cat. The doubling-up of impressions together with the need to keep the doubling secret excited me, tickled. Perhaps it was mutual, for Grant held me back for a moment alone after the meeting.

'Dinner tonight? At your place. I'll bring it.' He was scribbling something on the notepad on his desk and he didn't look at me as he spoke.

'Can't. Sorry.'

'Oh?' He looked up at me then. 'Someone else?' His eyebrows rose.

I left a little silence before I answered. I was choosing my words. 'Just following the boss's orders. Oiling the great social machine.' I laughed. 'With Monsieur Farjeon.'

'I see.' Tension bristled in the air between us. I thought he was going to touch me to defuse it. Instead, he said, 'Later then?'

'Too late. I'm a working woman.' I laughed again. It wasn't that I didn't want to see him. It was simply that I wanted to be with him at my best, not feel like a limp rag. But he looked so irascible at my answer, that I added, 'Tomorrow, perhaps?'

'Perhaps.' He mimicked my pronunciation. He was good at parrying, Grant. I liked that about him. He looked down at his schedule and took a long time over it, before answering, 'Tomorrow then, eight thirty.'

Our eyes met, fenced, subsided. 'I look forward to it,' I said softly.

I didn't have long to look forward to it, for just after midnight that evening, Grant appeared. I knew it was him as soon as I heard the bell. Perhaps I had been thinking about him. But I wasn't altogether pleased to see him.

'I was just about to get into my bath,' I said as soon as I opened the door. I pulled the towelling robe more closely round me.

'Perfect timing, then. I wouldn't have wanted to get you out of it to answer the bell.'

I suspected from the way he looked round the room, that he had half-believed he would find someone else there. I must have looked disgruntled, for he stroked my cheek softly and whispered, 'I wanted to see you. Wanted. I'll help you with your bath.'

'Do I look as if I need help?'

'No, but you might like it.'

I liked it. I liked the ruffle of his hands along my breasts as he took off my robe, liked the way he soaped me all over and ran his fingers in patterns along my skin, liked the way he rubbed me vigorously dry so that my body tingled. Later, I liked the weight of his penis as I took it in my mouth and the way it filled me when we came together and the purring sounds he made which merged into groans. The next day in the office, I liked his occluded eyes and the formal tones and the parry and thrust of working life with him. I liked Grant Rutherford.

Over the two years or so we had together, Grant and I would meet two or three times a week. Sometimes we would go to the theatre together or he would take me out for dinner, but usually we met at my apartment, which gradually filled up with things he bought for me on our travels. Oh yes, for it was my turn now for those intimate little weeks abroad. But we didn't go to France. The choice was mine and I chose Mexico, then Rio de Janeiro, then a trip down the Nile. I imagine by then, given the coincidence of holiday times, everyone in the office knew there was something going on between us. But we never let on and no one ever said. And by then, in any case, it was clear that I was increasingly good at my job and I was rewarded appropriately. One thing that pleased me was that I hadn't gone to bed with Grant before he had offered me a job and that I stayed on, at least for a while, after it was all over.

Grant and I laughed a lot together and over time, we gossiped and schemed. He was as hungry for my impressions as I was for his knowledge. In that sense, we were a good team. And he liked the fact that he couldn't be certain of me, that he couldn't be sure where else I might choose to assuage the desire he had so readily acknowledged I was there to provoke. Just as much as I liked the sense of risk and the fact that he wasn't around all the time. I was too hungry for life and its myriad experiences to want what I thought of as the stranglehold of coupledom. And the days were so full that I relished my moments alone.

On the infrequent occasions when I saw Grant and his wife at parties or events, I tried to vanish into another corner of the room. Once when it wasn't possible, he introduced me to her, but apart from a perfunctory politeness, which I returned, we had little interest in each other.

It was soon after that, I think, he said to me one night in that musing way he had after passion was spent, 'You're a strange woman, you know.' He was stroking my hair.

'Oh?' I curled away from him and looked into his eyes.

'You've never asked me when we're going to meet next. You've never asked me about my wife. You never ask me whether I love you.'

I took this in. 'Is that strange?'

He grinned. 'It's strange.'

I thought about it for another moment. 'Your wife is your business. You're here and I know we both like that.' I nuzzled the smooth skin of his shoulder, felt his arm lift round me to draw me closer, laughed. 'Don't we? And as for the rest, well, certain things don't need language.' I surveyed the firm planes of his face. 'I don't want to marry you, you know.'

'Don't you?' He looked a little hurt.

I laughed again. 'I'm far too young for marriage. I'll always be too young for marriage. Besides,' I grew a little more serious, 'I'm not too sure what marriage is for. Perhaps because I never had a couple for parents.'

He kissed me then, as if he were trying to make up for something. 'Maybe you're just foreign,' he murmured a moment later.

'Just?' I wound my leg round him.

We both laughed as we watched his penis rise. 'And you have everything of me you want.'

I surveyed him hungrily. 'There is something else,' I reflected.

'Oh?'

'You know that wonderful wine you brought us for dinner . . . Well, I'd love another glass.'

He leapt, groaning, from the bed. 'Whatever my mistress desires . . .'

While he was gone, I thought about it. I know it's not a thing one is meant to admit, but I liked being a mistress. Maybe it's just that in French the word maintains something of its old status. A mistress, after all is a superior being, a *maîtresse*, a teacher. The word has far more power to it than 'wife' or *'femme'*, which is also any woman.

Any woman, my mind stopped at that, and I suddenly saw Amy

78

Burton, the woman who had come to work for the art department a few months back. She was a pretty blonde, about my age, who preferred to wear her skirts a little too short for her slightly buxom legs. She was showing me the layout she had done for an artwork for one of the French accounts. I didn't like it much and I said so, rather bluntly, pointing out that the style was a little too jazzy for that particular account. Amy turned on me and lashed out, 'Grant Rutherford gives very good head, doesn't he?' Then with the flick of a leg she waltzed away.

At first I didn't know what she meant. I was still a little slow with American sexual slang. Then I thought she was throwing in my face her knowledge that I had a relationship with Grant, which was the only reason I felt I had the right to criticise her work. And then, at night, it came to me that she was telling me just the opposite, that we were so to speak bedfellows and that I had no right to criticise her because she had intimate knowledge of the way Grant 'gave head'.

I hadn't said anything to Grant about it and I had put it out of my mind. Until now.

Grant came back into the room balancing a decanted wine bottle, glasses, a bowl of cashews. He had – have I said this already? – an exceptionally fine body, trim and strong from those daily hours he spent in the squash courts doing deals with the boys. I admired him openly for a moment as I sipped the proffered wine. 'Grant,' I said then, 'You say you'd like me to ask questions.'

'Mmmm?' he chuckled, a little nervously.

'Well, you know Amy Burton, the lovely blonde in the art department?'

He had the grace to look just a little abashed and then meet my eyes with a smile. 'You mean the one with all the hair?'

'Well, what do you think of her work?'

'What do you?' He turned the question back on me.

'A little tactless,' I offered. 'She can't quite match style to intent.'

'Oh?' He scrutinised me.

'Mmm, she's a little brash for some accounts.'

'I'll check it out.'

'Nice wine.'

'Very.'

I swallowed another mouthful and nestled into his shoulder. 'Grant, is it true that you give good head?'

He started to laugh. 'Mostly when provoked by lean young writers.'

I remembered that some weeks back I had left a party with Will Sykes, partly with a sense that it was a favour long overdue, but mostly because I liked him. I hadn't known Grant was there, but perhaps someone had simply mentioned the fact to him. So that explained Amy.

'And otherwise?'

'You should know.'

I touched him. I knew.

Some weeks later Amy disappeared from the office. I thought of Madame de Pompadour and the power of mistresses.

PART TWO

�⚖ 12

The raw silk sofa has the same milky hues as the one in my first apartment in New York. But I have married it with the soft luminosity of golden mahogany. On the corner of the long refectory table which is my desk stands a claret-red globe of a bowl. Like some tribal fetish, it haunted me for days until I returned to the antique shop on the Rue du Cherche-Midi where I met Beatrice, and purchased it. Perhaps it was once used to carry blood.

I have spent the last weeks furnishing the site of my new life. I have bought a bed and a fridge and a cooker and a dozen leafy plants for the glazed hall. I have bought scatter cushions in bold African prints and a quilt of startling yellow with a single black zigzagging line down its centre. I have scoured exhibitions and come back with two oils by the same artist. His palette has the ochre and sienna and Titian reds of a lost Italian century, but his figures live in the tormented planes of a contemporary world.

Why I have done all this, I do not know. I have no intention of inviting anyone here. Perhaps one day Beatrice will come and give my rooms her benediction. But I haven't phoned her yet and I do not want her to realise that I have moved in on the other side of the street. Instead, I sit and gaze out of the fourth-floor window in the certain knowledge that sooner or later I will catch sight of her in the building opposite. This week, two of the floors are shuttered. From the emptiness of the Paris streets, I have deduced that we are in the midst of school holidays. Beatrice must be away. She will return. Then she will become my teacher.

Meanwhile I read. In my teens and when I first came to New York, Balzac was my favourite novelist. I devoured the key volumes of the *Comédie Humaine* – *Lost Illusions*, *Old Goriot*, *Cousine Bette*. The cutthroat gaudiness and worldly hypocrisies of Balzac's characters thrilled me. My mother would try to suggest that I was too young for that jaundiced realism, those cynical certainties about the ways of the world that I paraded triumphantly before her. She urged me to read the Brontës, but the passionate longings of the Yorkshire sisters made me squirm or filled me with hilarity.

Now I have gone back to Balzac, but the old thrill has disappeared.

I glance at my watch and leap off the sofa. Time has vanished again. It is almost four and my interview is at five. My interview.

The letter arrived just before I moved. Its Paris postmark confounded me, stoked the embers of paranoia. I couldn't imagine who in Paris might be writing to me. The few letters I received were from Steve in New York. Once there was an envelope from my publishers containing a few other envelopes. But Paris? And then I remembered. The ad. Women who kill. What on earth had induced me to respond to it? And why had anyone bothered to answer?

Yet they had, and the single sheet asked me to attend for interview on one of three dates from which I could choose. Maître Arnault would be available then. I slept on it and the following morning, I telephoned. I was curious.

Paris is full of naked women: they curl lazily into the walls of metro stations, throw their heads back in ecstasy at street corners, leap off billboards like prowling tigers, or stand proudly pregnant, their rounded lines mimicked by this year's new car. No one seems shocked. The female nude here still speaks the rich language of seduction, a lingua franca of beauty. In New York it has been silenced in public spaces, is relegated to the sleazy porn shops of 42nd Street, where it can only mutter the gutter expletives of rape and violence.

I walk along the Faubourg St-Honoré without pausing to glance at elegant boutiques or designer dazzle or even the regal façade of the British Embassy. Number 126 bears a gold plaque announcing the *cabinet* of Arnault, Foch, Cournot and Meyer. I take a deep breath, toss back my hair and let the elevator haul me up to the fourth floor. The office has nothing office-like about it. It feels like the well-appointed home of some nineteenth-century dandy with a fetish for leather-bound tomes and Grandville's human zoology. I half-expect an English butler, sleek as a seal, to appear from the door on my left, take my coat and settle me into the tawny chesterfield.

Instead a woman addresses me. I follow the swish of her impeccably tailored suit into the next room and am startled to find, when she turns round to face me from behind her desk, that despite the briskness of her walk, she must be at least sixty. Though the understated make-up makes no attempt to hide her years, she wears them lightly and with a grace which announces that she is still an attractive woman. For a moment I am baffled. The codes are not what New York has accustomed me to. This woman is too old to be attractive in so diffident a fashion and also too regal to be a secretary. She must be Maître Arnault. I had expected a man.

'I'll take down some of your details to begin with, if you don't mind.' She smiles at me with polite correctness, a pen at the ready.

'Of course.' I already regret having come, regret it even more as the sundry details of address, and status, and education, become a veritable grilling about the course of my career. At the same time the very speed of her questions and her pen mesmerises me, so that I answer as efficiently as she interrogates.

Some fifteen minutes in, it is she who ruptures the mood. She pauses and gives me a long, hard look. 'Are you certain this is a job for you?' she asks, a little querulously.

I stare back at her, shrug. 'Forgive me, Maître, but not only am I not certain, I still have very little idea what the job is.'

'Oh? Wasn't the job description sheet I sent you sufficient explanation?' She is visibly taken aback.

'There was no such sheet in the letter I received.'

'I see.' She puts her pen down. 'An oversight.' Then suddenly she laughs, a throaty, rueful sound. 'By the way, I am not Maître Arnault. He'll see you as soon as his meeting is over ... unless all this is a waste of time.' She reaches into a drawer in her desk and passes me a single sheet of closely typed paper. 'You had better read this.'

She watches me as I skim the page, but before I have got to the end of the first paragraph, a door to my side opens.

Simultaneously I see my interviewer spring up and a tall, loose-limbed man enter the room. He is wearing a dark, serious suit, but it floats carelessly round his frame and his shirt is open at the neck. His hair, more pepper than salt, is too long, as if he has forgotten to have it cut, and it falls defiantly over his forehead. As he stretches his hand out to me, I see that his eyes beneath thick brows are a deep blue, almost black in their intentness. They fix me, examine, probe, and I feel some truth drug is being applied which lays me uncomfortably bare whatever defences I may call into action.

He must be about forty, yet the smile is boyish, almost impulsive.

'Paul Arnault,' he grasps my hand firmly, 'and you are . . .'

'Maria d'Esté.'

'Of course.'

He waves me through the door into the next room. 'Just give me a moment with Madame Duval and I'll be right with you.'

The room is at once airy and oddly crowded. There is a large rectangular desk chaotically heaped with files, but at second glance, these appear to be ordered in fanlike clusters. By its side, like some reigning spirit on a pedestal, a man weeps, his sculpted face contorted in leaden sorrow. Above the fireplace and dotted round the room between the bookcases, there are images made up of a series of numbered photographic faces; and others composed of ears, eyes, noses, foreheads, chins, as if some mad cataloguer of human parts had been let loose with a camera.

I turn away from these dismembered faces but find myself irresistibly drawn back to the numbered series above the mantelpiece. The top four rows are all images of women, trapped in the stillness of Victorian photography. Their hair is parted mostly in the middle and pulled tightly back, their lips unsmiling, grim. These are not photographs they have posed for happily.

'Are you interested in Lombroso's classification?' Maître Arnault's voice startles me.

'Lombroso's classification?' I repeat inanely.

He grins and his features provide such a lively contrast to those that I have been staring at, that I grin back, despite my discomfort.

'Yes, Cesare Lombroso, the great Italian criminologist of the last turn of the century. In his search for the causes of crime, he identified a *homo delinquens*, a born criminal, whom he understood as a degenerate throwback to a less evolved species. Deviancy, for Lombroso, was a biological reversion to the primitive – that very primitive which threatens the civilised social order.'

'Really?' What I mean by this 'really' is, does he believe this rubbish, but I haven't made myself clear and he goes on.

'Really. He studied some 5907 criminals, and 383 criminal skulls, of which he took very exact measurements. According to Lombroso's revered predecessor, Peter Camper, the size of the facial angle formed by intersecting lines between forehead and upper incisors and ear to jaw determined one's place on the evolutionary scale. Classical Greeks and, of course, Europeans had an angle of eighty degrees and above.

Then one moves down through what he called yellow people to blacks and still further down to orang-outangs who only measured fifty-eight degrees.' He makes a low, rueful sound. 'Criminals, needless to say, scored very low. Physiognomy is destiny.'

I am shocked. I have the feeling I have walked into a madman's den. 'You don't believe any of this?' I say as I reach for my bag.

He bursts into laughter. 'Of course not.'

It is a contagious laugh and I join him, but he stops abruptly. 'The only thing I believe in is getting some semblance of justice for my clients. I'm a defence lawyer, you know.' He says it, not to me, but to someone who is floating outside the window. Or perhaps only to himself. Then he faces me again.

'But I find systems of classification fascinating. And we musn't behave with too much superiority towards old Lombroso and his science. How very different, after all, is it to try to locate an extra Y chromosome in prison populations or to carry out genetic finger-printing?'

'You mean it's just our technology that's more sophisticated? Centrifuges instead of callipers. But biology rules.'

'Exactly,' he chuckles. 'And then too, physiognomy still has its place in crime. Why else would the French police force today stop more people of one particular appearance – say North African – than any other?' He walks towards the many-faced print above the mantelpiece and waves at it recklessly.

'Now according to Lombroso, the degenerate criminal type had prominent cheekbones, a thrusting jaw, little hair on his face and a great deal on his head, a sloping forehead and drooping eyelids, not to mention a sombre and dissimulating expression and an effeminate aspect. As for the women . . .' He pauses dramatically and begins to examine me as if he were Lombroso himself, callipers in hand, in search of anatomical exactitude.

'The deviant, hence degenerate, women were always virile – too tall, too strong, too muscular, with determined jaw and cheekbones and – needless to add – an excessive sexuality.'

My hands grow clammy. Has he discovered my secret? I feel like some aberrant species of butterfly, pinned to the wall. I protest, 'But the women in these pictures have little in common except for the central parting in their hair and the style of the photographer.'

'Precisely. And the fact that they have been caught and condemned.'

87

There is that boyish grin again. 'But systems of classification have a way of helping us to see what we want to see. In fact, Lombroso's criminal woman was defined as everything that the sweet and simpering, feminine and passive Victorian Miss wasn't. Or wasn't meant to be.'

He looks at me seriously as if waiting for a response I don't have. Then his voice goes down a register, becomes oddly conspiratorial.

'Crime is our other, Miss d'Esté. That which we would prefer not to see ourselves as being. It is our murky cultural mirror. Rampant childhood desires, tangled dreamstates, float through the glass and lie in wait for us, threaten us on dark nights. So we need to define the criminal carefully, lock it away in order to distance ourselves from it; and in order to bolster and justify our sense of legitimacy in our chosen social order.'

He pauses.

I clear my throat uncomfortably.

'Why do you want to work in the area of crime, Miss d'Esté?'

The sudden specificity of the question startles me. Again I have the sense that he knows more about me than he possibly can.

'You're not planning to commit a murder?' he laughs, his face teasing. But the question hangs in the air.

'Not that I know of.' I laugh too, pull myself together. 'And as for working in the area of crime, I'm not sure I do want to,' I say with emphasis. As I say it, I have that odd tingling sensation on the surface of my skin. I recognise its murmuring. 'That one,' it signals and firmly I tell myself, there will be no more that ones.

'Oh.' Anger flickers across Maître Arnault's features. He taps a Gauloise out of a packet and lights it. 'Have I dissuaded you with my ramblings?'

I shake my head. 'The opposite, perhaps. But I need to know more about the job. A description failed to reach me.'

'I see.' He looks a little impatient and begins to talk swiftly about a book contracted years ago on the subject of women who murder, which case work has prevented him from finishing. Now on top of it, there is a report based on similar materials to be prepared for the European Commission, with particular emphasis on the differences between France and Britain.

'I need someone with a shrewd eye and a quick pen, who can summarise a great deal of material for me: hunt through legal texts, newspaper reports, interview lawyers, perhaps inmates. That's the gist. The person will have a large degree of independence and if things work out there may even be a co-author credit on the book.' He looks at me expectantly.

'I have no legal background,' I say perversely, since I now think I really would like to work with this man, whatever my skin signals.

'I know,' he chuckles. 'Madame Duval told me. That's why I'm interested in you. That's in fact why I advertised in the *Herald Tribune*. I want an outsider. You're the first candidate who's turned up whose mind hasn't been blurred by at least two years of study of French law.' He starts to pace the room with a caged restlessness. 'The French education system puts such a priority on abstract reasoning that facts become something beneath one's dignity. Justice, here, is blind only to facts. It's one of the primary problems of our legal system. I want someone who can tell a fact from a judge's or journalist's fancy, let alone from a theory. And then too, your English must be good, after all those years in America.'

'You've learned a great deal about me very quickly.'

He shrugs and looks at me. For the first time I have the sense that he is looking at me as a woman and I cross my legs.

'It's my job,' he murmurs. Is it my imagination or has he chosen this moment to play with the thick wedding band that encircles his fourth finger?

'Tell me more about the project,' I say.

'So that you can interview me?'

'Perhaps.'

We exchange tentative smiles and he goes on to tell me about how he has subdivided the material into types of crime: infanticide, murder of children, husbands, lovers, fathers – for women rarely it seems murder those they aren't close to. About half the book already exists in draft; and he has very precise indications about what needs to be looked into next, though there is plenty of room for any surprises his researcher may find. Apart from actual cases, what he is most interested in are comparisons between French inquisitorial and British adversarial methods.

'To see where justice works best.' He stops, aware that he has lost me. 'But I'll explain all that more fully when you start. For you will accept, won't you? I think we'll get on.'

'Can I sleep on it?' I need to decide whether I am fit to take on a

89

job. I have been engulfed in my own world for so long.

'Sleep on it.' He smiles, all charm and sweet persuasion. 'But first come and see the office. You can work from there or from home, between forays into libraries and travelling. Three, four, five days, a week, as you choose. You'll be paid accordingly. All that can be discussed with Madame Duval.' He gives me that assessing glance again. 'Though I would imagine that money is not your first priority.'

'Not for the moment,' I acknowledge, as he opens the double doors which lead into a narrow hall, then up a short flight of stairs into a long attic room. One wall is lined with thick manila files and books. The other has three windows which look over rooftops. A rectangular glass desk stands in front of the windows. Its pristine surface bears only a small laptop computer.

'That would be for you.' He switches it on and the menu appears. 'The draft of the book is in here, as well as files for each of the book's categories, details on certain cases, instructions on where material can be found, together with a possible order of attack.' He says all this with proud enthusiasm, as if he is showing me the gadgets in his latest car.

A giggle rises to my throat and I smother it. 'You have copies of all this?'

'Of course. We'll meet once a week, generally on Fridays unless I'm in court, for a reporting and planning session. And file-copying.'

This time I can't repress the giggle and I press the enter key to hide it. A sub-directory labelled 'Britain' comes up on the screen and an entry marked 'Crown *v*. Williams'.

'You know your way round the system?'

'I manage.'

'I only mastered it last month,' he admits a little sheepishly, then rushes on, 'So you'll do it?'

'I'll sleep on it.'

'We can have a one-week trial period if you like,' he says as we go back down the stairs. 'Start on Monday and let me know on Friday what you think.'

'Sounds sensible.' I turn to shake his hand. 'I'll let you know tomorrow.'

'Here, take these.' He picks two books out of his shelves and hands them to me. 'They may help you decide.'

'Thank you.' I glance at the top volume and notice his name on the cover. 'So you've done this before.'

'Never with quite so much difficulty.'

The streets are crowded with homebound traffic. It is almost dark. Maître Arnault has kept me for far longer than I imagined. Maître Arnault. Will I have to call him Maître, as Madame Duval does, if I work for him? Master. It rings so oddly in English. I have never called a man Master before.

On impulse I turn into a café and find a quiet booth on the side, away from the terrace. I owe myself a drink. My first interview in years and I have been offered a job. With all his ostensible knowledge, the Maître thinks I am whom I seem – a successful, competent woman who has left one country for another and is looking for a change in focus. He probably thinks I have come here for a man. Men usually think they are the motivating force for things. I shift uncomfortably in my seat and acknowledge they are only half wrong.

The wine is cool and dry, as dry and cool as the words on the page I randomly open of Maître Arnault's book. 'Justice is not morality,' I read. 'It has little to do with goodness and much with fairness.' I am tantalised, and read on, but this terse conceptual prose takes more concentration than I can give it here. I am about to open the second book when a voice deflects me.

'May we join you?'

I look up and see Maître Arnault. He is with an older man, comfortably grey-haired, and a young blonde woman with a fresh, pert air.

'Please.' I gesture needlessly and wonder for a moment whether this might be his wife.

'My colleague, Maître René Cournot, and Tanya Walker, who is with the firm on an internship. Maria d'Esté is considering coming to work with me on the women project.'

'Great.' Tanya Walker slides in opposite me. 'I always thought you had to have a woman in on this.' She embraces me generically, but her attention is all on Paul Arnault.

'You don't think Paul can handle the subject judiciously?' René Cournot chuckles and sits down beside her.

'Maybe judiciously,' she looks a little peeved, 'but not adequately or accurately from a woman's point of view.'

Tanya Walker has a distinct American accent and I have a distinct urge to flee. What if she recognises me? No. I still my irrational fear. She is from the mid-west. I can hear it in her voice. It is too late in any event. Paul Arnault has sat down beside me and my escape route is blocked.

'Yet I have defended quite a few women, I hope adequately and accurately. And at least successfully.'

'That's not the same.' Tanya Walker is emphatic. 'Women murder for different reasons than men. Men may kill sadistically for pleasure. Or retaliation. Or on contract. But women murder to survive. To write about them you have to feel in your body what it's like to be a woman confronted day in, day out by brutish, brutal, raping men who are twice as strong as you. Right?'

She looks to me for confirmation, but I refuse it. I do not know any brutal, raping men. I have probably met fewer of them than Paul Arnault. So why should I be able to imagine that situation any better than he can?

'I'm not sure,' I say.

Tanya Walker gives me a withering look. I have let down the team.

'Arguments from experience can be very limiting,' Maître Arnault jumps in. His impatience is manifest. 'You would deny me the right to defend anyone whose experience isn't mine.'

'Courts are not books.' Tanya's cheeks have grown pink. 'Courts, the law, are male. The defence is men talking to men about women's experience mistranslated into male terms,' Tanya states with more conviction than I can bring to anything. 'Just look at the way prison terms for killing husbands are twice as long as for killing wives.'

'In the United States,' René Cournot intervenes. 'Do you remember when we went to court yesterday, all three judges were women, as was the prosecutor?'

'An exception,' Tanya says.

'Not such a great exception in this country.' Paul Arnault smiles at her with a glimmer of polite irritation and all at once I am on her side, filled with admiration for her youthful passion.

'You should really have Tanya working with you.' I turn to Paul.

'Should I?' He looks at me, momentarily aghast.

'I'm a lawyer, not a researcher,' Tanya flings at me with such cutting vehemence that I am reminded of all the times in my life when my supposed sisters have struck out at me rather than at the man who in the given situation should have been the immediate object of their anger. As if they hated men in the general, but women in the particular.

'Of course. I didn't intend any disrespect.' I do not want to enter the fray and retrieve my position. But I feel the men's tension, as vibrant as that of spectators awaiting gladiatorial combat in some antique forum. Tanya, I can see, is fidgeting, still uncertain whether I am going to kick back or lie back. She doesn't know that neither is altogether my style.

'It's sometimes so hard to imagine the difficulties another woman has had to scale to arrive at a superior position on the great ladder of success, how tightly that position has to be clung to,' I say with deliberate circumspection.

Tanya looks as if she is about to respond, then changes her mind. Irony is not her forte.

'Still, things have happily changed since Olympe de Gouges, haven't they? You remember, she said that by closing the doors of employment, honour, and fortune to women, you compelled them to open those of crime.'

'Olympe de Gouges?' Tanya asks.

'One of the feminists of our revolution,' Paul supplies for her. 'The one in 1789.'

'She's still right. For a lot of women,' Tanya grumbles.

'Yes, perhaps,' I nod. 'There isn't much honour or fortune about in some quarters.'

'You bet there isn't,' Tanya says jubilantly. 'In the US, four million women a year are assaulted by their male partners. Four women a day are murdered by husbands or boyfriends. And a woman is raped every 1.3 seconds. No wonder women turn to crime.'

'But isn't it true that whatever impression the media give, women in fact kill very little?' A blurb I once wrote for someone comes into my mind. I quote it verbatim. 'Less than fifteen per cent of all homicides in the US are committed by women. And of those, ninety-three per cent are battered by their mates first.'

'You know the States,' Tanya says, taken aback.

'A little.'

'Things add up somewhat differently here,' Paul intervenes.

'When were you there?'

'Oh, a little while back.' I reach for my bag. 'I'm afraid I must go.'

In the mirror above the booth, Paul's eyes meet mine as we rise.

There is something so unexpected about this that it feels clandestine, as if there were something between us to hide.

'Can I give you a lift home?' he asks in a slightly strained voice. He has felt it too.

I shake my head. 'I'll ring tomorrow.' I wave to the others.

'You can drop me,' Tanya says with a touch of petulance.

Paul catches up with me by the door of the café. 'Look, I'd almost forgotten. I'm in court tomorrow. A small case, but perhaps you'd like to come along and get a taste of things?' He hands me a slip of paper with an address on it. 'We start at one. Okay?'

'I'll try,' I say.

⚖ 13

The gold-tipped railings of the Palais de Justice glisten like ancient spears in the sunlight. Two hard-hatted policemen stand guard at the central gate and wave me away. There is no entry from here to those steep, cumbersome stairs and imposing portals around which gowned figures cluster. Access to justice is not a simple matter. Rules must be gleaned, hidden doors found, checks and turnstiles mastered, before one can penetrate the inner sanctum.

At last I stand in the noisy hall of the Cour Correctionelle. Determined voices vie with each other and the clatter of heels on marble. The purposeful look honest. Those who stand around silently with confusion in their eyes take on a furtive air. I imagine I am amidst the latter. In the temple of guilt and innocence, I am inevitably one of the guilty. For the third time since I was turned away from the main gates, I wonder why I have come. I still have not made up my mind about the job.

In fact I know why I have come. I have come because of Beatrice.

Beatrice is back. I saw her this morning, while I was drinking my coffee. She lives in the apartment that was shuttered until now, on the third floor. In the soft light, her hair shone like a beacon above the fuzziness of her slightly flattened face. She was sitting at a table with another person, a smaller person I think, shadowy in the arch of the white curtain. I watched her still, certain movements as she lifted a tray of dishes from the table, receded into darkness, returned. A man must have come into the room, for the next thing I knew Beatrice was lifting her face to be kissed. I couldn't make out the man's features, but he was taller than her and after he had kissed Beatrice, he bent to hug the smaller person who must be their daughter.

I picked up the telephone then and dialled the number Beatrice had given me.

Her voice was soft, soothing. She was happy to hear from me, was sorry that she hadn't taken my number or she would have rung me sooner. She wanted to get it down straight away. I could see her pacing back and forth in front of the windows as she spoke. The telephone in her hand was cordless. As she repeated the number I gave her, I could even see her lips move. Then she looked up and I pounced out of sight, my heart bounding. I didn't tell her I lived opposite. It is too soon. I gave her Steve's address when she asked and she was delighted at the proximity. She quickly named a café on the Boulevard St-Germain where we could meet tomorrow afternoon.

Beatrice, I thought when I hung up, has a sense of purpose. She is candid. She wouldn't play about and shilly shally over job offers. She would go where she was expected.

A policeman holds open the door of Courtroom Twenty-six for me. He doesn't ask me for reasons or for identification. There is nothing improper about my presence here. The public benches are full. Youths scribble in notebooks. Old men and women who look as if they have come for seats, shelter, entertainment, gaze towards the front of the chamber.

The make-up of the court is perplexing. My entire knowledge of these things is based on American courtroom soaps and near-antique re-runs of Perry Mason. Apart from the hush in the air and the presence of gowned figures, nothing here is familiar. On the raised bench at the front there are three people, two immaculately coiffed women with an older man between them. They all wear what I take to be judge's black robes, complete with lacy white ascots at the neck. So, too, does a woman on a platform at the right. But it is the man in the centre who is speaking, his eyes darting from a thick file in front of him, to rest sternly on a tiny urchin of a woman who stands shuffling from foot to foot between two policemen in a raised box to my left.

'Who is that?' I whisper to the scribbling youth at my side and point to the man.

'The president of the tribunal?' he asks. 'Juge Jacques Delaroche. The prosecutor is Madame Hamon,' he fills in, pointing to the woman on the raised platform, 'and counsel for the defence is Maître Paul Arnault.' I follow the line of his hand and glimpse the back of Paul's head. He is sitting at a table, below the accused, the tiny uncomfortable woman, who now murmurs something and the president asks her to speak up.

'You came to Paris from Marseille in 1991 to seek employment, is that correct?' the president intones, barely waiting for her squeaky 'yes' before he rushes on to say that the employment took the form of inviting men to her room on an irregular basis.

'Only my boyfriends, Monsieur le Président,' the woman demurs.

The judge coughs and there are snickers from the public which he does nothing to contain. Nor does her defence counsel leap up to protest. I am riveted, as much by the story that gradually unfolds, as by the sense that the judge here is behaving like a prosecutor, and what he is prosecuting seems to be a life, a character, rather than a specific crime which has yet to be broached. The life is a miserable narrative of an existence on the edge – prostitution, petty thievery, stints in prison, bad company. And then, at last, the substance of the present trial emerges.

'On the night of October 12, police came to your room looking for your boyfriend, Moncef Harbi, of no fixed address?'

'Yes,' the woman replies in her faint, docile voice.

'They found his clothes, if not him. They also found taped to the brackets of the ceiling light fixture six packets of heroin each containing two grams with a total street value of approximately FF96,000. You said to the police that you did not know of the existence of these packets?'

'Yes.' The woman suddenly rushes into adamant speech. 'I didn't know. How could I know. Look at me. I'm barely one metre fifty-five. The ceiling is three metres up at least. Monsieur le Président,' she adds for good measure.

'There are such things as ladders in Belleville,' the president mutters in his dry tones. He fixes her with his gaze. 'You also said,' he leafs through the thick file in front of him and reads, '"Moncef couldn't have put it there. I would have known." Yet you claimed not to have known of the existence in your wardrobe, a wardrobe one presumes you opened at least twice a day, of a shoebox which contained a quantity of syringes.'

'I knew of the box. I just thought Moncef's shoes were in it.'

There is tittering in the courtroom, but the judge pays no attention to it.

'And you expect us to believe that, just as you expect us to believe that you had no idea where Monsieur Harbi, officially unemployed, found the money to pay your rent and buy you expensive presents? And believe that on the occasions when he asked you to deliver parcels for him and you received substantial sums in return for those parcels, you had no idea what the parcels contained?'

'I didn't open them. I didn't open the envelopes with the money either.'

'Yet Monsieur Harbi now tells us that not only did you know what was in the parcels, but that you also quite often designated the clients.'

The woman is silent for a moment. She pulls at the chain at her throat. Then she cries out, 'He didn't. You're lying.'

Even from my distance I can see the judge's eyebrows arch dramatically.

'I mean he's lying, Monsieur le Président.'

Her skin seems to have turned translucent. She looks as if she is about to faint. Indeed the judge tells her to sit down.

There is some shuffling of papers and then he begins again, telling the accused about her history of drug abuse, naming witnesses who do not appear but who appeared during the *instruction*, the investigation. At regular intervals she is asked to confirm or deny what he is telling us. At last, the woman my neighbour has identified as the prosecutor takes central stage, and with machine-gun rapidity sums up the case against the accused, whose eyes now are turned only to the ground.

I have the odd sense that I have been party not to a trial, but to an inquisition in which the accused's guilt is a given from the start and all that we are waiting for in these proceedings is a confession, so that sentencing can take place.

A memory leaps into my mind. I am walking away from the grim stone frontage of the cathedral of Notre Dame towards the Palais de Justice. I am with my mother and someone else and I must be quite small, for each of my hands is in one of theirs. But not that small, for the someone else who is a man is saying something about Jeanne d'Arc and the inquisition and I am listening because I admire Jeanne d'Arc who ran away from home to be a boy. Then the man talks about how once the Notre Dame had as its only neighbour on the Ile de la Cité, the palace of justice; and he says something I cannot follow about judges and priests vying with each other for power or sharing it.

Now the sense of his words suddenly hits me. There is more than a similarity between judicial authority and religious authority. There is an aping of forms. What else have I just witnessed but a contemporary replay of the inquisition? Why else all these robes, these ritualised postures and orders of procedure if not to make of the court as sacred a site as a church? I wonder at this. How necessary is it? What would happen if all the pomp and circumstance, the hush of ceremony, were removed? Naked, without its trappings, would the law crumble? It is merely human, after all. Yes, the trappings, the formal rites, are necessary to dignify the law, to raise it above the everyday.

Paul Arnault has at last stood up to speak. He, too, is gowned, the robe flowing round him as he paces for a moment, so that he seems bigger than I remember him. When he returns to his place beneath the accused, I catch a glimpse of his profile. He looks pensive, as if he is only now preparing his words. When his voice comes, it is both mellow and resonant. It has an authority which is only increased by its bursts of passion. I trust this voice. It is as I listen to it that I know with certainty I will work with him.

An underlying principle of the modern European court, Paul argues, is the presumption that the defendant is innocent until proved guilty. Guilty beyond reasonable doubt.

'We are here not to try the morality of Mlle Villiers, nor to judge whether she has led a blameless life – that is not a matter for the courts – but to determine her involvement in a specific set of criminal acts. Let us suppose for a moment that Mlle Villiers is not the owner of the past we have heard so much of here, but is instead a hardworking young female student in her second year at university. She is the daughter of fine, upstanding, middle-class citizens. Like so many young women, Mlle Villiers has her own studio and a boyfriend who more often than not shares her bed and who doesn't bear a North African name. She loves this man and therefore trusts him. She doesn't look through his trouser pockets or his shoeboxes. This is not a thing nice middle-class girls are brought up to do. Nor does she harbour any particular suspicions when her boyfriend asks her if on her way home, since it is on her way, she can drop a parcel off for him. She is happy to do him a favour.

'When the police arrive one evening and find drugs in her studio, she is amazed then appalled, though she speaks to them politely. All this really has nothing to do with her, nor can she imagine that it has anything to do with her boyfriend. Since she is a nice, polite young woman, the police, I suggest to you, believe her, at least about herself, and either they warn her about keeping bad company or there is a simple charge against her, of possession.

'As we have heard, Mlle Villiers does not share a history with this nice young bourgeoise. But it is not her history which is on trial. It is my contention that if we rid ourselves of the spectacles of morality and prejudice, look merely at the evidence in the case, we will find that at most it leads us only to the lesser charge of possession, if that. For the rest, I hope, Monsieur le Président, that you will rule accordingly.'

'Good defence,' says the young man at my side as we crowd out of the courtroom into the busy hall. It is as if he is commenting on a particularly adept football play.

'Is this Maître Arnault well known?' I venture.

The look on his pointed, foxy face suggests I have come from a contemptible planet where football is non-existent.

'One of the best.' He offers me a cigarette. 'But you rarely catch him in here. He's more often over there.' He gestures vaguely in a direction behind my back. 'The Cour d'Assises. For the big jury trials. Nice that he took this little case on.'

He warms to his task of explanation. 'You never know quite what kind of defence tack Arnault is going to take, the traditional complicitous one or . . .'

'Complicitous?' I intervene.

'You know,' he mimics a serious old man's expression, 'Dear judges, we are all gentlefolk and belong to the same club. We really must try to understand this poor bastard in the dock who's had such a rough life and do our best for him.'

'Or?' I laugh.

'Or the more daring frontal attack on the courts and the system of justice as a whole.' He arches his body like a pugilist and launches a fist into the air. 'You, Mr President, like the law you represent, are a reactionary shit of the first order, and understand nothing about justice or the world. The jury on the other hand . . .'

He grins.

'I get the picture. And Maître Arnault.'

'Arnault weaves his way sinuously between both. It's quite an art.'

The subject of our conversation suddenly stands before us. My companion's mouth drops and I imagine mine does too, but I manage to shake his hand.

'I'm glad you could make it,' Paul Arnault murmurs.

'Me too.' I feel as young and embarrassed as the youth at my side, whom I have been pumping under slightly false pretences. 'This is . . .'

'Jean-Michel Courtet, Maître,' the youth supplies eagerly.

'He's been educating me.' I smile my thanks.

'Oh yes?' Paul Arnault shakes his hand politely if a little absently and then whisks me away.

'Have you time for a drink?'

I nod.

We weave our way through the hall and out into the crisp afternoon. The murky brown waters of the Seine flow briskly along the Quai des Orfèvres. The Boulevard is noisy with traffic and Arnault doesn't speak until we have crossed it and are sitting in green wicker chairs in a brasserie opposite the court.

'Did you find that interesting?'

'Very.'

He looks out at me from those intent blue eyes as if he is expecting more.

I stir the froth on my coffee. 'I will take the job, if it's still going.'

His face relaxes into smiles. 'Good. I'm very pleased. I couldn't have begun to work with the other candidates. You'll start on . . .'

'Monday. Is she innocent?' I change the subject.

'Innocent?' He repeats the word as if it is new to him. 'Which of us is ever wholly innocent?' He is staring at me as if he knows that I, for one, am not, and I look down at my cup. 'My task is to see that my client is defended, well defended, on the specific grounds of the charge.'

'So you think she was dealing,' I prod him.

He shrugs. 'Not as seriously as the charge made out.' He surveys me as if he is trying to determine who I am and where my values begin and end. 'Mlle Villiers was rounded up as part of a wholesale series of arrests in one sector of the city. They might as well just have put bars around the entire area and thrown away the keys, for all that it has to do with hard evidence. Or justice. I'm defending a number of those rounded up on the night. Some of them are real villains. Others are there, shall we say, by co-habitation.'

The boyish grin plays round his lips. He glances at his watch. 'I think we could manage a proper drink now, don't you? To celebrate my new researcher.'

'What your new researcher wants, no, needs to know, is whether Mlle Villiers is the bad girl the judge described or the good girl you characterised for us?' Why am I pushing him like this, I wonder?

'You know very well it's not as simple as that.' He is suddenly stern.

'Do I?' I mumble.

'Look. It's like this. There's a tendency on the part of the courts to categorise women into neat little parcels. There are the good girls, the angels, who wear their blouses buttoned up beneath neat suits, who marry by the law of the land, who take care of their two-and-a-half children and their husbands, who address the judge demurely and respectfully, and who as a consequence are so pure that it is difficult for the court to attribute any crime to them; and if it does they always apologise for what they have done, so sentences are less severe. Then there are the bad girls, the demons, who show a little too much leg or bosom, who look as if they might actually enjoy the animal act or who do it in any event, and not with legal husbands and who, as a consequence, appear as monsters who cannot love their children and are inevitably guilty of any crime. And seem worthy of punishment whether they are or not because they behave aggressively to the court. Lombroso's born criminals. My sad little Mlle Villiers.'

'And we blame the victims for the crime,' I muse and then parry, 'but there are these different kinds of women. Real differences between good and bad.'

'Differences, of course.'

I am startled as he reaches out and undoes the top button of my blouse which I must unconsciously have buttoned while he was speaking. It is such an intimate gesture, that for a fraction of a second our eyes lock in silence.

Then he rushes on, 'Differences, yes, but not absolute moral differences and not necessarily visible by the signs the court so stereotypically decides to designate them by. In private, no self-respecting Frenchman, or woman, would dream of assessing the world like that. Put them together in public, give them the representative function of law, and suddenly the weight of convention bears down on them and they grow blind with prejudice rather than justice.'

I want to argue with him, but I don't know how. I want to tell him that if you had stood Beatrice and me at the age of ten in front of judges, they would have known in two minutes flat who was good and who was bad. My mother did and she was hardly ground down by the weight of prejudice.

He is looking at my throat and I realise I am again playing unconsciously with my buttons. Does he suspect that I am a bad girl trying to be good?

I laugh to ease my embarrassment and then to contradict my own thoughts, say, 'You mean a murderess is just an ordinary woman in a temper?'

'Enid Bagnold.' He quotes the source, pauses. 'Sometimes. sometimes not.'

'Where do I begin on Monday?' I ask, so that he will stop looking at me.

'I think you had better read through what I've written, so that you can get a handle on the kinds of things I'm looking for. Note anything that isn't clear and we can talk it through. Then there are some English dossiers, reports and books begging to be summarised, discussed. After that, in a few weeks' time, depending on scheduling, there's a trip to the Old Bailey to be made, a case involving a woman who murdered her husband. I'll give you a precise list of things to look for in covering that.'

I am suddenly excited, more excited than I have been for a long time. There is something to look forward to.

⚖ 14

The terrace at the Deux Magots is crowded with elegant women and dapper men. They hardly pause in their animated conversation as the bells of the old church of St-Germain peal out the hour.

Beatrice is punctual. I barely have time to read another page of one of the dozen books I purchased on Friday after leaving Paul. All night, until sleep overcame me, and all of today I have bathed in the horrors of true crime, appalled and perversely delighted at the excesses women could inflict on their fellows.

In her grey tweed suit, her crisp white blouse buttoned, as Paul would undoubtedly have noted, right up to her neck, Beatrice makes me feel a little ashamed. She looks so substantial, whereas I have deliberately dressed down, an old pair of jeans, a baggy sweater. As if I want her to outshine me.

She kisses me on both cheeks and sits down at my side. 'So, today you must tell me all about yourself,' she says, her face serious, once we have got preliminaries out of the way. 'When did you go to New York?'

'In 1979, just after my Bac.'

She reflects on this as if it is a major statement and then looks pleased. 'Nearly fifteen years ago.'

I remember that Beatrice was always a little slow at sums and nod, smiling.

'And what did you do?'

'I worked, various jobs, and I ended up as a public relations consultant.'

'And you were very successful,' Beatrice says. It is not a question. She looks me full in the face and her voice turns soft. 'You were always successful. So certain. So beautiful. I was amazed that you could be my friend. Do you remember the time that terror of a Simon hid my clothes after swimming and I was standing there shivering?'

I had forgotten, but it comes back to me now.

'You guessed right away what had happened and marched off and berated him so soundly that my clothes turned up within thirty seconds.'

'We were a horrid bunch,' I murmur. I am afraid she will choose to note my own particular misdemeanours, for she could not but have been aware of them. I take a hasty gulp of water and try to think of another subject, but Beatrice is right there, in the playground.

'Like when you all stuffed me into the rubbish bin in the yard?' Beatrice looks at me guilelessly from those mellow brown eyes.

'Ghastly girls. Me too,' I mutter.

'I didn't mind. Not about you.' She gives me her steady smile.

I wonder at her composure. If the tables were turned, I would never be able to forgive the slight, the shame. Not even after all these years.

'I wanted to be part of the group at any cost,' Beatrice admits candidly. 'And I must have been a vile, smelly thing. Probably belonged in the bin,' she laughs. 'Then your mother put me in the bath.'

My mother suddenly floats between us, a tangible third presence. We can both feel her there.

'That first Christmas you both gave me books. They were the first books I ever had of my own. Poems by Jacques Prévert and Jules Verne's *Voyage*. I covered the books in thick brown paper, so nothing could happen to them.'

I am touched. How could I have behaved so sadistically towards poor Beatrice? 'And now you have a great many books,' I say, to make up to her.

She nods.

'And a daughter.'

'Two children. There's Nicolas, as well. He's fourteen.'

'So you've been married for a long time.'

I want to know about her husband, but she turns the question back on me.

'And you?'

'I never married.'

For the first time I see a look of astonishment on her face. 'Never?' she repeats and then adds, 'But you've been with a lot of men?'

I gulp. Beatrice, I can tell, is not one to take relations lightly. There is a solemnity about her, an appropriate weight. 'A few,' I say.

'And now?'

'Now I've come back to France.'

Beatrice smiles radiantly as if it is the best decision I could ever have made. Faced with that expression I begin to feel it is.

We chat over a second cup of coffee and a second bottle of Badoit. I tell her how I have taken on my mother's name, in memory of her. She doesn't give me her married one. Perhaps she doesn't use it. Instead, she tells me about her work for SOS-Racisme and also for the homeless, and invites me to come along with her to a meeting. She is concerned, committed. The presence of my mother hovers ever closer, but when I imply this little resemblance to her, Beatrice appears oblivious to all my mother's good works. She would, however, like to visit her grave, she says, touching my hand lightly. We agree to do this together one day soon.

But now she has to pick up her daughter from her piano lesson and she asks me whether I would like to walk with her. It is near my apartment, she tells me, and for a moment I am confused, until I remember that I have given her Steve's address. I wonder whether I should invite her up, wonder too, whether perhaps she will invite me. I would like to see her in her home, meet her husband. But I do not have a good record with husbands. Perhaps Beatrice guesses this, for she doesn't mention it. Or perhaps she simply hasn't really forgiven me. Whatever she says, she doesn't altogether trust me. I will make it up to her. With her help, I will become the person she can forgive.

We walk along the Boulevard St-Germain. At an intersection, a low-slung Jaguar pulls up short with a squeal of brakes. The young man behind the wheel gives me a rakish once over, grins provocatively, and signals with a lavish gesture that we are free to cross. Beatrice takes in this little exchange. She gives me an artless glance as if she suspects that I know the man, then begins serenely to cross the street. I shorten my stride to match her stately steps and suddenly a feeling I recognise as envy engulfs me.

Envy. I isolate the sensation, examine it. Why should I feel envy for Beatrice? I have never before wanted the solid married life. I have never regretted the adventure of singleness, the sense that any moment might bring the unexpected which could be acted upon. I have never wanted to be half of another. Not for me those nights punctuated by snores and days of chores, irking trivial responsibilities endlessly repeated. Nor would I ever wish to be talked about in those tones of boredom or complaint which men so often use about their wives. No.

Yet the feeling is there as I glance at Beatrice's serene face, her sure, even tread on the pavement. The petty, niggling, unpleasantness of envy. I catch myself thinking that if only I had been plain, like Beatrice, my life would have been radically different. I, too, would now have a circle of dear ones around me. I, too, would have a father for my children. I, too, would know where I was going and be expected. And my conscience would be at peace.

At sixteen, my revulsion at Beatrice's homely dumpiness was acute. Yet with that plainness, she was forced to make something fine of her life. She is now someone to be reckoned with. I, on the other hand, am no one. Pampered by my prettiness, I gorged myself on the array of dishes on offer until I was replete, but without substance. I envy Beatrice.

I wait outside a solid stone house on the Rue de Varenne while Beatrice fetches her daughter. Their footsteps match as they emerge from the cobbled courtyard. The girl has dark curly hair, held back with a velvet Alice band. She is slender, slightly fragile. There is nothing of Beatrice about her, except perhaps for the staring expression. I only realise I had hoped for an incarnation of the playground Beatrice when disappointment tugs at me.

The hand the girl stretches out at Beatrice's prompting, is tentative.

'Marie-Françoise is a little shy,' Beatrice says. With an absent air, she straightens the white collar on the girl's navy-blue dress.

'How old are you, Marie-Françoise?' I ask.

'Eight,' the girl says. Her voice is high-pitched.

'You're tall for your age, aren't you?' I improvise, knowing nothing about it. I know nothing about children. I am not usually interested in them, but I am interested in Marie-Françoise. She is Beatrice's daughter. I want to find Beatrice in her. I want to be good to her.

The girl gives me a suspicion of a smile.

'Run along ahead of us,' Beatrice orders.

'Shall we stop and have ice cream? You like ice cream, don't you?' The girl looks unsure.

'Marie-Françoise has given up ice cream for Lent. We should get back in any case.'

'I'll walk with you,' I say. I don't want to let them go yet.

'She's become very religious these last years,' Beatrice notes with a touch of pride.

I don't remember Beatrice being a believer. 'Is her father religious?' I ask.

'No.' Beatrice gives away little. 'It must just be the age.' She changes the subject, tells me instead about the anti-racism demonstration tomorrow. I could come along if I liked, bring friends. She is taking a group of children from her school. I tell her that if I decide to come, I will meet her outside the school at two. I do not tell her I have no friends here.

At the corner of their street, which is also mine, we part.

'I'll take you out for ice cream after Easter,' I say to Marie-Françoise. Her dark eyes flash with greed, but she looks to her mother before replying.

'We'll see,' Beatrice says matter-of-factly. Then she turns her serene face on me. 'Perhaps tomorrow, then?' She hugs me as if to reassure me.

I nod, and make my way back to St-Germain. I wonder why I am so interested in finding Beatrice in Marie-Françoise. Do I want to redeem my sins against the mother in the daughter?

I think of the few children I have known. There was only one of Marie-Françoise's age: Michael's daughter. Michael was in the throes of a divorce and on the occasional weekends when she was with him, he would bring his adored Corinne along to see me. I imagine he thought it would help convince me to marry him, which was what he wanted. He thought she was wonderful. But the child, quite rightly, loathed me. She would scowl at me behind his back and turn up the television so loud that it blotted out all possibility of conversation anywhere in the apartment. I was briefly intrigued by the sheer force of her hatred and experimented with various seductive measures to see if I could lessen it. Needless to say, they failed, and since I was more interested in Corinne's loathing than in Michael's love, it was not a relationship that lasted very long.

I choose a quiet café, find a table at the back and plunge again into my true crime stories. They are as wild and cruel as the fairy tales I read as a child and it comes to me now that it was never the happy end which fascinated me, those moments when the prince kissed Sleeping Beauty awake or Cinderella waltzed into true love, but rather all the moments of horror in between: Donkey-Skin's brutally incestuous father; the poisoned apples and chalices that witch-like stepmothers prepared; the blindings and imprisonments and parched desert journeys of long-haired damsels who could with the flick of a page become the torturers of once-wicked sisters and ugly old crones.

The story I am reading now has all the accoutrements of a fairy tale. We are in the remoteness of New Zealand. Two girls, one stocky and plain, with something of a limp, the other tall and willowy with the face of an English rose, become not the worst of enemies, but the best of friends. They feed off each other's imaginations, ride together, write stories together, create a world which is richly their own, and then plot their escape from humdrum surroundings and interfering parents. They will live together, be prostitutes, cabaret singers, pay their travels across the globe. But the father of the English rose announces he is taking her off and the mother of the other girl says that there is no question of her accompanying her friend.

A few days later, the mother is found dead, beaten to death with bricks and stones on a lonely path. Caught in their interlocking fantasies, the girls have murdered her.

They really have. At the end, since this is true and not a fairy tale, there is no glorious transformation. The only happiness is society's. And it is the grim resolution of the law: separation, punishment, imprisonment. For its own peace of mind, society demands judgement and a kind of retribution. It is strange, but I cannot remember any courts in fairy tales.

As I sip my coffee, I wonder about these two girls. Would I have recognised them as potential murderers? Would I be capable of their act? If things had been different, would Beatrice and I have been capable of that ferocity? I think of the vileness of the children when together in the playground and everything seems possible: the wild joint fantasies, the sense that an unbounded world is ours and ours alone, the violent desires. Everything except that final passage into the act itself – the step where fantasy brutally abuts in reality: the hand which lifts the brick and launches the first blow, the blood, the scream. I cannot imagine playing out the frenzy of the act itself.

Beatrice would think I was mad pondering such things. But I would like to talk to someone about it. Perhaps it is a subject I can raise with Paul Arnault, though he might wonder at the sensationalism of the reading material I have immersed myself in, in preparation for my job.

⚖ 15

Rain beats with noisy insistence against the zinc panelling of the office windows. The digital clock on the shelf reads 15.58, so precise a time that it needs interpretation. My first Friday meeting with Paul Arnault is scheduled for four thirty. That is an hour I can grasp.

I have not seen him for more than five minutes since our Monday session, when in businesslike fashion he again laid out the measure of my task. Since then, during my days in the office, I have bumped into Tanya Walker, who greeted me with distinct coolness, clients sitting in the waiting room, René Cournot, who courteously presented me to Maître Gustave Foch, another partner he happened to be speaking with. It is Madame Duval who is my mainstay. It is she who took me out for lunch on my second day and in precise tones which had nothing of gossip in them gave me the low-down on who was who in the office. Gradually, too, she has introduced me to everyone. But their comings and goings are so distant from my attic room that I am hardly aware of them. As for Maître Arnault, if his previous insistence gave me illusions about the nature of our working proximity, these have all evaporated. Apart from Monday, the few times I have seen him, he has done no more than smile absently and ask me in a way that anticipated no answer, how things were going.

I am not unhappy. The draft of the first part of the book is riveting, as is the material I have been immersed in, though some of it is slow going. I have had to buy myself a legal dictionary and a primer on penal law just to keep up. To get the lie of the land, I have also made my first foray to the law library.

As for the rest, I went to the demo on Sunday, though not with Beatrice. There were street players and music and a fair number of people, all but matched by the number of police. I saw Beatrice there, but she didn't see me. I didn't want her to. She was surrounded by a little group and holding up one pole of a banner which read, 'To be a racist is to be off-colour'. She had that serenely radiant look on her face. It made me think of Jeanne d'Arc in the schoolbook etchings. Perhaps the young man holding up the banner's second pole had the same thought for he kept shooting little admiring glances in Beatrice's direction, as if sustenance were to be found in her stance. I considered it for a moment, but I decided he couldn't be her husband. For one thing, he seemed too young to have a son of fourteen. And there was no other man around I could readily designate as a husband, though I tried to find one.

Nor have I seen anything distinct through the windows, except the flashes of a television screen and once, Beatrice's profile. They draw the curtains in the evenings and I have been home so little this week. Still the proximity, the sense that she is there just opposite, that I know what time she turns the lights off, consoles me. Once, in that half-sleep of early morning, I caught myself thinking that my mother lived over the road and that my father had come back. When I realised the mistake my dreams had made, I was happy.

But I have to be wary of mornings. I wouldn't like to meet Beatrice as I leave the house before I have told her I am here. And there is no way of preparing. I can't see her front door from my windows. Soon, soon, as soon as I feel a little stronger, I will tell her.

I have dressed with particular care for my meeting today, a soft black woollen dress, stockings, an agate pin at my neck. I don't altogether know why I have taken such care except that I feel like a student about to be tested. I wonder if the Maître remembers that this is the end of my trial week.

Like a dutiful student, I now copy the file of notes I have prepared for him and look over the list of the material I have gathered in the course of the week, together with attendant queries. Armed with my folders, I knock at his office door.

The 'come in' is muffled and it is only when I open the door that I realise he is on the telephone. He flashes a mechanical smile at me and waves me towards the chair in front of his desk. I try hard not to listen to what he is saying or watch the impatient intentness of his features. I would not like that impatience directed at me. My notes provide a foil for my nervousness, but my eyes keep wandering towards the series of ears, chins, moustaches, brows, which crowd the walls, like so many wandering parts in search of a human whole.

'Don't let Bertillon worry you, Maria.' Paul's chuckle takes me by surprise. 'I don't think you'd recognise yourself in the line-up, even if you were there.'

'Bertillon?' I smooth my dress to cover my uneasiness. The only Bertillon I can think of makes ice cream.

'Alphonse Bertillon, creator of the first photographic police archive, precursor of the identikit. He had a mania for anatomising the human face and detailing minute differences. The trouble was, the faces wouldn't sit still so the precision of measurement and description had somehow to make up for time's passage. Otherwise yesterday's criminal might be confounded with today's lawyer. Or politician or baker or researcher. How have you got on?' he asks without an intervening pause.

I swallow, pass over the diskette I have copied for him. 'That's this weeks' pickings,' I say. 'Summaries of the Ruth Ellis and Myra Hindley cases. There's a lot more work to do on the latter.'

He slides the diskette into his computer and his face lights up with boyish pleasure as soon as the screen lights up with my words. The technological magic visibly delights him. I'm not certain if my synopses do, but he reads on in silence while I try not to fidget.

After some minutes, he grunts and looks at me. 'Ruth Ellis's advocate didn't exactly do her much good, did he?'

I don't quite know how to answer this. I am not an expert. How does one adequately defend a woman who confesses to having murdered her betraying and exploitative lover?

'He didn't approve of her, if that's what you mean. The reports make that clear. She wasn't as you explained to me one of the good girls who wear their blouses buttoned up and apologise for what they've done. And he made no effort to make her appear such.'

'Nor did he cross-examine witnesses to any effect, which the British system allows so much more leeway for. Your quotations from the trial make that clear. That's good. You've done that well.' He smiles at me briefly then gets up and starts to pace.

'You do realise that in France, far from being hanged, Ruth Ellis would have got off with a brief sentence and probably have become a local heroine. The *crime passionel*. Sexual passion is the one form of madness every French juror can identify with and understand.'

His expression makes me feel I am being baited. He wants my opinion on this, but I don't know what to say. Is passion a form of madness, a frenzy which parallels the state in which crimes are committed? I don't want to acknowledge this and yet perhaps the difficulty I have in imagining the actual murderous act of the two New Zealand girls is related to the difficulty I always have in imaginatively recapturing the sensations of the sexual act once passion has fled. I cannot put this to him coldly, here, in this file-cluttered room, so instead I quote the judge in the Ellis trial.

'Mr Justice Havers would have it that, "The jealous fury of a woman scorned is no excuse for murder. That is the law of England."'

'So it would seem,' Paul chuckles, and looks down at the screen again.

'But things have changed,' I add for good measure, still a student on trial. 'Partly as a result of the outcry over Ruth Ellis's sentence, hanging was abolished in England a few years later.'

'Are you enjoying the work, Maria?' he asks me suddenly.

I nod.

'So you'll stay on?'

'If you want me to. If what I'm doing is what you want.'

'It's just what I needed. At this rate the book will be finished more quickly than I dared hope.' He looks at me seriously in a way which would have made my pulse race, if I still had that kind of pulse.

'Now tell me what you thought of the draft. You're my first reader, you know.'

I tell him, honestly, that I found it riveting, though there were things I couldn't altogether grasp. My notes provide questions and he explains various processes of law to me. I learn that the most important person in any case can easily be the behind-the-scenes *juge d'instruction*, the investigating magistrate who, like a chief inspector and more, puts together the dossier on which the trial, and too often the sentence, is based. The jury trial itself is, as far as he is concerned, too often structured mainly for drama and spectacle and the president, the chief interrogating judge, is its star, grilling all parties for days on end and then also sitting on the nine-person jury and guiding its decisions, along with two fellow judges.

We talk then of the wave of *crimes passionels* which swept France from the 1880s through to the First World War, and I tell him I find it extraordinary that so many women were treated so leniently by so many juries.

Paul eyes me quizzically. 'You'd be harder on them?'

'Perhaps.' I shiver as I imagine the number of times a jealous wife might have taken a gun to my head, if years in a state penitentiary had not acted as a deterrent.

He shrugs. 'They thought of love then as an essential dominating power. In thrall to that power, it was absurd to speak of full personal responsibility for an act. Then as the century turned, the unconscious came into fashion – a deeply unsettling unconscious which was understood as a mechanism which could release nervous charges so powerful that they would momentarily seize absolute control of any ordinary person's behaviour and thrust her into what was called an *état passionel*. On top of that, the social psychologists talked about an urban frenzy, which gripped people, took them over. The claustrophobia, the noise, the intensity of burgeoning city life, could overload a woman's already fragile nervous system and make her prey to violent passion. So, as the experts testified in court, "no responsibility", and for the jury that meant, no conviction,' he grins, 'though of course far fewer men were absolved than members of the weaker sex.'

The last words are a deliberate tease and I know he expects me to bristle and react in the usual way. But we are not talking about usual situations. 'Women are often weaker,' I say.

He gives me a provocative glance, then seizes on my gist. 'Not in nerves, but in physical size, yes. And that can have a very real impact on behaviour, which the courts, as our esteemed Tanya Walker points out to me daily, are slow to take on board. For example, a battered woman will not defend herself in the same instantaneous way that a man might. And the courts have trouble understanding what can be a long-delayed violent reaction as self-defence. I like to draw an analogy with terrorism in such cases. No one thinks that if, after weeks of torture, the captive turns on his sleeping terrorist jailer, this is anything other than a legitimate form of self-defence.'

He looks suddenly at his watch. 'I had no idea it was so late. Will you excuse me a moment.' He picks up the telephone.

I walk to the other side of the room and read the spines of books while he punches out a number. It is almost eight and I realise that he must be phoning home. Despite myself, I listen, hear him talk to someone called Pauline who is to convey his apologies to Madame and tell her he will be there within the hour.

'I am sorry to have kept you so long,' he says to me absently as he rifles through the files on his desk and picks out two. 'Do make sure you keep a note of your hours for Madame Duval.'

'I'll make sure.'

He looks up at the sound of my archness.

'I mean it.' He is stern, then smiles. 'And next Friday if you're free, perhaps you'll let me take you out to dinner after our session. It'll give us longer. I'm afraid I can't even offer you a drink this evening. I'm late. But a lift. You're on my way home, the Rue d'Oudinot, isn't it?'

I am about to contradict him when I change my mind. 'Just drop me anywhere on the St-Germain,' I say.

His eyes are on me as I gather up my things. There is a momentary tension between us. I know this tension. It is to do with transitions. Transitions between one kind of time to another kind of time. Work to life. Narrow passages difficult to negotiate.

'A date?' he asks, just as I say, 'I'll get my jacket upstairs.'

I don't answer him.

'Meet me at the door of the car park round the corner. Ten minutes.'

I am there before him, and while I wait I wonder whether this little step towards greater intimacy is wise. He is there before I can decide, balancing two vast bouquets of carefully arranged flowers. He hands one to me. Lilies starkly white and waxen against the lustrous green of their stems. Interspersed with them, the frothy white of gypsophila.

'For all the overtime,' he says.

I murmur thanks, wonder what the choice of flowers suggests. The other bouquet, I notice, is in stark contrast to my own. A mass of ranunculas, pink and soft and pretty as a spring garden. His wife is not like me.

⚖ 16

The trees which line the northern avenue of the Cimetière Montparnasse are dotted with early buds. The sun bursts upon them sporadically from rushing cloud and leaps off the granite and marble of the tombs. As I wait for Beatrice by the gates, two English tourists in anoraks stop and ask me in heavily accented French whether I can point them to Baudelaire's tomb. Beatrice is right behind them. She is dressed in black and carrying a large pot of daffodils. I had not thought of flowers. Flowers are for the living, I imagine. Now I feel a little ashamed. But Beatrice kisses me and gives my hand a special squeeze.

We walk without speaking towards the d'Esté family tomb. A group of blue-clad nuns comes at us from a side lane. They are chattering away in an incomprehensible language, their unadorned faces girlish, animated, beneath the stark white bands of their headdresses. In response to Beatrice's polite nod, one of them waves at us gaily.

'Have you ever thought what it might be like to live only in the company of women?' I say to Beatrice once they have passed us by.

She gives me a curious sideways glance. 'Not really. Though they seem none the worse for it.'

'I think I might like it.'

'You!' She is visibly astonished by the notion.

'Why not me?'

'I don't know.' She shifts the pot into her other arm and, suddenly realising it must be heavy, I take it from her. She smiles, puts her arm through mine. 'Do you remember Dominique, the boy who sat next to me one Easter term, and how madly in love with you he was?'

I have forgotten Dominique, but now his face comes back to me, together with the quiff of Tintin hair he had, which stood right out at the top of his head.

'He would stare at you all the time, hoping you'd glance back at him, and in his spare notebook, I would see him drawing you.'

'I think you're imagining this, Beatrice.'

'No. Didn't you notice? If you ever spoke to him, he would blush beet red. He was even nice to me when he saw what good friends we were. He would offer both of us sweets at lunchtime. The other boys teased him horribly. Do you ever see any of those children any more?' she asks after a moment.

I shake my head. 'Do you?'

She looks away. 'Never.'

We have arrived at my mother's grave. Beatrice gazes at it solemnly, then bends to position the daffodils on the tomb. She stays like that, half-kneeling, for a few moments and when she rises I see there are tears on her face.

'When I was little, I loved your mother more than anyone,' she murmurs. She stares at the grave for some time in silence as if she is communing with someone and the sight of her there, her face wet, brings the tears to my eyes too. Suddenly I feel I must tell her, say it aloud.

'That date, 1978,' Beatrice says. 'Is that the year she died?'

I don't know why she asks this, since it is engraved on the tomb. I nod. 'In October.'

'Not so long after my mother.'

'I'm sorry,' I whisper. 'I had no idea.' It is the first time Beatrice has mentioned her mother. I want to ask her more, but she rushes on now, clearly changing the subject.

'Was she very ill at the end?'

This astonishes me. For some reason, I had assumed Beatrice knew. 'No, no, it was very sudden. She was knocked over by a car.'

'How terrible for you,' she says. Her eyes are very large and dark as she looks at me. It is my turn to take her hand. 'She missed you very much, you know, after you left Paris.' I lead her away from the grave. I need to make up to her what I robbed her of.

'I missed her.' Beatrice's voice cracks. 'And you, both of you.'

'Beatrice,' I say, wishing the sun hadn't chosen this moment to bathe us in its glare, wishing that I were in the darkness of a confessional. 'Beatrice, that last year, I wanted you away, I wished you away. I'm sorry. I . . .'

'I know.' She cuts me off.

'My mother loved you too much.'

'It wouldn't have made any difference.' Her voice has an edge of

117

bitterness I don't recognise. She doesn't really forgive me. I will have to do penance so that she forgives me.

'She would have enjoyed seeing your children, seeing you so well,' I mumble, and think to myself that she would have been mortified to see her own daughter.

Beatrice doesn't speak until the gates of the cemetery are behind us. Then it is as if nothing amiss has occurred.

'You know what I would like,' she says, looking up at me. 'I would like a cup of hot chocolate. I've had such a busy week. There's been a conference on top of everything else. So many people from everywhere. I imagine you went to lots of those in New York.'

The next day, just as the light is dying, an episode to do with Beatrice comes back to me with all the unshadowed clarity of the noonday sun. It must have taken place just before Beatrice broke her leg. Rachel, my other close friend, and I decided to tail Beatrice after school, follow her to the home we had never seen. Our satchels over our shoulders, our giggles repressed to each other's 'shhh', we followed her through narrow streets and then across a wide boulevard we weren't supposed to cross to a street dotted with shops. Perhaps it was the Rue St-Denis. In front of one of the buildings, Beatrice was stopped by a plump woman wearing a very short skirt. The woman kissed her on both cheeks, but we couldn't hear what they said to one another, and then Beatrice scurried through a door and disappeared.

'That's where she lives,' I announced to Rachel and gazed with something like disappointment at the nondescript building.

'And that must be her mother,' Rachel said, a note of triumph in her voice. 'Just look at her stockings.'

I looked. The stockings were criss-crossed things, like dancers wore.

'Her mother is a *pute*.' Rachel pronounced the taboo word with pride. 'A prostitute.'

'Don't be silly.'

'I bet you.' She tugged at my arm and pulled me into the recess of a shop door. 'Just wait.'

We waited and, sure enough, a few minutes later a man appeared and after a second's worth of conversation, the woman with the net stockings and the man disappeared through the same door as Beatrice. I felt my mouth fall open.

'I told you.'

'You don't know that's her mother.'

'I bet it is.'

'Isn't.'

'An aunt, then. Why else would she kiss her?' Rachel was stubborn. 'I'm sure it was her mother,' she insisted again, after a moment. 'I'm going to ask her. Tomorrow.'

'Don't.'

'I will too.'

We didn't talk much on our way home. I think I wasn't too sure what a prostitute was, though I didn't want to let on. But I knew it was bad and over dinner that night, I said to my mother, 'Rachel says Beatrice's mother is a *pute*.'

My mother gave me one of those dark warning looks which always made me feel that if I breathed another word I would cross over into a world from which there was no return.

'Don't be ridiculous,' she said. 'Wherever does the girl get such ideas?'

'We saw her,' I ventured. I didn't want to be stopped. Perhaps I also wanted to see how far my mother would go to defend Beatrice. 'With net stockings and with a man.'

My mother glared. There were two bright pink spots in her cheeks. 'Beatrice's mother is a poor, harassed woman who works part-time in a laundry and part-time cleaning other people's houses. And I think you and Rachel have better things to do than imagine lies about other people's lives. Like maths, for one. You've had quite enough dinner, Maria.' She sent me to my room.

I think I believed my mother, but I did nothing to contradict the rumours Rachel excitedly put round at school.

It was soon after this that Beatrice broke her leg and came to live with us. I asked her one night, 'Beatrice, do you know what a *pute* is?'

She looked at me with her big round eyes and thought for a moment. 'No. What is it?'

'I'm not sure either,' I mumbled, hid my embarrassment in a book.

Perhaps she read my mind, for she said then, 'I wish my mother were like yours. And that I had no father.'

For some reason this irritated me and I cut her off. 'I do have a father. He just doesn't live in France.'

'I'm sorry.' Her lower lip quivered as it often did if I was harsh with her. This irritated me more than ever and I stomped from the table only to be sent back seconds later by my mother, who was rightly convinced that my homework wasn't finished.

I gaze out of my window at the sliver of a moon and think of Beatrice and my mother. Suddenly I am rapt by the sight of a couple embracing in one of the attic windows opposite. Their shadowy silhouettes are folded round one another, their faces locked. Passion is so much of their stance that I can feel its heat leaping through the air, kindling my skin. It is a long time since I have felt this particular warmth. It confuses me. As too does the intensity of my spying on another's intimacy. I look away and then despite myself turn back. I want that woman's heat, that blending into the body of another.

I stare, watch the woman ease out of the embrace, and all at once from the lilt of her hair round her neck, the movement of her hand, I am convinced she is Beatrice. Beatrice. The notion devastates me. In all my musing on Beatrice, I have never associated her with passion. Is this one-time *chambre de bonne*, where the good bourgeoisie kept their maids, the site to which Beatrice and her husband retreat to play out their marital passion far from the children's eyes? I try to see the man's face, but he is unclear to me. And then, as if they sense the avidity of my watching, a curtain is drawn.

Sleep evades me that night and when it finally comes, I am bitterly complaining to my mother about Beatrice. The single white streak in my mother's hair has disappeared. She is young, her face unlined, but her voice is the same – reasonable, persuasive. I have so much still to learn, she tells me. And then she runs off with a cheerful wave of the hand.

'I'm going to meet your father,' she says.

⚖ 17

Despite the notice which announces it as a one-time upmarket marriage agency where Peter, Earl of Savoy, brought together the most beautiful of continental aristocrats in order to pair them off with English lords, the Savoy Hotel has an old-fashioned solidity, as comforting as Sunday lunches of roast beef and Yorkshire pudding served on trays of heavy silver. It hushes the voice, implants the sturdy decorum of tweed skirts and twinsets and averted eyes. I like this London of stiff backbones and soothing invisibility, though it was Paul Arnault's decision that I stay here, close to legal London, and not too far from the Old Bailey. Miles, however, from the Colindale newspaper library as I discovered to my dismay this morning when I trekked out there; and to my frustration this evening as the tube shuddered and screeched me back. The erratic sprawl of London never ceases to amaze me.

I have been in the city for two days. It is the first time I have been here this long without ringing Robinson. When I used to fly over from New York, Robinson's was always amongst the numbers I dialled first. Robinson Muir, whom I have known since I was a slip of a girl, even before I met Beatrice, and who with a hiatus or two has remained a friend ever since. Robinson, who still occasionally calls me 'Mare', after the horse we both rode on that childhood farm in Kent. But it is well over a year, perhaps two, since I last spoke to Robinson and I don't know whether I have the courage to do so now. The trouble with Robinson is that he always elicits honesty – not in words, necessarily, but within oneself.

I lie in the hot porcelain whiteness of the bath and think of Robinson in his perennial tweed jacket and worn jeans, a scarf in some outlandishly bright colour always dangling from his neck.

Robinson turned up in New York when I was nearing the end of my third year at Rutherford, Owen and Marks. We had done little more for some time than exchange the annual Christmas card, and I hadn't seen him since before my mother's death. He had come to Paris then on a school trip, a shy, gangling teenager who didn't know where to put his feet or how to speak without hiding his mouth. Now he had filled out, was a square-jawed man with dreaming eyes, a shock of ash-blond hair, and a firm long-legged tread which always reminded me of the wellies we used to wear on his parents' farm. He had won some kind of fellowship and was doing post-graduate work in bio-chemistry at Columbia University.

We met for a drink at a fashionable downtown bar, all chrome and dazzling lights and glossy sculpture. The drink turned into another and another and merged into dinner, which ended up with coffee at my apartment. We had years of catching up and growing up to get through and conversation with Robinson was always like a stammering haphazard journey with destination merely an excuse for any number of vertiginous sidetracks. Perhaps he had learned the art in Cambridge common rooms. Not that he was smoothly articulate. Anything but. I often had the sense that his words when they came had burst forth from some deep well of silence where he was most at home.

It wasn't that first night that we went to bed together. I suspect he thought I would be insulted if he didn't take my measure first as a separate intellectual being and rushed things. Robinson had morality and there were any number of fine gradations on his moral scale. It took me a little while to grow attuned to them.

But go to bed we eventually did, though perhaps the first move was mine. There was an inevitability to it, as if all those childhood games, that hide-and-seek through fields and woods, that burrowing into hay, had been but a preparation, a protracted teasing, which could only abut in this. He proved at once the most alien creature I had ever met and as familiar as the dungarees of his I had grown into like a second skin that first summer at Millhill Farm.

Making love with Robinson was like coming home: not to a home I had really known, but to that home we all carry within ourselves, wordlessly dreamt of, sensed, unspoken. Bed, with Robinson, was a place which pre-dated speech. It was all languorous slowness. It was all touch and deep silence and that ferny, moist smell he had, like a forest in the depth of night.

That was another thing. With Robinson, the lights were always off. He didn't look at me. I realised quite quickly that all those knickers and bodices were invisible to him, or if not invisible, then something of a nuisance. Sex was a serious matter. A dark matter. And because of its dark solemnity, it took on the aura of a mystery. We never referred to it in the course of our long conversations, as if it didn't exist. But it was always there, like a secret rite, waiting to be engaged upon. If he occasionally stretched out his hand and touched my cheek in the course of the day or inadvertently brushed against me, I would feel the reverberation of his touch deep inside me and I would long to be back in that place which was the consecrated space of our mingled bodies.

Needless to say, none of this coalesced very smoothly with my relationship with Grant Rutherford. For the first few weeks it didn't seem to make that much difference. Grant and I were after all old hands by now, and our love-making was like the titillating comic prelude to the main drama, which was the serious business of discussing business. But pretty soon, even the comedy became distasteful. My body wasn't in it.

Then one Sunday lunchtime, in the midst of one of those monologues, which veered between humour and passion, about his work at the laboratory, Robinson suddenly looked down at his napkin and said, 'There must be many men in your life.'

He said it in his off-hand voice, which I had learned signalled discomfort. Robinson was most off-hand when he was most uncomfortable and he was most uncomfortable discussing the intimacies of life.

I smiled, I hoped enigmatically. But he was waiting for an answer and since I could never lie directly to Robinson, I murmured, 'Some.'

He took my hand then, a rare event in daylight, and mumbled, 'I . . . I wish there weren't.' His eyes when he turned them on me were stormy. But there was something else in his face, a distaste, as if he had inadvertently swallowed some rancid milk.

I squeezed his hand for an answer and vowed to myself that I would speak to Grant at the very nearest opportunity.

It came a few days later. We were having a late dinner together in some quiet green-and-white restaurant in Little Italy. We had just been to an opening at an uptown gallery and had momentarily run out of gossip about whom we had seen with whom, when I took a deep breath and plunged.

'Grant, I think perhaps it's time we stopped seeing each other after hours.'

He gave me one of his probing looks and obviously didn't like what

he saw, for he loosened his tie, and that little muscle that sometimes appeared in his cheek when he was angry at meetings went to
work.

I babbled over his silence. 'We've had a good run and it's not as if
it's all that important to us any more and . . .'

'Speak for yourself.' Grant interrupted me. After a moment, he
asked, 'Who is he?' He had his stern face on, the face he used to turn
on me in my early days in the firm, and I suddenly felt very young
and bashful.

'An old friend. I've known him since we were children.'

'Really.' He paused. 'It won't last a month.'

'It has already.' I was bold. I didn't like his tone.

We stared at each other, sparring partners until the last. The icy
glint in his eyes matched his voice when eventually he said, 'And you
intend to stay on at the firm?'

'I really didn't think that was at issue.'

'Come on.' Grant screeched his chair away from the table and
manoeuvred me out of the restaurant as quickly as bill-paying could
allow. 'We can have coffee at your place.' It was a threat.

We drove back without saying a word, but with great surges of
horsepower and squealings of brakes. For some reason, I had really
not anticipated Grant's anger. There must have been a blind childish-
ness about me at the time. When he had parked, I said, 'I don't think
you should come up, Grant. Not tonight. Not in this mood.' I tried
a little laugh to lighten the tone of things. I wanted him to approve
of me. I wanted things to go on as before, but for one small matter.

He tried to kiss me and I didn't struggle. I gave him my lips. They
were colder than the November night.

He stared at me for a moment in the shadowy lamplight. 'I see,' he
said, then added, his voice gruff, 'I want to meet this man.'

I was appalled at the notion. 'That won't be possible.'

'Why ever not? Are you ashamed of him?'

'Of course not.'

'Then I'll take you both out to dinner.' He leafed through the pages
of his diary. 'Say next Thursday. You can confirm with Anita when
you come in tomorrow.'

Anita was his secretary and it was the first time one of our after-hour
meetings was to make its way to her attention. It was his way of
signalling a change: from now on my access to him would be through

his secretary. Grant had an inimitable way of scoring points. It was probably what had kept our relationship alive for so long.

'I'll let Anita know when I can.' I underlined that I had understood.

Grant chortled. 'And you'll give her the young man's name. Unless there are reasons for keeping it private, of course.'

'There are no reasons.'

'So you're to be an honest woman, at last?' Grant needled me.

'Have I ever been anything less? To Mr Grant Rutherford, at least?'

I opened the car door and as I did so he took my hand and kissed it with mock courtesy.

'Never,' he said seriously. 'And I trust it will stay that way.'

'My boss wants to take us out for dinner,' I said to Robinson that weekend.

'Oh? Is that a good thing?'

I giggled. 'I'm not sure. But I guess we have to accept.'

Grant took us to The Four Seasons, as if he were pointing out to me the distance we had travelled since we had first dined there. Or perhaps it was an uncustomary nod towards sentimentality. I don't think Robinson had any notion that he was anything other than my boss, though unusually for him, he did drape his arm loosely over my shoulder as we made our way towards Grant.

There was a tense, guarded courtesy about the two men which I half-managed to dissipate by talking too much and drinking too much too quickly. Then they locked antlers. Grant suddenly displayed a hidden and tortuous knowledge of genetic research and the perils of genetic engineering, whereas Robinson, who was looking exceptionally handsome in a dark suit I had never seen him wear before, waxed lyrical over the rise of Saatchi and Saatchi, only then to attack the nefarious grip advertising had on politics, the dangerous reliance on image and sound-bite.

'I'm with you there,' Grant surprised us both by saying. 'But if that's what the electorate want . . .' He held up his arms in a helpless gesture and chuckled.

'To know what you want, you have to have choice, real choice, not competing slogans devised by the same kinds of manipulative minds.'

'Do you mean politicians or advertisers?'

Grant was all veiled innocence, while I racked my brain for an anecdote which would deflect the growing hostility. Then Robinson suddenly excused himself and vanished into the men's room. Grant looked at me in silence and with a glimmering impatience. After what felt like a long time, he took my hand in something of a paternal gesture.

'He's a handsome young brute. But you're far too clever to be a romantic.'

I didn't have time to weigh the sense of this or answer, for Robinson chose this moment to reappear and I had to extricate my hand as innocuously as possible from Grant's.

We left soon after.

Robinson's only comment about the evening was to say that Grant seemed to know his business well and he was obviously a good boss if he wined and dined his staff and their mates in such grand fashion. I don't think there was any irony in the statement, but Robinson didn't stay at my place that night as he had for so many previous ones. Nor did he make any sign until about a week later. Needless to say, I was distraught. I also didn't understand his silence.

When he finally rang me again, he behaved as if nothing untoward had happened. Explanations, reasons, were never in Robinson's line. Instead, we fell into bed together, and despite work and all the other commitments, it felt like months before we re-emerged. The magic of our mingled bodies engulfed us, cocooning us in our passion. Somewhere in those months, I was offered a job with another firm. I took it, happy to leave Grant and his prickling little asides, his queries about the imminence of wedding bells. Once even he said he wished I would hurry up over it, so that we could get together again. I scowled at his cynicism, though part of me thought it might be true.

It was late spring when Robinson himself mentioned the prospect of marriage. We were in the Adirondacks on a week's holiday. A friend had lent us his house, a cabin really, on the slope of a densely wooded hill with a stream rushing over rock somewhere in the distance. Everything was scented with pine and woodsmoke, even our love-making. We were like children again, traipsing amidst the trees, dipping our feet into the freezing water of the stream and running wildly to warm ourselves. We took to making love outdoors. In the daytime too. Robinson would spread his anorak on the rough forest floor and we would lie there looking up at the streaking sunlight, listening to the birds' call as we had listened to the mooing cows, until we found ourselves in each other's arms, our limbs entwined, the act gradually, mysteriously, enveloping us, dictating its own rhythms, its own postures.

On the evening before we were due to leave, we were sitting at the little card table we had set up in front of the cabin and munching cheese and apples, catching the fading pink of the sky, when Robinson suddenly said to me, à propos of nothing, 'You know, by the end of September, I have to be back in England. You'll come with me, won't you? We'll get married. I love you.'

He was looking at me, but his words visibly embarrassed him, and I started to kiss him, as much to rid him of his embarrassment as anything else. And then he carried me indoors onto the camp bed with its rough grey blanket and thinnest of pillows and our senses took over, obliterating any need for a verbal reply. That night I remember thinking that if I had been an artist, I would have been able to draw Robinson by blind touch alone, the hollow of his foot, the taut arch of his calf, the slight bristle of his thighs, all the way up to the tendons of his neck, the precise curve of his jaw and lips, the thick grain of his hair. And myself, too, from the pressure of his fingers.

But the next day when I woke from the cradle of his arms, there was a niggling difference about everything. It was as if with the word 'marriage', time had entered into our togetherness, a future time which had nothing to do with the vibrant present tense of our passion. I recognised that if I had ever been in love, I was in love with Robinson. Though what the words meant when I examined them was none too clear. They seemed to imply a 'forever', but this forever ought really to have been a timeless extension of the present, whereas when Robinson spoke of the future, he talked about a great many concrete things.

He had moved in with me now, and whenever the opportunity arose, he made plans for us. He talked of a house we could rent in the countryside outside Cambridge, just where a single hill dipped. There was a pond and with luck a pair of swans might appear. He talked of a dog we would get who resembled Small in every detail. He talked of the manifold courses the university offered which I might wish to engage on. He even talked of children.

At first, I tried to imagine myself in this idyll, but I was uncomfortable. Something in me balked. It came to me that for all his lip-service to my separate being, Robinson could see no reason why I might choose to be who I was; why I might want to stay in New York and pursue what to him was meaningless work with only money as a reward. Over that summer, other things about him began to irritate me: the fact that he would often position his chair so that he could look into the middle distance and not at me; the fact that he never noticed what I was wearing, so that I began to feel I had no identity for him but that nakedness of the nighttime act; the fact that whenever we had even a minor disagreement, he wouldn't argue, but would simply withdraw into himself, and punish me by refusing his body. His silent presence was nonetheless there and gradually, too, I grew resentful of the unceasing regularity of that presence.

I wasn't aware of this all at once. September came round and Robinson simply assumed that by the end of the month I would travel with him to England, or join him soon after. It was towards the middle of the month I think that Grant rang me and invited me to lunch. He wanted to discuss a work problem. I hadn't seen him for some time and it was over that lunch, filled with humour and compliments and unspoken questions, that it came to me that really I preferred being the other woman. The woman whose time was her own to control.

Robinson taught me that. He also made me reflect on what it was that made passion with him so addictive for me, so particularly potent. I realised that with him, I lost myself utterly and I like to lose myself. There is an exhilaration to it, a wild irresponsible freedom, like the pounding of waves against a rocky cliff. And a risk. Not knowing where limbs and boundaries end and others begin, whose lips have uttered which moan, whose heart has taken up that hammering. Who is me and who is the other. The act is poised on the precipice of disintegration. Yet one wakes from the journey to find features swimming into focus again, a leg, a hand, a voice, that moves to one's command.

And that is the contradiction. The sexual act apart, I value my control. And I want it. I have no desire to prolong the merging, to find myself halved in couplehood.

I tried to explain some of this to Robinson, when I said I wouldn't come with him, but I don't think he understood. Perhaps I wasn't very clear. Perhaps we were both just too young, on either side of our mid-twenties. He was hurt. His face stony, he told me I thought too much, as if that were somehow an impure activity. Then he left in a silent huff and I cried, mourning the absence I had thought I wanted. He wrote to me not too long after to tell me he was getting married and I sent him a note of what were almost honest congratulations. Then some two years later, he wrote again to tell me the marriage was all but over and he was coming to New York on a brief visit. We met, both a little wary, a little older too, and wiser. Robinson could sometimes look me in the eyes when he took my hand.

We became friends and the friendship has lasted. Sometimes when the conditions are right, we even go to bed together. When bed is good with Robinson, it is like with no one else. That may just be the legacy of lying in the heat of the barn together, so long ago. The legacy of innocence. Perhaps, too, it's that as you grow older, it's nicer to lose yourself with someone whose features you trust as they come into focus again.

The bath water has grown cold around me. All its heat has gathered inside me into a shaft of pure longing for Robinson. I would like to lie with him. I would like to lose myself. What else have these last months been but the attempt utterly to lose the self I had become? The longing is stronger than the fear of confrontation and before it can evaporate, I wrap myself in the huge hotel towel and make for the phone. Fate will determine the rest.

Robinson is there. His voice has the familiar hesitancy masked by formality. I am about to identify myself as Maria d'Esté when I realise that Robinson only knows me as Regnier and this slippage makes me stammer a mere, 'It's Maria.'

There is a pause, then Robinson swears at me. 'Maria. Where the hell have you been? I've heard nothing from you in ages.'

'I've been in Paris.' I elude explanations. 'I'm in London now, for a few days. It would be nice to meet.'

'I wish you'd let me know ahead of time.' There is a querulous quality in Robinson's voice that I don't recognise, and for a moment I panic. Robinson has given me up.

'Don't worry if you can't manage it, Robinson. Are you well?' I pull the towel more tightly round me. I am cold.

'Perhaps Thursday evening. Where are you staying?'

'At the Savoy. I'll book a table in the Grill Room, just in case. At eight.'

Robinson whistles. 'I'll leave a message at the desk.' Then he adds, 'Or perhaps you'd rather come up here. On Saturday?'

'Let's play it by ear,' I say. I have never wanted to see the Cambridge

Robinson would have settled me in. Even less so, now. 'I'll look out for your message. Under my mother's name, please. Maria d'Esté.'

I ring off quickly with a sense of depression, console myself with the thought that Robinson and I have never managed to speak adequately on the phone. Like children and lovers, we exist for each other best in proximity.

⚖ 18

Even on a bright day, the Thames Embankment does nothing to welcome strollers. The murky waters of the river are too wide, the pavements barren, but for the swoop of a scavenging gull or pigeon. All of life seems to be enclosed in the ranked, jostling cars and distant towers. The northern side of the street, with its flower-strewn garden and leafy alcoves, is better. London is a city of parks, as if the only purpose of brick and stone and concrete were to breed green and golden dreams of country.

I pass under a fringe of plane trees and find the gateway to the Temple. There is a sudden hush in the air, as if I have crossed into a different city, a separate time zone. Rich lawns slope away from meandering lanes closely banked by rows of old brick. Old gas lamps mark the way – doorways painted with names, a library, the warm stone of a church, and fountains, their jets of frail water catching the sunlight. Even the brisk tread of the dark-suited advocates does nothing to rupture the cloistered tranquillity. The law is its own sanctified precinct.

I wander and lose myself, then hurry along, remembering that I am here for work – work I am once again supremely grateful for, since it has allowed me to find this place I had no idea existed.

My appointment is for ten thirty and I find the elaborate doorway with the chambers' name just in time. Inside, it is slightly dank and gloomy. A narrow, precipitous stairway leads me up to the second floor and a warren of doors. Jennifer Walters is ready for me. She is a woman of my own age with eyes as bright and shiny as wet pebbles and a humorous lilt to her lips. Her suit is requisition black, but it is well-cut and the collar of her white blouse has a lacy frill to it which matches her thick waving hair. As she rises to shake my hand, I see that she is surprisingly small and all energy. Her voice, when it comes, has a warm garrulousness to it. I like her instantly.

'So you've made your way across the hundreds of years and watery miles which separate us to get a little look-in on the strange workings of British justice?' She laughs engagingly. 'Tough going, I imagine.'

'Just as tough for me on the other side.'

'Ah, but we've no code books here with thousands of nicely numbered entries. Only thousands of lovely, dusty precedents.' She gestures dramatically at the thick tomes on the walls.

'Amongst which you'll point me to the relevant ones?'

'Here it is. All ready and waiting.' She hands me two sheets of paper filled with neat jottings. 'According to the express orders of the master, or should I say "Maître"' – she rolls her r's along with her eyes – 'nice bloke, the Maître. Though his English leaves something to be desired.'

'Which is why I'm here.'

'You mightn't find any of this crystalline, nonetheless.' She gives me an appraising glance. 'Legal rulings are not known for their transparency.'

'In this instance, I'm only a translator with a computer at the ready.'

'And as for the rest?'

I tell her more about Paul's women who kill than she can have garnered from his letter and she listens intently. Then it is her turn. With a succinctness which in no way diminishes her fervour, she explains to me that the current battle in Britain is to have a plea of self-defence accepted in cases where battered women have murdered their husbands as a result of cumulative and daily provocation, but have waited to do so until the man is asleep or prostrate in an alcoholic stupor. Judges are too ready to say that such a change would institute a licence to kill, but the experience of other countries shows otherwise.

'I don't know about France, but here judges seem more easily to grant that a wife's nagging can act as provocation to murder, than the continual and brutal treatment of a drunken husband.' She grins. 'Guess they've had more experience of the former.'

She names cases and dates and I quickly jot down the ones I know nothing of. Then she gives me some necessary background to the trial which is opening tomorrow and for which she is counsel for the defence. She says she can let me see the notes when it is all over.

My hour is up. As I rise, she smiles at me wryly.

'And don't forget, if you get stopped by a British bobby, we have Habeas Corpus here.'

I don't know what she is talking about and while I painfully try to translate from the Latin, she goes on.

'Yes, here our bodies are our own. When we can get access to them, that is.' There is a distinct twinkle in her eye as she adds, 'Give my best to Maître Arnault.'

It is only when I am sitting in the Law Library that something I am reading illuminates her parting words. In France, there is no Habeas Corpus; the body of the citizen belongs to the State and can thus be held captive before any official hearing. In Britain, the body is the subject's alone.

But it comes to me that Jennifer Walters was doing more than pointing out cross-Channel differences. There was some kind of implication about Paul, a suggestion that my body belonged to him perhaps, whereas hers didn't, but might have done.

My palms grow oddly moist at this sequence of thoughts. I have deliberately deflected any notions of Paul as a sexual being over these last weeks. And they have been weeks of growing comradeship, our Friday afternoon sessions extending into long evenings of heated debate, so heated that if I were still the woman I once used to be, there would be only one resolution for the friction of these arguments. Two or three times I have caught the question in his eyes, but I have turned away, despite the temptation. All that is behind me. There will be no more adventures. I conjure up Beatrice, as I would clutch at a talisman. Nonetheless, the passing weeks have made me take note of the temptation: its presence confirms that I have rejoined the living after a year in the barrenness of the desert.

On the Friday before I came to London, Paul and I ended up at Le Dôme for dinner. The wine-red plush and languid curves of the belle époque interior provided an incongruous setting for that day's subject. We were discussing infanticide, that crime in which a newborn is killed moments after its first breath. There were three cases at issue. In the first a jobless middle-aged woman, already mother of two and on the poverty line, had taken the child she had just given birth to alone in her ramshackle apartment and deposited it unceremoniously in a street bin. In the second a seventeen-year-old with a strict father and pregnant stepmother, had flushed her own infant and placenta into the family toilet and proceeded to faint in the very bathroom in which the birth had taken place. In the last a provincial bourgeoise managed to kill her newborn, product of a hidden rape, while her husband carried on working across the hall.

Paul is arguing that in all these cases the women were utterly unaware of what they were doing. They were as unconscious of their pregnancies as they were of the murderous act.

'The child for them doesn't exist,' he says. 'The birth is like stomach ache or vomiting or a period, a purely physical event, so they can flush or throw or wash its product away.'

'I don't believe a word of it,' I protest. 'Of course they knew. And if they preferred not to know, someone would have pointed out the pregnancy to them. Stop behaving like a defence lawyer. We're not in court.'

His eyes leap and glow more vividly than ever in the warm light that billows from the airy lamp above us.

'And you can stop behaving like a narrow-minded judge. Just try to understand for a moment. We're talking of women who live in silence, surrounded by silence. Unlike most women, they have no fantasy life about the child in the womb. It doesn't exist for them as a visualised, imagined being. They don't take its unborn presence in psychically. The child is never named in speech, so it simply isn't there. And because it hasn't been there before, it isn't there after either, as a real being.'

I shake my head stubbornly. 'I still can't see it.'

'Well then, imagine the pregnancy as a cancer. A cancer can exist for years without your being aware of it. It isn't there until it's named.'

'A cancer doesn't protrude a foot in front of you, so that chairs have to be moved back, tables.'

I gesture dramatically at where my stomach would be and catch a little lick of desire in his eyes. It vanishes at my icy glance.

'So you tell yourself, if you tell yourself anything at all, that you're putting on weight, that you'll eventually go on a diet.'

'But all these women lived with husbands, parents. Or they had boyfriends.'

'And they were all complicit in the silence. Look, we're not talking here about families, couples, who discuss problems. They avert their eyes, their feelings from one another. The seventeen-year-old had just been moved to a new school and a new parental set-up. She had no friends. The provincial woman had kept the humiliating, obviously traumatic, rape secret, even from herself. Silence about the rest was almost an inevitable progression. If any blame is to be attributed, it lies as much with the families as with the women.'

He pauses, looks at me almost beseechingly.

'I'll give you that,' I say. 'But I still think that somewhere they know.'

'Somewhere. But not somewhere conscious. Not somewhere that exists in words. If you don't understand silence, Maria, you can't understand half of what we call crime. Action, violent action, doesn't happen in words.' He stares at me for a moment as if he's reading me. 'I know. For someone who lives in speech and with an internal dialogue, the inner silence in which crimes happen is almost unimaginable.'

'I don't see why what you call silence should equal diminished responsibility.' I am still adamant, unbending. I am so, I realise, because I understand too well what he is saying. I recognise it. But I judge it harshly.

Paul raises his glass to me and suddenly chuckles. 'I'm glad I haven't got you on my next jury. Half of my work in a trial is to try to put into words what hasn't been in words before. To make it comprehensible to the jury. To put words to the irrational. Obviously I'm not succeeding now. I bet your parents talked to you non-stop when you were little, aired problems, commented on each of your foibles.'

'My mother.' I correct him, because I want to argue every inch of the way. 'There was no father.'

'Oh? You never mentioned that.'

I have unwittingly opened the way to a barrage of unwanted questions, so with an aggressive edge, I turn the tables on him. 'Why are you so interested in murder, Paul?' My life is not a subject I want to discuss with him.

His face stiffens into a closed mask at my question. 'It's my work,' he replies dully and concentrates on his plate.

There is something in his posture which makes me feel remorseful.

'I'm sorry. I'm giving you a hard time,' I mumble.

He looks up at me and smiles a melting smile. 'No, no. It's important to argue these things through. That's why it's nice to have you here.' He chuckles, 'Half the time, I'm only trying things on.'

I meet his smile. 'I've noticed.'

I have. Paul is often most vociferous in arguing opinions which patently run counter to his own. I enjoy the play of it and the energy.

I imagine Jennifer Walters did too, whatever the status of Paul's English.

⚖ 19

But for its copper dome topped by a gilt figure of Justice, the Old Bailey, London's central criminal court, has nothing of the grandeur of its French equivalent. Inside everything is grey shabbiness and pallid, furtive faces as if court and prison waiting rooms had doubled up to become one and the same. I remember having read somewhere that the huge Newgate prison was once a stone's throw from here. Perhaps that has tainted my vision.

The public seats in the courtroom I am directed to are all but filled. I squeeze in at the end of a row next to a plump woman in a bright turquoise suit and crimped blonde hair. There is an overwhelming scent of cheap perfume coming from her. I am tempted to move, but she addresses me before I can do so.

'This your first time here, duck?'

I nod.

'Mine, too. It's ever so exciting. Poor old Martha, though, eh. D'you know her?'

It takes me a moment to make out that she's speaking of the accused and I shake my head.

'No? Poor old thing. Right old sod, he was, beating her and the kids black and blue. Deserved it, he did. Still she oughtn't to have cut him up like that, head 'n all. Guess she weren't in her right mind, like.'

I warm to the woman. Change her accent, put in a few high-sounding terms and she would make an excellent expert witness. Even her perfume becomes beguiling. 'Are you a neighbour?' I ask her.

'Used to be. Until he took her off. Didn't like her having friends. Poor old thing.' She shakes her head sadly.

There is increased activity at the front of the hall and I make a quick note that the layout of dock and bench and jury seats and witness stand are unlike the French, but like what I know from American television. For the moment though, I would rather listen to my neighbour.

'Are you a witness?' I ask her.

'Me? No way. Solicitor came to see me though,' she says with a touch of pride. 'I told him I weren't no good at public speaking, but if Martha really needed me . . . I went to see her in the nick. Very quiet, she was. Too quiet, like. I offered to look after the kids. I liked them two brats when they were little. But they'd taken them off into care. Not right, is it, after how hard she tried to give 'em the best and keep them out of the old geezer's way?'

'No, it isn't.'

'You foreign?' She looks me up and down with sudden suspicion. I nod. 'French.'

This cheers her. 'My eldest went to Paris last year, with her school 'n all. Said it was beautiful. You know Paris?'

I nod again, just as a voice from the front calls, 'The court will rise.'

This doesn't deter my neighbour. 'Like your blouse. And that pin. Just wait until I tell Cyn, that's my eldest, I sat right next to a French woman.' She beams at me and I smile back.

The entrance of the wigged judge, as resplendent as a cardinal, silences us. He sits down with regal slowness and nods at the room. A pair of spectacles sits at the end of his nose and he peers at us, like an ancient owl, then clears his throat. The jury is sworn in. I notice there are an equal number of men and women. Then a small pale woman appears in the dock. She is all jutting bones and wispy hair, looks fifty though I know her to be thirty-four, and so frail that I can hardly believe she had the necessary strength for her act. A policewoman is holding her up. The handcuffs she unlocks seem utterly futile. The tension in the room mounts palpably.

'Poor old Martha,' my neighbour whispers again, shaking her head.

I take out my notebook and try to jot down significant details, but at first there is so much legalese I haven't quite assimilated yet that the going is rough. The prosecutor's droning monotone doesn't help matters and I wonder whether the jury can hear him better. What I make out most clearly are the 'My Lord's and 'Learned Counsel's. But then the witnesses begin to come in and things grow clearer. Unlike the French courts, the material witnesses come first. There is no primary attempt to establish the personality of the accused or the victim. We are in the realm of hard evidence: scene of crime reports, police testimony, the washing-line rope which was used to tie the husband to the bed, the kitchen knife which pierced six times, the body stored in the cupboard for days and then dismembered and disposed of over the coming weeks.

It is this last sequence of events which seems to count most heavily against Martha Roberts. Jennifer Walters bobs up and down, to intervene, to cross-examine, her voice as large as her frame is small. Her language is mercifully straightforward.

'In your long experience, Inspector, could a woman of Martha Roberts's stature have inflicted the blows we have heard described, unless she were in a state of frenzy, a state of acute mental stress which took her outside herself? Look at the accused, please.'

All eyes turn on Martha Roberts and the inspector mumbles, 'It does seem unlikely.'

'Did the jury hear that?' the judge asks, constantly solicitous of the jury's well-being. 'Might I ask you to repeat what you have just said, Inspector?'

The inspector dutifully repeats his words and is politely thanked.

'Are you finished with this witness, Counsel? Then we'll call a break until two thirty.'

The court rises as the judge walks heavily from the room. My neighbour attempts a wave at Martha Roberts then turns to me. 'Noticed a pub opposite. Fancy a bite?'

I follow her to the pub, buy us two meat pies which would make a French chef hang up his hat for all eternity, and sip the lager my neighbour, whom I have now learned is called Lorna Stott, has provided.

'It's 'cause of the kids, isn't it?' she says to me.

I don't follow her.

''Cause of the kids she did it. Didn't tell, I mean. And cut him up and all. 'Cause of the kids.'

'You mean because he was doing horrid things to them?'

'That too.' She nods sagely. 'But she knew if she told, confessed 'n all, they'd take them away from her. So she said he'd gone on a trip instead. But then she couldn't live with it, like, and she told in any case. Poor old Martha.'

'Yes, I'm sure that's right.'

She looks up from the meat pie she has been swivelling round her plate and which she obviously finds as unpalatable as I do, and says brightly, 'If my old Steve had treated me like that pig of a Tom treated her, I'd of left him straight off, I tell you. But she couldn't. Beaten into the ground, she was. Thought she loved him, too.

'Oh yes,' she insists when I give her an incredulous look. 'He wasn't so bad in the first month or three. Good-looking bloke in those days. And then the kids came and it was too late. Trapped, she was.'

She chuckles in the midst of her mournful expression. 'Maybe it's a good thing mine went and died before he turned pig. You married?'

I shake my head.

She gives me a curious look. 'You so good-looking 'n all. Don't they go in for marriage in France, then?'

I laugh. 'Some do. Some don't.'

'Ya, well. Not what's it made out to be, is it? What you doing here, then?'

I tell her and by then it's time to troop back to the courtroom. What interests me in the course of the afternoon is that Jennifer Walters's defence seems to be bringing us round to the same interpretation of events as my wise neighbour's, who watches and listens as avidly as I do and pokes me with her elbow whenever she is particularly excited by a point.

We hear from the friend whom Martha ultimately confessed to, some four months after the killing. Stanley Moore. He is a printer, a thin stalk of a man whose grey head seems too large for his body. His voice is nervous but gentle as he describes how he met Martha at the local clinic when they were both waiting to see the doctor. They started going out for drinks together, an occasional movie, took the kids to the circus. Then one night, when he had mentioned how well they got on and perhaps they might think of hitching up, Martha started to cry. Unstoppably. And in the midst of tears, the story came out. Yes, he was shocked. At first he didn't believe it. It was so out of character. She was such a quiet, sweet woman, so concerned for her children. He had had to convince her more than once that it was all right to leave them for a few hours in the care of a neighbour's daughter.

Then she had given him a vague picture of her marriage, no horrendous details, mind, she wasn't a complainer, but he had got the gist, and then he had believed her, had understood she had been driven. He had told her to go to the police.

'It was you who told her to go to the police?' prosecuting counsel asks, but only to emphasise the point.

Mr Moore nods and rushes on, explaining that Martha had quickly agreed. One couldn't live with something like that. But it was as if it were the first time she had thought about the whole thing since it had happened, as if it weren't her who had done it, not the real her.

'But it was Mrs Roberts, by her own admission,' the prosecutor quickly underlines.

Mr Moore nods.

'Was that a yes, Mr Moore?' The judge nudges him.

'Yes, Your Lordship.' Mr Moore speaks his answer.

Jennifer Walters bounds to her feet.

'When Martha Roberts confessed to you, Mr Moore, you had the impression she was talking about someone else, as if the person who had committed the crime were someone else. Is that correct?'

'Yes.'

'So that although Martha Roberts knew it was she herself who had committed the crime, she could no longer imagine how she had done it.'

Mr Moore hangs his large head, then looks up suddenly.

'That's right. She had been beaten out of her right mind.' He waves his hands about angrily.

Jennifer pauses for a significant moment, then asks, 'Do you still see the accused, Mr Moore?

Mr Moore looks across the room into the dock as if he wants to catch Martha's eye, but Martha has her gaze fixed to the floor.

'I visit her every week,' he says.

Only when he leaves the witness stand, does she look after him. She has the air of someone who is drowning. I can almost hear the gasps in her breath and I imagine that her life is passing before her eyes and it is too late to unmake any of its limited choices. And the last hope, this gentle, chivalrous man, cannot save her from the waters.

When we are called to rise, for a moment I cannot get to my feet. My neighbour has to prod me before I remember where I am and that this first day of the trial has come so quickly to an end.

As I leave the Old Bailey, I look back at the gilded figure of justice – sword in one hand, scales in the other, a blindfold round her eyes. Why is justice blind, I wonder? The hope must be that differences between rich and poor, differences in status, colour, gender are invisible to her: she is utterly impartial. Her sword cuts straight down the middle. But her blindness can surely also make her arbitrary, capricious, as random and mercurial in her choices as that other blind figure in the ancient pantheon – Cupid.

Love and justice. Riddles I live through, but cannot solve.

⚖ 20

At night the Thames acquires a magic which eludes it by day. Twink-ling lights bring the shores closer together, build a second city in the water's depths, blur the squatness of buildings, illuminate the graceful arch of bridges.

From our table in the Grill Room, while Robinson studies the wine list, I see it all. I also see how well the years sit on him. The deeper etching of lines on his face has done nothing but give it a greater austerity, a seriousness which seems truer to him than the lustre of hair and eyes, offset by the dark blues of shirt and linen suit. He has dressed for the occasion, in homage to the Savoy I imagine. So have I.

Perhaps that accounts for the unease between us; despite the warmth of the initial embrace, we are as awkward with each other as adolescents on a blind date, tiptoeing into questions across the tense hush of silences. It is unlike us. But perhaps, Robinson, like me, has something to hide. Or perhaps it is simply the weight of all those bedrooms above us which neither of us knows whether we want to share or not.

'Will a Bordeaux do, a Château d'Issan?' Robinson asks with all the earnestness usually saved for major questions.

'Admirably.' I try an ice-breaking smile which turns into a titter. 'I'll start, shall I? The yearly round-up – or is it more?'

'More.' He looks gravely into the middle distance.

I rush on. 'I've given up New York. Or rather it's given me up. And I've changed jobs, you'll be pleased to hear. I'm doing something a little serious for a change.'

'None too soon, I'm sure,' he grins and for a moment I have that old urge to argue with him about the relative merits of the profession I stumbled into. But I don't. I tell him instead as wine is poured and grilled mushrooms consumed, about my new job, about the trial I went to today.

Robinson listens with his usual attention, but his shoulders are still taut and he still hasn't met my eyes. It's like it was in the beginning. He prefers not to see me. Something I read – about the distance that separates people who prioritise seeing from those who hear – leaps into my mind and I lose my thread. Robinson is one of the listeners. Like a puritan iconoclast or an ancient Hebrew, he rejects the image as mere superfice, a gaudy distraction, a shallow travesty of the pure inner and invisible truth, which can only come as voice. God's voice to Moses on the mountain, loading him with obligations. Whereas I, whatever my mother's admonitions, am a creature of appearances, heir to a Catholicism of incarnate gods, plump or lean, painted or hewn, but always visible.

'It's all a little morbid, isn't it?' Robinson says with a slight air of distaste.

For a second, I don't know what he is talking about.

'My murderesses, you mean?' I suddenly feel proprietary about them.

He nods.

'You think I was better off with what you used to call my "murderers of the mind", all those vile image-creators and media types,' I bait him.

He doesn't rise to it. Instead he methodically cuts his lamb chops into small, tidy pieces, just as he used to do as a boy. Then, without warning, he grips my wrist, pinions it to the table, so that I am aware of his fraught urgency before he puts words to it.

'Mare, are you upset that I've had a child? Is that what it's all about?'

I stare at him.

'I wrote to you in New York to tell you. You didn't respond. Not a peep. Nothing. I couldn't believe it. I wrote again. Still nothing. I even rang. Unsuccessfully. And now . . .'

My brain feels like a tangled oak, thick with too many branches, interlopers, parasites. I cannot make my way amidst them to find what I have lost or lopped off. Did I receive a letter from Robinson with this startling announcement? Did I hide it seen or unseen under some forgotten bough?

The pressure of Robinson's hand is still on my arm. I cover it with my own.

'I never had a letter from you, Robinson. Any letters. I moved. A harried time. Perhaps they were never forwarded. Or . . . But how terrific for you! How absolutely wonderful.'

The 'wonderful' doesn't quite carry the emphasis I want to give it and I squeeze Robinson's hand.

'He is wonderful. Jamie. He's almost a year old now, a tough little chap.' Robinson releases my wrist and looks me in the eyes for the first time. There is a warm pride in his face, and something else, a gratitude. It is as if he had given me a present and my lack of acknowledgement had filled him with unease. He had wanted to please me, to have me share in the pleasure of his present, and now at last I am. Or at least he thinks I am.

For my part, I am suddenly uncertain, even annoyed. And I feel oddly shocked, as if the notion of Robinson as a father disturbs the natural order of things. It is ridiculous. After all, since that abortive first marriage, there have been a number of women in his life. And Robinson must be thirty-six now, ripe for fatherhood.

While Robinson sings the praises of little Jamie, I niggle over my disquiet. Is it that I have secretly harboured a sense that after all else was lived and loved, Robinson and I would somehow settle into comfortable old age together, surrounded by fields and flowers? Like his parents – the only real couple I had ever known closely in childhood.

'And Jamie's mother?' I ask.

Robinson flushes. It is rare with him, so I know he is embarrassed.

'Nina? Haven't I told you?' He fiddles with his fork. 'She works in the lab. Used to anyhow, until Jamie. She's from Chile.' Robinson glows as he talks about Nina. In his face, rather more than in what he says, I read his admiration. He is in love with her motherhood, with her too, perhaps, but it is all one package.

This note of cynicism in my thoughts appals me. 'She sounds great,' I rush to say. 'And you live together?'

Robinson is astonished at my question. 'Of course. In the house. Ever since, well, ever since Jamie manifested himself.'

The oldest trick in the world, I catch myself thinking and wish I weren't.

'You must come up and meet them both. For the weekend. Or on Sunday. Please come, Mare.'

I swallow hard. 'Yes, I'd like that,' I say to make up for my thoughts. 'I'd like that very much.'

Robinson beams and the gladness in his face makes me realise that I do want to see him in his new life. And suddenly, he in turn is all ease and alacrity, rushing me out of the hotel to somewhere friendlier, he says, a pub perhaps, or just a stroll across Waterloo Bridge.

Outside, in the darkness, he puts his arm over my shoulder and holds me close. We walk silently, step in step. Half way across the bridge, we pause to look at St Paul's.

'I'm so pleased, Mare,' Robinson says softly. 'I thought you were angry with me. Angry that I hadn't told you sooner. About Jamie and Nina, I mean. That's why you hadn't written, or rung. And then I was angry at you. For being so hard. Callous. We go back such a long way, after all. Longer than anyone.' He brushes my forehead with his lips. 'And it means a lot to me. You do.'

This is the longest speech about our sentimental life that I have ever heard Robinson make and it brings a catch to my throat. I squeeze his arm.

'It means a lot to me too, Robinson.'

We stand in silence, letting nearness and memory wash over us. Then Robinson surprises me again.

'I know something has happened to you, Mare. You've changed. Quite a lot, I suspect. And I want to know about it. I'd like to stay with you tonight, but you know I can't.'

'I know.'

'At the weekend, we can have a stroll together. You can tell me.'

'I don't know that I'm able to, Robinson. Not yet.'

We walk slowly back to the hotel. At the door, Robinson kisses me lightly on the lips and hands me a train schedule.

'Just ring to say when you're coming.'

I nod.

'And perhaps we can arrange a visit with the parents. Haven't had a chance to tell you, but they've abandoned Kent to move closer to us. I know they'd love to see you again.'

I think of Stephanie and Chris and a pleasurable warmth steals over me.

'Sounds good.'

It does. I look at Robinson's receding back and think that together this Nina and Jamie must be quite a pair. They have taught Robinson a whole new range of sensibilities. Or at least the ability to express them.

As I walk towards reception, I also sense that I have done well to take my courage in hand and see Robinson. Life is gradually seeping into me, filling up the holes. A life with a difference. Robinson has felt the shifts. I too am aware of them.

At the desk, along with my key, the attendant hands me a sheet of folded paper. I look at it in perplexity. Who could possibly be addressing me here? The note is in French, I realise, and I quickly look down to the bottom of the page. Paul Arnault. He's here. My nerves jangle. He doesn't trust me to cover the trial on my own, it seems. Should I happen to be available before eleven thirty, the note tells me, I can find him in the bar. Otherwise, we can breakfast together.

I glance at my watch, make a quick visit to the powder room to adjust my mind more than my face and go in search of Paul. I spot him, or rather the copy of *Le Monde* which hides his face, almost instantly in the softly lit bar. I pause to survey him. There is that odd combination in him of an easy, almost sprawling grace, and an intentness, as if he is absorbing the paper in front of him rather than simply reading. I take a deep breath.

'Hello. Checking up on me?'

He is startled and springs so hastily out of the deep chair that the people at the small tables on either side of him gaze up at us.

'Maria. I'd given you up.'

'But here I am.'

'So I see.' He looks at me in that way he sometimes has which seems to take in every part of me and then bends to kiss me on both cheeks.

The people on either side of us turn away. I can almost hear them mentally muttering, 'The French again.'

'Can I get you something? A cognac? A whisky?' He holds up his glass to the light. 'It's a fine one.'

I shake my head. 'Coffee, I think.'

'Coffee it is.' A peculiar expression crosses his face, but he calls over the waiter with alacrity and despatches the order in impeccable Franglais. It makes me smile.

'You enjoy my English?' Paul is never slow.

'Very much.'

'But you aren't altogether pleased to see me?'

I don't answer for a moment and he adds, 'I've intruded on your evening, your plans?'

In a way he has. I would have liked to have been alone to think over my meeting with Robinson, but it comes to me that this isn't the emphasis of his question. Before I can say anything, he runs on.

147

'I'm sorry if I have. I just thought that since the only meeting I had scheduled for tomorrow was cancelled, I'd fly over and watch a bit of the trial, catch Jennifer Walters if I could.'

'And check up on the progress of my research.'

'Nonsense.' He glares at me for a moment. Then his face softens. 'I just didn't want to miss our Friday round-up.'

I can think of nothing to say.

'Is the food in the Grill Room good?'

'Fine.' I look at him in astonishment as I say it, suddenly aware that he must have seen me with Robinson. He admits it as soon as it pops into my mind.

'I spotted you in there. I didn't like to intrude. Pleasant evening?'

'Don't worry. It isn't on my expenses list.'

'Why are you being so prickly, Maria?' He lowers his voice a notch and forces me to meet his eyes. 'If you want to go back to your friend, feel free to go. These aren't working hours. We'll meet tomorrow.'

Laughter takes me over. From the midst of it, I burble a 'Sorry', and 'Maybe I need that drink after all.'

When it comes, I collect myself and tell him a little about the things I've managed to get through so far this week and then in more detail about the first day of the trial. He interrupts me at every turn, inciting me to understand better what it is that I have witnessed and by the time I have drained my whisky, I am not only excited but oddly grateful that he has come. I tell him so and he flashes me a melting smile.

'I'm glad,' he says. 'Very glad. But now we'd better get you off to bed. Or Madame Duval, who looks after my interests with an eagle eye, will start questioning the overtime.'

'Don't be silly.'

'I'm being silly.'

He squeezes my hand briefly as we leave the bar, sees me up to my room. At my door, he murmurs, 'I'd hoped . . .' He skims my hair with his hand and I look into those blue-dark eyes.

'Oh, never mind what I'd hoped. Sleep well.'

From the sense of his fingers in my hair, I think I know what he'd hoped. But I'm glad he hasn't said it. Not tonight.

For the first time it occurs to me that Maître Paul Arnault is an expert at signs. He reads them well. He is a man of great tact.

⚖ 21

We are sitting cramped round a small table in the corner of a crowded wine bar not far from the Old Bailey. Jennifer Walters, Paul and I. Somehow Paul has managed to catch Jennifer and arrange this fleeting lunchtime encounter. Maybe he set it up from Paris.

We are munching ham and cheese sandwiches on that soft brown bread I used to love, and the wine is passable. But I feel sad at having had to abandon Lorna Stott to a solitary meat pie in order to serve as an interpreter when Jennifer and Paul's language skills break down. That's not the only reason I'm here, of course, but it feels like it. There are so many words flying between them at such rapidity that even though I can translate each solitary unit, the sense of what is being said eludes me. They are arguing some technical point that came up towards the end of the morning session. The jury was asked to leave while prosecutor and defence hammered out something inaudible before the judge.

I glaze over and translate what Jennifer has just said. She bursts into raucous laughter. 'Can't be that dreadful, can it?'

I smile, shake my head in embarrassment. 'I just don't understand a word I'm saying,' I confide in her.

She gives me a wicked wink. 'We hope no one else does either.'

'She doesn't mean that.' Paul breaks into his best Franglais. 'I'm sorry we're exhausting you, Maria.'

'I've told you before, Maître. You'll just have to do something about your legal English.'

Looking at them, I wonder again where professional camaraderie ends and something else begins – though I should know well enough from my own long experience that there are no clear demarcation lines.

'And you about your French.'

'Which is even worse, now, I know. By the next time I come to Paris again, it'll be better. Promise.' She grins at us both.

I leave them for a moment to find a loo and when I come back they are intent in conversation. As she sees me, Jennifer picks up her bag. 'I'm afraid I have to dash. Got to see my solicitor. The prosecution may have dug up one of their recalcitrant witnesses.' She glances at her watch. 'You probably have another thirty minutes or so. Though I don't know how interesting this afternoon will be. You should come back for my defence, Paul.'

'I wish I could.'

There is a great flurry of hugs and kisses between them and after she has gone, Paul says, 'Wonderful advocate, Jennifer.'

'Wonderful woman.'

'That too.'

My curiosity gets the better of me and I spill it out. Perhaps the wine has got to my head. 'Are you, were you, in love with her?'

He laughs a big laugh. 'Utterly. Totally. For a whole week.'

'I would have thought she deserved more,' I say as lightly as I can, since my throat has suddenly grown constricted.

'Oh she does, she does, but not, alas, from me.' There is a little tug of irony at his lips. 'What Jennifer and I have is what I think is called an amorous friendship. One of those delicious affairs of the heart for which the time is never quite right. And because it's so delicious as it is, we go on never quite allowing the time to be right. So we've never been to bed together, if that's what you're asking.'

'I guess I was.'

I don't like the way he's studying me, so I ask, blatant in my indiscretion, 'Because of your wife? Or her husband?'

He doesn't flinch, but he pauses, as if he is thinking about it. Then he says, the smile quite gone from his face, 'No, I don't believe so. I suppose neither of us wanted that from the other. Enough. We're friends primarily. We love arguing over legal questions.'

There must be doubt written all over me for he rushes on, 'And don't let Jennifer fool you. Her French is better than she pretends when she's in England. I met her at a conference in Paris. Years ago. My father was alive then. He was a judge in the court of appeal and he was giving the opening address. You should have heard Jennifer hammer away at him over lunch.' He laughs. 'I sometimes suspect he was the one she was really in love with.'

'Amorous friendship,' I repeat inanely.

'You must know what I mean.'

'Yes.' I waver as I think over my history. 'And no. Perhaps not altogether.'

'No, I can see why not,' he murmurs. His eyes linger on my face. 'Why?'

'Tell you over dinner. You are having dinner with me tonight, aren't you?'

'Aren't you flying back?'

'Not if you're having dinner with me.'

As we rush back to the Bailey, there is a new note of openness between us. We have crossed a line. The line of intimacy. Strangely, it makes me feel buoyant.

Lorna Stott has kept seats for us, but there is time for no more than a brief hello before the judge comes into the court. Something about the way he peers at his notes and then down at us makes me think he is feeling bad-tempered this afternoon. Perhaps his lunch doesn't agree with him. Can lunch affect the workings of justice? The irreverent notion pops into my mind and I remember how in my New York notebooks I had worked out which editors should be called at which points in the day for optimal effect. One in particular was notoriously disagreeable just after lunch, as His Lordship seems to be now. The baleful look he gives the prosecutor who has just put an inaudible question to him would have me quivering in my heels. Happily the jury's faces still display the same eager interest. Justice will not rest on a single man's digestive tract.

'This is the witness Jennifer was worrying about,' Paul whispers to me as a ruddy-cheeked man in a brightly chequered jacket ambles towards the witness box.

Mr Daniel Carter's voice has a high-pitched whine to it and gold flashes from his mouth as he speaks. He seems as creditable to me as a latter-day Mephistopheles, but I try to control my dislike as an impartial observer or good juror must. Mr Carter, it seems, was a close friend of the victim. Over the last years they would meet two or three times a week. In the course of those years, Mr Carter tells us, his friend – 'the best bloke in the world' – had occasion to mention that his wife made his life a right misery. Every penny he earned went on her, the house, and the children, so that Tom was lucky if he had a pound a week left to put a little bet on the horses. And she was a complainer, was Mrs Roberts. Never stopped from the sound of it. On top of that there was a suggestion that last year, or perhaps it was the year before last, she'd had herself a little fling. Not an easy woman, no, and with a tendency to fly off the handle. Why, he knew that himself. When he'd gone to inquire after Tom, after he'd vanished, she wouldn't even open the door to him. Just shouted at him through the door that Tom had gone off on a trip. He hadn't believed her of course. Tom would have told him if he was planning a little holiday. And yes, Tom was a gentle man. Wouldn't hurt a fly; never in all the years he had known him had he seen him get mixed up in a brawl of any kind.

'Any questions, Mrs Walters?' the judge asks Jennifer.

She leaps up with alacrity. 'Am I right in assuming, Mr Carter, that your and Mr Roberts's meetings usually took place at the Horse and Groom?'

'Not always.' Mr Carter is truculent. 'Sometimes we went to the Freemason's.'

'Another pub, is that correct?'

'Yes.'

'And did Mr Moore ever stand you a round?'

'Oh yes, he was a generous one, he was.'

'So that we would have to conclude that not every scrap of his wages went to his family. Is that right?'

'I guess so.' Mr Carter is not pleased to agree.

'How many pints might you have of an evening, Mr Carter? Four, five, six, maybe more? You're a large man.' I am certain Jennifer has given him an admiring glance. And it has its effect.

'Thereabouts.'

'And Mr Roberts kept up with you.'

'More than kept up. Tom was even bigger than I am.'

'Six or seven then?'

'Depending on the night.'

'And on the night he complained to you about his wife and told you she was having a "little fling with someone", can you remember how much he had had to drink?'

Mr Carter shrugs. 'Too long ago now. Don't remember.'

'Of course.' Jennifer pauses. 'Mr Carter, did you often see Mr and Mrs Roberts together, go to their home?'

'Not often.'

'How often? Three times a month? Twice? Less?'

'Maybe.'

'Would it be correct to say that in the last year or so of Mr Roberts's life, you rarely went beyond the front door?'

Mr Carter emits a grudging, 'Yes.'

'So that your knowledge of the Robertses' home life is largely based on what Tom Roberts told you of it?'

'Tom wasn't a liar, if that's what you're saying.'

'No, of course not. Nonetheless, your picture of that family life comes largely from Tom Roberts.' Jennifer looks significantly at the jury, then down at her notes. She pauses for a moment, then fixes her gaze at the witness. 'Except perhaps for one instance. Mr Carter, I want to ask you about a night in January two years back, a night when Mr Roberts did invite you home. Do you remember the night I mean?'

Mr Carter shuffles about in the witness stand. He is squirming. 'I'm not sure I do.'

'Let me refresh your memory then, Mr Carter. It must have been quite late, after closing hours, and Mr Roberts invited you not only into the family home, but into the bedroom where his wife lay asleep.'

Mr Carter starts to splutter. 'I didn't mean anything by it. I didn't. Tom said his old lady liked a bit of fun, bit of a tussle and it might as well be with me as with a stranger. And we'd had a bit to drink. And . . .' He suddenly clams up. He realises he has said too much.

There is an audible gasp in the courtroom, a creaking of seats as people shift uncomfortably.

Jennifer's voice is very cool. 'On that evening, Mr Carter, did you see Mr Roberts hit his wife?'

'He said she liked it that way, liked being knocked about. It was just a bit of fun, wasn't it. Sex is different.'

'Did Mrs Roberts look as if she liked it, Mr Carter?'

He doesn't answer straight away. Something at his feet has taken on an inordinate interest.

'Did she?' Jennifer insists.

'I don't know.'

'You don't know. If you had changed places with her, would you have known? Would you have liked it?'

Mr Carter looks up abruptly. His face has turned a sickly colour. The red stands out in splotches.

'Would you, Mr Carter?'

'No.'

The monosyllable is mumbled but it falls into the silence of the room with the heavy thud of a boxer's fist.

'So you can't be altogether surprised that Mrs Roberts might not open the door to you and embrace you warmly when you came to ask after her husband?'

'No.'

'Thank you, Mr Carter.'

'And that was intended to be a witness for the prosecution!' Paul whispers to me, full of enthusiasm for Jennifer's performance.

'He may still be,' I say warily, for the prosecutor has now risen to his feet.

Lorna Stott nudges me. 'I'm worried for Martha. She's gone all funny. Shouldn't they do something?'

Martha, who has sat through this last witness with the fixed rigidity of a plaster cast, now seems to have crumbled. I can no longer see her face, only the policewoman bending over her.

But the prosecutor has begun to speak and I start scribbling notes again.

'Mr Carter, after this unfortunate January evening, did Mr Roberts ever mention that his wife might be threatening him with revenge?'

Carter gives the prosecutor a blank look and shuffles his feet. Then he blurts out, 'Well she took it, didn't she?'

The prosecutor isn't happy. His witness hasn't given him evidence of any forethought on Martha's part, a long, intricate plan, coldly nurtured.

But now there is a commotion at the front of the court. Jennifer has approached the judge and after a brief whispered exchange, he announces that the accused has unfortunately been taken unwell and since it is so late in the day, rather than call a recess, there will be an adjournment until Monday.

Paul and I walk. The sky is a deep milky blue, fleeced with clouds, the light so dazzling after the gloom of the Bailey that I feel I have escaped from a place of confinement.

At first its shadows trail us. Paul's talk is all about the trial. He wants to discuss what he might have missed. He is fascinated by what he calls the unpredictability of British procedure. In France, he reiterates, if the investigating magistrate has done her work properly, everything is preordained. But in Britain there are surprises round every corner. It keeps one on one's toes. And it means the presumption of innocence is at least something of a reality, not an empty formality.

I counter him, I don't quite know why. I tell him it seems to me that justice is a bit chancy if the accused's case rests solely on the merits of a single defending counsel. Not every barrister is as brilliant and well-prepared as Jennifer Walters.

He laughs at this and soon we shake off the fetters of the Bailey. The light demands play and we play tourist. We stroll down Ludgate Hill to St Paul's, admit as we circle its flanks that we have never seen the interior and walk in to gaze up at the vast and striking dome, opening just where it should close onto another empyrean. We meander through city streets, brash in their newness, get lost in narrow cobbled lanes dotted with the stately remains of an older London, as well as with spindly acacias amongst tubs of spring flowers and the occasional dustbin. We stop in a pub, laugh our way down to the embankment and round again, up to the Savoy. We change for dinner. It is warm and on a whim, I put on a sleeveless creamy linen frock with a matching jacket and when I meet Paul down in the lobby, his suit is the exact colour of my dress. We exchange a smile which is all pleasure. At Orso's, we sit in the corner of the room and laugh some more over a good bottle of Meursault, delicately grilled vegetables, herb-fragrant bass, a tangy concoction of raspberry and lemon. And then we wander again, through the warmly crowded streets of an evening Covent Garden.

It is on one of these streets, in front of an art bookshop displaying a reproduction of Manet's bright-eyed reclining Olympia, that Paul first puts his arm around me, lightly at first, his fingers just resting on my shoulder, but when I don't edge away, more firmly, pulling me closer to him so that I can feel the outline of his body. We fit. There is always something of a miracle about that fit, perhaps because it can never be altogether predicted. Visual cues are not enough. It takes touch, a disposition of limbs, a texture of skin, a scent, the sound of a breath, a time, a place. Too many variables make it rare. I recognise its rarity.

Paul and I stand there for a few moments, fitting.

'I would like to love you, Maria,' he whispers in my ear. 'You know that. Would like to, very much. Please say yes.'

His breath is warm on my neck, his hand taut where it has slipped down to my waist. Olympia gazes out at me, her eyes and nudity a challenge. Laughter ripples into my throat. I don't want to think. Not now. Not tonight. Despite everything. Just this once. As if life hadn't changed. Once more.

'Once,' I say.

He turns me towards him, lifts my chin so that I have to look into his eyes. His face is shadowy in the lamplight, hard with something I don't recognise. 'Once may not be enough.'

'One night. Here. Away from everything.' I sound as if I am driving a bargain, like a whore. I don't want to bargain.

He kisses me. His lips are firm, sweet with the fragrance of the Meursault. Perhaps it is the seal. We walk back to the hotel in silence, our steps quicker now, but not too quick: we need to savour our linked arms, taste this new urgency.

As the door of my room closes behind us, we stop to look at each other. We are standing about three feet apart, but there is something in the darkness of his gaze, the tension of his features, which makes me shiver with excitement or fear, I don't know which. I take a step towards him and he meets me half way. We pause, our eyes locked. He stretches out his hand. I take it and he pulls me towards him. We kiss – lightly, a little timidly, hardly touching. And then he buries his hand in my hair and groans. With that sound, desire seems to fill the room. It is hot, fierce, winging through us and carrying us away.

Is it because it has been so long that everything feels new? His lips on my mouth, on my bosom, mine on his, the shimmying out of clothes, the arch and sweep of the male body against the palm of my hand, the rough and soft of skin, the indentation of his chin between my breasts, the curl and press of limbs and those waves of sensation too high, covering me, bringing tears to my eyes. I can taste their salt. I am crying. This is not the well-known game of pleasure. He is not playing with me or I with him. This has the mark of the real. Passion. I do not remember it. Perhaps it cannot be remembered.

We are lying side by side, our heads on separate pillows, our hair and skin moist. Except for our joined fingers, we do not touch. We are looking into each other's eyes. The tears have dried on my cheeks. We should speak now. In the glow of the soft bedside light we should speak soft words. But the words don't come. They are the habitual matter of our daily exchanges and they won't come. Instead, he takes my hand to his lips and kisses my fingers one by one. Each kiss is like a word, each subsequent caress, a phrase, slow, savoured, which this new skin of mine understands and answers, until we are wrapped together again and I forget to decipher meanings.

Afterwards something akin to awe takes hold of me and I search his face, hoping to find its source. There is a beauty about it now which I have never seen before. A dreaming stillness where I had once only seen the drama of mobility. The hair falls over his brow above eyes which are so darkly liquid that they threaten to swallow me if I don't turn away. But I can't seem to.

His mouth curves softly.

'Found what you're looking for?' he asks as if he has read my mind.

'Perhaps.' I return his smile. 'Though I was hoping for a drink as well.' An imp of the perverse makes me want to break the magic, perhaps to test if it is only a figment of my own hungry flesh.

'How inconsiderate of me.' He laughs, leaps to his feet, reaches for the phone.

I watch him. It is odd how without his clothes, he still looks dressed, clothed in a greater ruggedness, his shoulders and legs muscled like a swimmer's, his stomach taut. While he pulls his trousers on, I go in search of my robe, sorry for a second that I have only this old striped burgundy silk with me, a man's gown, bought for comfort and colour. As I brush out my hair I chastise myself for that ancient reflex which makes me want to appear attractive. There is no need. There will be only this time. Only once. I swallow hard. I have promised myself.

He is sprawled in the armchair by the window when I come back. He is watching me, a little warily. Perhaps he too has remembered the bargain.

'Room service should be here in a moment.'

'Good. I'm thirsty.'

Our voices sound raw, untried, as if we have forgotten how to use them. He stretches his hand out to me and draws me into his lap, strokes my hair, my back. I curl into him, have a sense that if room service doesn't come quickly, we will never hear them. But he is in no hurry. He speaks.

'Am I allowed to tell you how beautiful you are, or would that be too repetitive?'

'You can tell me,' I tease him, pull away a little.

'You're beautiful, almost more beautiful than Olympia.' He catches my tone.

I laugh. 'Did you imagine we'd end up like this?'

'I hoped. But I didn't imagine. Not this.' He touches my bare skin beneath the robe and I shiver. 'Not this,' he repeats, meeting my eyes.

The waiter fractures the moment. There is a silver tray; long-stemmed goblets and glasses. There is a bottle of champagne in a vast bucket and a bottle of Vichy. There is a bowlful of strawberries and crisply starched white napkins atop white plates.

We lean back against pillows and drink a series of comic toasts – to the Savoy, to London, to the Thames, to spindly acacias and over-flowing dustbins. Then, with a hint of solemnity, Paul raises his glass once more. 'To the *Herald Tribune*,' he intones, 'which brought you to me.' He drains his glass and draws me towards him, so that I feel at once shielded and intoxicated, both little girl and desiring woman.

Some time in that long night, he looks at me steadily and says, 'You know, Maria, this isn't just a sudden aberration. A piece of opportunism. I've wanted you ever since that first time. In my office. You were looking up at Lombroso's women. Looking up guiltily. Whether in hope or fear of finding yourself, I couldn't quite tell.' He chuckles but there is no mirth in it and a tremor comes into his voice. 'I thought to myself, she's so beautiful. Some man hasn't been able to resist the desire to defile her. I could help put her back together again.'

It takes me a moment to take in the full measure of this.

'Do you still think that?' I ask.

He is quiet for so long that I suspect he has fallen asleep. Then he says, 'I'm not sure.' He pauses. 'Are you going to tell me?'

I don't answer and he doesn't press me. Instead he murmurs, 'Why back then, in front of the Manet, an eternity ago, did you say "only once"?'

I stiffen. My laugh is too shrill. 'Because I'm a dangerous woman.'

'I can see that. Feel it.' His hand is on my thigh and he moves it gently upward. 'I'm not afraid, you know. And you can't still mean it.'

'I mean it,' I answer and kiss him with more passion than I should be permitted.

When I wake, sunlight is pouring round the corners of the curtain, cutting the carpet in bright swathes. Paul's eyes are on me, so warm that I close mine again and let him wake me properly with lips and limbs. I don't want it to have all been a dream.

Our love-making over, we are shy. I lock the door to the bathroom while he orders a breakfast so late it might as well be lunch. While I soak in the tub, I think that I want to memorise every moment of our togetherness, give him all the generosity I can muster, so that our time here will stay with me as a talisman. For once I will have behaved well.

But when I come out he is not there. A pit opens in the base of my stomach: could he have taken me so literally at my word, a lawyer following the letter of the law I have laid down? The coffee tastes acrid, the toast as dry as desert sand. I choke on it. But this is what I wanted, what I ordered, I console myself. Why does it taste so bitter? I should have imagined better what it would be like with him and evaded the initial temptation. I should have written a goodbye into the contract. 'Article two, subsection thirty-six of Maria's general code for lovers, twentieth edition: always say goodbye with a smile before leaving. Wordless abandonment by either party constitutes a felony. (See section three.)' I try a smile in the mirror which doesn't return it, so instead I pull on an old pair of white jeans, a white shirt, and gaze blindly at the newspaper which has come with breakfast.

I am so lucky, I tell myself as I make out the headlines of others' suffering. So spoiled and lucky. So why does a tear spill out on the page? I will fly out to Sarajevo or Rwanda and share with others the good fortune of my luck and goodness. I will read my unselfishness in their eyes. I will become a doctor without frontiers, a flying nurse, a comrade in misery.

An image of Beatrice materialises before me and I still my overblown heroics. There is no mockery in Beatrice, of others or herself. No heroics. There is only a quiet selflessness. A hardworking patience. I still have so much to learn. My mother always told me that. I am only beginning. But at least I have begun. Perhaps I shouldn't have succumbed to Paul. Beatrice would not have gone to bed with another woman's husband. But I was right to say 'once'; and only I have been hurt by it.

A knock at the door startles me from these raving half-thoughts. I go to open it and am even more confused to find Paul standing there. His hair is wet. He is freshly shaven and he is wearing a different shirt, a deep sea blue against the cream of his suit. I stare at him without moving.

'Are you going to invite me in for coffee or am I now contractually barred from entry?'

I stand back to let him by. He kisses me lightly on the cheek and ruffles my hair.

'I thought you'd gone,' I say.

'Gone?' An eyebrow rises in consternation. 'I went off to wash. And to buy some necessaries. I didn't presume to hope I was staying over, so I hadn't come adequately prepared.' He smiles at me with such a mixture of self-irony and tenderness that I find myself in his arms.

'And I got you something, too,' he whispers. 'Something silly, to remember London by.' He hands me a package which I open with childish eagerness. Inside, amidst the tissue paper, there is a silk scarf, black and white with large dollops of yellow. The colours coalesce into an image of St Paul's.

Laughter plays over Paul's features. 'I couldn't resist the thought that you might, just occasionally, don my name.'

'And do I wear this beatified you to the office or to bed?' It comes out despite the fact that I am trying to be a different person. To hide my confusion, I tie the scarf loosely over my shirt.

'Both, I hope. It looks nice.'

I refuse his eyes.

The coffee in the flask is still hot and tastes strangely better than when I first tried it. By the time I have drained my cup, my resolve is firm again. I must act on it quickly.

'When is your flight?' I ask.

'Look at me, Maria.'

I look at him, but I cannot face the troubled perplexity of his expression.

'Isn't it good between us? Very good?' he murmurs.

'Too good.'

'I see.'

I don't know what he sees. I wish I smoked so that I could do something in this silence. I pace instead, stare blindly out of the window.

He has come up behind me. His hand is on my shoulder. 'Maria, if it's my wife that's worrying you, you musn't. It's not like that between us. We have a . . .'

'Tacit understanding.' I turn on him. 'They all say that.'

'Of course!' He scowls at me. 'They all say that.' His tone is flat.

There is a look of desperation on his face. 'But this is not "they all"; this is me. And you. In the law they teach us each case is unique, individual, whatever the similarities with other cases.'

'We're not in court, Paul,' I smile. I don't want to see that despair. I squeeze his hand. He kisses me, too hard. We are both breathless.

'This once I can't accept, shouldn't it really in all fairness, at least extend to one whole weekend?'

His hand is in the small of my back. I like it there. I would like to keep it there. 'All right,' I mouth at him. 'One whole weekend.'

It is only after he has kissed me again that I remember. I slip away from him. 'A slight hitch, though.' I play with the scarf he has given me, try to squeeze another cup of coffee from the flask. 'I promised to visit a friend in Cambridge.'

'What kind of friend?' His voice is rough.

'A very dear old friend. My oldest friend. He . . . There's a baby I haven't yet seen.'

Paul is studying me. 'Would I be in the way?'

I consider this carefully, then shake my head.

Paul grins his boyish grin. 'What I like about you, Maria, is that even though you tell me nothing, I suspect you of honesty.'

⚖ 22

Birds flit and swoop from hedgerows bright with dog roses. Cow parsley flutters in the wind that lifts our hair, caresses our faces. Every now and again the sweet fragrance of hawthorn floods our nostrils. I am happy, happier than I can ever remember being. My hand is on Paul's thigh. He has placed it there and if I close my eyes I can feel each twist and turn of the narrow road through the tensing of his muscles. I am cocooned in sensation.

Somehow, in the hour we spent apart, Paul managed to hire this pert white convertible complete with map and find the picnic hamper which rests on the back seat. The toys I bought are in the boot with our bags. We have taken a circuitous route, so lazy and circuitous that the distance from London to Cambridge could well prove as long as an afternoon and the total of criss-crossing country lanes.

At our side now, there is a little wood, dappled with light. Through the trees I can see a carpet of shimmering blue. Paul slows the car and squeezes it onto a narrow verge.

'Hungry?' He touches my throat, folds his hand over mine.

'Ravenous.'

His smile curls deliciously and I have to kiss it. Something happens in that kiss, I don't know what, perhaps it is simply the pressure of his hand, but our languor disappears and suddenly we are hurrying, rushing into the shelter of the woods, clasping each other, falling onto the first mossy bank so that he can come into me there where I have wanted him since he left.

It is all so explosive and quick, that afterwards he is apologetic.

'Blame it on the bluebells,' I giggle, ruffling his hair. I am happy, but perhaps he is more accurate when he grumbles a little and says, 'So many emotions to squeeze into "once".'

I am feeling giddy. I don't want the gloom. I am about to thrust clichés at him, 'Better to have loved and lost . . .', when I stop myself. After all, I have never done much of the losing. Except that once. I force the image away, hide my face in the hamper, bring out trimly cut sandwiches, salmon and cucumber, roast beef, cheddar cheese, a bottle of wine.

It is after he has uncorked the wine and poured us each a glass that he asks, 'And what if I were to fall in love with you, Maria? Had fallen in love?'

'Don't be silly.' I laugh. 'I'm just a pretty face. Long legs and a pretty face. I'm not worth it. And you're a serious man.' I am deliberately, assiduously frivolous.

He is studying me again in that intent way of his. 'Shouldn't that be up to me to judge? I've worked with you for, what is it now, two months, argued with you, watched you . . .'

'Ssshh.' I put my fingers to his lips. 'Don't.' I have the sense that if he goes on, I will start to cry. 'Tell me a story instead. About your childhood.'

He puts his arm around me and we lean into the trunk of a tree.

He tells me about a bluebell wood in Brittany. His parents had a country house there and every year from when he was very small, he would go to the wood with his brothers, with friends. Then one year, the wood was gone, had simply been razed to the ground, and amongst the stubs of burnt-out trees, only one or two valiant flowers poked their heads. He was too old for crying, eight perhaps, but that night and every night for a week, he had cried secretly in bed.

'My first loss.'

The tears bite at my eyes. I gather the remains of our picnic back into the hamper. 'So we shouldn't be sitting here. It makes you sad.'

'Not at all. I've found the wood again. With you. And it's as magical as I remember it. In fact, it's made me remember it.' He smiles softly. 'Now tell me about your first loss.'

I am bemused. I can't think of anything. At last, I mumble, 'My father, I guess. But I don't really remember him at all.'

'Lost and half-found again in an endless number of men,' he suggests.

'A veritable brigade,' I laugh, but the laugh goes wrong. I look up at him. The diagnosis is startlingly simple, yet it has never occurred to me. I don't like it.

'Too facile,' I say and make a face at him.

'Much too facile,' he agrees readily, but a moment later he asks with an edge, 'Are you sure it wasn't a platoon?'

'An army.'

The turn of the conversation irritates me so I want to irritate him. I don't like inquisitions.

'And did you, do you, love any of them?'

'All of them.'

There is a napkin left on the ground and I screw it into a ball and fling it at him.

He catches it in mid-air. 'And what did you love about them?'

'Let's see.' I am angry now. 'Tom had a really nice dimple in his chin; Harry's hair was as blond and fine as desert sand; Dick had a lovely dick, all thick and stubby. Shall I go on?'

'Please.' He is relentless.

'Tim had a brain; Josh had a matted chest as soft as moss; Seamus had a gift for metaphor and a voice to go with it; Grant purred as deliciously as a big cat; Bill improvised magnificently on any number of instruments; William rubbed my back in the bath, until all thoughts disappeared; Steve tickled me with malicious wit; Arnie could plot monstrous amorous campaigns; Leo was good; Oscar's laugh was as big as his belly; Tony, well Tony was just Tony and had huge chocolate eyes with thick dark lashes.' I am inventing madly, I could go on like this for days. 'More?'

He shakes his head, 'I get the picture. Humpty Dumpty. And little Maria couldn't put all the parts together again.' He pauses. Dark eyes flash at me. Too dark.

'And me? What do you like about me, Maria?'

Suddenly I want to be cruel.

'You? Why, you're Mr Once.'

I get up and walk away. I am livid, raging. I go deeper into the wood, run, stumble, slip, improvise directions. When I look back, he isn't following me.

By the time the wood clears into meadow, my mind has cleared too. The sun is low in the sky. He will leave me here, I think. I will have to walk to the nearest village. Or hitchhike. I realise I have left my bag in the car. Never mind, it serves me right for playing the fool. I will ring Robinson and he will come and fetch me. I will write to Paul, no, to Madame Duval, and give up the job. It was all too good to be true, anyway. I didn't deserve it.

I skirt the edge of the wood and find myself back on the road. In the distance I see Paul's car. I walk towards it slowly. My heart feels heavier than my mud-caked shoes.

He must see me coming in the rear-view mirror, for he bends to open the door for me. We stare at each other. He looks as miserable as I feel.

'Sorry,' I say, just as he says it too. He puts out his hand to me. I take it and kiss it softly. I am crying. I did not know I had so many tears left.

In Cambridge we park the car and walk arm-in-arm along picture-postcard streets, through majestic courtyards, into splendid gardens. The May trees are heavy with flower, the ground beneath them snowy with petals. We stand and look up through branches so lush, they are dizzying. He holds me very tightly as if he is afraid I may disappear again. I don't want to. I can no longer recapture the nub of my fury.

We find a hotel overlooking the river. I would like my own room, if only for an hour, so as to collect myself, but I don't dare say. He would misread it, I think, but in that uncanny way he has, no sooner have we put our bags in the room, than he asks, 'Would you like a little time on your own, Maria? I can meet you in that pub we passed, by the river, whenever you're ready.' I clutch at him then, kiss too deeply, as if I can already taste the sorrow of a future goodbye.

From our garden table in the pub, we watch ducks paddling, racing away from noisy punters, pink light fading in the milky sky. Later over dinner, we talk. He wants to know about my parents, my childhood, about me. There is a quality in his attention, a stilling of himself, which lulls me. This compounded with the sense I have that I want to make up to him for my earlier behaviour loosens my guard, my words, so that I find myself uttering things I have rarely spoken before – and never to someone who knows the sites of my words, the flavour of the background, the name of street and school.

I tell him about my mother, her busy, if solitary, life, her white blouses, her goodness, her bravery, the trail of refugees in the spare room, the injustice of her sudden death.

'And the shock,' Paul murmurs, then asks, 'And Monsieur d'Esté?'
For a moment I am confused.
'Your father? The one you lost.'

'Guy Regnier.' I smile. 'D'Esté is my mother's name.'

'You don't use his?'

I look away a little nervously. 'I used to. I've just changed recently, in honour of my mother perhaps.' As I say it, it seems to me to hold at least a grain of truth.

'And what happened to your father?'

I tell him the little I know. I tell him in almost the same words my mother used. I tell him that my father left us when I was two, oh not for the usual reasons, but to answer a greater call – medicine, war, Vietnam. The story I tell surprises me: my parents emerge as heroic idealists, great and good, so different from myself that it makes me gasp inwardly.

Perhaps I have the same strained look on my face that my mother used to have when she talked of my father, for Paul says to me when I have finished, 'They sound wonderful. But for a child wonderfully resentable.'

I squeeze his hand, strangely glad that he has said it.

'And have you ever thought of finding out what happened to your father? It shouldn't be impossible any more.'

I stare at him. I have never, except for that once when the letters came into my hands, wanted to know. But now the notion appears tantalising. 'Do you really think so?'

'It's worth a try. There can't have been that many French doctors who stayed on through the war. I have a friend in the Embassy. If you like, I could ask . . .'

Later, when we are lying atop rumpled sheets, moist with each other, he asks me, 'Maria, what is it that you really won't talk about?'

'Anything.' I don't want to be serious. I run my hand along the warmth of his skin, pause in that smooth crevice I love where hip and thigh meet. He pulls me on top of him so that I am forced to look into brooding eyes.

'We'll have plenty of time to talk after our "once",' I say, snuggling into him.

'You can't stop life like that, Maria.'

'Can't I?'

I don't altogether like the sound that comes out of me.

*   *   *

Robinson and Nina live in a tiny village outside Cambridge. We drive there for lunch. I have spoken to Robinson and told him of Paul's presence. He didn't sound overjoyed.

The house is white and old and graceful and slopes a little precariously in one corner. There are lilacs in front, a spreading copper beech on the side and in the distance, a meadow where horses graze peacefully.

I hesitate before ringing the bell. Paul squeezes my arm. I don't know what I have said to him that makes him think I need reassurance, but he knows. What he doesn't know is that this might have been my life.

Robinson comes to the door. He is in jeans and shirt sleeves and I feel his nervousness as clearly as I feel my own. He embraces me, perhaps for Paul's benefit, and I enthuse about the house before introducing them. They shake hands and assess each other while I assess them. They are of a height within a fraction of an inch, though Paul looks taller where Robinson looks sturdier. In fact, they are so unlike, one fair where the other is dark, one laconic where the other is mercurial, that any attempt at comparison would only produce travesty. Their only point in common must be me and I suspect they both know it, for by the time we have made our way through the house and into the sun-dappled back garden, Paul's hand has stolen proprietarily round my waist. I am happy to have it there. I have had visions of feeling like the maiden aunt peering in uncomfortably on the happy family.

A golden retriever, whom Robinson introduces as 'Big' so that I have to grin without being able to explain to Paul, comes lolloping up to us. He is closely followed by a rounded woman with smiling eyes and dark curling hair. She is balancing a toddler on her thigh, all flashing eyes and plump charm like his mother.

'Welcome,' she says with a Latin lilt to her voice. 'Say hello to our guests, Jamie.'

Jamie stares at us, then puts up a pudgy arm to wave and in an attack of shyness buries his head in his mother's bosom.

We all laugh and start to talk at once.

'Lovely boy.'

'Come to Daddy, Jamie,'

'Can I get you a drink?'

'I've got a present for him. In the car.'

J'y vais.

Paul goes off to the car, while Nina fetches white wine.

'He's beautiful,' I say to Robinson.

'And just like his mother. I know,' Robinson chuckles. 'But he has my character.'

'Oh?'

'Blindly stubborn. According to Nina.'

Our eyes meet and we laugh. It's all right. It's going to be all right.

When Paul arrives with the presents, there is general commotion. Not knowing what to choose, I have, as always, decided on plenty – a big box of Lego, a teddy so plump and tawny that he is the epitome of cuddle, a giant milk van, complete with bottles and driver's seat. For the adults, there are cakes and claret.

'Christmas in May.' Nina is all ebullience.

'Every day of the year, *j'imagine*, if Maria can organise it,' Paul says.

I notice an exchange of glances I cannot read between the two men; then at the side of the garden, beyond a strip of privet, see two old people appear. My breath catches. Chris and Stephanie. An image of a striding big-boned couple flashes through my mind, but these two move in white-haired slow motion, as if the ground wasn't where they remembered it.

By the time they reach us and we have all exchanged greetings and Jamie has fallen twice out of the milk van, the shock has dulled and I am able to see Stephanie and Chris in these two ageing bodies, now smaller than my own. Her eyes are still clear and candid and he still spreads his hands carefully on his lap as if they belonged to someone else. And they both take in my presence with the same easy warmth, making me feel I have left them only yesterday. Though at one point, when I stretch across the table to pass Chris another slice of lamb, he says, 'Who would have thought gawky little Miss Know-it-all would turn into this superb creature!'

I rarely flush, but I feel the warmth rising in my cheeks now.

'Was she really little Miss Know-it-all?' Paul asks, his English suddenly acute.

Stephanie nods vigorously, 'And we always thought that one day she and Robbie would . . .'

'Mother!' Robinson cuts Stephanie off.

Nina laughs. 'But he found this other wretched foreigner instead.'

Our eyes meet and in that look I realise she knows everything. For some reason, it doesn't displease me.

'Terrible wretches, aren't we,' I smile at her.

'Ghastly.'

It is only after lunch and when we have tucked Jamie in for a nap with his new teddy, that Robinson and I have a moment alone. We stroll down to the edge of the meadow and watch the gambolling horses.

'Is Paul the change in you?' Robinson asks. He is nervous with his curiosity.

'I shouldn't think so,' I say lightly.

'Aren't you ever going to settle down, Mare?'

Now that he is, he would like to see me settled too. Marriage, children, they're like a missionary faith. Once people like Robinson have become true believers, they insist you join their ranks. Or maybe they simply want you on a shelf, marked unattainable.

'I like Nina very much,' I answer him. 'And the house is splendid.'

'Would you have been happy here?' he asks softly.

He needs to know and the question touches me. I give it the seriousness he has put into it.

'Not as happy as you and Nina, Robinson. You know that too.'

It is only when we are speeding down the motorway back to London that I notice Paul has removed his wedding band, has probably removed it this morning.

I touch his finger where it should have been. 'That was nice of you.'

He darts a glance at me. 'They're nice people. Like family.'

'Yes.'

There doesn't seem to be much more to say. The flurry, the tensions of the afternoon, have driven us apart. It is better that way. It will make Paul's going easier.

'And Robinson?' he asks abruptly after we have covered some miles.

I shrug. 'Robinson is the past.'

'And the future?'

I don't answer him. I don't answer him until he puts the question again. We are back at the hotel and there are very few minutes left before he leaves for Heathrow. We are sitting, staring at each other in the front seat of the car, our hands clasped.

'I haven't much future, Paul.' I kiss him softly on the lips. 'But thank you for this gift of the present.'

I bound out of the car, but he doesn't release my hand for a moment. 'I hope the trial is over quickly,' he says.

⚖ 23

The trial lasts another week, but I do not return to Paris immediately. I have the legitimate excuse of more library work to do, but of course the motor for my reason is Paul: I do not want to face him too soon, much as I miss him. He is a slow ache inside me. I cherish it, as I would have cherished him.

As soon as he has left, I move out of the Savoy to a bed and breakfast near the British Museum. I do not want to sleep in the bed we have been in together. Nor do I see why my extended stay should cost quite so much. I may not be good, but I am not an abuser of favour.

I see Jennifer Walters after the trial. We go and visit Martha Roberts together. The woman is oddly calm. All the tension I sensed in her before has vanished. She has left us for another space. The only emotion she manifests is in the sudden and tight clasp of her hand round Jennifer's. She answers the few questions I put to her briefly and as if they concerned someone else.

Afterwards, Jennifer says to me that it neither went as well for Martha as it might have, nor as badly. Six years: with good behaviour she will be out in much less. Jennifer is matter-of-fact, about her own role too. Though she did her best, she couldn't get Martha to perform as well as she might have in the witness stand. Martha went cold. Her tears were all spent. She could neither cry, nor recapture in words the emotions, the fear, which had driven her to the act. So she came across as hard. And juries don't like hard women. The impression of hardness always conjures up the notion of scheming, of forethought, of full possession of mental powers. Nor did Martha manage to convey her abasement, the brutality of her husband, out of pride perhaps, or because it was no longer fully present as a threat. Compound all that with the lateness of her confession, the head in the closet, and the jury couldn't bring itself to exonerate her.

'But why did she keep the head?' I ask. It is something I, too, cannot understand.

Jennifer shrugs. 'Don't know. Maybe she couldn't think how to get rid of it. Maybe it had a talismanic force for her. Maybe she still loved him and it was a memento. Maybe she wanted to be found out and punished. All of those, I imagine. And people do, you know, want the punishment. They feel guilty, even if the murder was deserved. Whoops,' she stops herself and grins, 'I shouldn't say that.'

My time is up.

'Give my best to the Maître,' Jennifer says. 'You'll report to him?'

'Weekly diskettes. Sometimes bi-weekly.'

She smiles wryly. 'I suspect he's rather fond of you, the Maître.'

'And of you.' I return the smile and wonder for a moment whether Paul and I could settle into what he called an *amitié amoureuse*. An amorous friendship.

At first Paul rings me every night. I do not like to think that he is ringing me from home, but in any event, I am rigorously professional. Every night he tells me, in a voice that makes the ache inside me bigger, that he misses me. When I say that I am staying on in London, he says he will join me for the weekend. I refuse. I am firm. I make it clear that if he suddenly turns up, I will leave the job altogether. I do not want to leave. I like to finish what I have begun. And I am learning too much – about crime, about punishment. Perhaps it will help.

I do not altogether know why I am quite so firm with Paul, except that I have made the vow and I know I must keep it. When I bump into an English advertising acquaintance in front of the British Museum, that knowledge grows clearer again. The woman's eyes and voice light up with that familiar gleeful sympathy as she utters her, 'Maria, whatever's become of you?' and I want to hide again. I am reminded of how well-gossiped the Anglo-American networks are and why I chose to come to Paris.

It is odd, but as the days pass I miss Paul more acutely. Images of him have grown into a loop which plays over and over in my mind, freeze-framing of its own accord. They are hardly all images of bed either. It's a puzzling, complicated old business, this tangled matter of sex and love, where they come together, where they float apart. I can't ever wholly separate them: the separations seem to come from outside, from notions about morality; from time, from patterns of social life; from sloganising pundits.

If only it were all as simple as some of them want to make it, I could have become celibate years ago, a veritable nun in black gown and splendid headdress. Seriously. If sex were merely a matter of orgasm as so many of them clamour, if that were the whole edifice, the touchstone of good and bad, we could have done away with it years ago. As far as I can make out, it takes about sixty seconds of well-administered fingers and fantasy to arrive at that lovely little thrill. But the supposed Big-or-Little-or-Medium-O is a mere incidental, isn't it? We're not crude input-output machines, with buttons marked O for mechanical release – not even men, I suppose.

No. There's an awful lot more to it than that. Other people for one, the adventure of them, the discovery. The voice on the telephone or beside you. Bodies taking over from words and words flowing back, secret, intimate. The little things, the curve of a shoulder, the flutter of a breath; and big things, the caring, the pain of separation. Play and passion all in one. Pleasure and exchange. Imagination and memory.

Those are the good things. Paul has reminded me that I was once a creature of the bright side.

PART THREE

♎ 24

I arrive in Paris early on a Friday morning three weeks later. My case is stuffed with photocopies, the laptop half a megabyte fuller. I am pleased with myself, with Paris too. The grit and sprawl of London had made me forget the sparkling majesty of this city. My journey homeward takes me along boulevards lined with chestnut and plane trees, past the formal splendour of the Place de la Concorde, the iridescence of the Invalides. I find myself wondering why I ever abandoned all this for the wilderness of New York.

Despite the layer of dust, the apartment, too, is welcoming. I shower and change quickly and on a whim ring Beatrice. I know she will not be there, but I want to announce myself to her housekeeper or answering machine. Beatrice's knowledge of my return will steady me. I told her I was going off on a research trip, though I didn't tell her for how long or what I was researching. I have a sense that Beatrice wouldn't approve, would judge me prurient, or might ask why.

Beatrice's voice on the answering machine is calm and sweet and perfectly paced. All is well with her world. I tell her I am back and ask whether she would like to come out for dinner or a drink sometime soon. Having done that, I feel prepared for the office.

Paul is not expecting me. I didn't want him to. Active waiting is not a pleasant emotion in these circumstances and he has only ever been good to me. I think I led him to suspect I was returning Saturday. He may not even be there.

Madame Duval, whom I check in with first, is as impeccable and efficient as ever. I give her an assortment of carefully selected expenses chits, along with three pretty canisters of Harrod's tea. She is visibly touched by the present and full of questions about London. But she stops herself. Maître Arnault will undoubtedly want to see me and he has only an hour or so before the day's meetings begin. She pauses and warns me that he's not in the best of tempers. It's always the same, she sighs, when he's working on a case which involves Tournier, a *juge d'instruction* he finds particularly trying. She buzzes him a little hesitantly, then tells me to go straight through.

Paul is sitting behind his cluttered desk. He is unusually still, pale, too handsome. I hadn't thought the sight of him would so affect me.

He stares at me, as if I were a ghost, but doesn't rise. 'I worried that you mightn't come back,' he says softly.

'I'm here.'

He is suddenly all motion. He comes towards me, but I move away. I cannot allow myself to be touched. I lift my case to my bosom. 'I've brought lots of clippings, photocopies.'

He raises his arms as if I were a policeman holding a gun to him. 'Okay, no hands.' He laughs strangely. 'Next thing I know you'll have me up for harassment.'

'Don't be ridiculous.'

'Men at the desiring end of an unwanted relationship are always ridiculous.'

I would like to say that it hasn't been unwanted, but he goes on.

'All right then, let's see what you've found.' He clears a space on the table at the end of the room, shows me formally to a chair opposite him, finds a pad, a pen. I lay out the materials and we talk, politely, coolly, though I have a sense that if our fingers brush against each other, we will explode. We have not got very far when the phone rings.

'Thank you,' Paul murmurs. 'Five minutes.' He turns to me. 'Are you going to have dinner with me tonight, Maria?'

Despite the look on his face, I shake my head.

'So you meant it?'

'I meant it.'

'Who . . . ?'

I stop him. 'It's not what you think, Paul. It's not like that. There isn't anyone.'

'Why then?'

He looks so wretched that in utter self-contradiction, I think that if he asks me again or for tomorrow, I will break down and say yes. But I am in France, where the order of mistresses is even better regulated than in New York. Weekends are not part of that order. I used, on the whole, to be glad of that.

'It's a promise I made myself. It's for the best,' I say softly. 'We can meet this afternoon, if there's time. Or Monday, to go through the rest of this.'

'Can't. And I'm in court Monday. Will you come?'

'If you'd like me to.'

'I'd like you to.'

I gather up the things, stop for a moment at the alternate door which leads to my office. As I look back at him, it comes to me that it's a lot harder being good than I ever imagined. Particularly when selfishness has been a lifetime habit.

My desk has a neat stack of new folders on it, together with some diskettes. 'For your comments and perusal as soon as poss. Diskettes first', says the note attached to them. I am pleased by the ordinary businesslike tone of this and I set to work. Perhaps the two of us will manage it all gracefully, despite the difficulties of the initial encounter. He is a sensible, intelligent man, after all. And serious.

The first diskette is labelled 'Draft Chapter Five (incomplete)'. Paul has been working in my absence. This is the section on husbands and lovers, and the English material I have collected will have to be woven into it.

I switch on the screen. A single paragraph sits at its centre, somehow as startling as an erotic image, despite its source in Aristotle's *Nichomachean Ethics*:

'Pleasures are an impediment to rational deliberation, and the more so the more pleasurable they are. For instance, the pleasures of sex; it is impossible to think about anything while absorbed in them.'

At the bottom of the screen, Paul has written, 'Is this accepted truth true in your experience? Comment please.'

I stare at the citation and don't know how to comment. I read on, am increasingly aware as I read that Paul has used this draft to talk to me in my absence. There are little notes dotted throughout the text, probing questions, asides. He is trying to understand – my behaviour, me. I am at once subtly flattered, touched and troubled. Mostly the last. I do not want to be laid bare, understood; but I want to be kind. Perhaps the greatest kindness would be for me to leave.

It is the end of the afternoon before I finish reading the draft. I go back to the beginning and under the quotation from Aristotle, I write, 'Pleasure is quick. Life is long. One man's pleasure is another woman's pain.' I want to write more but a knock disrupts my thought.

'Finishing off?' Tanya Walker pokes her cropped head round the door.

'Just about.' I gesture her in, am pleased to see her, relieved that she isn't Paul.

'I wanted to hear about your trip.'

Tanya has taken to making abrupt incursions into my office. I suspect she's lonely and even if I'm not the ideal female friend, or one she's terribly interested in, I'm at least not a superior whom she has to impress. Then, too, she has a kind of political zeal for Paul's project; she's afraid that we'll make a hash of things, that we won't situate women's murdering acts against the appropriate background, that we'll describe the perpetrators as exceptional monsters rather than typical women driven over the edge by men. She has lectured me any number of times on this score.

What I find extraordinary about her lectures and wonderfully contradictory is the way she can combine the high moral tone with a relish for gruesome detail. She is both fascinated and terrified by violence, which is always sexual violence, and her fascination means that there is potential terror everywhere. Like a talking tabloid, she brings me stories about deranged men running over their wives at high speed, or immersing them in vats of acid; about serial killers stalking suburban streets in search of schoolgirls, or jealous lovers trailing former girlfriends in order to hack them into pieces. When it is women who stab husbands or lovers, cut off or cut up their parts, there is a vengeful glee in her stories, as if here we were in the sphere of rational action.

Tanya reminds me of New York, where sexual violence is both fact and fantasy of everyday life, one feeding off the other in an ever-increasing spiral of fear and menace. Sitting with her, looking out over this sedately elegant Paris street, I am taken back to the incomprehension I felt in my first days in Manhattan when people would counsel me to beware: of walking in the streets alone at night, of taking the subway, of strangers, of men in general. To beware of the violence round the corner, a violence which always had a sexual tinge. I was taken aback by this. I had been brought up to think of violence as what the police did to North Africans or what unjust states perpetrated on their inhabitants; or simply and most terribly, as war.

Despite all my years in America, I am still at root my mother's daughter. When I feel the rare urge to generalise about violence, it is not sex I think about. I cannot bring myself to see men's violence towards women in anything but terms of individual pathology. I suspect this is the real reason Tanya lectures me. She doesn't like the fact that I have no general views.

But today Tanya isn't lecturing. She is listening to details of Martha Roberts's trial and as I recount them, her pretty, regular features settle for a moment into peevish discontent.

'Sounds great. Wish I'd been there. I wanted to come, but Paul dissuaded me. He keeps saying it isn't my field. You two got something going?' Her tone is breezy.

'You're letting your imagination run away with you,' I laugh, notice in consternation that the telltale passage is still on the screen and rapidly switch it off.

'So you are finished. Feel like a movie? I could use some entertaining.'

'Great idea.' It is so long since I have done anything as ordinary as go to a film with an office acquaintance that I grasp at the proposition with real delight.

As we pass through Madame Duval's office, Paul is standing by her desk. There is a sheaf of papers in his hand and the face he turns on us freezes into a frown.

'Off for the weekend?' he asks. Tension strains the politeness in his voice.

'Off to a movie,' Tanya announces. 'Want to join us?' She is bold.

'Can't.' He passes a hand wistfully through his hair. 'Got to finish up here.'

'Too bad. Another time.'

She is so pleased with herself that she is still grinning when we reach the street. 'I've never dared to do that before,' she admits. 'You give me courage.'

'Safety in numbers,' I murmur.

'I think that boring wife of his keeps him under lock and key, you know.'

'You've met her?' It comes out before I can restrain myself.

'At René Cournot's.' Tanya crows a little. 'He has an annual party around Christmas time.'

I try to deflect her by pointing to a beautifully cut frock in a boutique window. But Tanya won't be put off.

'Ordinary little woman, she is. And he treats her with extraordinary consideration. I can only think that either she's appallingly rich or he's a very guilty man.'

'And you'd like to make him guiltier.'

'Wouldn't you? What are men for?' She laughs with more gaiety than I've ever heard from her.

'I imagine I've done enough for mankind in that direction.'

She eyes me critically for a moment. 'I bet you have.'

It is when we turn the corner into the Champs Elysées that Paul is suddenly upon us. His tie is askew, his hair dishevelled. He has been running. And his voice is a little too full of a forced jollity.

'Changed my mind. Thought a movie with two beautiful women was just what I needed before settling into a weekend of manuscript.'

'Well, well, well,' Tanya smiles while I struggle with my composure.

We sit in the dark and watch the life of an English butler, locked in an ethic of service, an ideal of propriety, unfold. Paul sits between us. At one point his hand curls round mine. It is warm, soft and taut at once. I do not draw away. I am crying. I am crying because the butler has just realised that his life has been given over to hollowed-out forms. His service has been meaningless, travestied by his master's embracing of fascism. He is a relic to nothing. And it is too late for the love that has passed him by.

I am crying because Paul's hand is on mine and I would like to keep it there and I can't keep it there.

Afterwards, on the terrace of a café shadowed by Napoleon's triumphal arch, I am angry. I am angry because we are made to feel pity for the butler, in some way superior to him – because we all supposedly know that feeling comes first and life is love.

'But the butler has harmed no one.' I am adamant. I scowl at Paul.

'Nor has he lived, made choices.'

'Because life equals a few little rolls in the hay. Passionate little rolls in the hay.'

He shrugs. 'Rolls in the hay are not love.'

'And why isn't service a kind of love?'

'Serving fascists?' Tanya intervenes.

I shake my head so hard that my hair tumbles over my face. 'No, just putting our own little selves second. What's so sacred about our selfishness? Our vaunted individuality?'

'Maria's about to be born again,' Tanya laughs.

'That's not what I mean. My mother . . .' I stand up abruptly. 'Too long a day. I'm not making sense. Must be exhaustion.'

Paul is swift to rise. 'Shouldn't we see you home?'

'No, no, I'll be fine.' I reject his concern, dash off with minimal grace and flag down a taxi before they can follow me.

On Sunday morning, Beatrice and I meet in front of the Musée d'Orsay. She throws her arms around me and kisses me enthusiastically.

'You don't know how exciting this is for me,' she says. 'I've only ever been here once since it opened. It does me good to have you in Paris.'

'Only once?'

'Yes.' She looks a little shamefaced. 'There's always so much to do, so many tasks that come first. And on Sundays, there are the children, who never want to go and see boring old pictures. But this weekend they're away with their father. And I haven't got a single meeting.' She claps her hands girlishly.

In fact she is altogether girlish today, now that I look at her properly. Against the light drizzle, she wears one of those round hats with a little upturned brim. It is navy blue, like her suit which has a pleated skirt. A white blouse with rounded collar peeps out from her jacket. She has done her hair differently too. There is a wispy wave at the cheek, and her eyes as she looks up at the pictures are hugely bright.

'Do you remember? Your mother used to take us to museums. No one has ever explained pictures to me like she used to. Maybe you can do it for me again now.'

I laugh, but I do as she asks, filling in where I can, telling her stories about artists' lives. There is that rapt look about her which is etched in my memory. Is it only now that I notice the slight wistfulness about the lips?

We are standing in front of Manet's 'Olympia'. The original. I don't really want to pause here, but Beatrice has wrapped her arm through mine and won't budge.

'She's so beautiful,' she says softly. 'It must be wonderful to be as beautiful as that, so defiant in nakedness.'

'Though she didn't have that wonderful a life, it seems. She was probably a prostitute.' A tremor comes into my voice as I catch the look Beatrice turns on me. And I suddenly recall the part the word 'prostitute' played in my childhood spying on Beatrice. I rush on to burble about Manet's brilliant opposition of light and shadow, his rejection by the academy, his disappointment at being seen only as the head of the Impressionists.

'I still think it must be wonderful,' Beatrice murmurs.

Maybe it is the wide silence of her eyes, but I then remember a story about another Olympia, a childhood Olympia, perhaps Manet knew it too. 'Do you know the story of the sandman?' I ask Beatrice. 'That evil demon who comes to steal children's eyes if they are open when they shouldn't be? There's an Olympia there, too.'

Beatrice shakes her head.

I grin. 'This Olympia is the most beautiful creature in the world and the hero, Nathaniel, I think his name is, falls madly in love with her merely by spying on her through a window. Then one day he discovers that this ravishing silent Olympia is really a doll, an automaton created by the man he has always thought is her father and a famous oculist who has provided her glorious, hypnotic eyes. And the two of them are dismantling her. Nathaniel rushes over to save his lady love. But he is too late. Olympia's eyes are bleeding on the floor and the oculist turns on him and tells him they are really Nathaniel's eyes, stolen from him in childhood by the sandman, who is the oculist in disguise.'

'That's a horrible story.' Beatrice shivers.

'Yes, it is.' We move away from the picture at last, but for the rest of our visit, I am haunted by the sense that I have too much in common with Nathaniel, that Beatrice is the doll I spy on, a doll left over from childhood who has grown into independent life. And my eyes will be taken from me for my secret spying on the forbidden.

Over lunch in the brasserie opposite the museum, Beatrice confides in me.

'I've been twice to your mother's grave in the last few weeks. I like to talk to her. She gives me solace.'

'What do you need solace for, Beatrice?'

She shrugs, looks away for a moment. 'Sometimes the responsibilities get on top of me.'

'But the responsibilities are good. They anchor you.'

She laughs. 'You say that because you're free. But tell me about London. Did you see your lover there?'

The question startles me as much as the tone. It has an avidity I don't associate with Beatrice and I must stare at her oddly for she rushes on, 'I'm sorry. You stayed on so much longer than you'd said, so I . . . It's indiscreet of me. It's just that I have so few friends of my own, friends I can talk of such things with. And you've become one. Again. A friend of my own.' She smiles at me shyly, then looks away. Her fork is poised in mid-air, as if she has forgotten about it.

'I did see an old friend,' I admit, wanting to give her a confidence in exchange for hers. 'From New York days. That was very nice.'

'New York?' Her eyes are on me again, soft and brown. 'Tell me, when you were in America, did you ever go to Hollywood?'

She is a little breathless and I remember that on the last few occasions we met, we talked a great deal about the United States. At first, she began by lambasting American foreign policy, towards Bosnia, towards France, and then there was a shift and everything was inquisitiveness – about daily life in Manhattan, about the Grand Canyon, about the Everglades. And now about Hollywood. I tell her about my visit to a studio with a producer we once represented, about Venice and Malibu and strips of silver beach.

Beatrice's food sits untouched in front of her. 'It would be nice to go there one day,' she sighs.

'Paris is nicer. But if you want to go, nothing is very far these days.'

'I know. It's just that I have no English. And . . .' she shrugs, despondent.

'That's no problem. I can teach you. We can start straight away.' I laugh, hold up fork, knife, spoon, get her to repeat after me the names of everything on the table. We are giggling. Schoolgirls again, back in my mother's kitchen, before my perversity tore us apart.

Over coffee, Beatrice stops the English lesson. 'You make a good teacher,' she says. 'You should come and help out with the refugee children. I give them extra French, you know. At the centre in the Thirteenth. Late on Wednesday afternoons. Could you manage it?'

'I don't see why not.'

Beatrice has her busy, responsible look on again and she takes a piece of paper from her bag and writes an address down for me. 'Four o'clock. A little earlier, perhaps, so that I can set you up.'

It is when we are already out on the street that she turns to me and says, 'And it really is time you came and met my husband, the family. Now that we're friends.'

There is an air of entreaty on her face and I have the sudden sense that she is afraid. But I can't tell whether she is afraid that her family will alienate me or steal me away from her. I put my arm through hers as a promise against either.

'You love them very much, don't you?'

She squeezes my arm. 'We're having a little party. For my husband's birthday. Saturday next. You must come.'

'That would be nice.'

All at once curiosity seizes me, as acute as it once was about Beatrice's parents. Its strength makes me uncomfortable and I fail to notice that we are walking up the Rue d'Oudinot and that Beatrice is hesitating in front of Steve's place. I was going to tell her today that I had found an apartment opposite hers, but now it's too late. I squirm at my secret, am troubled too, because if I invite her up, she is certain to notice how unlived in the place looks.

'I need to pop round the corner and get a few things.' I try to salvage myself. 'Then you can come up for a cup of tea.'

'Okay.' Beatrice has no suspicions. 'But we could have some of this.' With a smile she holds up the bag of treats I have brought her and Marie-Françoise from London. 'And I can only stay for a moment.'

The apartment smells a little stuffy, but doesn't look too bad. I fling open some windows.

'Haven't had a chance to air it properly since I got back,' I mumble.

'It's a fine place.' Beatrice walks round the salon appreciatively. 'It's amazing that you've managed to find so many good things in so little time.'

'Oh, it all belongs to an American friend.' I see my opportunity. 'I'll have to find my own place soon.'

'Why bother?' Beatrice smiles as if I have just let her in on an intimacy. 'This is so nice.' She pauses in front of my favourite picture, moves back to find a better angle and brushes against a side table. A pile of post the *gardienne* must have piled up in the weeks of my absence begins to topple to the floor.

'But you haven't even had a chance to open your letters.' Beatrice stops the fall. 'I really mustn't keep you.'

'Junk mail,' I say. 'Not worth the time it takes to open.'

I don't know whether it is as much of a surprise to her as it is to me, but we both start to laugh.

After Beatrice has left, I sit back in the sofa and start to sift through the post. It is mostly junk, but there are two large envelopes from the office in New York, each containing an assortment of forwarded letters. I am reminded that I have not yet written to Steve to inform him of my new address.

There is a letter from Steve at the top of the pile and I read it first. He gives me a round-up of New York gossip – births, marriages, deaths and who has been lunching with whom and replacing whom in an assortment of key posts. He tells me I am much missed, and if I should decide to come back, open arms and racing hearts will greet me. He also tells me that he and Chuck will be in Paris in late June.

I am touched by this letter; beneath the flamboyant fast talk and intent superficiality, Steve has proved a loyal friend. And I can almost hear him chortle as I tell him what I'm now up to.

The next two letters are from my publishers: the first containing a royalty statement which is not minimal; the second asking me whether I would consider doing another book, given the success of the first, and suggesting some possibilities. I daydream about this for a few minutes and it is while I am locked in the daydream that my eyes focus on the next envelope, redirected from publishers to office. I know that writing – plump, childish, green-inked with thick slashes beneath my name. I don't want to know that writing,

Cold beads of perspiration gather in my armpits. That writing has found me, that writing which pursued me for months, a letter a day, malicious, furious, demented, coiling round my thoughts, my life, like a nemesis. Trapping me, because every one of its spiteful words was in essence true.

I don't want to open this letter, but my fingers are already tearing away at the envelope. And as I tear, a crack appears in the well-guarded perimeter fence I have erected around an area of my life. Atop brick and barbed wire, the bare rickety sign still reads, 'Do Not Enter'. But the crack is widening, opening to engulf me. I am through. Arms flailing, eyes tightened against grit and stone, I am through on the other side.

⚖ 25

Autumn-bright leaves dance and swirl amidst the murky browns and greys of Manhattan's Flatiron District. In my office, the noisy old radiators make the atmosphere tropical. The plants have noticed: their tendrils creep over pictures, assault chairs and curios. I haven't the heart or time to restrain them. It is October 1991 and Nichols, Regnier and Peele Associates now occupies a whole floor of this converted century-old warehouse. Steve Nichols, who invited me to join the agency just over three years ago, is next door to me. Harold Peele, who handles the corporate accounts and the occasional city politician, runs the little empire at the other end of the long corridor. Despite the Wall Street Crash of 1987, we are doing well. People seem to need images even when money is tight.

Unwritten company policy has it that every year one or other of the partners will carry what we call internally a 'guilt' account – that is, provide advice and a measure of services free or all-but-free to a worthy cause or small charity. This is Steve's idea: for years he has been helping various Aids groups, though in his jaunty way, he is quick to announce that the rationale for the 'guilt' accounts is that there is nothing like helping to help our own image.

This season it is my turn. Out of the batch of letters which come in regularly soliciting our help, we have chosen three which tickle our conscience and our fancy; and the last of the candidates, a group seeking to provide shelter for the homeless in Spanish Harlem, is due this afternoon.

Promptly at three, reception announces the people from the Hundreds Project. Instead of the anticipated two, four traipse into my office, two men and two women. They are about my age, but they feel younger. All but one are jean-clad and all but one, as I shake their hands and note Spanish names, look at me with a suspicion which borders on hostility. The exception wears a trim navy-blue cord suit and carries a large rectangular portfolio. He has the dark good looks of a silent film hero with heft and he smiles warmly. His name is Sandro Jimenez.

All my style prejudices must come to the fore, since I fully expect Sandro Jimenez to make the presentation. But no sooner has one of the women, Valeria, pulled a thick sweater off, than she begins to speak. She is quickly interrupted by the second woman, who is in turn cut off and contradicted by the other man. And so it goes on in an uncontrolled three-way relay until all I want to do is shout for a single voice and a single coherent picture instead of this chaos which nonetheless bears the tangible whiff of deep commitment.

'Perhaps one of you might make it clear just what it is exactly that you're trying to achieve,' I manage to say during a pause in the relay.

'May I?' The one called Sandro Jimenez looks at his colleagues and then at me and gestures at the portfolio beside his chair.

'Please.'

He places the portfolio on the easel stand which just about escapes the green tendrils and begins to show me photographs: large, stark, black-and-white prints of streets in the East Hundreds, derelict, devastated sites, weed in concrete; people sleeping rough, covered in newspapers, slumped in doorways; children playing in wasteland; young men, cold hands too big for their bodies, old men with dead eyes beneath crazy hats lining up for soup in front of churches, missions. Meanwhile he talks with soft passion of a block in the lower East Hundreds, calling out for reclaiming; small rooms but with light and privacy for young, homeless men, who could help, be trained in construction work, in a neighbourhood reclamation project which could gradually be theirs; vouchers for food and shelter instead of cash for drugs. The photographs are replaced by architectural drawings, illustrations of finished sites, bright in colour, fresh, welcoming.

I am hooked.

'And how far have you got?' I ask.

Three of them start to speak at once. I throw up my hands in a gesture of desperation and I hear Sandro say, a note of quiet authority in his voice, 'Carmen, explain about the churches.'

There is silence for a moment, then Carmen starts to tell me how two of the churches in the area have pledged their support for the project, how in the short term they will provide food and shelter for a proportion of those selected to work on the reclamation. Then, at a nod from Sandro, the other man, José, tells me how after much persuasion, they have had the go-ahead from the relevant authorities, have obtained all the necessary permissions and a small grant. Finally, Valeria explains that they have begun to select the most reliable amongst the drifting youths in the area, have talked to them about the project, nurtured interest, promises.

At last, I have something of a coherent picture and I smile gratitude at Sandro.

'And who are your architects?'

A shy half-smile flickers over his face. He points to himself.

'I see. And the firm?'

'No firm. Just me.'

'Sandro's one helluva architect,' Carmen enthuses.

'Terrific,' Valeria echoes her.

'I don't doubt it. But that may not be enough. What have you built, Mr Jimenez?'

He lifts his hands dramatically in the air. 'What haven't I built! I've worked on brownstones, office blocks and warehouses, on suburban ranch houses, bungalows, swimming pools, apartments.' He bends towards me as if he is about to convey a secret. 'But this is the first time I will have planned from beginning to end.'

Sandro's hands, thick, rough, the nails splayed, so unlike the suit he gracefully wears and his silent movie hero features, alert me before José begins to speak.

'Sandro's worked in construction since he was fifteen. And last year he graduated from architectural school. He comes from the neighbour-hood.' He says this last as if it is the ultimate testimonial, then adds, 'You should look at what he did to my apartment.'

'I see.' I am silent for a moment and in that silence Sandro stares at me, while the others all start again to speak at once.

'She doesn't believe in us,' Sandro murmurs in a lull, 'and if she doesn't believe in us, *amigos*, we have one big mother of a battle ahead of us. And one big lot of homework to do.'

I think it is this last comment which, pictures and plans aside, begins to convince me.

'What is it that you want from us?' I ask, though I know perfectly well.

'Dollars,' they shout in unison like an audience at a game-show, and then Sandro goes on, his voice urgent. 'We've gone as far as we can, and now we need help. We know we need publicity to get the money, but we don't know how to get the publicity to get the money.'

'You need a lot more than publicity,' I mutter. 'You need organisation. You need to designate someone with charm and punch to head the group. You need an action plan and financial projections. You need clearly to define stages and attach a target cash figure to each.' I pull a glossy multicoloured graph from my desk and wave it in front of them. 'You need ecstatic letters from your civic and church leaders and local dignitaries. You need a report on conditions in the area and how beneficial what you're aiming for is going to be. And that's just the beginning.'

'We've got the last,' José says, offended.

'Good.' I pause and stare at each of them in turn. 'And you're not only going to have to work harder than you've ever worked, but you're going to have to learn to trust the people you team up with.'

'I trust you,' Sandro says softly. He turns to the others. 'She's going to help us.'

'That's not certain.' I cut him off brusquely. 'I have to report back to my partners and before I can do that with any confidence, I need all the background materials you can provide me with.'

Sandro stays behind when the others trail off. He stares at me from those dark liquid eyes as if he hopes the staring will mesmerise me. It isn't without effect.

'Look, you have to forgive the others. They didn't want to come here. I pushed them. They don't like the idea of hype. I know it's essential. We have to learn. But they're a hundred per cent. The project means everything to us. To the neighbourhood.'

I have the sense that he wants to put his hand on my arm as if that will enforce my commitment, but he draws back. 'When do you want the reports by?'

'Friday.'

'Okay.' He pauses, clears his throat. 'I think, if you could make the time, it would be good for you to see the place. To come down there.' His eyes are so intent on my face that for a moment I can't focus on what he is saying. 'And your partners too, if they like.'

I look down at my appointments book. 'Difficult, this week. Perhaps Saturday morning. Ring me on Friday.'

'Right.' His eyes smile. His lips smile. There is an innocent charm about him as he shakes my hand and I reflect, in the way I have with clients, that the cameras will love him.

*   *   *

Saturday morning, Sandro picks me up in a dilapidated Pontiac which judders over pot-holes as if each one is its last. He takes me to a part of the city I only know from cab windows – cabs wanting to circumvent midtown traffic as they hurtle me to the airport. We pull up in front of a mission which, like everything around us, has seen better days. To the right, there is an open lot, dotted with burning trash cans and supermarket trolleys heaped with cardboard and plastic bags. A few men hang about, as inert as the rubble around them. Perhaps he is afraid I won't come out, for Sandro rushes to open my door with old-fashioned courtesy. There is a shyness about his speech, his gestures, which makes me feel as if I am some fragile figurine he is bringing home to introduce to family and neighbours. And he is nervous about the introduction. One or other of us may not pass the test.

Three men of indeterminate age sit on the mission steps, puff on cigarette stubs, pass a bottle to and fro between them. They don't look up as we approach. Only when Sandro greets them by name does life flicker into glazed eyes and rubbery lips. As we step into the gloom of the mission, the close, cloying smell of huddled misery hits me with the force of an uptown express. I need to lean against a wall, but there is no wall to lean on, only Sandro's arm.

'Okay.'

I nod, pull my coat more tightly round me, try to breathe only in shallow spurts. Sandro guides me along what emerges as a shambling queue of men. Some of them seem to know him, hail him, look at me curiously, call out, 'Pretty lady', or grunt with hostility, 'Princess come'ta visit'. Most have moved beyond curiosity and keep their eyes listlessly on the ground. At the end of the line, there is a man, half-hidden by a vast coffee urn.

'Padre, this is the friend I was telling you about.'

The padre's eyes are as blue as a china doll's amidst the wrinkled crevices of his sallow face. He holds my hand a fraction too long, assessing me, while he utters a welcome. His praises for the Hundreds Project are interspersed with words for each of the men who approach him for their paper cup of coffee. Each, it actively occurs to me for the first time, has a name. Each has a story that I am not sure I want to hear.

Between greetings, questions, comforting phrases, the padre manages to convey to me how the Hundreds Project could be the beginning of an essential transformation of the area, how it would bring hope, work, sanctuary. He tells me too how he has known Sandro since he was a boy and has complete trust in him and his team. In the midst of all this a leather-jacketed youth, who has been overseeing some squabble in a far corner, comes up to us. Sandro drapes his arm over his shoulder, introduces him with pride as one of the future works team. The boy gives me a crooked smile, then exchanges some quick-fire Spanish with Sandro, before raised voices from the other side of the room call him away. As I look after him, I find myself having to make a conscious effort to keep the scene before me visible. One flick of the lids and that big city survivor's tunnel vision I have practised for years would render all the ugliness and misery imperceptible.

Perhaps Sandro knows this, for a moment later we are in the crisp, jarring cold of the open air. We go round to the side of the mission where Sandro unlocks a door bearing the sign 'Hundreds Project' to show me a small, cramped office. The walls are covered with check lists and the group's plans for the area. This reassures me, as did the materials delivered on Friday which had more professionalism than Sandro's colleagues had led me to expect. We stay for only a moment before setting off on our tour of the area. As we walk, Sandro begins to speak in soft, suasive tones. Gradually his voice eradicates burnt-out buildings, the squalor of fenced-up sites and insidious poverty. Stone by stone, I begin to see the structure of his dreams – simple, functional housing, not displeasing to the eye, the greenery of parks, well-equipped sports and playgrounds. But like some journalist of the more cynical ilk, I won't succumb to the dream. I tell him that I can imagine buildings, parks. What I can't imagine is the broken people we've met in the mission being set to work, trained. And what guarantee is there that these workers won't rip off and sabotage to feed habits while good will and funds evaporate?

By this time we are sitting in a dilapidated little coffee shop where a tattered poster of a distant seascape provides the only colour and Sandro the only spot of beauty. But the look he turns on me is hard. If the neighbourhood doesn't participate, doesn't take pride in the project, he tells me, within a year what is reclaimed will look little different from what we just saw. No, it won't be easy, and no, the recruits, except for a few, aren't part of the mission's floating population. The team has been very careful in its selection so far and the criteria have been well thought through. And there will be skilled men brought in, to teach by example.

He takes a gulp of the watery coffee and then, as suddenly as if he had lifted a tragic mask to his face, blunt despair distorts his features. 'You're right. There are no guarantees. And the longer it takes to get going, the more likely it is that all our groundwork in the neighbourhood will have been for nothing. Less than zero. And a lot of guys will have been fed apple-pie hopes only to be thrown back to eating out of trash cans one more time.'

He doesn't say anything else and I don't know whether it is at that moment or later as he drives me wordlessly back through the disintegrating streets, but all at once it is I who believe in the dream, am convinced of its need, its vitality, its urgency.

'Okay, Sandro. Let's give it a whirl,' I say. 'I'll sort it with the partners and your team had better prepare itself to scale some awesome heights.'

The car lurches as he lets out a whoop of jubilation. He grips my wrist so hard that I have no doubts left of his experience on construction sites. 'I knew I could count on you as soon as I laid eyes on you.'

'Lucky it wasn't hands,' I mutter and rub my wrist, but we are both smiling.

At my place, which is now a top-floor SoHo loft vacated by a painter Romewards bound, Sandro and I begin to detail an action plan. Four pages of it in his small, meticulous hand result by the time darkness takes over the afternoon.

It is only when I switch on lamps and lights that Sandro looks around him. He whistles beneath his breath. 'This is some nice place you've got here. Design it yourself?'

I shake my head. 'It was more or less like this when I took it over, all except the movables.' I follow his gaze and imagine how the place must look to him. Against prevailing fashion, this is my colour phase. When I first moved in, the sheer size and whiteness of the space terrified me and I filled it with as much colour as a Fauve canvas. Two overstuffed sofas, one coral, the other clear iridescent blue, face each other in the space where we now sit. In the far corner of the room, my office bathes in deep Provençal yellow. Creamy stone columns of irregular size form an entrance into the dining area dominated by a long oak table and again snatches of yellow, coral, blue. After the gloom of the mission, it must seem as if we have flown into the vividness of the Mediterranean. The climate suits Sandro. His face glows as he fingers a tapestry, smooths a sculpting.

'I do a little sculpture, when there's time,' he announces. 'Maybe you can come and see it sometime.'

'I'd like that.'

He flashes me a look of gratitude, wanders around some more, eyeing the place with what it occurs to me is professional interest as I fetch drinks.

'Maybe I'll give you a piece. There's one that would look good, just here.'

'You shouldn't give. You should sell.'

'Why? I do it for pleasure. I'd like to share the pleasure. With you.'

I don't respond and after a moment he asks me, 'Do you live here alone?'

'I'm afraid so. Does it seem wasteful?'

'I wasn't thinking of that.'

The look he gives me reminds me that Tom Abrams, my current beau, must be due any minute. I say beau, advisedly, since Tom and I aren't lovers. Tom is a family man whose family has abandoned him and he's still feeling raw about it. I suspect he'd like to start a new family with me, but he's cautious, since I give few signs of being the family type and he's only recently convinced himself that he's in love with me. The added caution is to do with Aids: Tom is infected with the new purity. Despite what the media tell us, this secondary infection hasn't been in my experience quite as contagious as the first, but Tom has it. Not that he's the proverbial money and jogging man. He's just careful, and his dreams are about hearthside chats over brandy with the children snuggly tucked in upstairs. He's older, too, and I like him, like the chats which are mostly about where he's got to in life and where he's gone wrong, with all the emotions close to the surface. He suits me at the moment, a rest after the last affair which ran precariously close to my being cited in the divorce courts. Then, too, Grant Rutherford, who has never stopped following my doings, both professional and personal, from a middle distance, has cropped up in my life again for what he likes to call another instalment in his undying French Affair.

Between the two of them and mounds of work, I have ended up again with too few of those precious evenings on my own.

'I'm afraid a friend is due in just a bit,' I say to Sandro. 'And I should go and change.'

'Of course, no problem, thank you.' Sandro drains his glass hastily.

'Wait a minute. It's just occurred to me. Tom is an architect. Cartenuto, Reynolds, Abrams, Steele. You should talk to him. We'll need a known firm to vet the project. Perhaps act as an umbrella. Tom may have some ideas.'

Sandro blanches, stiffens abruptly. 'We don't need any vetters. Any umbrellas. My roofs won't leak.'

I am hardly blind to male pride but Sandro is behaving as if he were Placido Domingo and I had recommended he take on some small-town Kansas tenor as a coach. His chin juts forward as I stare at him, his shoulders are tensed.

'Look, Sandro, we're not talking leaky roofs here,' I say at last. 'We're talking big money from a lot of people. Which means making a lot of friends. Inducing confidence. You could be Mies van der Rohe himself, and at this stage of the game, I'd suggest the same thing. Okay?'

For a moment he doesn't budge, then inch by inch fluidity returns to his body.

'Okay. But not today.'

'Up to you,' I shrug. But it is already too late. The bell has rung and Tom is at the door. He gives Sandro a surprised look. I introduce them, throw Sandro in at the deep end, and leave the two of them together while I go off and change. When I come back, they are deep in conversation, Tom firing questions, Sandro answering. They are so intent that they don't even notice me. I am pleased. I perch quietly at the far end of the sofa and watch. Sandro's zeal is evident in every gesture – I find myself making mental notes – but he will have to temper his over-sensitivity, a slight tendency to react to questions as intrusion or insult. It is only a modulation. The fire is good. The pride is good.

'I must go.' He suddenly stands up, turns to me. 'I'm imposing on your evening.'

'Perhaps Maria can arrange for me to look at the plans.'

'Of course. Next week sometime.'

After Sandro has left, Tom says, 'Interesting young man. Where'd you find him?'

'I'm afraid he found me,' I laugh. 'Or rather the agency.'

Over the next months I work harder than I would have thought possible with the Hundreds group. With Tom's help we find a better-placed architectural firm who will check figures, vouch for the project and allow their name to appear as consultants. Leading architects write one-line testimonials. We whittle down the aims of the project into one terse page of prose which Steve, with his inimitable flair, translates and spices for different markets – journalistic, philanthropic, civic, trade. We devise a fundraising campaign, complete with visuals, which concentrates on the number one hundred and follows the number into tens and hundreds of hundreds of dollars. Another complementary board shows building targets achieved in hundreds of days, together with the cash figure needed for each stage of construction. We find companies who will initially donate materials in exchange for appearing as patrons and in the hope that eventually donations will turn into cash orders. An up-and-coming fashion designer agrees to create work clothes for the trainees, bright green overalls with the number one hundred on the back. We take rolls of human interest pictures and cull the best for a publicity package, which goes out to all and sundry.

With Sandro, I select five of the most photogenic future trainees and coach them in interview techniques. I do the same with the core group and particularly with Sandro and Carmen: I show them how to get aims across clearly, passionately and succinctly, since media time is short; teach them how not to be waylaid or stumped by interviewers' tangents or hostility; how to use statistics effectively; how to smile and charm, hide nerves and sit quietly. I call in favours: get celebrities to give their names in support of the project; talk to journalists and feature writers, begin the process of creating a buzz – a feature here about the area and its ills and possible solutions; a profile there of Sandro, his neighbourhood and dreams; a few radio interviews; a local TV slot, a piece in the architectural press. Sandro doesn't need much coaching. He's a natural. The women interviewers, particularly, love him.

I start to take Sandro round with me to the places and parties where he will meet the people he needs to know, the great, the good and the rich. One night he doesn't turn up at the appointed time. Nor is there any word of explanation. I am angry – all the more so because it was a sit-down affair and I had managed to get him placed next to the wife of a corporate head with a good record in city charities. The next day I leave an irate message on the project's answering machine.

When I come home from the office, Sandro is waiting by my door. In the lamplight, his face looks ashen beneath the dark curling hair.

'Sorry,' he mumbles. 'Couldn't get there last night. Had an accident. At work.'

'What happened? Come on up.'

As the creaking elevator takes us up to my apartment, I examine his face for cuts and bruises. I have visions of him beaten up, left for dead on one of those derelict sites. My knees feel weak.

'What happened?' I ask again when we are through the door.

'Nothing serious. But I had to go to the hospital and that took forever.' He seems ashamed.

It is only when he takes his coat off that I notice his hand is bandaged, that he is moving his shoulder oddly. He holds out the bandaged hand. 'Fractured my thumb,' he grins.

'In a fight?'

'No. What makes you think that? I try not to have fights.'

'Well, how then?'

'Told you. At work.'

'In the office?'

He looks at me as if I have just landed from another planet.

'On the construction site. A pile of breeze blocks.' He makes a careening motion.

'I didn't know you'd started.'

'Started what?'

'The building work. You should have waited. We would have had an inauguration ceremony. Ceremonies are important.' Now that I know he hasn't been left for dead on an empty lot, I am angry again.

'What're you talking about? I'm working on a construction site downtown. How do you think I make my living? Going to parties? Started again three weeks ago. Ran out of money and had to start again.'

Now he is the one who is angry and I am ashamed, aghast at my own blindness.

'Those damn suits you told me I needed didn't help.'

'You should've said,' I murmur, handing him a drink.

We look at each other for a moment and suddenly he starts to laugh. 'But I'm really sorry about last night. Carmen told me your message was furious. I'll write our hostess a note of apology. You can dictate it.'

'Does it hurt?'

'Only when I move.'

'So you can't write.'

'Wrong hand. But I can't work for another few weeks. So I'm all yours.'

'Do you need money?'

'Accident insurance.' He is suddenly stiff.

'What about dinner then?'

He smiles softly. 'Now that sounds tempting.'

'With Tom. We're meeting in an hour.'

His face closes. 'No, just remembered. Can't really cut . . . Got to get back.'

I call Tom and cancel.

Three weeks later, after much effort, I persuade Sandro to allow a photo to be taken of him on the construction site and to be interviewed. The feature comes out under the headline: 'Construction Worker – Architect of Dreams'.

In April we hold a fundraising party. On the strength of the guest list, we convince a hotel to give us a banqueting room and a less than elaborate buffet. The walls are covered with photographs of the project. The mayor, after a little stringpulling by Harold Peele, agrees to speak and is flanked by celebrities. Carmen talks about the training programme. Sandro gives the closing address. He is good, very good and in his bow tie and dinner jacket, he looks as luminous as his words. I watch the guests while he speaks and I have that little zing of adrenalin which tells me it's going to work. We already have our first two promises and once they have voiced their donations, others begin to follow. José and Valeria stand by the target board and, with only a little self-conscious drama, place green stick-on exclamation marks next to the rising hundreds as the pledges are made. Cameras flash, applause sounds and mounts, and by the end of the evening we have raised sufficient funds for the first chunk of the scheme. Sandro voicing thanks, to our firm and myself, not least, faithfully promises that each of the contributors will have their names etched into the wall of the building.

We are ecstatic. In the emptying room, Steve hugs me, hugs Sandro and Carmen and Valeria and José. I hug everyone, including our five model youths who are here in their green suits. But when I hug Sandro, something odd happens. Maybe it's because he holds me too close. Maybe it's because my dress leaves my back bare. Maybe it's just the general excitement, but we don't quite let go in time and a little circle of silence forms around us as the others watch and we still can't quite let go.

Sandro takes me home. He doesn't speak. He grips my hand tightly at every red light. It is I who burst into sporadic babble, tell him how wonderful he was, how wonderful everyone was, how he must make sure to keep a photographic record of the progress of trainee labour and building work, how the campaign has to be kept on the boil, how in another eight months another fundraising drive will have to be organised. I am breathless with my babble and the pressure of his hand and the something which has lodged itself between us. When I sneak a look at his profile, it is remote. Remote in beauty, I think, and chatter some more to cover the remoteness.

When the door of the loft closes behind us and he looks at me for the first time since we left the crowds, I, too, grow silent. He pulls me towards him and kisses me. It is a deep, hungry kiss and though I am not aware of much else, I am aware that it has waited a long time in both of us and that before it is over we are both all but undressed and he is gazing at me from those soft dark eyes.

We never make it up the rickety curved staircase to the bedroom that first time. We fall instead onto the blue sofa and only at the last moment do I drag up from somewhere the presence of mind to reach into my bag for a condom. He doesn't seem altogether pleased, but he puts it on himself, won't let me touch him there. He has no tricks, Sandro, but when he is in me, I moan with the pleasure of him. He is all strength and depth and a slow, slow dance.

Later, in bed, he tells me he loves me and I smile and curl into him and stroke the tawny smoothness of his skin and tell him he doesn't need to say that. 'But it's true,' he tells me solemnly. 'I love you.' I am still smiling when I wake up to streaked daylight and find him gone. I know he can't wait to get to the project, to tell everyone, to begin. I find myself whistling a silly tune as I dress. I feel strangely young again and I have a mad whim to go up to East Harlem and see him, touch his lips with my fingers.

At noon, he rings me at the office and asks me, a little shyly, if he can see me later, about nine, since there is so much to do. 'I'll fix some dinner,' I suggest, but when he arrives, dinner is forgotten. Sometime in that long night, he murmurs, 'You've made me, Maria. Recreated me. Like a goddess.'

I am not good at gravity. I joke instead, tell him I don't require worship, but it comes to me over this and subsequent nights that Sandro's love-making is a kind of worship.

When I make an impromptu visit to the site, some days later, it is I who feel worshipful. The street is abuzz with noise and activity. Dust and rubble may be everywhere but it feels purposeful. Scaffolding has gone up; cement mixers are turning; youths in green overalls are everywhere. A large placard announces the project. From somewhere above me, I think I hear Sandro's voice and I look up to see him perched on the roof. I wave, blow him a kiss. Perhaps for the first time in my life, I have the sense that I have contributed to something real.

I do not see Sandro every day. We are both working flat out, he, to make maximum use of the good weather, I, to catch up on what was left to one side during the frantic last month of the Hundreds campaign. But imperceptibly, his clothes move into the loft and at one point, with only a fractional hesitation, I give him a key. It makes things easier when I have to be out late of an evening. Though Sandro accompanies me often enough, particularly since I have made it clear to him that he needs to cement the contacts he has already established as well as make new ones. Sometimes, at these gatherings, when I look across the room and see Sandro making profligate use of his charms, I have to rush over to him and touch him to make sure he isn't some fantasy I have dreamt up to assuage both desire and vanity.

One afternoon in July when my part of New York has begun to close down, Sandro rings to ask whether I'd like to meet him at the project office after hours. When I get there, he is alone and we fall into each other's arms.

'You know, Maria,' he murmurs, 'I've wanted to give you something for a long time. I'm so grateful to you. For everything. But I'm always so broke. I thought ... Maybe ... Come.' He takes my hand and leads me round to the back of the mission, down some steps into a kind of storage room. But what I see in the half-light are not old tables and heaped chairs, though there is a camp bed made up in a corner. Instead I am surrounded by desultory figures hewn out of stone, roughly chiselled – men, women at prayer, angels with stumpy wings, like funeral masonry but unfinished, the shapes still trapped in stone. Despite myself, I shiver.

'Natural air-conditioning down here.' Sandro wraps his arm round me. 'What d'you think? This is the one I imagined in the loft.' He points to a muscular kneeling man, arms lifted skyward, but pulled down by the weight of the outcrops at his base. 'Then, after I met you, I did that one.' He gestures towards one of the angels I have already glimpsed. There is a grace about the figure, its half-open cloak, but its wings are too heavy for flight and I have a vision of its toppling under their weight. It is only after a moment that I realise the figure is meant to be me, but I have been silent for too long and now Sandro says, his voice grim, 'You don't like them.'

'It's not that.' I squeeze his hand. 'It's just a lot to take in. They're so strong. You know what it's like with art.' I pause, let the word hang, begin to ply him with questions about the statuary. I learn, in the course of much that is less interesting, that Sandro's father was a stonemason, that he died when Sandro was thirteen, that Sandro inherited his tools. At the end of this, I say to Sandro that I would like the male figure very much.

'You're right,' he answers a little despondently, 'the one of you doesn't really work.'

As I fall asleep in the heat of that evening, my hand on Sandro's chest, it occurs to me I know next to nothing about him. Yes, I know oodles about the project. Yes, I know that Sandro is uncomfortable about the fact that I earn so much more money than he does and he prefers to eat in so that he can bring groceries up to the loft. Yes, I know that he comes from the proverbial wrong side of the tracks. Yes, I know his body intimately and perhaps, through that, a little of his being. And now I know about his father. But about Sandro's life itself, I know very little. I am not unhappy about this, I reflect. I look forward to the surprises.

Later that week I debate with Sandro about the benefits of escaping from New York heat to the Cape for a brief and much-needed holiday. He can't leave and he is glum at the prospect of my going.

'Look,' he says, suddenly shy, 'I've had this idea. I thought you might write a book. A handbook. About PR. With all the millions of details. For people like us. Use the project as an example. It wouldn't harm us and it would help hundreds of other groups. And you could start now, during the quiet season.'

I gaze at Sandro and know that if he touches me, I won't go anywhere and that he doesn't need this idea to persuade me. I also think the idea is in itself an interesting one.

'I could write in a nice cool hotel room overlooking the sea,' I tease him.

'But you won't have me there to advise you.' Sandro is serious, doesn't take well to teasing. 'It's got to be clear and simple.' He puts his arms around me, lifts me out of the sofa. 'Stay, Maria. Please.'

I stay. I map out a possible book and start to write a few brief sample chapters. I test them on Sandro, who, true to his word, puts questions, clarifies. I enjoy the process. I work every day, often from home. Friends ring occasionally, Grant amongst them, to check on my state of mind, but mostly I write. And shop for groceries to make dinner for Sandro. He comes almost every night, only sometimes ringing to say he's so tired, he isn't human, or he really has to spend the evening with the team. I don't mind. I'm happy. It comes to me that this is what marriage must be like when it's good. And then it comes to me that if I have thought that, then maybe the time which friends have always warned me about has come too, and after all I am ready to settle down. Or more simply, I have found the right partner. Like the sentimental seventeen-year-old I never was, I start to daydream a mingled future for the two of us. I am in love.

Come September and the rhythms change. I am busy again, but I try to keep some evenings for the book, which Steve, too, now tells me is not only a brilliant idea, but will help the agency. He reads through the chunk I have written, zaps up my prose and shows a section to a few publishers. By the end of the month, I have a not insubstantial contract. I offer half the advance to Sandro, who turns away from me as if I had hit him.

'But it was your idea. And the idea is half the labour,' I plead.

'Put it towards my share of the rent.'

'What? For the next five years?'

'If that's what it is.'

There is something bothering Sandro, but I don't know what it is and he won't tell me. Only at the end of the month does he confess to me that three of his initial trainees ran off with an expensive load of materials and tools at the end of August, that he has had to replace them with outside labour, that the project budget is askew. I urge him to swallow his pride and go and talk to the consultant architects and devise ways of putting things back on course. And there must be insurance. Sandro, I have begun to realise, is not particularly good with money. Probably his mother didn't have him sit with her over the books from a young age like mine did. In fact, I know she didn't. I have learned after much resourceful questioning that Sandro's mother died a year after his father and that his elder brother overdosed not long after. It was not a model middle-class family. But I value Sandro's achievements all the more for that, as I never hesitate to tell him.

In November, just before I have to leave for London on a business trip, I hand over the completed book to Steve for editing. Steve takes us out to celebrate in style and I don't know whether it is Steve's presence, or the champagne, but we are all as buoyant as we were on the night of the fundraising dinner. Later, too, Sandro's love-making is as hungry and intense as it was on that first night.

'I should leave more often,' I smile at him, just as he says, 'Wish you weren't going . . .' When he looks at me like that, I don't want to leave him either.

When I come back from London he has filled the loft with flowers and he holds me very tight. Remarkably, too, he has cooked dinner for us, set the table with candles, a white cloth.

'I love celebrations,' I say as I hand him the stacks of presents I have bought.

'I wanted this to be a special evening,' he murmurs, smooths my hair. It is then that I notice the odd light in his eyes.

'Is everything all right, Sandro?'

He takes my hand. 'I wanted to ask you to marry me tonight.'

'Is that a question?' My stomach performs a happy somersault.

'But she won't let me. She won't give me a divorce.' He is looking above my head.

I stare at him. 'Who won't let you?'

'She won't. My wife.' He groans, buries his face in his hands.

I gaze in incomprehension at those large hands I know so well. I see grooves, roughened knuckles, the pallor of scrubbed nails. My voice comes out in a different octave. 'Are you telling me that all this time you've been married, Sandro? That you've hidden it for over a year?'

I scrape my chair back from the table, topple a wine glass in the process.

'It's not how you think, Maria.' He is behind me. 'I hardly talk to her any more. She's a Catholic. She won't divorce. I only go see her because of Juanito.'

His hand falls on my shoulder, restraining me, and I turn round to face him. 'Juanito? There's a child, too?' I am choking. I don't know why I feel like this. Duplicity is hardly new to me. Yet I feel it. Sandro has lulled me into different hopes.

'A boy. He's almost four.' He looks at me miserably. 'He loves me. I have to go there. See him.'

'And you never told me.'

'I thought if I told you, you would stop seeing me . . . I thought I could tell you once I was divorcing, and could marry you.'

I am sitting on the sofa now and he buries his face in my lap. He is weeping. Silent sobs which make his shoulders heave. I don't know how long he weeps, how long we sit there but suddenly I find I am stroking his hair and my lips are moving. 'It doesn't matter,' I say. 'It doesn't matter.'

Yet it does matter. The lie sustained over all those months matters. I can taste it. It tastes bitter, foul, treacherous, like rotten fruit. Made more rotten by the knowledge that the notion of marriage had ripened in my mind, as perfect and fragile on its branch as an early cluster of golden pears.

I choke on them. I get up. 'I have to go,' I say. 'I have to get some air.'

Sandro is right behind me. He puts his hand on my shoulder as I reach the door. 'No,' he says in a tone of distraught nobility. 'It is for me to go.'

We look at each other. The expression on his face is one of utter desolation. I don't know who makes the first move, but suddenly we are in each others' arms and the ignorant chemistry of our bodies takes over. There is a savagery in our passion, an edge of desperation which cuts and scars. When it is over, he stares at the ceiling and whispers, 'I'll make her, Maria. I promise. Soon.'

I find myself laughing. 'I don't care about marriage, Sandro,' I say. 'Never have.' He gives me an odd glance and I continue laughing.

Later I extract the story of his marriage from him. It comes in painful fits and starts, but it is a predictable enough story of teenage sweethearts and shotgun haste followed by miscarriage.

'Then, after Juanito came . . .' Sandro's voice breaks and he buries his face in the pillow.

'What?' I prod him softly.

'She didn't want me any more.'

'It's not unusual.' I am matter-of-fact. 'So you don't sleep together?'

'Not after you and I . . .' He grips my arm. There is a wild look in the face he turns on me.

In the morning, on my way to the office, I tell myself that in essence nothing has changed. I have known for months about Sandro's pride and deep secrecy, and this is simply another in the series of instances. Yet the bitter taste in my mouth persists.

It persists despite the festive season, despite the flurry of parties. Despite the fact that things are going well at the project and everything is almost on target. There is a new tough female accountant in place, and a foreman so good Sandro almost feels redundant. He should be pleased. But he isn't. Perhaps he tastes the bitterness too.

He is to have Christmas with his family. I tell him I don't mind. I am going to friends. The night before Christmas Eve we spend quietly at the loft together. I cook a salmon, chill champagne, put on a Brahms cello sonata. We exchange presents. Sandro gives me an elaborate Victorian necklace he shouldn't have spent the money on. I give him a stack of architectural books with thick glossy pages. Since my last jaunt to Paul Smith's in London, I have lost the taste for clothing him.

That night in bed, Sandro says to me, 'I want to give you a child, Maria.'

'I can think of other presents I want first,' I murmur and I know he is hurt, has always in any case disliked my dutiful pill swallowing. But I find myself thinking that perhaps he is really asking me to stop wanting him, like his wife after the child. And I do want him. That's the rub. I always want him.

We don't make love again that night.

On New Year's Eve we go out to a party together at a neighbouring loft. It is a grand place and there is a live band playing salsa and a great many of my friends. I dance with Sandro and wish that the grace of his body could obliterate the bitterness in my mouth. I dance with others too. It is while I am dancing with others that I feel his eyes cutting into my back. He is standing at the edge of a group and following my every gesture, my every turn and smile. His face is stormy. I recognise that look. Yes. A laugh begins to curl and flutter inside me. It grazes the bitterness on my tongue, spills out as I meet the black vigilance in Sandro's eyes. Each time I turn and see those eyes, I flaunt myself with greater extravagance. When the bandleader begins the countdown, I stand between Grant and Sandro and at the midnight stroke, I turn to kiss Grant first. It is a friendly kiss, though in fondness it goes on fractionally too long. When I give my lips to Sandro, his face is contorted. He holds me too hard. 'Whore,' he hisses.

The laugh finds me again, washes the bitterness from my mouth. I walk away, slip into the crowd, am generous with my kisses. Sandro's eyes don't leave me. They are black with pain. The pain of jealousy. I can almost feel it coiling across the room.

The pain makes me glad. My tongue tastes sweet. As I dance I give that sweetness a name. I call it vengeance. For some reason, I think of my mother and I wonder if she ever tasted that sweetness. It would have done her good. It would have served my father right.

I leave the party with a stranger. We go to a bar and drink, but without Sandro's eyes there to provoke me, I am not interested. I say goodnight to him at the corner of the street. As I walk swiftly home, a figure lunges out at me from the shadows and pulls me into a doorway. It is only when he presses me against the wall that I recognise Sandro. I stifle my scream and let him kiss me. I enjoy that kiss, enjoy the harsh flavour of despair which has begun to stalk his passion.

Later Sandro questions me about the men I have spoken to, laughed with. He cannot help himself. Any more than over the next weeks he can stop himself tracking me, grilling me about whom I have slept with in the past, maybe the present.

'I owe you nothing, Sandro,' I tell him, 'certainly not the truth.'

I do not altogether like being cruel to Sandro. Yet I take pleasure in it. I tell myself that I should stop, stop the whole thing, tell him to pack up his things and go. But that is not so easy. I don't want him to go. I want him to hurt. And I feel I am waiting for something. Perhaps it is simply an unencumbered reiteration of that marriage proposal. I no longer know.

Then, too, our lives are so intertwined. The second part of the campaign has begun and I feel responsible for its success. There is money at stake, good will, too many dreams. And my book is due to come out at the end of March. It is dedicated to Sandro. We are both caught up in a frenzied media whirl, linked together in the public eye, photographed side by side at the site, pictured with the core group planting trees, interviewed about the possibility of further reclamation projects. Suddenly I am a public person wih a vengeance. My picture appears in *People* magazine. I am featured here, there and everywhere, treated like a celebrity. People listen to the ends of my sentences and take them seriously.

I realise that I hate it, loathe being in the limelight as much as I like putting others there. But I play it to the hilt, flirt with both camera and photographer, just so that I can see the misery in Sandro's eyes. It is the misery now which binds us. I can see it plain as day in the photographs where we are together: he stands there like some noble caged animal, imprisoned in a posture which is half way between fury and passion, his eyes only and ever on me.

One night he is impotent. I tell him it doesn't matter, we're both tired. But he is so distressed that I try to take him in my mouth. I have never done this before with Sandro and now he lashes out at me, slaps me, curses me with any number of expletives.

I get up, dress quickly. I am seething. So angry that when my eyes fall on the sculpture Sandro has given me, I want to take a hammer and smash its heaviness into fragments. This pure rush of anger is a new sensation.

'Where are you going?' Sandro asks me. And I tell him that if he is going to call me 'whore', I may as well behave like one. I also tell him he doesn't know the first thing about loving, that he is only half a man, that he will never be an artist if he doesn't know how to be a man. I don't know quite what I tell him, but he doesn't answer back. Sandro has never had as many words as I have. And he doesn't stop me when I race away.

Out of some atavistic impulse I go to the Gramercy Park Hotel. I lie in bed, unable to sleep. I try to put some order in my thoughts, but they refuse any clarity, despite the fact that my anger has gone. Without Sandro there to vent it on, its heat has vanished. I am simply cold, listless. By morning, when sleep has still refused to come, I ring the office to say that I am unwell. I ask that my appointments be cancelled. I lie there some more and think again that it is high time I broke it off with Sandro. Then I think that perhaps I already have. Perhaps he has already packed his few possessions and gone back to his wife, glad to be rid of the whore he has named me. That refreshes my anger, kindles the ever-present desire. I don't like being left. It reminds me of my mother. I like doing the leaving.

At a loss, I ring Grant. Miraculously he is free and he comes to dine with me at the hotel. It is such a pleasure to see the familiar irony of his face, to get away from the trap Sandro and I have somehow created for ourselves, that I am drunk on a single glass of wine.

'Do *you* think I'm a whore, Grant?' I find myself asking him.

He looks at me shrewdly. 'Love life getting out of hand, is it? The pitfalls of passion and all that?'

I don't answer.

'Well, let me think,' he laughs. 'You don't take money. You don't even take husbands. So on serious reflection, I'd say no. Anyhow, I thought people these days just called it being a free woman.'

'I don't feel very free.'

'The trouble with you is they all fall in love with you. You're dangerous. You don't think sex is just another name for rape. Or power. Now if you were American, you'd have us all up for harassment in the workplace. Retroactively, too.' He winks at me. 'Though I take it the man we're worrying about is not your boss.'

'Are you being done, Grant?' I ask, suddenly concerned for him.

'No. I'm clean as a policewoman's whistle these days. Anyhow, I'm feeling too old. Except for you.' He looks a question at me.

I hesitate, but as I return his look I realise that despite everything the only man I can imagine myself in bed with is Sandro. I shake my head, smile. 'I think I'm too tired, Grant, even for you.'

'I'll pay,' he grins.

'Ridiculous.'

'You see. Not even a little bit of a whore. Just one damn fine seducer.'

I'm surprised at the way in which the meeting with Grant affects me. It is as if he has reminded me of another part of myself, a freer self, reminded me that the forever of marriage is not part of my repertoire. Yet as I curl between the sheets, I find myself longing for Sandro. I can no longer remember why I have been cruel to him. I can no longer remember anything except that I want him and that he may no longer be there for the wanting.

At the first glimmer of light, I race back to the loft. Sandro is there. He has fallen asleep on the sofa. His face in repose is gentle, like a child's. My heart turns over. I touch him softly on the cheek and his eyes flutter open. Dark pools of suffering. 'Forgive me, Maria,' he murmurs. 'Forgive me.'

I take his hand, hold it. We sit there quietly for a moment and when we begin to make love, there is a sweetness to it and I think neither of us knows whether this is an elegy or a rebirth.

Over the next days we circle round each other like convalescents. I have the sense that we are both reserving our forces. The fundraising dinner for the project is only a week away and we both recognise its importance, are aware that we must act as a team.

It is on the day before the dinner that the first letter arrives. It comes with the rest of the heaped post which my assistant hands to me in the morning, and perhaps I should know from the odd look of inquiry she flashes at me that something is amiss. But I think nothing of it. There have been so many letters seeking advice since the book came out that Andrea sifts the ones she can deal with before passing the rest on to me. This letter is different. It doesn't ask for advice. It leaps out at me with the force of a malediction. At first I think I am being confronted by the ravings of a madman. Then I realise with a shudder that this letter, which bears the word 'bitch' with three deeply-etched exclamation marks as its only salutation, is from Sandro's wife. I cannot tear my eyes from the outraged expletives, nor from the mixture of semi-literacy and pulp psychology. Amongst the curses, I am labelled a husband thief and family breaker. That angers me, but it is not that which scares me.

What scares me is the letter's reek of hatred mingled as it is with moments of prescience. I have turned Sandro into a marionette, Louise Jimenez claims; I pull the strings which have led him away from her. Not his work, his new life, as he has told her. I have made him abandon his child. I, the rich bitch, who can never love him half as much as she does.

I stare at the word 'marionette', so odd in its context, and wonder if it is true that I have turned Sandro into a puppet, robbed him of independent life.

But what scares me more is what I learn through the tangled syntax. If Louise Jimenez is to be believed, Sandro's secrecy extends even further than I imagined. It is only by seeing the photographs of the two of us together that she has deduced anything of our relationship.

She has deduced it from the way he looks at me in the pictures, not from anything Sandro has told her.

And then there is the threat. Louise Jimenez says if it doesn't stop, she is going to expose us. She will go to the padre, she will go to the papers, she will scream it from the top of the Empire State Building. I don't know why this scares me, since everyone in my crowd is aware of my relationship with Sandro. But it does scare me: there is a difference between awareness and scandal.

The letter also makes me feel dirty. Sullied by Sandro's double betrayal. My passion has been born and nurtured on the dirty sheets of lies.

I do not show the letter to Sandro that evening, much as I would like to. There is one more hurdle to leap and I am a professional. But I do not sleep with him. I plead tiredness, nerves, beauty rest, a headache. He sleeps on the sofa. He takes it with a measure of stoicism. There is no scene. Perhaps he is glad.

On the evening of the fundraising gala, I dress with particular care. We are holding a banquet this time, with paid seats, half of the price of which will go to the project. I am at the head table. I need to look my best. My frock is new, a simple black with straight classical lines leaving shoulders and neck exposed. Over it, I put a Japanese silk cloak, rich in colour. I try to smile naturally at myself in the mirror. I almost succeed. Sandro looks at me as if his jealousy no longer needs the spur of others. He clips the heavy necklace he has given me round my neck.

It will soon all be over, I tell myself.

I am on automatic pilot throughout that evening which glitters and buzzes but doesn't quite reach the heights we'd aimed for. Perhaps we put our targets too high; perhaps Sandro's speech doesn't quite have the ardent zeal of the year before. Something has gone out of him, a fire, a force. I don't dare meet his eyes, so I don't know for certain. In any case, three-quarters of the way is almost there and it has to be counted a success, but all I can think of as the core group hug each other goodbye is that last year Sandro and I began here and tonight I must tell him it is the end.

'We have to talk, Sandro,' I say, as soon as we are home.

'Not tonight, Maria, please.' He strokes my hair softly. 'Let's keep tonight as it is.'

I avoid his eyes. I make some hot chocolate, put two mugs on the table, and next to his the letter from his wife.

'Read it,' I say.

He glances at the writing and his face twists. He gives me an imploring look.

'Read it,' I repeat. My tone takes on the cruelty I thought I had dropped.

He reads the letter quickly, crumpling pages up as he goes. I wait for him to say something and when he doesn't, I rage.

'You've lied, Sandro. Lied from beginning to end. To both of us. One big lie.'

I am wild in the face of his silence. I start to fling things on the floor, his things. Anything I can lay my hands on – shirts, razors, toothbrush. And I mutter. I cannot quell the viciousness of my anger.

'After everything I've done for you. Why? Just tell me, why? And then get out. Take your ugly sculpture and go.'

He stares at me. His face is a mask. Then he slams his fist on the table, so hard that I stop my flinging and stand very still.

When his voice comes, it is raw, as if he were the one who had been doing the shouting.

'Because she has my son,' he says. 'Why do you think? And you . . .' He hides his face in his hands.

I gaze at his turbulent muteness and that hard cold voice takes me over.

'Well, you'd better get back to him then, hadn't you? Your son and that grotesquely illiterate wife of yours. Maybe they can cover you with that phony idealising respect you so crave. Here . . .' I rip the necklace from my throat and add it to the heap on the floor. 'Offer her that and just get out. Go. Now.'

He gets up slowly and goes to the door. He only turns back when he has opened it.

'I didn't intend it this way, Maria. I never intended it this way,' he says. Then he is gone.

I sit there and gaze at the closed door. For some reason I cannot believe he has gone. There is more I still want to say to him. I start to laugh or at least I think I'm laughing, but when I touch my face, it is wet with tears.

*　　*　　*

The next day in the office there is a phone call from a television news programme asking if Sandro and I can be interviewed at the site at four o'clock. I tell them Sandro should be available, but I can't make it. They fume a little and I tell them perhaps Steve can stand in for me. Grumpily they settle for that and I ask Andrea to get a message to Sandro and to speak to Steve, who agrees.

On his return from the site Steve comes into my office and flops into the armchair.

'What's up? Chief Architect Jimenez never showed.'

'Oh? Perhaps he's had enough of cameras.' I doodle on my notepad.

'He never showed at the site or the office either. Carmen told me. She did the interview instead.' Steve is examining me, looking at my doodles. 'Something happen between you two?'

I shrug. 'It's over.'

'Oh ya? Too bad.'

He is waiting for me to tell him more and I don't want to, but Steve has a way with waiting which makes some form of speech imperative, so I blurt out, 'He didn't tell me he had a wife and he didn't tell his wife he had me.'

'Oh. Nothing serious then. Just a mere matter of eternal triangles.' The joke falls flat when I don't respond. 'Hey . . .' He comes round to my side of the desk and puts his arm round me.

'I'm okay. But his wife is threatening scandal. Cultural wars. East Harlem *v.* Rich Bitches.'

Steve whistles. 'You rich?'

'Depends who's doing the counting.'

'Ya. Tell you what. Chuck and I'll take you out over the next few days. Keep the awesome profile smiling.'

'You're on,' I say and try the profile for him.

At the door he turns back. 'Timing isn't great, is it.'

I'm not sure whether or not this is a reproach. 'Hasn't been great for months,' I mutter.

'Got ya.' He gives me a commiserating smile.

When I go back to the loft late that evening, I feel utterly drained. The elevator isn't working. I trudge heavily up the stairs. Shadows leap out at me, making me fearful. From them I somehow conjure up the figure of Sandro and suddenly, as if I were some child in need of solace, I find myself wishing that he will be there, waiting, so that I can curl next to him in a simulacrum of innocence.

He isn't there, though the loft bears all his traces. I cannot bear them. I realise that I need to go away. I do not know how to cope with abandonment – even if I have urged it.

A few days later I go to Martha's Vineyard. I stay in a small hotel, walk miles across sand, let it wash through my toes, my fingers. The weather is clear, mild. I breathe deeply as if there cannot be enough air in the universe to fill my lungs. I read novels, dip into three at once, so that the stories grow rampant, confused. I try not to think and I begin to succeed. One morning when I go down to the dining room, I feel different. I realise it is because I have not stretched my hand across the bed in search of Sandro's body. There is a glimmer of freedom in that. I taste the freedom and like it, try to preserve its flavour. I hire a bicycle and pedal hard round the island. Out of the rush of wind in my hair, I try to imagine new lives for myself, far from the fevers of Manhattan. I begin to like the contours of these new lives. In them, I am strong, bold, untrammelled, undesiring.

I flop down on the sands and gaze up at the sky, the swift passage of billowy clouds. A smile curves my lips. It feels new, untried. I close my eyes and tell myself everything will be fine. Fine.

I don't know how much time has passed, or whether I have slept, but suddenly I feel that a shadow has settled over me, making me cold. I open my eyes. Sandro is standing over me, gazing.

'So beautiful.' He stretches a hand out to my face. I start back.

He crouches down beside me. 'You were right,' he says. 'I can't live without you. Can't.' He stares out to sea. 'It's over. I've left her.'

I look at him and hardly recognise his voice. There is something wrong with the set of his shoulders. And he has taken off his shoes. His feet are oddly pale.

When my tongue starts to move, I am not sure what it will say. It says, 'It's too late, Sandro. And it's better this way. It wasn't meant.'

'No!' He grips my arm with a fierceness which scares me. 'Not that. Never that.'

I shrug. I edge away from him, but he won't let me go. He covers me with his body and his voice in my ear is as dully insistent as the waves.

'It was meant. All of it. We'll be together now. Always. You'll have my baby, Maria. You will. My baby.'

I am rigid beneath him. I do not want his baby or his weight. I am suffocating. I am being ground into the sand. Buried. I struggle for air, struggle away from him.

'No.' I scramble to my feet. 'No, Sandro. It's over. We both know that. It's for the best.'

For a moment, he doesn't move, just gazes up at me from eyes so black that I am afraid I will drown in them. Then he gets up. His gestures are slow, heavy. They take forever. But finally he stands there, sombre, obtuse, hunched. And he stares at me. Stares, but neither moves nor speaks.

'Really,' I say. 'You'll see. It's for the best.'

He comes towards me and I start to shiver. 'Well, goodbye,' I say, but now my legs won't move. He has turned me into one of his stone figures. Like him.

With an effort, I break the spell. I stretch out my hand for the goodbye, but mostly to prevent him coming closer.

He clasps my wrist and pulls me roughly towards him. I am shaking. Shaking so hard that I don't even notice that my hand has risen until I hear the slap across his face. In the surprise of it, I turn and run. I run and don't look back. I run until I reach my bike, and then I pedal for my life.

At the hotel, I lock my door. I sit on the starched bed and practice breathing. When the knocking begins, I don't move. As it turns to pounding, I think I say, 'Go away, Sandro. I don't want to see you. Not now. Not ever.'

Perhaps I don't say it. In any event, the noise stops and when I wake the following morning, everything is very still. So still that by mid-afternoon, I dare to emerge from my room. I take a deep breath and slip out of the hotel. I walk. I walk and find myself looking over my shoulder and I chide myself. Then I sit and I gaze out to sea. I try to read but my eyes won't focus on the page, so I watch the waves.

It is then that I see the old man. He is walking alone on the beach. His shoulders are slightly hunched and his trousers are turned up against the surf. The current tugs at him, bounding, pulling, so much vaster, stronger, than the disappearing shore and those pale wavering feet. I have a sudden acute sense of the old man's fragility. I want to run up to him, take his arm, lead him away from the hostile waters.

The old man haunts me that night and the next day I find myself drawn to the very same spot. I wait. I am afraid. I think the sea may already have swallowed him. But after a while, he appears again. His trousers are still rolled up, though his feet seem a little paler. The same odd feeling comes over me, and suddenly I have an image of Sandro as I left him, hunched amidst the pale sands.

Restlessness fills me. I go back to the hotel and try to dispel it but it won't leave me. It is still there the following morning and I know then that I must see Sandro one more time, speak to him, explain if explanation is possible. I don't want to hurt him. Not really. I lie on the beach and try to think what I might say. By mid-afternoon, a sense of urgency takes me over and I can't think any more. My mind is all dull torpor. But my limbs move of their own accord. They impel me towards New York.

I arrive just after eleven, impatient with the Friday-night traffic as my cab prods its way through the streets. Spring Street is completely jammed and I pay off the cabby and walk the remaining block. I think I know as soon as I hear the sirens screeching. A shuddering takes me over. I run. In front of my building, a small crowd has gathered. I push and elbow my way through. I scream, howl, 'Sandro.' And then I see him, lying there on the pavement, his limbs awry, his head in an odd position, one hand stretched out as if in entreaty. The fragile carapace of his body broken.

I don't remember much of the following hours – the leap and thrust of the ambulance, Sandro under a grey blanket beside me; endless questions; Steve suddenly there, taking over, perhaps I phoned him, leading me back to his place; a pool of amber light in a white ceiling; brighter streaks through slats announcing morning, coffee scalding my lips, my feet too white on the floor, the bones too brittle for movement. Sandro's body on the ground. Life as frangible as the porcelain in my hand.

At some point I am aware of Steve speaking. Steve believes in speech, the curative power of talk. He talks. He tells me a story; a tragic story. The word 'tragic' is big on his lips. He tells me a story of a young man full of talent, of dreams, of ambition, of sensitivity, eaten up by the pace of the city, unable to live with the realisation of his dreams, torn apart by their fulfilment, made alien to himself, the new and unaccustomed glittering pressures replacing old familiar problems. He tells me a story of distances crossed, like an immigration from a familiar country to a promised land too rich to bear. He talks and I don't believe him, then I half-believe him, since Steve knows how to talk. At some time it dawns on me that Steve is giving me a story for consumption, a story I will need in order to answer the questions that will inevitably be asked.

Steve and Chuck tell me they will go to the loft and clear out Sandro's things if I like, see that everything is in order, bring me fresh clothes. I am afraid to go with them, yet I am drawn as irresistibly as moth to flame. I have already seen the note. The policeman, whom I gave my keys to, showed it to me on the night, right there on the sidewalk, so that I could confirm it was Sandro's writing. Not that there was much of it. Seven words. 'Too late. Better this way. Loved you,' all under a vast X, which crossed out everything – himself, his life, me. But seven words more than I want Steve to see. More than I wanted to see, too, accompanied by the policeman's cynical shrug.

When I open the door, the loft looks exactly as I left it. I half-expect Sandro to walk towards me with his shy, expectant smile. Only when I move towards my office area do I spy the difference. The sculpture: it has been hacked at, defaced, battered. The nose is missing, the face is mutilated, fingers and penis are gone. Stone litters the floor. Beyond the maimed sculpture, curtains billow. No one has thought to close the window. I turn away, say to Steve, who is shaking his head sadly, that I will wait downstairs. I have the sense that I will never be able to come back here again.

On Monday, I insist that I want to go into the office. Steve tells me I am mad, that I should rest, let myself mourn, weep. I have no tears and I tell him that I don't want to be alone, that there are piles of work waiting for me, that I need to find a new temporary place, arrange for all the stuff in the loft to be stored. I don't know quite what I tell him. My mind isn't working clearly. I am consumed by an emotion I don't recognise. I think it is only later that I name it as guilt.

I sit in my office and stare out of the window. A soft rain is falling. The drops hit the pane and shatter into rivulets before disappearing. Where do they go? I would like to catch them in my hand, but my window won't open. Why is it that the window in my loft opens? I veer away to shuffle papers on my desk. It occurs to me that the telephone hasn't rung all day. I ask Andrea about this and she hugs me softly, confesses that she has been fronting my calls, putting others through to Steve. She looks at me sadly and I do not have the heart to chastise her. I try to busy myself with last week's post, but my head is blank.

It must be the following morning that Steve comes into my office with a harried expression on his face.

'Look, I hate to bother you with this. But we have to talk.' He places an open newspaper on my desk. 'Steel yourself.'

I look to where he points and see the headline, '"Architect Murdered" Wife Claims'. I read. I read and find that Louise Jimenez sees me as a monster, thinks I have killed her husband as deliberately as if I had stabbed him with an eight-inch knife. I read and learn that Sandro Jimenez was a faithful husband and loving father, a dutiful man, a good Catholic, a great architect, and that I smashed up the family, tore him apart and murdered him. I stare at the photograph captioned 'Louise Jimenez' and see a small, pretty woman with dramatic eyes and too much hair.

'She's right,' I say softly. 'I'm a murderer.'

Steve slams his fist on the desk. 'And I'm Napoleon.' He is closer to anger than I have ever seen him. 'Look, I've been fronting for you, but you're gonna have to face the guys and gals of the press yourself tomorrow. Two strategically placed exclusives, I think. That should do it. It's important for all of us.' He waves abstractly at the extent of the office, paces, as if that will focus me. 'Just because Mrs Jimenez has watched "Fatal Attraction" one too many times and swallowed the monster myth, hook, line and stinker, doesn't mean you have to vomit it up too. Got it? Sandro was not Mr Victim of Our Times. He was just one talented macho guy for whom the going got too rough. And you're not Medea and Circe rolled into one. Okay?'

I nod and he sits down again, calmer now. 'The important thing is to remember your Jessica Rabbit.'

'Jessica Rabbit?' For a moment I worry that Steve has gone as awry as I feel.

'Ya. Remember? Roger's wife.' He sketches a perfect hour-glass figure in the air and heaves his chest forward comically. 'Jessica utters the immortal lines, "I'm not really bad. I'm just drawn that way." And you can't allow Signora Jimenez and all our nice scandal-slurping media pals to draw you that way. You gotta do your own drawing. Now here's the picture as I have seen it unfold before my own very wide and open eyes.'

Steve tells me the tragic story he began to tell me a few days before, but this time the love interest comes into play. He tells the story convincingly and if I didn't know the pretty lady in the cast too well, tears would be clutching at my eyes. He underlines that Sandro never told me of his marriage, that I tried to break it off, that the poor man felt trapped, that we both suffered. 'And don't forget the good that's come of it all. The reclamation scheme. Most people don't get to do that much in a whole uninterrupted lifetime. Clear?' He glares at me, all his strength of will in his eyes.

I nod, but the only thing I can think of is that interrupted lifetime and how I interrupted it.

Over the next days I play the part Steve has assigned me. I must play it well, for Steve is pleased with the result. I don't read the articles, not the exclusives or any of the others. I don't do very much, unless Steve orders me to. Mostly I stare out of the window. I am numb. Sometimes, I imagine what it might be like to make that leap. I look at my hands, at my feet, and see only brittleness.

At the funeral I wear a veil and hold Steve's arm and wish I were invisible. I haven't wanted to come. I cannot bear to think of Sandro's body in that box. I cannot bear the gawking eyes, the looks of pity or suspicion, the pointing fingers. There are two distinct groups in the cemetery, the people from the project, and the people from our side of town – a few friends and supporters, a few journalists. I do not like the glances either group casts my way. Valeria and José can barely restrain their hostility and march past me with their chins high. Carmen stops to squeeze my arm, but rushes away. I realise why a moment later as a small woman steps up to me and tears the veil from my face. 'That's her,' she shouts. 'Murderer. Bitch.' She starts to pummel my chest. I don't know whether it is those fists or the sound of a camera's click, but I push her, push her hard, as if I were once again a girl in a schoolground. A child shrieks and I see a small face, Sandro's face, atop a pudgy body held by an old man, and then Steve is pulling me away, urging me towards the car.

Two days later, the letters start, raging, raving, incoherent, but clear enough in their intent. Like furies in ceaseless pursuit, they proclaim me a murderer.

My dreams corroborate the claim. In the nondescript furnished studio I have rented, I dream of Sandro. We are standing in the loft. I hold a hammer and I am hacking slowly, deliberately, at the sculpture he has given me. He looks at me sadly then walks towards the window, hoists himself up onto the ledge, lifts his hand towards me. I can take it, save him. I don't. I walk towards him menacingly and in a harsh voice mutter, 'Jump'. There are many variations on this dream. Sometimes Sandro is hanging from the ledge and I prise his fingers away, one by one, until he drops. Sometimes, his hand is clutching my wrist and he pulls me with him, but I grasp at the fire escape and kick him away, watch him tumble. Once, I kiss him softly and smile before I say, 'Go'. I wake from these dreams shivering, wreathed in perspiration. And I cry. I cry as I have never cried before.

At the office, I wait for those letters to arrive, read them obsessively, then tear them up into tiny pieces as if this could eradicate the murder. I cannot work. I have neither the courage nor confidence to convince anyone I might ring of anything. When Steve forces me to come to openings or events with him, I am only aware of the voices gossiping behind my back, the false little gasps of sympathy, the fingers too smooth on my shoulder or arm.

One day Steve tells me I really have to have a holiday, a change of some kind. I look at him for what feels like a long time and then I say, 'You're right, Steve. I'm no good to anyone. I think I need to leave, go somewhere else. You'll have to find someone to replace me, buy me out.'

'You're not serious?'

'I'm serious.'

He tries to convince me otherwise, but having said it, it is now the single thing I know for certain. I must leave New York.

It takes some months to sort matters out, but the knowledge that I shall soon be gone makes activity possible. And in the activity, brick by brick, a wall begins to appear around my life with Sandro, a part of myself entombed like him, dead, unreachable because I cannot allow myself to reach it. Just before it is finally in place and I leave, I go to visit his grave. It is early morning, I don't want to see anybody, and there is a chill in the air. The leaves swirl round as bright and carefree as they were on the day Sandro first appeared in my office.

The tomb is plain stone and on top of it, by some macabre irony, someone has chosen to place the winged figure Sandro chiselled of me. It still doesn't look like me, but it weighs down his tomb as heavily as I weighed on his life. I stand and stare at the grave until my legs and eyes seem to have grown into it. I think I say I'm sorry. I know I make a vow. I will do penance. There will be no more hazardous affairs of the heart and the body. I will expiate my guilt.

When I get home, I send a note to the padre at the mission, together with a cheque, the proceeds of which I ask him to give to Sandro's family. I do not feel particularly better. Writing a cheque is not a difficult thing to do. Living is harder.

⚖ 26

Sun slants through the window and falls on the graceful sandalled feet of the walking woman. From the position of the light, I know it must be late afternoon. What I don't know is how long I have sat here, paced, dreamt my life with Sandro. I am wearing a white towelling robe I don't recall having donned. The pockets are stuffed with soggy tissues and there is a half-empty mug on the table in front of me, so at some point I must have cried, must have made some coffee. The bed, when I look at it, is rumpled, so perhaps I slept.

On the floor, by the sofa, lie the pages of Louise Jimenez's letter. Like a more powerful force, she has found me out in my distant shelter. The line of defence I constructed with Andrea – the instruction to return all envelopes bearing that inimitable script with a Forwarding Address Unknown – has been broken. There is no easy escape from my past, no way of eradicating it forever.

I pick up the letter and glance at the all-too-familiar opening curse, read the first lines again: 'One year. Three-hundred-sixty-five days since you killed him. And I bet you think you got away. But I'll never let you get away. Never.'

Suddenly I wish I could do something to assuage Louise's pain, still so raw after all this passage of time. Would it make any difference if I answered her? Proclaimed a truce? Told her suffering was not hers alone, that I too had had my life ruptured? No. I let the letter slip through my fingers. Words will not bring Sandro back, Juanito's father as she often calls him; and maybe Louise needs to carry on hating me so that she doesn't have to hate herself.

I sink into the armchair and memories of Sandro take me over again. I no longer know if their dizzying poignancy is accurate. Ends shape beginnings and middles. And at the end there is only Sandro's fractured body, his interrupted life. Whatever slice of the story I cut into, it races inexorably towards that single material truth. And my guilt, judged by Louise Jimenez and the popular jury of the press, but never in a courtroom. Perhaps a courtroom would have been preferable.

I doze. I must doze, for I dream. I am scaling the façade of a building, brick by brick. My hands are bloody, the skin scraped from them. I will never get to the top where I once lived. No one can help me, not even the man who stretches out his hand through a window.

The sound of a buzzer presses itself into my consciousness and for a moment I think I am in the loft and Sandro is at the door – back then before he had any keys. Only when I get up and the bell isn't where it should be do I realise I am in Paris and there is no reason for the ringing. But the bell is insistent and to stop its sound, I mumble a 'Oui' into the intercom.

'Maria. At last.'

It takes me a while to recognise Paul's voice and then I can't find mine.

'Let me up.'

'I can't.'

'What's wrong?'

'Nothing. I'm all right. Really.'

There is no answering sound and for a moment I sigh with relief. Then I hear the unmistakeable click of the elevator and seconds later he is there pounding at the door in front of me. I open it. He stares at me.

'You're ill.'

I imagine what I must look like with my tangled hair and my red nose and Steve's old robe, and I nod.

'Why didn't you ring in, tell us?' He closes the door behind him, examines me with those intelligent eyes. 'I've been worried sick, thought you'd gone, thought . . . I've been phoning. Madame Duval's been phoning. No answer. For days.'

'Days?'

I shouldn't have said that, I realise, for he is staring at me again, looking round the apartment. He puts his arm over my shoulder.

'Three days, Maria,' he says softly and with such concern that tears leap into my eyes.

'Three days,' I repeat stupidly. 'I had no idea. I'm sorry. Sorry.' I am crying and I have to fish into my pocket for those soggy tissues. 'Can I get you some coffee? A drink?' I burble through tears, hide my face.

'I'll get it.' He urges me into the sofa, picks up stray cups, letters that have fallen on the floor, the letter. Do I imagine that his eyes skirt over it before he places it neatly on the pile? I hear him opening cupboards in the kitchen, slamming the fridge. 'There's no food here,' he calls out to me. 'Haven't you been eating either?'

He comes out with a brandy bottle, glasses, a pitcher of water, peanuts I didn't know existed and which must be staler than my breath. He hands me a glass and goes to the telephone. I hear him identify himself, give my address, place an order for what sounds like a mountain of food.

Then he sits down opposite me. 'Okay, now tell me what's happened.'

'I have flu.'

'Flu? In May? Tell me another story.'

'Maybe it's hay fever, then.'

His eyebrows arch in scepticism. 'Maria, I may not be a doctor, but I'm pretty good at knowing which approximations of the truth are closer to the real thing than others. So I'm going to sit here until you tell me something I can begin to believe.'

'Why?'

'What do you mean, why?'

'Why are you doing this?'

'You know why.' He looks at me with a directness which makes me shiver. 'I care for you,' he says softly. He doesn't touch me, but it is like a caress.

'Can I have one?' I ask as he takes out a pack of cigarettes.

'Remedy for hay fever, is it?' He leans back into the sofa. 'Well?'

The cigarette makes me dizzy. I stub it out, cough. 'Will you excuse me for a minute.'

I go to the bathroom. I wash my face. I brush my hair. I look at myself. I look terrible. I jab on some lipstick, see my clothes heaped on the floor of the bedroom, put them on and still look terrible. Good, I think. I walk back to him, sit down. 'Okay,' I say. 'You want a story you can believe. Here it is. I killed a man. And I got away with it. Scot-free.'

I watch him watching me. I don't know how long he watches me, but there is no expression I can read on his face. At last he says, 'What weapon did you use?'

I have forgotten I am dealing with a lawyer. I laugh. 'Does it make a difference?'

'A big difference to what I decide to believe.'

'I used love,' I say. My voice is hard, grates even my ears. 'And then the lack of love.'

His eyes do not leave my face. 'A powerful weapon in the right hands,' he acknowledges. 'But in that case, too many of us are murderers. Mothers, fathers, husbands, wives, siblings – we would have to turn the whole country into a prison. Luckily the courts don't judge metaphor.'

'I am not talking metaphor, Maître Arnault. I am talking real bodies. One dead body in particular.' Suddenly my voice breaks and I start to weep. He is beside me, stroking my hair as if I were a child.

'Suicide,' he murmurs.

'But with a very active accomplice,' I blurt through my tears.

'It sometimes feels like that, I know.'

He is silent while I wipe my eyes. Then he continues, 'But it's also sometimes meant to feel like that. A violent act performed not only against oneself, but against those around one.' He pauses to look at me, but I won't look back and he goes on. 'Self-murder used to be considered a crime not so very long ago, but as far as I know there were never any accomplices named.'

'This one was named.' I don't know why I am suddenly angry, but I am and I take Louise's letter and thrust it at him. 'Here,' I say rudely. 'Practise your English.' I rush from the room. I pour cold water over my face again. I sit on the edge of the bed. I wait. I suddenly wish that he would come in here after me and shake me hard, slap my face.

Instead, when I finally go into the living room, he isn't there and my face tingles as if the slap had happened. Maître Arnault has judged me. I am not worth the confession he encouraged me to make. I should feel relieved. I laugh out loud, sit down with a thump so that the springs of the sofa squeal.

His face, as it suddenly appears from behind the kitchen door, scares me. 'Food's here. When you're ready.'

I jump up. 'I thought you'd gone,' I mumble.

'And I've told you before that I am well brought up and I usually say goodbye before I leave.'

He is watching me again, watching me as I take in the spread on the table which seems to include everything in a *traiteur*'s window, smoked salmon and langoustine and little pastry shells stuffed with green.

'I imagine you haven't eaten properly for days. And you need to eat. You're light-headed.'

'Is that the name for it?' I mutter, but I smile and tuck in. It occurs to me that I am ravenous.

'Not too fast.' He gives me a worried glance. 'And there's another course in the oven.'

I slow down and after a few more mouthfuls, gaze up at him. 'So?'

'So . . .' He knows what I mean. 'So if my English serves me, there's a wife and child in the case. Which explains a great deal.' He gives me a look which brings a flush to my face, and holds my hand for a moment. 'A very great deal. But it only gives me a fragment of the story. I'd like to hear the rest.'

Silence falls between us. In it I can hear myself chewing. I swallow hard. The food is suddenly as distasteful as my own story, but I start to tell him anyway, bluntly, coldly, so that I can get it over with quickly. It will be just as well if he hates me by its end. I do not look at him while I speak. I tell him about Sandro, how he falls in love with the glittering mannequin who can help him wheel and deal his way to his dreams. I tell him a little about the project and less about my work. I tell him how the glittering mannequin is glitteringly cruel; how she cannot cope with difficulties and rejects that love once Sandro has cut himself off from his family, his base. I tell him how an already broken Sandro topples from a window. I sit there and wait for him to say something, but he doesn't say anything for a long time.

'Well?' I demand when I can stand the silence no longer.

'Well, as a murder confession, it doesn't wash, Maria. No prosecutor would take you on. Not enough of a motive.' He gives me a funny half-smile. 'And as a personal confession, it doesn't altogether wash either. I can't find you in it. You were there, weren't you?'

I get up and start to clatter plates away into the dishwasher. Paul talks over it and I want to cut him off. 'You did love this man, didn't you? So when did it start to go wrong? Did he do something? Did you? Did he hit you? Did he defile you? Did you start sleeping with other men? Did you tell him his work stank? Did you goad him? Did you suggest he kill himself? Open the window? Push him?'

'All of those things,' I mumble. And then I turn on Paul, lash out as vehemently as if he were Sandro and my anger had just been born.

'He betrayed me, deceived. Lied to me. About his wife. And he started to hate me. He didn't understand why, but he hated me. And himself. And I hated him too, wanted revenge. He placed me on a pedestal and we both hammered at it until it toppled.' I am screaming. I try to moderate my tone. 'It was all tangled up. Love and hatred. Jealousy and love and hatred. A trap. And I wanted him gone.' I rush from the room.

He is right behind me. His hand is on my shoulder, restraining me. 'Guilt is a very bitter emotion, Maria,' he whispers. 'Punishment sometimes relieves it. Haven't you punished yourself enough yet?'

I meet his eyes. They are sombre. They understand too much and it occurs to me that this is my punishment. I would like to love Paul. I would like to touch his face now. I would like to curl into bed with him, feel the smoothness of his chest. But I can't. Sandro has stolen a part of me away, buried it with him in the grave. That part of me that dares, that is bold, that flaunts fate, that cares nothing about tomorrow, about others. He has stolen that and in its place given me fear, a sense of mortality. I am angry with him. I do not want this awareness of the fragility of things.

Perhaps Paul knows, for he holds me very close for a moment.

'Thank you for coming to find me,' I say.

He nods, kisses me lightly on the forehead. 'Just carry on being angry. It helps sometimes. And if you're not in the office tomorrow morning, I'm coming along with the fire brigade.'

'Not tomorrow.' I demur. 'I'm not up to it yet. Friday.'

'Friday, then.' He looks at me and I think he is going to kiss me and I am going to have to move away. But he doesn't. He just looks at me, smooths my hair softly away from my face. A sad little smile curls his lips. 'Don't be too hard on yourself,' he says and then he is gone.

That night I do not dream of Sandro. I dream of Paul instead. But he isn't Paul, he is a judge in scarlet robes and I am in the dock. But when I look round the courtroom, I am in the prosecutor's chair as well. I know it is me, though the face is Beatrice's and the face is speaking words I cannot hear, speaking for a long time until the judge interrupts. 'Insufficient evidence,' he proclaims, and I stand up in the dock. There is a rumble in the courtroom. I see I am wearing only a white towelling robe and suddenly with the gestures of a stripper I take it off, throw it towards Paul, but he is already gone and the prosecutor, everyone, is pointing at me and I am afraid. I laugh. Or cry.

The sound wakes me and I lie in bed until the dream traces evaporate. Then I lie there some more and try once again to pull together the pieces of my life. One of my mother's accounts books comes to mind and I list the pluses and minuses. On the plus side, I have work which fascinates me, a friend found again in Beatrice, a lovely apartment, a daily life which is more than bearable. And Paul, who must count as a friend as well, to whom I have bared myself, who has judged me and not found me a monster. That is a definite plus. It makes me more tolerable to myself. On the minus side, there is an enormous debt which can never be repaid in kind, but which through work, through a kind of penance, I may be able to convert into a plus.

I suddenly feel light. I leap out of bed, remembering smaller but significant debts, to Steve whose apartment I must scrub and polish so that it is ready for him. I will do that today and buy him a present, something to be left here in anticipation of his arrival. To Beatrice, whose language class I utterly forgot about yesterday. I will ring with an apology, invite her out to the theatre, one of those treats she has told me she has too few of; perhaps offer to look after Marie-Françoise for a day, so that she can treat herself.

As I change linen and scrub and polish and dust and tidy, I make a host of resolutions and the activity, the resolutions, in turn fill me with energy. While I shower, it occurs to me that perhaps after my work with Paul is finished, I might train as a lawyer. Not criminal law, no, but something more ordinary. Immigration law. I will speak to Tanya about it, to Beatrice, perhaps even to Paul. I am filled with plans. I imagine myself as Jennifer Walters, a briefcase under my arm.

By mid-afternoon the apartment sparkles and I am ready to go home. On the way I browse in bookshops and boutiques, looking for something for Steve. The day has taken on a holiday feeling. It is warm and the pavement terraces are crowded with animated faces. I pause in front of a man's shop. The mannequin in the window wears a plantation suit, the lightest of beige on white stripes, loose trousers, a panama. I have an irresistible urge to try it on and succumb to it, despite the shop assistant's barely controlled surprise. The suit makes me happy, the hat, as I tuck my hair beneath it, even more so. I laugh, posture in front of the glass, find a pale yellow shirt, am told trousers, sleeves, can be taken in and up within the hour.

I sit in a café and spoon frothy milk into my mouth, down pungent coffee, and set off to scour some more boutiques. In the Rue du Dragon, I find a long thin shop with a bizarre assortment of bric-a-brac, amongst which stands a green ironwork reindeer, some two feet high, its antlers tapering into candle-holders. I know instantly that Steve and Chuck, who have an eye for artful kitsch, will adore him. While the owner wraps the reindeer, I spy a small bronze figurine, scales in one hand, sword in the other. Justice, yet without the blindfold. The face is wise, peaceful, and the figure is altogether too rounded and charming – a soft, compliant justice. I hold her. She is only a little larger than the palm of my hand. For Paul, I think, who has been a merciful judge. I lug my purchases back to the man's shop, try on my suit and decide to wear it straight away. As I reach in my bag for my chequebook, my fingers touch the soft silk of the scarf Paul gave me in London. I tie it round my neck. A talisman.

On the street, a taxi has just dropped someone off and I leap into it. The reindeer can go to Steve's apartment straight away. I know exactly where it will stand.

When I get out of the cab, there is a man hovering in front of the entrance. He is half-hidden by a bouquet of flowers and I do not recognise him until he steps towards me.

'Another fifteen minutes and it might well have been fire-brigade time.'

I smile. 'I've been out.'

'So I can see. And I thought you might be in and not letting anyone else in.' He grimaces, then grins as he holds open the door of the lift. 'Hello. You look ravishing.'

'I feel better too. Thank you. For yesterday, I mean.'

'Thank you for wearing this.' He touches the scarf at my throat.

Our eyes meet and in that small cramped space the leap of mutual desire is too palpable. I look away.

'And you've been working,' he says as we go into the pristine apartment.

'I'm sorry you had to see it all in such a mess yesterday.'

'I'm not.' He squeezes my shoulder. 'The mess isn't separate from the rest, Maria. And better in the front room than hidden away in a dusty cellar where it's too hard to get at.'

I know he is telling me something, but I don't want to hear it now. I take off my hat, shake out my hair.

'And presto. She's a woman again.' He bows comically, hands me the bouquet.

'Did you ever have any doubts?' I laugh as I tear open paper, bury my face in sweet-smelling stock, pink and white and purple.

'Not on that score. Never.' There is a rough edge to his voice and I turn away. 'Maria, I . . .'

'I've got something for you too.' I burrow in my bag, bring out the small wrapped package. 'And we need some drinks. A vase.' I rush into the safety of the kitchen. I feel so open, so exposed to him today that the test his presence sets is almost unbearable. I want to reach out and hold him, be held. I take a deep breath, a second, go back to the salon. He is gazing at the statuette.

'Do you like her?'

'She's very fine. And it's nice to be able to look back into her eyes and argue. A placable justice,' he laughs, 'muse of defence lawyers.'

'You did such a good job yesterday of defending me to myself.'

'So you know it isn't a life sentence? You can come out of prison whenever you decide.'

I hand him a glass. 'I'd rather not talk about it today.'

'Okay.' He gives me a soft smile. 'Do you feel up to some work? There's a poem Jennifer once sent me that I came across again recently. I'd like to use it. Do you think you can help with the translation?'

'I can try.'

He hands me two sheets of photocopied paper. 'It's by W.H. Auden. "Law Like Love". Read it out to me. I'd like to hear it as it should sound.'

I look at him and I know the poem is another covert message, like the chapter of the book I read last week.

'Go on,' he urges and I read, read the mounting whimsy and doggerel brilliance of Auden's commentary on the Law – of law defined in disparate and interested ways – by gardeners as the sun, by 'impotent grandfathers' as the 'wisdom of the old', by their grandchildren as 'the senses of the young', by the priest as the words in his priestly book, by the judge . . .

'Read the stanza about the judge again,' Paul chortles.

> 'Law, says the judge as he looks down his nose,
>   Speaking clearly and most severely,
>   Law is as I've told you before,

Law is as you know I suppose,
Law is but let me explain it once more,
Law is The Law.'

'Sounds just like my father,' he chuckles. 'And now the next one, about the scholars.'

'Yet law-abiding scholars write:
Law is neither wrong nor right,
Law is only crimes
Punished by places and by times,
Law is the clothes men wear
Anytime, anywhere,
Law is Good-morning and Good-night.'

Two stanzas later, the poem's tone changes. The irony is still there, but lyricism steps in as the lover addresses his beloved and timidly, wryly, hazards a wonderful conceit, another definition certainly as good as the others.

'Like love I say.
Like love we don't know where or why,
Like love we can't compel or fly,
Like love we often weep,
Like love we seldom keep.'

I have been so intent on the poem and its translation that I haven't been aware of Paul's growing closeness, his arm around my waist.

I turn my face to him. 'You understand all this too well,' I murmur. 'It's just a ploy.'

'Not a ploy. I want you to understand it too. Share it with me.'

He kisses me and it is as if he hasn't stopped speaking, but the taste is stronger, like the last stanza of the poem, and I have to answer back, the argument is too compelling. And with it comes something I don't recognise, something fresh, like plump green buds. Perhaps it is hope.

When I finally edge my lips away, he holds fast to me, whispers in my ear, 'I'm glad you're still there, Maria. I was afraid yesterday, this last week, all those weeks you were away . . . I might have lost you.'

'I won't . . .'

'Shhh.' He puts a finger over my lips. 'Listen. I've thought about what you told me yesterday. Twisted it and turned it, tried to feel what you might have felt. And you can't condemn yourself. You can't give up on life until life gives up on you. Or love. You've decided you're dangerous – to others, to yourself. But not everyone is Mr Jimenez. I'm not. Nor would I hurt you, never like that. Trust me.'

The logic is as compelling as his touch. But I don't want it to work on me. Not here, where the ghost of Sandro has been so vivid in these last days. Not yet either. I have not paid my dues. And that unrepresented third party hovers in the wings, all the more threatening because I know I already care for Paul far too much.

'I'd like you to go now, Paul,' I say softly. My voice breaks in a way I don't want it to.

'Why?'

'It's too soon.'

'All right.' He gathers up his papers slowly, holds the little statuette in his hand as if he is weighing its density. When he looks up at me, his expression is wistful. 'Don't let it be too soon forever, Maria. Life isn't that long.'

I want to turn away so as not to have to meet the sadness in his eyes, but his hand grips my arm. 'It's because of my wife, isn't it? You're afraid.'

'That too.'

'Of course. That woman must have made your life hell.' He looks around the room as if he is considering something, then turns back to me. 'One day, when we have a lot of time, I'll tell you about my wife, Maria. She's a remarkable woman. And about our relationship. I think you'll see, every story is individual. Unique. But perhaps I need to trust you a little more first as well.'

I flinch at this, yet realise there is very little reason why he should trust me. I have taken his love and sent him away. I have taken his understanding, his friendship, and given him only unhappiness in return.

'I'd like to earn your trust,' I say.

He ruffles my hair, smiles. 'I shouldn't think that will be an insurmountable task.'

I kiss him. His lips are warm. They taste of life. I need life. I have been living with shadows for too long. And his eyes when I look into them are vivid, present. 'Soon,' I murmur.

He holds me close. The face he turns on me is filled with elation. He laughs. 'I feel as if I've just won the second most important case in my life.'

'Only the second?' I tease him, happy too in this new mood. 'And what was the first?'

'I'll try and remember it when the soon comes.' He meets my tone.

It's when we are standing by the door, loath to say goodbye, that the words pop out, surprising even me. 'Paul, do you think I'm too old to train? As a lawyer, I mean.'

He doesn't answer for a moment and I babble, 'Ridiculous notion, I guess.'

He laughs his boyish laugh. 'Not at all. Brilliant idea. Even if it ends up by dulling your vision.' He winks. 'You've been bitten by the justice bug. That's wonderful. I'll dig out all the documentation for you. Tomorrow, if I can. We're meeting at three as usual, right?'

I nod.

He pauses, looks at me with momentary concern. 'You'll be all right here? You won't panic? You'll have pleasant dreams?'

I smile at him. 'I'll be all right. I'll dream about Mr Auden and law like love and growing into a black gown with a little lace kerchief.'

He squeezes my hand. 'That sounds just the thing. Though I wish I could be with you.'

⚖ 27

Friday dawns as bright and fresh as if I were once again an eighteen-year-old aware only of the present and a tempting expanse of future. The streets shimmer moistly after their morning scrubbing. The chestnuts dance in robes of deep green and as I cross the river at the Pont du Carrousel, a hurdy-gurdy man churns out a sprightly air. I empty my change purse for him so that he can feel as light as I do.

In the office, Madame Duval is as solicitous as if I had just recovered from a major illness. 'Don't let the Maître work you so hard,' she says to me with the closest thing I have ever seen in her to a gesture of complicity. 'It doesn't matter if the book takes a few months longer. These men, they get so obsessional.'

I nod sagely and she adds, 'And he's late himself this morning. Rang in to say he had a few errands to run, so he won't be coming in until this afternoon.' She looks down her notepad. 'You're scheduled for three. So make sure you have a proper lunch.'

At the corner of the long table which is my desk stands a pot of daisies with a note from Madame Duval. 'To cheer up the subject matter'. Decidedly I am in Madame Duval's good books and I have no idea what I have done to deserve this. Nonetheless, it makes me happy and I settle into work with more energy than I can remember. Something in me has been released, some dusty threatening corner opened to sunlight and I can bring all of myself to the tasks at hand. Even Tanya notices when we share a lunchtime baguette.

'You look a whole lot better than you did last Friday. Someone hand you a big fat cheque? Or is it just sleep?'

'Pleasant dreams.' I smile at her. 'Why don't you come round on Sunday and see my new place. It's almost ready for visitors.'

The invitation seems to surprise her even more than it surprises me. I don't think I've realised quite how secretive I've grown.

'Sure. Though next Sunday might be better. I'd half-planned a trip to Chantilly.'

'Next Sunday then.'

I give Tanya the address and note that I must give it to Madame Duval and Paul as well. I have stopped hiding.

Paul arrives promptly at three. He is wearing a deep blue suit which brings out the colour of his eyes and he smiles at me with such evident pleasure that I feel like telling him, Cole Porter fashion, that he's the tops, he's the Coliseum, the Louvre Museum, Fred Astaire, camembert and all the rest of those peaks, so outrageously rhymed.

He puts a pile of books on my desk and embraces me. 'I know, not in the office. But just today. Today is special. Because you're here. Because you've made decisions. Because . . .'

'Because you're piling on the work,' I laugh at him.

He kisses me and I know I shouldn't be doing this, but I am and it feels good, it feels wonderful. And I think to myself that maybe his wife really is remarkable and that I'm just destined to be the other woman. And then I don't think anything very much at all until we move apart.

'We should go away together for a few days, Maria. Somewhere warm. In the sun.'

I imagine pine-fragrant evenings with him, the chirruping of cicadas, strolls in moonlight, the distant sound of waves.

'Soon,' I mouth at him, clear the ache in my throat, shake myself. 'First, I imagine I have to get through all those books you happen to have dumped on my desk?'

He chuckles. 'Those, my lovely lawyer-in-waiting, are your work, not mine. Though I might help you just a little with it if you like. It looks quite daunting.'

I glance down at the top volume and see *Faculté de Droit* printed in large black letters. 'Course brochures! How kind of you.'

'Wait till you've read them before you say that. In the meantime . . .'

'In the meantime, we've got a mass of stuff to get through.'

'Don't be in too much of a hurry. I don't want you disappearing out of my life.'

'I'm not planning to disappear.' I meet his eyes and the pull is so strong that, almost, I reach out to touch him again.

'Good.' There is a hoarse edge to his voice. 'That makes me very happy.'

We look at each other in silence until, with an abrupt gesture, I force myself to turn to my list.

'Have you had a chance to go through my notes on the Martha Roberts trial yet, Maître?' I ask with an attempt at Madame Duval's brisk efficiency.

'Barely. Shall we do that first?'

I nod and we begin to work, work avidly as the excitement of the material takes us over. I feel strangely free with him now: I can say anything because he knows what there is to know about me. It makes our arguments doubly exhilarating.

At one point, he is almost angry, shouting: 'Why are you so keen on punishment, so averse to reasons? Isn't ostracism, a fractured life, punishment enough? You'll end up a prosecutor if you're not careful.'

I flush. 'But Jennifer Walters said herself that . . .'

The phone rings and I reach to answer it.

'Madame Duval for you.'

He picks up the receiver and mouths a mocking kiss at me.

'Oh, of course. Send them up.' He turns back to me, smiles. 'I hadn't realised it was so late. My children have arrived. I'd like you to meet them.'

My mouth drops so far down, I think I will have to scrape it off the floor.

He laughs. 'Don't be afraid, Maria. They're nice. Usually that is.'

I don't have time to say anything before there is a knock at the door, quickly followed by a thin sandy-haired boy in jeans and denim jacket. He is at the awkward age and he stands looking from one to the other of us, unsure whether to cross the threshold or run.

'Come in, Nicolas,' Paul encourages him.

'Wait for me,' a voice pipes from the stairwell, and a little girl bursts into the room.

I stare at her and blink and stare again. Dark hair, a heart-shaped face, a navy-blue frock with a white collar.

Somewhere beside me I am aware that Paul is embracing the boy.

'And this is Maria d'Esté,' I hear him say and I shake Nicolas's hand, but my eyes are still on the girl.

'I've already met Maria,' the girl says shyly, then bounds into her father's arms.

'Hello, Marie-Françoise,' I murmur, not sure whether my voice will even allow that much speech.

She gives me a soft peck on either cheek and goes back to her father. 'You know each other?' Paul asks, a smile of delight on his face.

'I met Maria with Maman. And she brought me the most yummy flaky chocolate from London. In a big box. And I haven't said thank you yet. And she said she would take me out for ice cream.'

'I see.' Paul's face mingles astonishment and trepidation. I don't know what mine reveals but I have the distinct feeling that in a moment I might burst into tears.

'Yes,' I say, gathering up my papers so I won't have to look at him. 'Beatrice is my oldest friend. From schooldays.'

'How very extraordinary. I had no idea.'

'Is Maria coming to dinner with us?' Marie-Françoise asks. 'It would be nice. Since Maman couldn't come.'

'Why don't you and Nicolas invite her.' Paul's voice is odd. 'It would be grand. If she's free.'

'Oh yes, come.' Marie-Françoise is far more forthcoming than when I last saw her. 'It's Papa's birthday and we always take him to his favourite restaurant.'

'I don't think I . . .'

'Oh, please. It'll be more like a party if you come. You ask her, Nicolas.'

The boy shuffles his feet and gives me an embarrassed look. 'We're going to the Colbert. Food is tops.' He garbles his words, gets them over quickly.

'Well, that's decided then.' Paul is suddenly definitive. 'Now you two run downstairs and talk to Madame Duval while we finish up in here. Five minutes. No more.'

He waits until the door is closed, then takes my hand. 'I really don't know what to say, Maria. Beatrice never mentioned you. I . . . She never comes here. She doesn't like lawyers.' He laughs strangely.

I wrench my hand away from him. I feel as if the world I had just begun to put into place block by careful block has toppled. Like one of those over-reaching children's towers, the foundations weren't sound. I wasn't sound and this is my punishment. Beatrice and Paul. Paul and Beatrice. My friend and the man I have let myself love. Not separate sustaining columns in my life, but one unit, so that the new roof comes crashing down round my head. And I can't even be angry. Beatrice deserves him, this handsome, passionate and compassionate man, with his quicksilver intelligence. This man of integrity. Beatrice merits him. And he her.

'Beatrice your childhood friend.' Paul is musing. 'And you kept in touch over all these years. Funny that she never said anything.'

I can't tell whether he is more distressed by the revelation or by the fact that Beatrice has never told him. 'We only met again this year, after a long time,' I murmur. I gaze out the window. Sunlight sparkles over silver rooftops. In the distance I can see the blue-uniformed guard at his post behind the Elysée Palace. The world goes on.

'You know it has to be over now, Paul. I'll have to leave. The job. You. I can't do that to Beatrice. Your remarkable wife. My friend.' A strangled laugh comes to my throat.

'No.' He grips my wrist, forces me to look at him. He looks weary, bruised. He looks the way I feel. 'No, there's no need. It's not the moment for decisions. And it's my birthday.' He tries a smile which goes wrong at the edges.

'I know. I'm coming to your party, tomorrow night.'

'So you're the mysterious old friend who's sitting between Albert and Jean-François. I think Beatrice was saving you as a surprise for me. I'll have to tell her . . .'

'No, I'll tell her. I'll ring her as soon as I get home.'

'Which will be just after dinner tonight.'

He holds up his hand as I start to protest. 'No, please, Maria. First for Marie-Françoise's sake. She's been a little unhappy of late, I don't know quite why, and this is the first time for ages I've seen her bubble. Then for my sake – because I can't bear the thought of you going off and feeling miserable and hating me. Then for Nicolas's sake, because he doesn't like having to talk to me too much and having a beautiful woman there might make him cheerful. Finally . . .'

'Aren't you ready yet, Papa?' Marie-Françoise bursts in through the door. 'It's much more than five minutes. Much.'

'Yes, my little Miss, we're ready.'

'Oh, good.' She claps her hands. 'And Maria is coming too.'

I go with them. I don't know how not to. Marie-Françoise has her hand firmly in mine and she is telling me with great enthusiasm and in systematic order the chocolates she likes best. First the ones I gave her, then white chocolate with those little nuts all crunchy in the middle. Then praline. The list takes us almost to the Palais-Royal.

Paul and Nicolas walk ahead of us, the boy ambling self-consciously, surreptitiously seeking his image in shop windows, edging uncomfortably away when his father places a hand on his shoulder.

'And you can have all of your chocolates at once now that Lent is over.'

Marie-Françoise screws up her little serious face. 'Oh, no. Maman won't let me. She says I'm too greedy. And I don't like keeping Lent but she says I have to, because I'm so greedy.'

'I see. Well, your teeth will be the happier for it.'

'I could get false ones. Like Grandmaman. Once I saw them in a glass by her bed.'

We have reached the entrance of the Palais-Royal with its striped columns of varying sizes set out above and below ground for some mad Alice in Wonderland game, and suddenly Marie-Françoise releases my hand, races away.

'Papa, Papa. You have to make a wish. For your birthday. In the stream.'

Paul catches the child in his arms and lifts her up over his head, twirling her round. I notice the grim cast of Nicolas's features and I walk over to him. 'I think we could all do with a wish,' I say, and open my bag.

Paul stays my hand, distributes a mass of small coins. 'Okay, altogether now. Wishes come as soon as you land a coin on the column.'

It isn't easy. At first all our coins bounce off and fall into the stream beneath. These are wishes one needs skill and patience for. Then Paul and I and Nicolas manage to land one each. I tell Marie-Françoise she can share my wish and we all close our eyes. As I close mine, I think of the other wishes I have made and Beatrice's presence in them and I know my wishing days have come full circle and this time I can't wish Beatrice away, however much I may want to, and that is the name of retribution. Beatrice and Paul together. My just deserts at last. This is my punishment. And my penance. So I wish with as much honesty as I can muster that they will both be happy, and I squeeze Marie-Françoise's hand.

I open my eyes to see Paul looking at me wistfully and I suspect he knows my wish, but I walk ahead with Nicolas. That is why I am here, after all, for the children, and I try to find conversation which might take the boy out of himself. I remember my first walk through this park when I had just landed in Paris all those months ago, and I tell him how Charlotte Corday purchased a knife just there in the Arcade, a knife with which she murdered Marat. I can't work out whether the names mean anything to him but his eyes light up at the word 'murder' and he asks me whether I've seen 'Reservoir Dogs', which his parents won't let him see, and I know that for five minutes at least I'll have his undivided attention. But then Paul calls to us, interrupting the flow, and tells us to look back at the fountain.

There is a gaggle of boys gathered round it. One of them has a stick with a line tied to its end and at the bottom of the line there is what I realise is a magnet with which to fish up coins.

'Redistributive justice at work,' Paul laughs. 'It's the quickest form I've seen yet.'

Yes, I think to myself. That is what is happening now. To Beatrice and to me. And perhaps through Beatrice to Louise Jimenez and to all those women I have wronged. Justice redistributed more equably at last. No running this time. I will pay my dues. And in this new order perhaps I will at last learn, when I least want to, what it means to put my own desires last.

The restaurant is large and airy with globe lamps and white tablecloths and old-fashioned fans whirling slowly round the ceiling. I sit next to Paul but don't look at him. I face Nicolas and Marie-Françoise and I exert myself into cheerfulness, woo them with stories, am rewarded with giggles from Marie-Françoise and the occasional unwilling smile from Nicolas. He is an inward child, unresponsive, and it is something of an uphill struggle, though Marie-Françoise manages to get through to him.

At one point, she announces proudly in response to nothing at all, that Nicolas can talk to fax machines. 'Show them, Nicolas.' She prods her brother.

'Don't be silly.' He is rough with her.

'Oh, come on.'

'I'd love to hear,' I smile at him.

He shrugs and suddenly he emits a high-pitched squeal, so uncanny in its whining variations that it is as if he has been transformed into a machine. We no longer exist for him. In the rapt look on his face, I recognise Beatrice – Beatrice as a child, unaware of the playground around her.

'That's enough, Nicolas,' Paul mutters. 'You'll drive us mad.' He is hard with the boy, I have noticed, too stern, too quick to correct, which makes Nicolas withdraw even further into himself and Paul unhappy, though he doesn't seem to be aware that he has provoked the reaction.

Marie-Françoise claps her hands, gives me a triumphant look. 'Sometimes Nicolas does it into the phone when it rings. And people think they have the wrong number.'

'Do you, Nicolas?' Paul is severe.

I laugh. 'Maybe it's something I should learn. It could prove useful.'

The boy looks from me to his father. 'Maria has seen "Reservoir Dogs",' he says in a taunting voice.

'Maria is Maria and you're fourteen years old.'

'And you're forty today.' Marie-Françoise is jubilant, points behind us.

A birthday cake appears on the table, a stubby candle at its centre.

Joyeux anniversaire,' the girl starts to sing and we join in. 'Now you'll have to make another wish,' she laughs.

'To Paul.' I raise my glass, encourage the children to do the same, hold it in the air as he blows out the candle, closes his eyes to wish. I wonder what he is wishing, know, when I feel his fingers warm on my thigh, but the gesture so startles me that the glass slips from my hand, shatters into a thousand pieces on the tile floor. I stare at the fragments, the splash of red wine, as if it were an omen and suddenly I feel my mother's face above me as she looked on that day when the glass tumbled from her hand onto kitchen tiles. The day I questioned her about my father. It comes to me then with a certainty I never had before that my father left her for another woman.

'It's nothing,' Paul murmurs as I get up to find the women's room.

Marie-Françoise follows me and tells me a long complicated story about how she once dropped a plate and her mother was very angry and I think that I must get away and be alone and panic when I realise that I can't even get back to the apartment where my things are and how impossible the whole situation is and how I want to run, but I can't run, not again. Not this time.

'I have to leave you now,' I say with a brittle smile when we get back to the table. 'I had no idea of the time and I'm already late for friends.'

'We'll see you tomorrow. At the big party.' Marie-Françoise smiles at me, a little shy now that I'm leaving.

'Yes, tomorrow.'

'Don't you want some cake?' Nicolas surprises me by asking.

I shake my head. 'You have my portion.'

I go, as self-conscious in my leaving as if I were trapped in Nicolas's adolescent body.

At the door, Paul catches up to me. 'I have to see you, Maria. Alone. Later. We need to talk.'

I look into his eyes and almost lose myself, surface to see my own pain and panic reflected there. I shake my head. 'There's nothing to talk about, Paul.' I try to keep the quiver out of my voice, make it hard. 'Told you I was bad news. Let's just cut our losses and hold onto the memory of our good time. We had London, after all.'

'No.'

I turn on my heel, walk a few paces and turn back. He is still standing there. I don't know why, but I go back to him for a moment. 'And be nice to Nicolas,' I say. 'He needs you more than I do.'

It only comes to me later that it was a cruel thing to say. But by then I am back in the apartment and I have already left a message for Beatrice on the answering machine, an ebullient, excited message. Or at least I hope so. 'You'll never believe this, Beatrice. But I saw Marie-Françoise today and your Nicolas. And it turns out that all these months I've been working for your husband. Ha ha ha. Isn't it wonderful? Give me a ring.'

I sit in the gathering darkness and stare out of the window. I cannot tear my eyes away from the house opposite. Beatrice lives there, I know. Now I have to accustom myself to the idea that Paul lives there too. Why in all this time of periodic peeping have I never caught a glimpse of him? Is it simply that I didn't expect to see him and one only recognises the anticipated? No. I remember that night when I glimpsed Beatrice in a man's arms, up there above me, in the attic room. Dark now, like their apartment. Beatrice and Paul. My stomach turns over.

I have this sudden notion that I should write to Louise Jimenez and tell her what is happening to me. It might make her happy to learn of my misery, to see me being punished at last.

The lights come on in the apartment opposite. I see Beatrice's outline cross the windows. I draw my curtains. But she doesn't disappear from my mind. I imagine her pressing the button on the answering machine, listening. But I cannot imagine her reaction. I stand in the shower and let the water pour over me for a long time as if it could wash my life clean. I try not to panic. I tell myself Beatrice is still my friend, a better model than ever now that I know whom she has linked herself to. I tell myself that I can be responsible and finish my work for Paul without ever having to see him alone again. We can communicate over the computer. I hardly need to go into the office. He doesn't need my arguments. He only needs my notes. I tell myself that I will never have to admit to Beatrice or Paul that I have lived here, that I will be able to sublet the apartment and find another on the other side of Paris. I tell myself that come October, I will start to train and will become a useful member of society at last. I tell myself all this and believe very little of it, and cry.

The crying follows me to bed, moistens my pillow. Its moisture makes me feel very small, very alone, like a child. I suddenly wish my mother were there to stroke my hair, as she used to do when I was ill, until I fell asleep. Paul strokes my hair like that. But Paul is with Beatrice. And my mother is dead.

PART FOUR

⚖ 28

The heavy oak door yields to the click of the code. I push its solid weight and I am through to the other side. There is the surprise of a courtyard here, a green sanctuary with a glossy-leafed magnolia at its centre, yellow roses clambering up trellises on three sides. To my right the board, announcing the names of inhabitants. And there it is, as clear as thick black lettering can make it: Arnault. If Beatrice had invited me in on that first day of our meeting, everything could so easily have been different. I would now be pressing this bell without a spasm of clammy nervousness.

Beatrice rang me this morning, woke me in fact, her voice as serene and unruffled as ever. Her laugh tinkled, unsuspicious. 'And here I thought I was keeping you to myself. My very own friend. A surprise on his birthday.'

'He'll be bored to tears having to see me out of the office. It'll remind him of work. Perhaps it's better that I don't come.'

'No. You must. For me. And look your most glamorous. Nothing like what Paul once called my frowsy schoolteachers. I want to show you off.'

I have done as Beatrice asked. I am wearing my favourite summer dress, a close-fitting raw silk with an ivory tinge and an eastern flavour, buttoned to the neck in front, but with a hidden slash down the back. I have piled my hair high and put a comb through it, added some plum colour to my lips and a little to my cheeks. No one, I tell my mirror to tell me, would know that I am not in my prime.

A stranger opens the door to me and it takes me a moment to realise from her black dress that she must be a maid. She shows me through a square hall and hands me a glass of champagne just as we enter a high-ceilinged rectangular room, made wider by the addition of a glazed terrace akin to mine and overlooking the courtyard. The room has an unexpected grandeur: low-slung sofas, the gleam of old wood, a few good oils and at the far end, a vast table set with white damask

247

and sparkling silver. People cluster here and there and from one of these groups, Beatrice emerges. She is wearing a ruffled canary-yellow frock which doesn't altogether suit her, but her smile is as bright as her dress.

'I'm so glad you've come. I was beginning to worry.' She kisses me and I give her an extra hug.

'I'm sorry I'm late.'

'It's worth it. You look wonderful.'

'And you.'

'No, don't say that. It doesn't quite work.' She laughs a little breathlessly. 'But come and meet some people.' She squeezes my hand and whispers, 'I hate these do's.'

I stay close to Beatrice, try to absorb the innocence of her wholehearted welcome, try not to look round for Paul. I shake hands with dignified strangers and stylish women – a politician, some lawyers, a fast-talking economist, a high-ranking civil servant. I have the sense that I am in the midst of the ENArchy – that group of public administrators trained at ENA who make up the country's ruling elite. Maître Cournot is here and greets me effusively, presents me to his wife, a slender, silver-haired woman who could be his double. It is while I am talking to her that I feel a tug at my arm and look down to see Marie-Françoise.

'Hello.' She lifts her cheek for a kiss.

'Bed in ten minutes, Marie-Françoise. No arguments,' Beatrice reminds her.

'Can I show Maria my room first?' The child is slightly plaintive, more timid than she was yesterday.

'You'll have to ask her.'

'I'd like that,' I say.

'But you really must say hello to Paul first. There he is.' Beatrice puts her arm through mine. 'You know he changed my whole seating plan when he found out who you were. And invited another person.' She grumbles a little, then laughs. 'That's the trouble with men like Paul. They always take over. I don't want him to take you over. From me.'

I squeeze her arm to reassure her, hope she can't read my face. 'We go back too far for that, Beatrice.'

She flashes me a happy look.

Paul is standing in the far corner of the room, his back to us. He is intent in conversation with a smaller man, whose face I cannot see.

'Look who's arrived.' Beatrice announces me and he turns round abruptly.

'Maria, how very nice.' His voice is correct but I cannot meet his eyes.

'Maître Arnault.' I give him my hand and he takes it formally for a moment, only to drop it as if it burned.

'Paul, remember. Well, well, well . . .' I can feel his gaze moving from Beatrice to me and back again. 'To think that you and Beatrice have known each other since you were Marie-Françoise's age.'

Beatrice laughs happily and I think that I will not be able to bear this charade a moment longer.

'But let me introduce you to Monsieur . . .'

'Patrick Morin.' A tall stocky figure with roguish blue eyes and curling smile interposes himself before Paul can finish. 'I sometimes have the feeling that our gracious hosts contrive to keep me away from their most beautiful guests. Can it be that you're trying to save me for yourself, Beatrice?'

'Beatrice is much too generous for that.' Paul answers for her, his voice light, but the face he turns on me has no lightness in it.

I feel a tug at my hand and look down into Marie-Françoise's expectant face. 'Will you come now?' she asks softly.

I nod with a sense of relief. 'You'll excuse me. I promised to go and see Marie-Françoise's room.'

'Not for too long, I hope.' Patrick Morin is impish. 'I want you to bare your soul to me.'

'I'm afraid I left it at home,' I reply and turn towards Marie-Françoise, who is pecking Beatrice goodnight.

Paul calls after us, 'In just a few minutes, I'll come and tuck you in.'

Marie-Françoise grips my hand fiercely as if she is afraid I will be waylaid again. 'I'll show you the whole house if you like,' she says.

Curiosity takes me over. I am through the windows. I am inside the house I have been spying on as if my salvation inhabited it. But I have only had a partial picture of it, I realise, a mistaken perspective, for only one room in the apartment faces the street.

'This is the *petit salon*.' Marie-Françoise does the honours like a proud householder. 'And where we eat when Papa isn't here.'

I see what I have glimpsed through the windows: a round table, fleshed out in solid cream marble, behind it a countertop which separates it from a kitchen where a young woman is laying food out on plates; at the other end two plump sofas positioned for television watching with the screen tucked into an invisible corner, bookshelves, a sound system. In short a comfortable family room over which Beatrice presides. Was it a trick of light or deliberate myopia that prevented me from ever recognising Paul in here?

Marie-Françoise pulls me quickly through the crowded *grand salon* into a corridor which stretches along the second arm of the courtyard. 'And this is my parents' room.' She opens the door and I see a blue-clad bed, an old escritoire, a chest of drawers, all somewhat austere and impeccably tidy but for a tie left lying at the edge of the bed, its knot askew. I close the door hastily.

'And this is Maman's dressing room.' Marie-Françoise opens the next door along the hall to reveal a smaller space complete with a single bed, built-in wardrobes. I step over the threshold and breathe in Beatrice's perfume and a different atmosphere. The wallpaper is pink and white, with a motif of tiny rosebuds; the bed has a white lace-trimmed duvet and heaped matching pillows and the chair at the curved and mirrored dressing table is covered in the same fabric. Something about the room distresses me in a way different from the first. I don't quite know what it is. The maidenliness of it, perhaps, like a young girl's dream room in an age before pop stars and vivid colours. Or perhaps it is merely the divergence from my own taste. Purity, I think. Beatrice's purity, like the tiny pale crucifix which hangs surprisingly over the bed.

Marie-Françoise has grown weary of my looking and pulls open a corner door to reveal a tiled bathroom with a second door which leads to the main bedroom.

'Show me your room, now.' I turn away from unwanted thoughts.

'No, I'm last,' she says.

'So you can put off going to sleep,' I laugh.

She gives me a naughty look. 'Papa won't mind. Now this is Nicolas's room.' She hesitates for a moment, decides not to knock.

'Marie-Françoise,' a voice reprimands her, but it isn't Nicolas's voice. It belongs to a tall, straight-backed woman, as elegant as her evident years. 'You must learn to knock. Your brother is a young man now. *Excusez-moi, Mademoiselle,*' she turns to me and stretches out a thin be-ringed hand, 'but this little one grows more impossible by the day.'

Her smile, and the way she ruffles Marie-Françoise's hair, lightens her comment and the child's grin tells me that she isn't in the least taken aback.

'This is my *mémère*,' she announces proudly. 'And this is Maria.'

'Monique Arnault,' the woman fills in for me, smoothing a strand of impeccably coiffed silver-grey hair from an arched cheekbone. 'And you must be Maria d'Esté. My son has told me about you.'

I flush despite myself.

'You're helping him finish that book he should never have undertaken to write. Not that it's any of my affair, of course.'

I think she winks at me then, but it is so incongruous in that haughty face that I don't quite believe it.

'But you've come to see Nicolas, not me. I think this game of his which I've been trying to understand – with no success whatsoever – must just about be finished.'

Nicolas is huddled over a computer screen being traversed by some muscled Rambo figure engaged in superhuman hurdles and dizzying pitfalls, in any number of fistfights with any number of monsters.

'Ouee!' he shouts and I imagine the epic struggle is over.

'How'd you score?' I ask him.

He gives me the first genuine smile I have ever seen on his thin face. 'I got 2063.'

'Beat your record?'

'Not quite. Almost.'

'You understand these things?'

'Not really.' I smile at Madame Arnault's surprise. 'But I did some public relations once for a software firm that developed a series of games like this in America. Just think of them as mythic quests or combats recreated for the screen. Hero slays cyber-monster instead of many-headed Hydra.'

'Be nice if these heroes needed a little more cunning than brawn,' Madame Arnault mutters. 'We don't really want a new generation of simple-minded warriors, do we now, Nicolas?'

Nicolas looks away. 'It's just a game,' he mumbles. 'I do other things on it.'

'Yes, well, let's hope girls distract you soon. And you treat them better than these monsters.'

Nicolas blushes. Marie-Françoise pulls at my hand. 'My room now, or there won't be time to show you all the things.'

'Until later then.' I nod at Madame Arnault, wave at Nicolas.

Marie-Françoise opens the next door down the corridor with a touch of drama.

'So you're at the end,' I grin at her.

'Oh no. There's the guest room where Mémère is staying, so we won't go in there. And there's another room up in the attic where Maman goes to work in quiet, but I don't like it up there.'

'Oh.' My pulse makes an erratic leap.

'Look!' Marie-Françoise gestures elaborately and I see an apple-green room with a bunk bed tucked in high under the ceiling, a little desk beneath it and every spare scrap of wall between shelves and cupboards covered with pictures of dogs. 'I hope you like dogs.'

'I can see that you do,' I laugh.

She makes a funny face. 'Maman says it's cruel to have dogs in the city. So I have pictures instead. Which is your favourite?'

I can tell by her expression that this is a deeply serious question and I begin to examine the pictures one by one.

'This one, I think.' I point to a woebegone spaniel whose ears droop too low.

She nods sagely. 'That's Mr Kim. And this is my favourite.' She gestures towards a white husky with bright blue eyes. 'She's called Storm.'

'Storm, that's nice.'

'But sometimes Storm is very bad, so my favourite is Peluche.' She points towards a golden retriever.

'So you like big dogs best.'

'The more dog the better,' she says earnestly. 'Did you ever have a dog?'

I shake my head. 'But I used to go to a farm in England every summer where there was a huge old dog called Small or Petit.'

'Mémère has a dog in the country. He's called Rabelais because he eats so much.' She giggles. 'But maybe we could rename Arnold, Petit.' She stands on her toes and shows me a giant Great Dane.

'Good idea.'

'You didn't by any chance bring me any chocolate, did you?'

'Well, in fact, just a very little.'

'Goody.' She claps her hands and I bring a small beaded purse out of my bag into which I have stuffed a few chocolates covered in gold foil. She looks inside then puts the purse carefully into a drawer.

'I'd almost forgotten.'

'That's 'cause you look so pretty tonight.' She touches my dress softly. 'Thank you.'

I don't know why, but the comment and the touch make me want to cry and I wonder what I'm doing here immersed in conversation with a little girl, I who don't like children, and in a house where I shouldn't be, amongst people who inadvertently or not I've deceived, and I feel like hugging the child goodnight and running off again, disappearing.

'Still not in your nightie?' Paul's voice startles me from the door. 'Come on, little cabbage. Get a move on. Dinner will be on the table in five minutes. And you can't keep Maria in here all night.' He casts me a look of such pure longing that I shiver, then he bends to the child and in a trice has her frock off and her nightie on. 'Now off to wash and brush your teeth. Maria and I will wait here to give you a goodnight kiss.'

The child leaves us. I want to follow her and I cannot move. I want to fall into his arms. I want to be somewhere else, on another planet, where guilt and desire do not exist.

'It's impossible. I see that now,' he says in a voice so flat I do not recognise it. 'I've talked to Beatrice and I see that. But there's no guilt, Maria. No blame. Don't bring it here from somewhere else. Here there is only pain.' I meet his eyes and the pain sweeps over me. His. Mine. The pain I've kept at bay with dogs and children and chatter and Beatrice's innocent rectitude. I have to sit down.

'I'll bring all the files back on Monday,' I say in a voice as flat as his.

'No.' It is as if I had hit him. 'I can't lose you altogether, Maria. Not just like that. Please. Not just when it seemed . . .' he stops abruptly, clenches his fist. 'Stay. Perhaps . . .' He doesn't finish his sentence.

'What did you tell Beatrice?' I ask after a moment.

'Nothing. I listened. She told me you were her only childhood friend. She cares for you, admires you. Your mother. That's why . . . You won't say anything either, will you?'

Marie-Françoise bounces into the room. 'All clean.'

From somewhere I dig out what must be a ghastly smile. 'Beautifully clean.' I kiss her, watch as Paul lifts her into bed, collect what remains of my reason.

People are beginning to take their places at table when we return. Beatrice rushes over to me.

'I knew it. My family is already monopolising you far too much,' she says to me with her serene smile. 'Now come, I've switched all this seating round again and you're sitting over here. Close to me. With Patrick between us. Paul will probably be furious.'

'Does he often get furious?'

She pauses for a moment, reflects. 'No,' she says with an odd laugh. 'In fact he's infuriatingly considerate.'

I laugh, too, in an attempt at girlish complicity. I empty a glass someone has filled and laugh too much, begin to float, become a machine for social repartee. I do not look down to the other end of the table where Paul presides unless my eyes find themselves there involuntarily. As the food comes, I banter with Patrick Morin instead, juggle with the language of veiled and teasing seduction. I can do this in my sleep and Patrick is evidently as much of a past master as I am. The act is like a skilled interlude between the main parts of the drama, but at one point I catch Beatrice's eyes on me and have the sense that she thinks it is the play itself. I cannot tell whether she is appalled or fascinated. Perhaps both, but I turn away from Patrick to listen to the people opposite.

Their tone is far more serious. They are discussing the war in former Yugoslavia and the Hague War Crimes Tribunal which is slowly moving into operation under the auspices of the United Nations. One of the lawyers I have briefly met explains how this is an unprecedented venture in international law. Not a military tribunal, like Nuremberg, but a civilian one, which can judge any member of the population who has been shown to have been engaged in atrocities. New codes will emerge, new conventions to govern civil wars.

'But it's impossible,' the woman next to him exclaims. 'Precisely because it's a civil war. Once the process starts you'll end up having to put half the male population behind bars, more. Serb, Croat, even Muslim. A whole generation of young men between the ages of eighteen and twenty-five. And what happens when they come out seething with resentment because they've done time and not others – more hatred, more killing.'

'Yes,' Patrick nods sagely. 'We're talking about the emotions of vengeance here. And revenge is self-perpetuating. Better to sue for peace and let a new emotional order gradually take over.'

'What do you mean?' Beatrice suddenly erupts, her voice raw, high-pitched, her face fierce. 'Revenge is essential. If you had been with some of those children whose parents were killed, mutilated before their very eyes; if you had talked to those thirteen-year-old girls raped by drunken savages, like I have, you would know that they have to have revenge. They won't survive without it. The nightmares will go on and on. There has to be vengeance.'

Beatrice's words and voice are so charged that a hush settles over the length of the long table, a fidgeting discomfort. The directness of her emotion has forced nightmare through the thin walls of civilisation and we don't know how to look at each other any more, how to speak. People prod the pink skeletons of langoustine on their plates, raise napkins to mute lips.

At last Paul's voice breaks the silence. Beatrice is right, he says. She has given us the rationale for the War Crimes Tribunal, indeed for the very existence of law. Revenge yes, it is necessary – if not feudal revenge of the eye-for-an-eye kind. But retribution through the law, an impartial third party. Its judgements may not be able to restore the past, but it can start to patch some of the wounds. So that the social order can begin to limp again.

There is a muted chorus of agreement. Paul's mother flashes her son a proud look. People find their voices. I watch Beatrice. She is getting up. She looks slightly dazed as she mumbles something about the next course. I follow her into the kitchen, ask if I can help. She doesn't respond. She looks desolately at the trays the caterers are heaping. Suddenly she turns to me. 'I always put my foot in it when his friends are here.'

'What are you talking about, Beatrice? You didn't put your foot in it.'

'I did. It's always the same. I can't get it right. Even when I keep absolutely quiet.'

'It didn't seem that way to me. Anyhow, they're your friends too, aren't they?'

'Not really. They only pretend.'

'He doesn't pretend. He listens to you.'

She turns away from me. 'Yes,' she says in a flat voice, then walks towards the window, stares out, stares as I do into the house opposite. For a moment it is as if I am disembodied, have flown back to my own apartment and our eyes meet in fear across the distance of the street.

'Do you remember, Maria,' Beatrice's tone has grown dreamy, 'in your kitchen when your mother gave us dinner? I used to sit there and wait to see what you both did so that I could imitate you, make sure I did the right thing. But neither of you ever noticed. You just accepted me. As I was.' She veers back to me. 'His mother never makes me feel that. I always do the wrong thing for her. Even when I just move my little finger.'

I laugh, genuine mirth for the first time. 'She's your mother-in-law, Beatrice. That's what she's there for. Otherwise she wouldn't have a job.'

Beatrice grimaces. 'Do you really think so?'

'I really know so.'

She smiles, her face tranquil again.

'I wish I were more like you, Maria. So light, so easy.'

I laugh again and for the briefest moment I feel heroic, like one of those Racinian heroines who battle nobly between duty and passion. Then I gesture towards the window, 'That reminds me. I bumped into an American friend the other day and she asked me if I'd like to look after her apartment for a bit. It's somewhere on this street. We could be neighbours for a while.'

Beatrice claps her hands. 'How wonderful. I'll help you move if you like. I can drop in on you after school, like the old days,' she giggles, stops herself. 'When you're there, that is. What is it that you're doing for Paul, by the way?'

I look at her in astonishment. 'Research for his book. Translation. Don't you know?'

She shrugs. 'We never talk about his work. All these years . . . I'm not really interested. People commit crimes. Are or aren't punished for them. Over and over . . . It's too tedious.' Her shoulders stiffen. 'We'd better get back in there, I guess.'

Later, after we have made our way through magret and salad and an assortment of delicately scented ices and Patrick has extracted a promise that we will meet for dinner and the conversation has moved through the latest financial scandals and the prospects for Europe, Paul's mother taps her glass with a spoon and makes a well-turned and humorous little speech in honour of her son's fortieth birthday. Paul doesn't squirm. He thanks her with only a little irony for putting up with him for forty years. Then he runs his fingers through his hair, pauses and raises his glass in a toast to Beatrice who has brought them all together, his oldest and nearest. His tone is all respect. His eyes are warm. Beatrice flushes. I have a funny sensation at the pit of my stomach. Perhaps it is just another nail in the coffin of my all-too-recently awakened hopes.

It is when we rise from the table for coffee that Paul comes over to me. He is awkward, uncomfortable, as he leads me towards the quiet end of the room. 'I had hoped to introduce you to someone, Maria. I invited him especially for you, but Patrick, not that I blame him, has monopolised you. Now my friend doesn't have much longer. And I'm not sure the moment is right. So I don't quite know whether . . .'

I laugh. 'Another hesitation and I'll think you're trying to marry me off. Perfect remedy for all my lost loves. The wedded state. I could become as remarkable as Beatrice.' The wine has loosened my tongue.

He grips my arm fiercely, then remembers himself and lets go. Our eyes lock unhappily. 'That's not what it's about, Maria.' He takes a deep breath. 'Though I'm sure the other could be arranged without much difficulty. Not that I imagine you need an arranger.' He looks away. 'What I'm trying to tell you is . . . do you remember I said I had a friend at the Vietnamese Embassy? Well, he's here. And I asked him about your father. He knew him. Not well, but . . .'

I lean against the wall. I am not sure it is strong enough to hold me.

'What are you doing to this poor woman?' Patrick is beside us.

'Not now, Patrick. Leave us.' Paul scowls at him, places himself like a bodyguard squarely in front of me. I close my eyes. Sniff a bluebell wood. Taste his body. We talked of loss. My father. Father. Strange word. 'Papa,' Marie-Françoise says. 'Tuck me in, Papa.' Eyes all round, bossy and flirtatious at once.

'I'd like to meet him. Even for a moment.'

Paul nods. 'I think he might have gone next door,' he murmurs, and leads me to the front of the apartment.

On the sofa sitting beside Madame Arnault is a small, dapper man of indeterminate age. He rises as Paul introduces me, greets me in a voice so soft that I almost want to make him repeat the words.

'So you are the daughter of Guy Regnier.'

'Regnier, did you say?' Madame Arnault queries. 'I used to know a Guy Regnier, or at least my father did. A doctor, wasn't he? Brought up in the East, trained here before the war and went back after it.'

I stare at her and she chuckles. 'Don't look at me like that, young lady. I'm not a witch. My people were all doctors. Even I was once. And my father taught a good number of them, so it's hardly surprising. It's a small world.'

I am sitting down and I must look odd for they are looking at me oddly. Paul is beside me and he has taken my hand.

'It's just that Maria doesn't remember her father,' he explains. 'And I don't think she's met anyone for a long time who knew him.'

'I encountered him on only a few occasions.' Monsieur Tran looks beyond me and then for a brief second into my eyes. 'He used to be known as "*ông bắc si tôt lám*", the good doctor.'

Paul's hand feels very warm, so mine must be cold. I hold onto it. '*Ông bắc si tôt lám,*' I repeat like a child. 'The good doctor.'

'Yes,' Monsieur Tran smiles. His face is as smooth as porcelain and I imagine he must have been a mere stripling when he met this good doctor.

'If I remember the gossip correctly,' Madame Arnault intervenes, 'Guy Regnier was a kind of "doctor without frontiers" before the organisation existed.'

Monsieur Tran nods politely. Questions flood my mind, a slew of them in no particular order and of such mingled consequence and inconsequence that I don't know where to begin, and before I can Beatrice comes into the room and Paul springs up with so marked an alacrity that we all stare at him.

'Excuse me.' He walks quickly towards Beatrice and after a brief exchange follows her next door.

Monsieur Tran clears his throat. 'I'm afraid I must leave you too. But in a few weeks' time, a colleague of mine arrives from Vietnam who would be able to tell you far more about your father than I can.' He reaches in his pocket and hands me a card. 'Perhaps you could contact me then or I can ask him to telephone you. At Maître Arnault's *cabinet*, yes?'

I nod, then quickly add, 'Or at home.' I scrawl my number on a slip of paper. 'Thank you. Thank you very much.' I lean back into the sofa. I don't know how much time passes before I am aware of Madame Arnault's scrutiny. I try to smile at her.

'Yes, it must be strange not remembering your father. I remember mine so clearly, though it was long ago, that I can still see the way he peeled and cut apples for us into neat, surgical slices.' She stops herself short. 'And your mother? Who is she? If you don't mind my being inquisitive.'

'Françoise Regnier. Françoise d'Esté. She died years ago, when I was seventeen.'

'I see,' she muses. 'No, I don't think I ever met her. Your father though, if my memory serves me, was a very attractive man.' Her eyebrows arch, her lips curl, and I suddenly see the flirtatious young woman in her. 'Yes, after the war, several of my friends, I remember, had their hearts set on him. Forgive me, I'm prattling. And you'll want to join the young people.'

I don't move. 'Tell me more,' I say.

'Well, there isn't much more. He went off, quite suddenly. Couldn't stand France after the war, I guess. Not a good time here. In '49, was it? I'm not quite sure. So you were born out there?'

'No, no, in Paris.'

'He came back, then. But by that time I must have been having my children and my father had died. Guy Regnier was really his friend.' She glances at me curiously. 'Or was it that your mother came back without him? Sensible of her.'

'No, he did come back to France, but then left for Vietnam again. When I was about two.'

She lets out a deep breath. 'I see. Difficult. But here I am troubling you with too many questions. Shall we go back next door?'

'I think I'll just slip away now. I . . .'

She pats my hand. 'Of course, my dear.'

'Will you thank Paul and Beatrice for me?'

She nods, gazes at me again as I stand. 'To think. Guy Regnier's daughter. Yes I can see him in you. You have his colouring, the bones.'

I am almost through the door when Paul catches up with me. His face is sombre, tired. 'Was that all right? Are you all right?'

'I'm not at my most self-possessed, if that's what you mean.'

That look of longing comes into his eyes. But he doesn't touch me. I kiss him lightly on the cheek and he steps back as if I repelled him. 'Happy birthday.' I pretend gaiety, feel only confusion. I turn away.

'Maria.' He calls me back. 'Don't mention Monsieur Tran and all that to Beatrice.'

'Why ever not?' I am suddenly angry. 'How many things am I not supposed to mention to Beatrice?'

'Please.' His knuckles on the door jamb are white. 'I'll see you next week.' He closes the door so quickly that I stand there looking at smooth surface where I should see Paul. I clench my fists, wish I could hammer at it, hammer at him.

I race down the stairs, race as if I were Cinderella running from the ball. But there is no prince running after me and if I were to drop my slipper, he would undoubtedly hand it to his wife on a silver platter and convince her it were hers. I race across the street, look furtively up at the lighted window opposite, and sidle into my door, the gestures stoking my anger, making it as hot and unreasonable as if the situation weren't also of my own making.

I do not turn the lights on in my apartment. I stand in the dark and gaze into Paul and Beatrice's bright home. My anger persists and I stoke its coals, prod at its embers. I know where the anger comes from. I have been abandoned. I have been given up for another. Is it the first time? Paul has given me up for Beatrice. Oh, not without difficulty. There will still be a little of that. But given me up nonetheless. Tried to return my father to me in his place. A little ghostly sleight of hand, so that I am not left with nothing.

Not nothing. But only the dead. My father, whose features I have to dredge up from the memory of an indistinct photograph. My mother, who has grown fuller, more real to me since my return to Paris than perhaps she ever was in my childhood. And Sandro too, yes Sandro, whom I abandoned to his death.

I draw the curtain and nurture my dead.

⚖ 29

When I was small my mother and I used to play her own version of geography. She would twirl the globe which stood in a corner of my room as fast as it would go. Then, when it was spinning so fast that the whole world was just a blue blur, I would close my eyes and place a finger somewhere on its cool surface and stop its spinning. Wherever my finger landed was the subject for that game. We would work out how long it took to travel to that elsewhere, whether by plane or boat or train or bicycle or camel. We would talk about the climate at that particular time of year, the food that grew there or the fish that swam, the languages people spoke. When I was a little older, the encyclopaedia would come out and we found out more about kings and queens and wars, raw materials and religions, mixtures of peoples.

Strangely, my finger never landed on Vietnam.

Now I go to the library on the Boulevard Raspail and I read about Vietnam. I find out about the Van Lang dynasty eight centuries before Christ and the Au Lac which replaced it. I find out about Chinese domination and independence struggles as far back as the tenth century, feudal wars between the Macs and the Les which divided the country into north and south. By the time I reach the nineteenth century and the period of French colonialism, a pattern seems to be in place which gathers inevitable momentum with the crushing speed of industrial technologies. The twentieth century adds the ideological card. I read more carefully now, learn that the French were ousted in 1954 after a long and acrid war, that the Geneva conventions which might have unified the country were disputed by the Americans who backed tyrannical and unpopular southern governments. I learn about the violent repression of Buddhists and the growing American presence. Finally I learn about the brutal and terrifying war. The war that shadowed my childhood, the subject of half-understood headlines and raised adult voices, some of them occupants of the spare room. I learn and I wonder how Monsieur Tran acquired his calm face and sweet smile. I learn and wonder about the man who was my father and I wish that I had found a better destination for my adolescent callousness than the hearth in which I burned his letters.

But all this is only the second or third thing I do. The first thing I do on the Monday after Paul's birthday party is ring Beatrice to thank her and announce that I have all but moved into the new apartment. I am literally a stone's throw away. I invite her to come and visit whenever she has a moment. I also tell her that my old telephone number will be transferred here in a few days' time and that one way or another I will see her on Wednesday to help out with the language teaching. Then I ring Madame Duval to tell her I've moved and that I'll be working from home and library for most of the week, will only be in the office to pick up and drop things off. She tells me not to worry, that the Maître will be so much in court over the next few weeks that she hardly expects to see him and she can't imagine he'll have much time for book work.

Paul hasn't told me this. I don't know whether he forgot in the midst of everything else or whether it was deliberate. By mid-week I suspect the latter. Paul is drawing a clear and rapid demarcation line between us. My role is to get on with work. I have no need to know of his plans or whereabouts and Madame Duval can easily serve as a link. This is as it should be.

I sit in the dark and look out of my window and see if I can catch a glimpse of that other life which isn't mine. With the fragments of irony that are left to me, I examine my situation. This is the first time that I have chosen the wife over the husband, when, needless to say, I have desired the husband. But this is also the first time the husband has given me up so willingly. That, too, is as it should be. But it hurts. I look in the mirror in the morning and see that it hurts. The mirror laughs, tells me that perhaps, by will or accident, I am at last changing. The metamorphosis I so wanted has begun. The better me. Penance. It doesn't seem to make me very happy. But then I imagine happiness was never part of that particular equation.

I make plans. I am going to be very busy. If I work flat out I can easily get through the material Paul has already outlined by mid-summer. If he needs more, if he needs trips to Spain or Italy, he can find himself another researcher. Meanwhile I need to sift through law faculty courses, register for October, if it isn't already too late. I check bank balances and determine that if I am scrupulous, if I do some occasional part-timing, I may just about manage to become the student I never properly was.

I ring Steve in New York, find myself buoyed up by his voice, tell him I have got my own place and can't wait to see him and Chuck. I will get them opera tickets, take them out to dinner. He tells me various people have contacted him for my number – Grant Rutherford, amongst them. Can he give it out now? I say yes without hesitation. He tells me, too, that he has recently been down to East Harlem, that the second building of the Hundreds project has opened. It's all looking good and the team with a couple of new additions is in fine spirits. He pauses significantly. 'And they've named the new building after Sandro.'

'That's brilliant,' I reply. My voice is husky, but there isn't a tremor in it. Nor have I broken out in cold sweat. I ask Steve to send the team my warmest congratulations, say I will write to them myself.

When I put down the phone, I note that I have indeed changed. I am not afraid. I have stopped running and hiding. I think of Sandro and I do not instantly see a fractured body that I have helped to push out of a window. Instead I think how pleased Sandro would be to have a building named for him. I think how proud of him his son will be when he grows up.

It is when I switch on my computer and see Paul's prose on the screen that I realise how much it is he who has helped me to arrive at this point. Could it only have been a little over a week ago that I was sitting in Steve's apartment, cut off from everything but misery and ghosts? And Paul saw me through it, wooed me out of it, made me think and feel differently, gave me hope, opened me out, gave me love. Made me love. Him. And not just then, but over the months. A process of coming back to life. If not to the life I briefly hoped for.

But glancing through this chapter again, I am caught in a time warp. It was written while I was still away in London and Paul's asides are delicate little probes, attempts to understand me, or persuasive arguments about the power and necessity and sometimes madness of love. Like coded notes to his coy mistress. In the interim, the mistress has all but ceased being coy only to find that the Maître has decided that love is no longer in the offing. I know this is only a partial story, but while I read, it feels like the truth. And the feeling makes me cruel, makes me want to rile. I make little bracketed barbed comments in

Paul's text, date them, quote the last line of 'Law Like Love', 'Like love we seldom keep'; suggest that law is really far more like marriage. Like marriage, it comes complete with contracts and code books, engages respect and policing, grants occasional licences for peripheral passions, incurs penalties when broken.

On Wednesday afternoon I go into the office to drop off books and files and pick up new ones. Perhaps if Paul had been there or perhaps if he had even phoned me in the intervening days, I would have erased my caustic comments, but all there is from him is a message through Madame Duval reiterating what she has already told me. So I leave the diskette with her.

From the office, I go to the school in the Thirteenth where Beatrice teaches the refugee children. It is a working-class area and the school is a run-down sixties civic building, dusty in its functionalism. Beatrice is already there, writing phrases in a big round hand on a chalky board. She embraces me warmly. Then she primes me, takes me through some of the areas she's already covered with the children, stressing that what they need is everyday speech – buses, trains, shops, playground, doctor, pharmacy – and whatever points of grammar arise from that. She shows me the neighbouring classroom where I will be stationed for the hour.

By the time we return to the first room, the children have begun to gather. I look at them and realise that I have not prepared myself sufficiently. I have not prepared myself for the impact of these lost, haunted eyes, these weary faces. Nor have I considered missing limbs, frail, scarred bodies, expressions which are at once pleading and absent or angry. I look to Beatrice for help, but she is already greeting the children, introducing them to me. I force a smile to my lips, shake hands with two mothers who have tagged along for the lesson, one thin and gauntly arrogant, the other small, with a timid expression. Beatrice's outburst at the dinner party comes back to me.

There are about a dozen children in all and Beatrice chooses six of them to come with me. One of the mothers seems to belong to my six and we traipse along to the neighbouring classroom. I begin by telling them about myself, my name, my age, where I come from and then coax them each in turn to do the same, the mother as well. They are all from Bosnia, four of them from Sarajevo. I swallow inadequacy and put on what I imagine is a teacher's face, tell them we are in a playground, dramatise, give them phrases to repeat, write them on the board, choose a boy who must be about ten and who speaks slightly more fluently than the others to engage in an acted-out dialogue with me. He has a patch over one eye and from the way he bumps into desks and chairs, I sense that he doesn't see well with the other either. I tell him I'm a naughty girl and he's a good boy and I'm going to break in on his game. We begin. It goes something like this.

'Salut.'

'Salut.'

'What are you playing?'

'Ball.'

'Can I play too?'

'Sure. Catch.'

'Ouch. That was too hard.'

'No it wasn't.'

'Yes, it was. I'm going to tell teacher.'

'No, you're not.'

'Yes, I am. Try and stop me.'

Suddenly the boy makes a rat-tat-tat-tat noise through his teeth and aims a pretend machine-gun at me. The gaunt woman, his mother, shouts out something I don't understand from the back. One of the smaller girls starts to cry. I realise my teaching methods leave a lot to be desired. I pat the little girl's head, thank my dialogue partner and tell him that was wonderful, except for the machine-gun. I start again on the less dangerous business of repetition.

At the end of the lesson mother and son come over to me. She is obviously lecturing him and at the end of her lecture, he says 'Sorry Miss' to me. In English.

'You speak English?' I reply in kind.

'A little,' he nods.

'You too,' the mother bursts in. 'I am sorry for Jasha. He has lost his manners.'

I grin at them both. 'Mine weren't too good either.'

The woman suddenly smiles, shakes my hand. 'Thank you. Until next week.'

I walk with them towards Beatrice's classroom, ask the woman if she too is taking French classes. She tells me the Alliance Française is too expensive and she is teaching herself out of a book. She laughs with a hint of bitterness. 'And they have put us in a house which is like all of Bosnia. So there is no one to practise with. But here we manage to live together, Muslims, Serbs, Croats. No problem.' She throws her hands up in the air. 'There is a story, no!'

'There is a story,' I repeat.

She looks at me curiously. 'You are a teacher?'

I shake my head. 'Just helping out. And you?'

'I was a, how do you say, dentist assistant. Now I am a nothing.' She laughs harshly. 'No, not right. I am sometimes a cleaner. Do you need a cleaner? I am a good cleaner.'

'Perhaps,' I murmur uncomfortably, then face her. 'Look, would you like me to help you with your French? We could do an hour after the children's class. Or you could come to me. With Jasha.'

I cannot read the expression on her face. After a moment she says, 'You are not afraid we will dirty you with our miseries?'

I shake my head, feel like telling her that I'm already rather dirty as it is. 'Here.' I jot down my name and phone number for her. 'Just ring me and we can arrange it.'

She takes the paper and studies it. 'You know I am a Bosnian Serb,' she says with a stiff defiance, then holds the paper out as if she expects me to take it back.

'And what is your name? I didn't catch it.'

She is still staring at me. 'Vesna Dimic.' She suddenly smiles, looks young, pretty. 'I will phone you.' She ruffles her son's hair. 'And Jasha, he is not so bad. Just a little confused.' She gestures towards her eyes, grimaces. 'It would be better if he hadn't seen before. Not now, when he needs to. Say *au revoir* and *merci*, Jasha.'

'Distressing, isn't it?' Beatrice says to me as we make our way home.

I nod.

'Are you going to come back?'

'Yes, of course.'

She puts her arm through mine. 'I'm glad.'

'But now you must come up and visit my new place.'

'For a cup of coffee. I need it. By the way, has Patrick phoned you?'

'Twice.' I grimace.

'I knew he would,' she says triumphantly. 'And you're going to go out with him?'

'Perhaps.'

'He's a very good journalist, you know.'

It's as if she's trying to sell him to me and I wonder for a moment whether Beatrice has put two and two together about Paul and London and me.

'And you'll tell me all about it, won't you? If you . . . if you go to bed with him?' She blurts it all out in a rush and flushes. I have the odd sense that the words are new to her lips, as if she were a child experimenting with swearing.

We have turned into our street and I let her question pass, stop instead in front of the house to punch out the door code.

'But you really are just opposite, Maria. That's wonderful. And it's beautiful,' she says as I lead her into the flat. 'Just perfect.' She smooths the sofa with her hand, touches the wood of the table, sniffs flowers, opens the door to the bedroom. 'Exactly what I would want if I lived alone.' She sighs a little as she sinks into a chair.

'Lucky accident, isn't it.'

'You're always lucky. You bring me luck too.' She gives me her beatific smile and I hide my face, busy myself with making coffee. 'One day I'll tell you all about it,' she says dreamily.

'Was Paul pleased with his party?' I ask with forced casualness.

'I think so,' Beatrice laughs, dropping a sugar cube into her coffee. 'To tell you the truth, he's been so busy I've hardly had a chance to talk to him. And on Friday, he's off to Brittany with the kids for the long weekend.'

'Aren't you going to go?'

'He's taking his mother home,' she says, as if this is explanation in itself. 'If you're here, we can do something. Go somewhere.'

'The Miró exhibition, perhaps.'

'Yes.' She gets up. 'I'd better run home. Marie-Françoise will be waiting.' She pushes the curtain back from the window a little and looks out.

'She's a lovely child,' I say.

'Maria, look.' Beatrice is suddenly excited. 'You can see into our front room from here. I can wave to you in the mornings over breakfast. We're almost as close as when I stayed with you. Do you remember? When I had my broken leg.'

I stand next to her and look out. 'Oh yes,' I say with a tone of surprise, feeling like the errant deceiver I am. 'Isn't it amazing.'

The next morning I see Beatrice and Marie-Françoise standing by their front window, waving at me. I open mine and wave back. When

I stop and return to my breakfast, I have a strange feeling that a reversal is taking place. The feeling persists over the next days. I have a sense that I am being watched, secretly, ardently, though I am not certain who is the watcher. Increasingly, I draw my curtains.

Marie-Françoise pops in on her own that afternoon after school. She wants me to show her my house, she says seriously, and I do so with equal seriousness. Then she hangs about, visibly unwilling to leave until finally I ask her if anything is wrong. She shakes her head at first, then shrugs. 'Maman is not in a good mood,' she confides to me.

'Oh.'

'A very bad mood.'

I smile at her. 'Perhaps she's tired. Perhaps she finds it difficult having your *mémère* around. Sometimes it's hard for mothers.'

Marie-Françoise thinks about this, then nods, while I think that I am relieved to hear that even serene Beatrice has moments of visible bad temper.

'Problem is I got a two in my *dictée* and Madame Delfort says Maman has to sign my notebook,' Marie-Françoise murmurs.

'Two out of ten?'

'Yes.' A frown creases her brow. Tears are held back.

'And why is that?'

'I think I wasn't paying attention.'

'Well, you'll just have to tell your mother that you were day-dreaming and you'll do better next time. A lot better.'

She considers this. 'All right.'

'And I imagine you'd better get home now, or your mother will be worrying.'

'Oh, I told her I was coming.' She wriggles out of the sofa. 'Can I come back next week? After the holiday.'

'Whenever you like and I'm here.'

'Well, thank you for having me,' she says in her little girl rote voice.

I grin. 'Thank you for coming, Marie-Françoise.'

After she has gone, I reflect to myself that in the logic of things, Nicolas should come and check me out next, closely followed by Paul. But it occurs to me that there is more wish than logic in this. Paul probably hasn't touched base long enough even to learn that I'm here, and even if he had, the last thing he would want to do is visit. The trouble is, I miss him. Even my research seems to have grown less compelling now that he isn't there to argue it over with.

On Saturday Beatrice rings me early. She sounds a little shy, breathless. 'You know you suggested we go to the Miró exhibition. Well, what I would really like to do – say no if you think it's a waste of time – is go shopping. I need some summer clothes and I thought you could help me choose. You have such good taste.'

'You have good taste, too, Beatrice,' I demur. 'But if you like . . .'

We traipse through the streets of St-Germain, go up as far as St-Placide and then down again the other side. It isn't easy for me. Beatrice seems to have developed a desire for bright colours and patterns which drown her quiet looks. I pretend I am back in New York and grooming a client for television, and persuade her into creams and tans, classical blacks. I wonder at one point if we are both wrong. I am trying to restore the gentle, demure girl of my childhood and she wants to create the dramatic persona who can stand up to her mother-in-law. We settle somewhere in between: two simple, well-cut dresses, but with a patterned African wrap and some thick glossy beads for added effect. Beatrice gazes at herself as I show her how to arrange the shawl in different styles, and seems pleased.

The days pass. Tanya comes to visit and tells me she has been following Paul's current case, went to court to watch him at work. 'Pretty good,' she says grudgingly. 'Sometimes very good. But I think his client's going to lose. And boy did he bite my head off afterwards because he'd seen me there. Told me I had no business coming without telling him beforehand. So I gave him a piece of my mind and told him he was neither my Lord nor Master, not even my boss. And guess what? He apologised.'

I wish I could give Paul a piece of my mind, though I don't know quite what piece I'd give him.

More days pass. I go out to dinner with Patrick Morin and make witty noises, but don't let him past the front door. Vesna Dimic rings and comes round with Jasha. She is timid and hostile by turn, until I bring out a set of children's language tapes and French songs for the boy and set him up with earphones. Then she confides in me that what she would like most of all is to get him a musical instrument, a piano or a guitar. He likes music and he will need it, she tells me. He is due for another eye operation next month, but no one knows how much sight he can hope to regain. She doesn't tell me how he lost his sight. She doesn't talk about the war at all. I don't press her. Sometimes one needs secrets, even from oneself. To keep one's face in place and one's legs moving. I know. Instead we talk about all the food we can eat and clothes we can buy in French. This fantasy gorging tickles her and she goes off smiling – Jasha, his tapes and the walkman I have lent him in tow. She isn't effusive in her thanks. Gratitude, I realise, is only an easy emotion when one has a lot to give. Instead, she says that next time, she and Jasha will bring me some *ćevapčići*, so that I can taste some local cooking.

I work. I ferry files to and from the office and go to libraries. I see Beatrice and Marie-Françoise, who even drags her brother with her one day. He is so uncomfortable that he only manages three sentences during the time they stay. But he flashes me a rare smile as they go through the door.

I do all these things and while I do them I know that I am waiting. Though what exactly I am waiting for isn't clear. Perhaps it is simply a confrontation with Paul. It comes to me at one point that he may think the confrontation is already over and I am waiting in vain. But I cannot get rid of this sense of waiting.

One evening, I think it is the day when Nicolas has come to visit and it must be late for it is finally dark, I am sitting at the table in the front room reading, when I have the distinct sense that comes upon me from time to time that I am being watched. I look out and I see Paul silhouetted against the window. There is a light somewhere behind him and it is the first time I am certain it is him. I stare for a moment and then something takes me over. I don't draw my curtains. Instead I begin slowly to undress, unbutton my shirt, pull down my trousers, shake out my hair. I walk back and forth in front of the windows and take off my bra, my knickers, throw them flagrantly towards the window. I am performing a strip, like in my dream, but more leisurely, more methodical. I tell myself I am only doing this because I so hate the passivity of waiting.

The next day Madame Duval rings me. She tells me the Maître would like to see me on Friday. The trial is finally over. I tell her that Friday would be very inconvenient. Could the Maître name a date next week? She says she will call me back.

A few minutes later the phone rings again and a tiny ache of triumph goes through me. I am certain it is Paul. But the voice that greets me isn't Paul's and it takes me a moment to recognise it.

'Hello, beautiful. I've just landed. Are you free for dinner tonight?'

'Grant?'

'The very same.' He chuckles. 'So cancel all the beaux and let me take you out.'

I let him.

We sit in the art deco ocean liner which is the restaurant of the Hôtel Lutetia and float over our lives. Apart from the grey which is winning the battle against the brown in his hair, Grant is unchanged. He still openly assesses me over the tops of his spectacles.

'Odd to see you in your native habitat,' he says to me after I have grilled him about New York. 'You never used to want to come here when we travelled together.'

I laugh. 'Do my plumes look less bright?'

'No, not that. But you're quieter.'

'Maybe it's just that I have no one to be noisy with.'

He chuckles. 'I don't know whether I should be sorry about that or not. But you're not still succumbing to the easy seductions of despair, are you?'

I think about this. 'I didn't find it so easy,' I say at last.

'No, of course not, that was crass of me.' He takes my hand.

'But yes, I think I've climbed out of the pit.'

'So Mr Jimenez is properly buried at last.'

'And properly remembered. Maybe that's just as important.'

We are quiet for a moment. Then he says, 'And you feel at home here. You have no thoughts about coming back? To New York, I mean.'

The question startles me and I have to consider it. Finally I shake my head and tell Grant about what I've been doing, about the notion of studying law which has arisen from it. I don't tell him about Paul, but he is in my mind as I talk and I wonder whether my decision is really only to do with him and will crumble without him. It suddenly becomes terribly important to me to hear how Grant will respond to my plans, he who knows me so well.

When I finish, he whistles under his breath. I have a feeling he is going to give me a piece of throw-away irony, scupper my best-laid plans with a swingeing remark about belated adolescence. But he doesn't. He looks at me seriously and says, 'I take it all back. No slough of despair. You've come a long way.'

It is over coffee that he asks me whether I might consider doing the occasional piece of work for him from here, a little consultancy – French clients again. I could meet one lot of them in the coming days. He'd make sure I was well-paid. And it shouldn't interfere with studies.

'You're doing this to help me out?' I quiz him.

'Have I ever been that generous? No. I've been trying to get hold of you on and off for months. You could have saved me a trip.'

'Done.' I grin at him. 'It couldn't have come at a better time.'

Later, he insists on seeing me home. He doesn't care that it's a five-minute walk and the streets are safe. Anyhow, he wants to inspect the site of my new life, he tells me. I don't protest. I like having Grant's protective arm round my shoulders, I like showing him into the apartment. It makes me feel as if my various lives are coming together.

'Nice,' he says as he looks around. 'Very nice.' He settles into the sofa. 'Now all you have to do is offer me a drink and invite me to stay and I'll be a supremely happy man. Who does stay, by the way?' he asks before giving me a chance to answer.

I turn my back to him, busy myself with drinks. 'No one.'

He waits until I have sat down. 'Is that part of the new you?' He is studying me.

I laugh. 'I'm not sure.'

We look at each other for a few moments. Then he comes over to me, lifts me out of my chair. 'Shall we see if it still works between us, Maria?' He kisses me. It is a warm kiss, warmly familiar, and it warms me. I think of Paul and put Paul out of my mind and hold Grant closer. Then in the midst of the kiss, I have an odd sense, as if there are eyes burning into the back of my head. Someone is watching. I am certain of it. I move to draw the curtains, peer out. There are no lights on in the Arnault apartment. Perhaps I have imagined it.

I go to bed with Grant. I go to bed with him to prove that I'm still a desirable woman, to prove that I still know how. And to prove to myself that I'm not in love with Paul. Bed is not always a good place for tests and I don't think in this case that I altogether pass.

The next morning the phone rings just after nine.

'Maria.'

I hold myself very still.

'Madame Duval tells me you can't come in today. Are you sure? We could meet somewhere else if that would make it easier. I need to go through some things with you.' Paul doesn't ask me how I am. He is formal, cool.

'You'll find all the work I've done is with Madame Duval.' I match his tone. 'And I'm afraid I'm busy. A friend has come in from the States.'

'One of the platoon?' His voice changes register.

'Its general.' I hang up. I am shaking.

The phone rings again a moment later and I am tempted not to pick it up but I haven't the strength of will.

'I'm sorry. I'm just finding it very hard, Maria. I'm trying, but I'm finding it very hard. Let's have a walk together. I'll meet you in front of the Jeu de Paume. Any time you say. Now.' I hear him swallow.

'In an hour.'

'An hour.'

He is already there when I arrive, pacing in front of the gallery door. There is a sombre air about him and when he sees me, it doesn't change. He doesn't wave. He just stands completely still. We look at each other across the distance of steps and I start to tremble. He comes slowly towards me, takes my hand and holds it, holds it so tight that it hurts. We walk into the Tuileries Gardens, our hands clenched. When I steal a glance at him, his face is taut, as closed and distant as the ranks of inexorably cropped trees which line the aisles of the park. He doesn't speak until we reach their shelter. Then he is curt.

'Why did you do it, Maria?'

'Do what?' I wrench my hand away, read my own thoughts in his. 'Sleep with Grant? I did it for you. To free myself of you. It's like closing a door. Hard. The way you closed it.'

He clutches my arm. 'And is it irrevocably closed now?' I look into his eyes and he kisses me, too hard, as if he is breaking the door down. I break with it. I have to sit down when he releases me. I sink onto a bench, stare at the monumental curves of the sculpture in the fenced garden in front of me. The flanks seem too soft, too tender to have been hammered out of stone.

'That's not what I meant, Maria.' Paul is sitting beside me. His voice is soft and hard, like the stone. 'I know I'm not your keeper. I have no rights. There's no contract between us. Not even a promise. As you pointed out so succinctly in your barbed little asides to my last chapter. What I meant was, why did you move in? Across the street? Now?'

He takes my hand, strokes it finger by finger. 'It's like slow torture having you there. So close. So visible. So inaccessible.' His hand closes over mine.

I want to lie, but I can't lie to him. And I don't know how to explain. 'Beatrice, for Beatrice,' I say.

'You mean she asked you to? Told you about an apartment?'

I shake my head. 'I wish it were dark,' I mumble. 'Let's walk.'

He walks stiffly by my side, then after a moment shrugs, puts his arm tentatively round my waist. I don't move away and we stroll silently for a while, step in step. Sunlight bursts erratically through leaves, then vanishes into gloom. In the gloom I start to tell him.

'I moved in there before I met you. I only went to the other place, the one you know, sometimes. That's why you couldn't reach me on the telephone that time.'

I wait for the horrified glance of suspicion, the chastising words. But he doesn't say anything, only, 'Go on.'

'Beatrice didn't know either, not until after your party. It became too hard to tell her once I hadn't to start with. I got hoist on my own secrecy.' My voice is too bitter.

'But why?'

'Good question. It just seemed right at the time. When I bumped into Beatrice, after all those years, Beatrice who had always been so good, so serene, and who I'd been such a pig to, Beatrice who was the closest I ever came to a sister. Beatrice who was still so good, so gentle, so . . . so everything I wasn't. Beatrice, whose life seemed to work. Well, I just wanted to be close to her. Maybe I thought I'd learn something. About how to live. After Sandro. Or she'd spread some magic dust my way. I don't know. It seems mad now. I'll move soon. As soon as I can.'

His arm tightens around my waist. 'It's not working like this, Maria. I can't seem to . . . Come away with me. For the weekend. Any weekend.'

I am glad he has asked. I have wanted him to ask. But now that he has, I know that I can't. Much as I may regret it when I'm alone. I can't do that to Beatrice. I hold his hand anyway, to savour his closeness.

'It'll make things harder,' I say, shake my head.

'It couldn't be any harder.'

We have come to one of the little cafés which dot the gardens and I smile at him tentatively. 'Coffee?'

He nods. He isn't smiling. 'A week, then. Two, over the summer. We could go to the sea. The Mediterranean. Italy perhaps.' He looks at me and in the burst of sunshine through the trees his eyes look very blue, as if they already had the sea in them.

'It isn't the length of time. It's Beatrice. She trusts me. Trusts you too, I imagine.'

'We often have separate holidays,' he murmurs.

'Anyhow, by July, I'll have finished my work for you. And I'll disappear from your life. '

I cannot read his face. Too many emotions cross it in rapid succession. The waiter arrives. We order coffee. A toddler comes bounding down the path. She is all tiptoes and plump thighs and brown curls. *'Glace,'* she calls over and over. 'Ice cream.' There is a rapt smile on her face. Just beside our table, she trips and lets out a howl. I pick her up, dust off her frock. *'Glace?'* I repeat. She stops in mid-howl, twists her still open mouth into a tentative smile, nods. *'Veux une glace.'*

'Our lady of ice cream,' Paul says to me. He calls the waiter over. Before the little girl has made up her mind about flavours, a woman comes rushing down the lane. 'Véronique,' she calls, 'where have you got to?'

'Ronique,' the little girl repeats happily.

The woman looks at her severely, apologises to us, explains that she was talking to a friend for a moment and the child ran off. She moves to take her away, but Véronique starts to howl again. Only the arrival of the ice cream cone pacifies her. Then she waves to us merrily and goes off with her minder.

'Maybe if I took up howling with that kind of persistence, I'd get somewhere,' Paul chuckles.

'Only with your mother.' The child has lightened our mood.

'Certainly not with my mother. I was thinking of you.'

I let it pass. 'I liked your mother.'

'She liked you. She spent one whole dinner reminiscing avidly about your father. Have you found out any more, by the way?'

'I thought you told me not to talk about any of that in front of Beatrice.'

His face changes. He looks away. 'Beatrice wasn't there.' He swallows his coffee in a gulp. 'Maria, I know I said that night, it wasn't possible. Between us. But I want it to be. I don't know how, but I want it to be. And I don't want you to disappear.'

I cannot bear the nakedness of his expression. I conjure up an image of Beatrice. 'Is that the howl?' I say with all the lightness I can muster.

'Part of it,' he scowls. 'Do you want the rest?'

'I'm not sure.'

'Do you care for me at all, Maria?' His tone is flat, the tone I can imagine him using with a client, lethally matter-of-fact. I don't like it. I am about to be flippant and then I remember what it's been like these last weeks when the busy-ness I've constructed for myself is over and I'm alone. I try to match my tone to his.

'You should know the answer to that.' I let myself meet his eyes and think that I shouldn't have. They obliterate Beatrice's image and a little demon in me begins to ask why it is that I care about Beatrice so much anyway. But Paul brings her back.

'Beatrice and I don't sleep together.' The words are half-swallowed beneath his breath. He looks away. 'Not that I suppose that will change anything.'

I don't know that I believe him. I think of that scene I accidentally witnessed in the attic room and I don't believe him. Men are always saying things like that to their other women, as if one was supposed to feel sorry for them, instantly and gracefully assuage their desires. It isn't worthy of Paul. 'You and I don't sleep together either,' I grumble, laugh, add, 'Poor Beatrice. I wish you hadn't told me. You must have betrayed her a thousand times. A whole brigade of women haunting the wings.'

'An army. Don't undervalue me.' His irony bristles. He puts a pile of change down on the table, gets up and as he does so I remember the time those words passed between us before, the other way round, and I ran in anger, and I know he is going to do the same now.

'It's no good today.' He looks at me briefly. 'Enjoy your weekend with Grant. I'll see you at the office. Monday at three, isn't it.' He turns away without waiting for an answer.

I watch him, the quick stride down the path amidst the ranked trees. I watch him turn the corner, disappear. Something goes wrong in the pit of my stomach. Maybe it's desolation. I run then, run after him, but when I turn the corner, he is nowhere to be seen. The park is crowded now with lunchtime strollers and I can't see him. Tears clutch stupidly at my eyes. I slow my pace. It's no good today and it will never be any good today between us. And it's no good today because there are no tomorrows. No real tomorrows. Only stolen time, lost weekends. I never used to think about tomorrows before. Sandro's legacy. And it's no good today with Paul because Beatrice hovers over us and all the tomorrows. Beatrice whom he says he doesn't sleep with.

And what if he wasn't juggling with the truth, but sharing it, conveying an intimacy, while I responded with breathtaking callousness? I could ask Beatrice. She would tell me. The thought buzzes through my mind and stings me with self-loathing. For all my stupid efforts, I am clearly beyond redemption. My only forte is self-pity. The easy seductions of despair, Grant said. Yes. I shake myself.

I have been walking in such a daze that I only gradually realise that I am crossing the Pont de la Concorde. So my feet have decided that I will not follow Paul to the office and try to make amends. They are probably right. I stop to look down river and follow the graceful curve of the Seine as it winds round the Ile de la Cité. I can see the dome of the Palais de Justice from here, the twin towers of Notre Dame. I wait for the familiar buzz of pleasure the sight usually gives me, but it doesn't come. Not today. It's no good today.

As I turn away, I see him. I don't know how long he has been standing there, but he is standing there now, leaning against the balustrade and gazing down river as I was a second before, utterly wrapped in his thoughts. He doesn't notice me as I come up to him, doesn't see me until I touch his hand.

'Maria. I'm so glad.' The melancholy vanishes from his features. He covers my hand gently with his. 'I was making a wish and suddenly you're here.' He looks at me whimsically. 'Shall we have lunch together, after all?'

I nod.

'Breaking your prior arrangements?'

'Just prior excuses.'

He squeezes my hand then lets it go. 'Left bank or right?'

'Left.'

We walk side by side. He doesn't touch me now and we don't speak until we have crossed the river and reached the Boulevard. Then he says, 'I lost the case, you know. It hasn't helped my mood. The trouble is I don't know whether it would have been lost anyway or I simply wasn't paying enough attention. So I'm sorry if I growled before.'

'For what it's worth, Tanya told me it was a lost case days ago.'

'Nice to know the office is gossiping about me. Did she tell you that I growled at her too?'

'I'm afraid she did.'

I can feel him casting a long look at me. I step onto the pedestrian crossing, heedless of the oncoming traffic. He pulls me back brusquely, his hand hard on my shoulder. 'This isn't London, you know.'

I laugh and I don't know whether it is the mention of London or the brushing against him which makes me decide but I say it quickly, before I can change my mind.

'Look, I know this little place on the Rue d'Oudinot. It's very quiet and we can talk in peace. The only trouble is we have to bring our own food.'

I don't think he understands me straight away and when he does, he gazes intently at me for a moment. Then things happen very quickly. There is a stop at a *traiteur* in some little street, a short ride in a taxi during which all I am aware of is the closeness of our bodies and his hand on my knee and the growing wetness of my knickers. And then I am standing in front of the picture of the sandalled feet of my wandering woman and I tell her mine have brought me back to her willy-nilly and that I don't want to think about tomorrows. I don't like the me who thinks of tomorrows any more than the one who doesn't and once more won't make any difference anyway and it will make him happy and he more than deserves any little happiness I can give him. And then I stop making excuses to her, for he is standing behind me and his arms are around me and I turn in them and say, 'Once more', but he stops my words with his lips and I'm glad. I'm tired of the thoughts going round and round in my mind, like moths trapped in a small dark room where the light is just on the other side of the glass. I lose myself in the light.

So much time has passed, I had forgotten the sheer fit of us, the marvel of his skin, rough then smooth against my fingers, my bosom, the clasped limbs, the pulse and heave of him inside me, the sound of his breath in my ear. At some point, I think it is when I am on top of him because his eyes are very blue beneath me, I whisper, 'Remember, whatever happens tomorrow, today I love you.' Or maybe I just imagine that I say it and that he says it back to me, but it feels very loud.

Later, we are silly, like children, and he feeds me ice cream straight from the container and calls me, '*Notre Dame des Glaces*', and we find some music on the radio, water music I think it must be, for I feel myself melting into him as we make love slowly, softly, as if all the time in the world were ours.

Later still, or perhaps it is at last, we are dressed again and I am running late for my meeting with Grant and his clients and he for his homecoming and we are both sad. We sit round the low table where we once read a poem together and he picked up the pieces of me, and sip coffee and he says, 'It's true what I told you before, Maria, whatever you think. About Beatrice and me.' His eyes are intent and he holds me with them, won't let me look away. 'We're not taking anything from her by being together.'

'You can't know that.'

He shrugs. 'I'll try and explain it to you. One day, soon. When we have a lot of time. It will take a lot of time.'

I don't think I want to know this. That sense of betrayal is beginning to churn again in my stomach.

'Perhaps you shouldn't tell me. Or perhaps I just shouldn't see Beatrice any more.'

'No.' It is almost a cry.

I stare at him and he looks away.

'She would be too unhappy to lose you,' he murmurs.

'More unhappy than you?'

He doesn't say anything for a moment, but runs his hand tensely through his hair. 'Differently unhappy,' he says at last, then tries a grin which doesn't quite work. 'You'll just have to make do with us both.'

I don't shake my head, but I have a feeling at the base of my spine, a little shiver which runs up it, and I know that it isn't possible.

He insists on seeing me to my door, says he will even see me up if I like, after all, we work together, there is no problem, but I feel like a thief skulking round corners, feel door codes are too good for me. 'Maria.' He walks into the building with me, lets the door fall shut behind him. 'Thank you.' He holds my hand, won't let it go. I kiss him quickly on the cheek. He clears his throat. 'If . . . tonight . . . if . . . please draw your curtains,' he finishes abruptly.

A sullen ache jolts through me as I realise what he means. 'Is that really what you think of me?' I lash out. 'Really?'

He stares at me intently. 'It's not what I think of you, Maria. It's just that I'm sadly aware that I have no rights. Or that my rights end where his nose begins. And yours . . . Which, of course, is the usual case.'

'And you think we're talking about rights here? You think if you had those nominal rights, a bit of a marriage contract, a piece of scribbled paper, it would make any difference?' I am so angry my voice has risen abruptly.

He looks sheepish. 'No, of course not. Don't take it like that. Please. It's just that I could be with you then. I want to be with you.'

I gaze at him, unconvinced. He takes my hand and holds it again. 'Don't you understand, Maria? I'm just translating feelings into lawyer's language. They don't live together very happily. Bad co-habitation.' His eyebrows arch in self-irony. 'I'm just telling you I'm jealous. That's all. It's not an emotion I'm comfortable with.' He performs an exaggerated squirm, mocks himself.

I like the irony, the fact that he can joke about jealousy. So different from Sandro. I smile. 'So next time you have to defend a *crime passionel*, you can do it with a little more conviction. You'll have lived the motive.'

He smiles too. 'As long as I'm doing the defending and not being the accused.'

We hug each other lightly and he is gone.

It is then that I go to open my letter box and find the note bearing the stamp of the Vietnamese Embassy.

⚖ 30

I am sitting in a red plush booth in a Vietnamese restaurant near the Avenue du Maine. Paper lanterns swing from the ceiling. The mirrors are old, put waves in one's face. The waitress walks and talks so softly that there is a hush in the air. Not that she talks to me. She smiles a timid smile but she talks to the man I face, who orders dinner for us. He is tall for a Vietnamese and he wears a cotton suit in worker's blue. That's how he described himself on the phone when we agreed to meet. I told him I was quite tall too and had a lot of auburn hair and would wear white. He laughed. 'You can always ask for me by name,' he said. 'Pham Ngog Thuan.' I repeated it lamely, thought his French was far better than my ability to pronounce a name.

I repeat it again now, and ask in momentary confusion whether I should call him Monsieur Pham or Monsieur Thuan.

He smiles. It is a nice smile, a little sad perhaps because it never reaches his eyes which are soft and black. There is a catlike quality about him, a nimble grace, and his hands move quickly, are small, dainty, for his shoulders.

'Why not call me by my French name,' he says. 'Pierre.'

'I can manage that. And you must call me Maria.'

'Maria. Maria Regnier. Dr Guy Regnier's daughter,' he muses. 'He had a photograph of you in his office. But you were only knee-high. I couldn't have recognised you.'

The notion of me at whatever height in my father's sight makes me feel odd. I existed for him. Warmth floods my cheeks. 'You worked with him?'

Pierre shakes his head. 'I didn't have that privilege.'

'Tell me about him.'

'You probably know many of the things I can tell you.'

'I don't know anything.' I think it comes out as a wail and I try to retrieve myself. 'My mother didn't talk much about him. Not that she ever really gave him up,' I rush to defend her, 'but she didn't talk. Probably didn't think it was good for me. So what I know wouldn't even fill the tiniest obituary. And what I'd like to know is everything, anything. Did he smile a lot, did he have a bad temper, what flowers did he like, did he find another woman after my mother?' My voice rises. 'I just want to have some sense of him as a man.'

Pierre sits through this barrage without stirring. He is looking at me, seriously I think, though I can't tell since his face doesn't move. Meanwhile, a mass of small plates, filled with dumplings and spring rolls and tiny shrimp, have arrived on the table and he courteously urges me to eat, heaps my plate, begins to chew slowly.

After a moment, he says, 'Perhaps the easiest thing is for me to tell you a story.'

'Please. Any story.'

He nods. 'Guy Regnier worked in the Hôpital Grall, the big French hospital in Saigon. It's still there, has probably always been there. He worked mostly in surgery, but he was an expert in burns, skin grafting. The hospital catered largely to the French, but also, particularly after '54, to the richer Vietnamese – not to the Americans, they had their own.' He pauses, looks at me quizzically. 'Do you know anything about the recent history of Vietnam?'

'A little. Very little.' Like a dutiful student, I give him a check-list of what I have garnered from my reading.

'That'll do.' Pierre smiles that smile that doesn't reach his eyes. 'So you know that the war with the Americans really took place in the countryside, not in Saigon, though the city was bloody enough in its own way. Guy Regnier wasn't a particularly political man, a humanist perhaps. But he did know that the Saigon government was brutal and corrupt and his sympathies during the American war were with the Viet Cong. Because he had a deep loyalty to the Vietnamese people among whom he'd grown up.'

He stops as if I were about to question him or argue the point. I don't. 'Go on,' I urge.

'Well, one day, it must have been in 1967, one of his rich Vietnamese patients, a regular, took him aside and asked him whether he might consider making a little overnight journey into the countryside with his black bag and all the burning tricks of his trade in tow. It wasn't that far, but it wasn't that safe either. In fact, it was downright danger-ous and he would have to be blindfolded as well, for his own safety.

The Viet Cong didn't trust Europeans much and just in case anything went wrong and on his return he was asked questions, he could legitimately say he had seen nothing. The rich man would accompany him part of the way.

'So Guy Regnier went off into the night with his black bag and blindfold and ended up in a little village where a number of young men, boys really but high enough ranking guerillas or he wouldn't have been sent for, were suffering from severe burns. And worse. And he helped them. Saved a few of them. And others, later. For he went back when he was called to other sites. Went and tried to shrink his height and cropped his hair short so that he wasn't so visibly who he was.'

I move the food round my plate and smell seared flesh and sit very still. 'Thank you for telling me the story,' I say as the silence between us seems to grow as fat as the lump in my throat.

Pierre nods. 'I was one of those boys. In the first village. So I have a particular debt to Guy Regnier.'

I stare at him. I want to touch him, sniff him, see if I can find the scent of my father on him. 'You look well,' I offer inanely.

His lips curl. 'It was a long time ago. Though I don't think you'd like the sight of some parts of me even now.' He winks, I am sure he winks, though his face is serious again so quickly that perhaps I imagine it as I try to imagine those scars. I want to touch them too.

'And you knew him before you went into the countryside,' I say. 'Because you saw my picture in his office.'

He nods. 'Now tell me about you, and about Françoise Regnier. One story deserves another.'

'Nothing so dramatic,' I mumble and I tell him quickly about my mother. Perhaps I emphasise what I call her good works too much, or the number of Vietnam committees she sat on, for he looks at me strangely.

'And she never remarried?'

I shake my head, then tell him about her sudden death, and a little about myself, my life in America, my return here. There doesn't seem to be much to tell. Peace breeds fewer stories than war.

We have reached coffee, but I don't want to let him go. I want to hear more about this Guy Regnier who has taken on flesh and bone through his words, has grown into something more tangible than the phantom of my mother's narrative. I clear my throat and manage to bring out again the crucial question Pierre has refrained from answering.

'And do you know whether my father remarried? Had other children, perhaps?'

He sips his coffee, doesn't look at me straight away. 'I don't believe so,' he says at last.

Maybe it is because he has taken so long to answer, but I have the sense that he is being polite, isn't being altogether truthful, doesn't want to hurt my feelings. We are strangers, after all. I let it pass. I play with my napkin. Then I ask him, though it is oddly hard for me to bring out the words, 'And do you know how he died?'

It is the first time I see something like open emotion on his face, a fleeting frown and then a twist of the lips.

'You do.'

'Not exactly.' He shakes his head. 'All I know is that it happened on one of those clandestine night-time journeys into the countryside. I suspect his guide didn't turn up on time to take him back to the city. And then it was too late.' He pauses, looks into the distance. 'Bombs. I guess you could say he died of bravery.'

The silence between us grows. The waitress hovers. But I still don't want to let him go. Somehow it is as if he carries my father within him. Timidly I ask whether he would like to come back to my place or perhaps go to a café. There is so much more I would like to hear, even though I don't know what questions to put.

As we are walking, Pierre says, 'Maria, did your mother ever tell you that Guy Regnier had another child?'

I stop in my tracks, stare at him. 'Another child?' I echo, shake my head. 'After me? But you said . . .'

'Before you.'

'Before me.' The headlights of the passing cars look too bright. They dazzle me. I want to go into a quiet corner. I need to think about this, feel it. Another child, before me. Another woman, before my mother. The missing link I always sensed. 'Was that another reason he went back to Vietnam?' I say at last.

'Yes.'

I am lost in my own thoughts. I wonder why my mother never said anything. I put it down to her puritanism. She wouldn't have liked the thought of my father with another woman, even before her. A prostitute perhaps. I think of the statistics I have read. Or perhaps she was simply jealous, knew that my father had left her not only because of work, of idealism, but to go back to the mother of his first child. Then, as if it took a great deal of sophisticated mental algebra to arrive at this solution, I suddenly realise that this other child is my brother or sister. I taste this fact and it makes me strangely happy. My world seems to have spread, shifted its perimeter to include a distant country.

'Do you know this person?' I ask.

Pierre doesn't answer straight away and I suspect that he is weighing his answer carefully. Perhaps this person is someone he is not meant to know, or doesn't want to know. He works for the Embassy, after all. There may be things he can't tell me, can't talk about to foreigners. Vietnam has only recently opened itself to the west. Then I think that maybe this sibling, so new to me, is already dead and he doesn't want to tell me that.

We have turned into my street and I ask, my tongue stumbling over the new words, 'Is this person a brother or a sister?'

His laugh sounds odd in the quiet of the darkened street. Then he says, so softly that I instantly want him to repeat it, 'I am that person.'

We stare at each other. We are standing in front of my door and we stare at each other. 'You are my brother,' I repeat twice, tasting it. 'My brother.' I smile at him. I feel shy. 'Welcome to my house, brother.' I push open the door, gaze at him in the lift, wish I could read his eyes.

'Thank you, sister,' he parries as I usher him in. 'The last time I saw you, you were a pesky little creature who was always tugging at my trousers and shouting "Gimme", so the evidence of my eyes is hardly incontrovertible. But you're so much like Guy that I think that has to be proof enough. Sister.'

I giggle. I giggle as I bring out one of the bottles of champagne that Grant has given me to celebrate our new working partnership. I giggle as I pour it into glasses and hand Pierre one and we drink a toast to each other. I giggle as I watch him, and he watches me more openly now. Afterwards we talk. We sit side by side on the white sofa and talk into the small hours of the night.

I learn a great deal then. I learn that Pierre came to France with our father late in 1952 when he was two, that his own mother, Guy's wife, had died just after giving birth to him. It was not the right time to be French in Vietnam. The war against the colonisers was in full flood. On top of that, everything in Saigon reminded Guy of his wife, who it seems he had loved deeply and too briefly. He didn't want to leave Pierre behind with his grandparents. But his grandfather had extracted a promise from Guy that he wouldn't bring the boy up to be solely French. The war would end some day and he must bring him back to his country. Which Guy did, when Pierre was twelve.

In the interim, there was my mother and me.

Pierre remembers my mother. He remembers her as being very kind to him and very proper and sometimes very stern. He remembers Guy worrying about him feeling left out when I was born. And he did feel left out, though only a little. It was at school that there were problems. He came home with too many bloody noses and each one worried Guy more. Guy and Françoise started to argue. Guy wanted to take all of us back to Vietnam. It was his country, too, after all. He was born there. And he could be more useful there than he was in Paris. Françoise could teach. They needed teachers everywhere. And then there was Pierre and his bloody noses. It would distort him to grow up here. The country was racist.

And then Françoise would retort that she wouldn't go to live in a country where the slant of her eyes was a sign of her politics. She wouldn't be identified with the colonists, present or former. And Guy would answer that the days of the French empire were over and she must think of Pierre, for whom life would be better in Vietnam. And she would tell him to think of me, and how difficult things would be for me. And how dangerous it could all be. The arguments went on and on until the very day they left.

'Your stepmother is a stubborn woman,' Guy told Pierre after they had gone. 'Almost as stubborn as me. But she'll come round.'

'I think he believed that for years,' Pierre reflects. 'He always thought you would both suddenly arrive on the next flight from Paris.'

I think of my mother and am glad that she wasn't betrayed in that easy way my own guilts had led me to imagine. I am glad for both of us.

'And then history took over,' Pierre says.

He fills in the gaps in that history for me. He is racked with guilt because in some way he feels responsible for our father's death. Though he knows it could not have been otherwise. When the twelve-year-old Pierre first arrived in Vietnam, it was no easier for him than it had been in Paris. He didn't speak much Vietnamese and, despite the slant of his eyes, he was more French than anything else. Gradually he learned, but the more he learned about his country, the less he wanted to become a part of the South Vietnamese army he was destined for. So he fled, ran off into the countryside when he was seventeen, joined the Viet Cong, rose in the ranks.

'And it was because of me he never went back to France,' Pierre murmurs to me. 'He wouldn't leave me there. Every time he read or heard of a fresh bombing in the villages, he thought of me. He saw me in every injured child, was poised to save me. And he did, more than once. I would come to see him from time to time when I could, clandestinely, and I would tell him to go home. And he would look at me severely and tell me he was home. Home was a place one earned. He was a good man.'

'*Ông bác sĩ tốt lắm.*' I repeat the words I have learned and he stares at me. 'Monsieur Tran taught me,' I smile. 'The good doctor.'

'Yes.'

We sit and talk and are silent in turn, mulling over distant lives which are suddenly as close as our own bodies. At one point I say to him, 'So you were the "P" in his letters. I thought once that P might be a lover,' I laugh. 'And then you fell out of the letters.'

'I told him he was to say nothing about me. Letters could be read by the wrong people. Reprisals taken.'

I think it is after this that I tell him about Françoise, that she was pregnant when he left, that there could have been another one of us.

'That is sad,' he says. 'Very sad. I don't imagine Guy knew.'

I grin. 'Stubborn woman.'

'Stubborn all of us, perhaps.' He looks at me, stands. 'I really must go. Work tomorrow. We'll meet again soon. Sister.' He bends abruptly to place a moist kiss on my forehead. There is something strange about the gesture. And then it comes to me: it feels like a repetition. If I sit very tight and make myself very small, perhaps I can almost remember it. A kiss from big brother to little sister, ordered by parents, not quite wanted, but there nonetheless.

I stand to his height. 'Very soon. Saturday, if you like. I'll cook dinner for you.'

He smiles.

Pierre. I lie in bed and taste the name and repeat the word 'brother' to myself.

Tentatively I mouth the word 'father' and I think of a father who is Pierre's father, as well as the father conjured out of my mother's words and silences and gestures. I then think that I have spent a great deal of my life looking for male stories to fill up the gaps in the story I inherited.

I think of my mother and my father and that brief and fragile little unit that was our family and its fracturing and how the pieces somehow feel as if they are now back in place. Like some beautiful porcelain bowl of eastern design, copied in the west, broken and now put back together again, the cracks still showing, but whole. I can stroke it, mull over its intricate patterns, keep things in it – letters, jewellery, safety pins, lose them and find them again, those mundane but essential little objects of everyday life. I like the bowl. I no longer have any rancour about its splitting. Neither towards Françoise or Guy. Things break. One can't always stop them. There is no blame.

⚖ 31

The reason I don't rush into the office on Friday morning, throw my arms around Paul and gleefully announce that he has found my brother for me is because of what happened with Beatrice on Wednesday. It is difficult enough to face her after what he has told me, but it is even more difficult to confront him with the hidden knowledge she has given me. Like some overblown shuttlecock I am bounced between them, trapped in a desperate game of no one's making, gorged with too many intimacies. The game will have to end very soon.

On Wednesday Beatrice and I taught in the school in the Thirteenth as usual. After the lesson, Vesna came up to chat to me outside the classroom. She was wearing the dress I had given her and I told her how well she looked in it. She said 'Merci' in that sharp way of hers, then told me she and Jasha wouldn't be coming over at the weekend or be in class next week. He was having his operation. I kissed her stiff cheek and wished them both luck, told Jasha I had a special surprise for him when the ordeal of hospital was over.

Beatrice was watching me through all this and when I turned to her, there was the first real scowl on her face I had ever seen.

'You shouldn't get so friendly with them,' she said.

'Why ever not?'

'It's not professional. They won't thank you for it.'

I shrugged, told her I didn't mind, told her I liked Vesna, thought of her as an Antigone leading her blind son out of the gates of the city. She was tough, I said. It was the only way to survive. I didn't tell Beatrice that I thought I was a little like Vesna. We had both seen too much life, though what she had seen was a million times worse and her armour was thicker, had to be.

I don't mind Vesna's superficial lack of graciousness. Beneath it all, we understand each other. I know that from her reactions. The day I gave her the dress I asked her whether she had heard that during the winter, French women had been called to band together and send their Bosnian sisters something that would lift their spirits – perfume, frilly knickers, feminine things. She laughed uproariously. She loved the notion. 'Let them send us anything, except guns and the men who use them,' she said. When I had previously asked Beatrice what she thought about this call for frilly knickers, she was scandalised. 'Medicine is what they need. Warm shoes.'

I'm afraid that for all my efforts, I am still not like Beatrice.

Anyhow, on Wednesday my comments about Vesna didn't altogether pacify Beatrice, but she conceded the point. She also asked me, as if to make up for her irritation, whether I would like to take on a second class in a different school. I agreed, though I said my time might not be so flexible in the autumn.

Then she came home with me for a drink and her mood visibly shifted. As soon as we were up in the apartment, she started to pace excitedly around the front room. When she had swallowed a few sips of wine, she turned to me and said, 'You know, I saw you. Saw you naked one night, undressing.'

She put her hand up to her lips and it was almost as if she were hiding a girlish snicker.

'Oh?'

'And kissing a man. He looked very handsome.'

I had thought it was Paul doing the spying. Beatrice must have told him about it. They talk about me. The thought makes me shrivel up inside. I hate it.

'I must remember to draw my curtains.'

'Oh no, I don't mind. Really.'

She was a little breathless, her eyes all round and shiny. I filled her glass again.

'What's it like for you with a man?' she asked then.

'Depends on the man, I guess. Sometimes it's wonderful. Sometimes . . .' I grimaced. 'And for you?' I returned the question since she seemed to be waiting for something.

'The same.' She turned away. I knew from her gestures that this wasn't the whole truth and that probably she has only ever known one man. Paul. But she has known him. Knows him still, whatever Paul has wanted me to believe.

I wondered for a moment what it would be like only ever to have slept with one man and concluded you would probably spend your time speculating about all the others, which was what Beatrice was doing now. But if that one man was Paul, it probably wasn't so bad. I felt rotten as I had this thought and I laughed too cheerily, and then found myself leading her on, since we were being girls together and I'm not a very good girl. 'Doesn't your husband mind when you sleep with others?'

'I don't think so,' Beatrice answered. 'We're very grown-up about it.'

I know my Beatrice and this didn't sound like her voice or her words. She'd learned them. These were words Paul had given her.

But I carried on. 'And you don't mind about him? With other women, I mean.'

'Not really. Would you?'

I thought about this. 'It depends,' I said again. 'Probably though. It's so hard to generalise.'

'Yes.' Beatrice nodded enthusiastically, suddenly hugged me. 'It's so hard to generalise.' Then she hesitated. 'I only mind when he stays out all night. I don't like being left alone with the children and then suddenly hearing a noise in the night. I like to be told when he's coming in.'

'Yes, I can see that.'

Beatrice gave me her best smile then and I felt like a worm whose wriggling was really not worth the earth it turned.

She got up after that and started to pace again while I thought of Paul's other women and everything she must have been through. Then she startled me by saying in a small voice, 'Maria, do you think I could try on one of your dresses? It's just that I have this do to go to and . . .'

'Of course.' I would have gladly given her my entire wardrobe at that moment.

We went to look through my closet and I pulled out a few things that I thought might just fit her and she tried them on hesitantly. They weren't quite right. Our shapes are so different, but Beatrice seemed ecstatic as she squeezed into a few of my dresses and I was happy to see her with her own eyes. Finally she chose a flimsy, flowing olive-green two-piece which didn't look too bad.

It was while she was trying on clothes that she said to me, 'You know, Marie-Françoise has been asking me whether you might like to go up to Brittany with them all one weekend. To visit Grandmother.'

'I couldn't do that.'

'She scares you too,' Beatrice laughed. 'But don't worry, Paul will be there. He'll protect you.'

I could hardly breathe.

Beatrice trusts me so implicitly that even as I remember that moment, I can hardly breathe.

After Beatrice went, I sat very still for a long time and felt very afraid. And the fear must have followed me into sleep for I had a terrifying dream. It still pursues me. The dream is about Marie-Françoise. We are standing in my living room in front of the billowing curtains and I am getting undressed. Marie-Françoise is looking at me. Her eyes are black with a searing hatred. But it is not Marie-Françoise who looks at me. It is me as a child. I recognise the untidy plaits.

'Don't stare at me like that,' I say to the child who is both of us.

'Okay.' One by one, she slowly takes out her eyes and hands them to me. 'Is that better?' she asks.

This is why I cannot throw my arms around Paul today. Last Monday it would have all been different. It was different. On Monday the current between us flowed so strong and fast that it could have sailed us to the South Seas without a stop. Only the knowledge of Madame Duval's august presence just a heartbeat away kept us from tumbling on the floor and succumbing to its rush.

We worked instead. At my behest, we did an update, so that I could map out what research there remained for me to cover. It isn't so much. Perhaps Paul is cutting corners because he knows I need to be free for the autumn. But in any case he wants to get the bulk of what remains of the writing done over the summer. He said to me then with that compelling look on his face, 'And if you were to come away with me, Maria, it would be sure to get finished.'

'And the children?' I asked.

'The children are well taken care of, all their holiday plans firm.' He started to enumerate them: a few weeks in Brittany, a computer camp for Nicolas, Marie-Françoise to the coast to see her cousins.

And Beatrice? I wanted to ask, but I didn't want to say her name, didn't want her to exist for us at that moment. All I wanted was to bask in the fantasy of it. So instead I touched his hand and said, 'We'll see.'

And today the winds have changed. The current today is between Beatrice and me. And though it isn't so strong, I have the sense that it could easily flood the house.

So I don't rush into the office and tell Paul. I phone Madame Duval instead and say something has come up and could she convey to Paul that I won't be in. Then I set to work. And day-dream about Pierre and my father and my mother. In the afternoon, on an impulse, I walk up to the Cimetière Montparnasse. This time I bring flowers, not a bouquet since she wouldn't like the waste, but a large potted rose which will last and last. I talk to her. It is easy to talk to her now. I tell her I don't mind her having being such a proud and stubborn woman, but she could at least have told me that I had a brother. She tells me I was too young to tell to start with and then as time passed, it became too hard. She tells me some things aren't secrets but somehow they never get told. It's in the nature of family life. All life, maybe. But she is happy I have met Pierre now. If it hadn't been for Guy's stubbornness . . . I laugh.

Before I go, I confess to her that I find it a lot harder than her to tell right from wrong and then act on it. She doesn't answer me right away and then in her best schoolteacher's voice, the one she used when I used to despair of maths problems, she says, 'Just keep trying, Maria.' I am about to turn away, it is not my favourite voice, when she adds, more softly, 'Your father used to say that the only thing he ever found clear was the position of the liver and the pancreas. And usually when the owner was dead. For the rest, we all just muddle along best we can.'

I say goodbye to her. I feel oddly at peace. I know that I have imagined her words, but they felt real enough. Perhaps memory has dredged them up from somewhere.

I have only been back in the apartment for some ten minutes when the doorbell rings. Marie-Françoise, I think, and wonder whether I have any ice cream left. But the voice on the intercom is Paul's and for a moment, I hesitate. I don't want him here. Here where I sat with Beatrice just two days ago. Her perfume is still in the air. But I let him in. There are some things that can't be said over an intercom.

When I open the door he is all smiles and warmth and irresistible charm. He is still on the shore where I last left him and he doesn't know I have crossed to the other side. He hugs me and I move away before it becomes something else. He doesn't notice my withdrawal. He is still smiling.

'Lovely here. Airy,' he says as he follows me into the front room. 'First place I've seen you in that's your own.' His eyes play over me. 'And I like your jeans. The ones you wore to Cambridge.'

I draw the curtains with a swish and he frowns slightly. 'I know you're uncomfortable, Maria, but I've only come to give you this.' He puts a diskette on the table. 'You said you wanted to hurry along with things and I thought you might have some time at the weekend to look it over.'

I nod.

'And I wanted to find out how things went last night with the man from the Embassy. Am I allowed to sit down?'

'Please.'

He doesn't choose the chair Beatrice always sits in, which is something of a relief. He sinks into the sofa instead, gestures comically. 'And will you offer me a drink? A glass of water will do.'

'Of course.' I stand there for a moment, watching him, and his brow creases. 'What's wrong, Maria? Has something happened?'

'Everything's happened.' My voice is too shrill.

He is beside me in a moment, his arm round my shoulder. I shake it off.

'Your father? Was it bad?'

'No, yes.' I flounder, then tell him because I want to tell him above anyone else. I tell him quickly about yesterday evening, about my father, about the brother I have found whom I never knew I had lost.

'But that's extraordinary, Maria, wonderful. Absolutely wonderful.'

'And all thanks to you.'

He shrugs. 'A lucky contact.'

'Thank you for the luck.'

'Here, I brought you something. I guess now it will be all the more fitting.' He takes a brightly wrapped package from his case and hands it to me.

I shake my head. 'You shouldn't give me things.'

'Why not? I want to give you things.'

'You shouldn't.'

He drops the package on the table. It makes a small plop. Those intelligent eyes examine me. 'Something else has happened, Maria. You've changed again. I don't understand.'

'Nothing's happened.' I start to pace. 'It's just that I've seen Beatrice.'

'So.' There is a wary look on his face.

'So you lied to me. Lied to me about the two of you.'

'I didn't lie to you.' He is adamant. 'I don't lie to you. I just omit things. Have to omit things it isn't discreet to talk about. Why believe her rather than me?'

'And then all those women.' I start to pace. I am angry for Beatrice. As angry as if it were me he had wronged. 'You've been cruel to her. It's cruel, no matter what kind of arrangements you've made. Even if she's remarkable. She doesn't like it. Not Beatrice. She isn't your New York or Paris sophisticate. She's afraid at night. She's a gentle soul. Naive. She doesn't know how to tell you. She's afraid of you. Of your mother.'

I go on and on. I can't stop and he sits there rubbing his forehead as if there is a pain in it that won't go away.

'I wish it had never started between us. It would have been better all round.' I say it bluntly and then I curb myself, think how much Paul has meant to me all these months, think how without him I would never have found Pierre. I go into the kitchen, make noise with glasses, find the mineral water I never brought out. He is still sitting there when I get back, still rubbing his forehead.

'Would you like an aspirin?' I ask lamely.

He doesn't answer me. Then suddenly he says, 'So you prefer to believe Beatrice, trust her rather than me?'

Our eyes meet and I turn away before his take me over. 'I . . . She's an old friend,' I protest. 'She's good.'

'Yes.'

He goes. He doesn't slam the door, but he doesn't say goodbye either. And I stand there looking after him. After a moment the temptation to lift back the curtain and peer through the window is overpowering. I don't. I lie on the bed and close my eyes very tight and try to think of other things.

What I think about is my old adage of the clean break, the value I had learned young of finishing things off swiftly and sharply, of being able to say 'it's over' and sticking to it. No regrets. No mess. And how increasingly I don't seem to be able to make the breaks clean enough. Maybe life is just too dirty.

And it has a funny way of going on just when you think it can't any more. We muddle along. Paddle in murky everyday pools far from the sea.

Over the next days I cook dinner for my brother and we talk and he tells me about his wife and two children and how he is only in Paris for three months, but may come back. I learn that he is in charge of the development of a new tourist zone for the Vietnamese government. Steve and Chuck arrive and we laugh a lot and wine and dine and go to the opera. Paul's mother rings me up and insists that I come to Brittany for a weekend. When I tell her about my guests, about Pierre, she insists that I bring them all along. The house will love the life. We fix tentatively for the first weekend in July.

Meanwhile, I take Nicolas to 'Wayne's World II' and enjoy his enjoyment. Marie-Françoise eats so huge a sundae at a café we go to that she tells me she thinks she's probably had enough to last her a year. Jasha's operation is a partial success and I give him a guitar which seems too large for his body but which he strums with rapt delight. Vesna tells me that she has found a job for the summer managing a small Serbian restaurant while its owners are on holiday. She hugs me and tells me I can bring all my friends to eat. Maître Cournot throws a party to mark Tanya's return to the US and she confesses to me that she thinks her moral fibre has crumbled in France and she isn't fit for the stringency of the mid-west. Beatrice looks more radiant than I have ever seen her and I assume Paul has decided to concentrate on making her happy. When I go into the office for our now twice-weekly meetings, he is quiet and courteous. We work very hard and talk only of work. He doesn't touch me, hardly looks at me. I sit there afterwards and wait for the glow which is supposed to come with goodness and I ache for him.

Sometimes, late at night, I take out the pin which was in the box he gave me, for I opened it at last, and finger it. It is a formalised flower, its petals of lapis lazuli, as blue as the bluebells in our country wood. Lost and found again. Paul has returned many things to me, my father, my brother, bits of myself. And I have lost him in the process.

We muddle along.

PART FIVE

⚖ 32

The train speeds through the countryside, eating distance as smoothly as if it were churn butter. Cows graze and turn limpidly into sheep who are metamorphosed into villages which disappear in the blink of an exclamation to leave only expanses of sky over tufted fields. It is my first journey in a TGV – a Very High Speed train – and I feel as young as Marie-Françoise who is at my side, but far more excited. She is an experienced traveller, I a novice.

Between exclamations, we play cards. Nicolas sits opposite her and opposite me is Paul. He didn't know until yesterday I was coming and I wasn't sure he was. He rang me to cancel our Friday meeting, said he had completely forgotten it was the start of the summer break and he always took the children up to his mother's to get them settled in.

'But I'm coming too,' I said.

There was a pause, a low grumble. 'No one seems to tell me anything any more. Not even my mother.'

'Maybe she thought we talked.'

'I suppose she did.'

'There are others, too. My friends from New York. My brother.'

Another pause. 'Well, that will be nice. The three-twenty train. Taxi in front of the house at two forty-five. Bring a bathing costume. It might be warm for a change.'

In fact, Steve and Chuck decided to drive up and take the opportunity to visit a bit of France. They offered to take Pierre along so he could do the same. I didn't think he'd accept. He met them once, but I couldn't tell what he made of them – a gay American couple who talk enough to make up for all of his silences. And there are limits to what one can ask a long-lost brother from the other side of the world. I didn't think the Embassy would approve either, after all theirs was meant to have been a puritan revolution. But Pierre accepted the offer. Maybe he thinks Steve and Chuck will be useful to him in the future. I told him that between them they knew everyone who was worth knowing in New York. Maybe he just likes the idea of consorting with the former enemy, though he knows better than I do that many of them weren't.

Apart from the excitement of finding him, I like my new brother more all the time.

So there are only four of us on the train and Paul has been so silent for the last hour that it feels more like three. Now he bleakly mutters, 'Gin', and lays his cards on the table.

'Not fair,' Marie-Françoise blurts out. 'I only had one more jack to go. Not fair.'

'Not fair? What do you mean, not fair!' I exclaim, starting to tickle her so that she wriggles and squirms and finally bursts into bright laughter.

Paul suddenly gives me a dazzling smile, the kind he used to woo me with. 'What do you say to a little walk?' he asks. 'I think it's about time for the other kind of gin.'

'Can I have a Coke, Papa?' Marie-Françoise, all charm now, smiles up at her father.

'One a day for the whole weekend.' Paul ruffles her hair, 'And Nicolas can have a little something with the grown-ups, if he likes.'

Nicolas flushes bright red, but when he gets up I notice his shoulders are high. He isn't hiding so much these last weeks. A change is slowly creeping over him. Maybe it's the computer camp. He told me about it when we went to the cinema, told me it was really all because of me that he was allowed to go. His grandmother had taken my words to heart and told his father it might not be such a terrible thing. And Paul wasn't all that against it in any case: now that he had a computer of his own, he was coming round. He had even told Nicolas he would have to teach his father a trick or two when he came back.

'And your mum?' I asked him.

'Oh, she doesn't care what I do, as long as I don't bother her,' he said to me.

I told him I was sure that wasn't true, but he just shrugged and I remembered then that Beatrice never seemed to pay any attention to him when we were together. More than that. Never even looked at him. The family's ugly duckling.

The train may be smooth to sit in, but when we walk its speed is evident in bumped shins and hips. Paul looks back at me over the children's heads and mouths an 'ouch', shows me how to position my hands on each forthcoming seat to keep my balance. Something seems to have woken him from his brooding slumber. Maybe it is simply the sight of the sea, darkly blue now in the distance.

I asked Beatrice why she didn't come up with us since we were to be a whole party and her mother-in-law would have little time to make her uncomfortable. It would be jolly. She looked at me blankly. 'You've forgotten, Maria, I'm sure I told you. I go off on holiday on Monday. I need some time alone to prepare.' She smiled dreamily then. 'Three whole weeks to myself, on an island. Bliss. Maybe I'll stay longer,' she laughed. 'I'll be just like you.'

Beatrice, I have to say, has been looking wonderful in anticipation of her holiday. She went on a diet so my dress would fit her better and it worked, so I told her to keep it, gave her another. That wonderful serenity is back in her face too. But she's been growing a little forgetful. She forgot to turn up to the French class on Wednesday and I ended up with both groups; then she forgot to buy Marie-Françoise a pair of trainers for Brittany and asked me whether I'd pick up a pair on Thursday. Perhaps her duties are really getting on top of her.

By the time we finish our drinks we have almost arrived and we have to make a dash back to our seats to collect our things. When the door slides open and releases us onto the platform, the air is moist, already salty. Paul takes a deep breath and smiles. 'All right, scamps, find us the biggest taxi.'

We pile into a cab willing to take all of us and ride lazily through the dips and turns of a lush green countryside which reminds me of nothing so much as England.

'Been here before?' Paul asks.

I shake my head.

'Hope you like it.'

'Of course Maria will like it. It's beautiful,' Marie-Françoise answers for me.

The house is tall and solid and whitewashed. It sits at the crest of a hill off a small winding road. Squat wind-curved trees surround it and when we reach the top of the hill, the sea is a surprise on the other side. It bounds against rocks, curls white and spits against a cliff.

The sun sits on the horizon, a plump yellow ball washing the sky pink in its wake.

'I like it,' I murmur to Paul.

He looks at me in a way I thought the last weeks had obliterated and then Madame Arnault is upon us, waving from the porch, urging the children in, holding a large and tugging golden retriever by the collar.

'Rabelais!' Marie-Françoise falls on the dog and lets him lick her face.

'Your grandmother first.' Madame Arnault smiles at me, before giving her cheek to Marie-Françoise and Nicolas in turn. 'Welcome.' She kisses me lightly, then moves to embrace her son. 'The others haven't arrived yet, so you've plenty of time for a wash, a stroll through the grounds, a drink. I'm so glad to have you all here.'

She looks less daunting than she did in Paris. Perhaps it's the casual slacks and fawn sweater. Perhaps it's just because we're in her own home.

'I've put you in the guest wing, my dear, far from the children, so you can sleep in in the morning. And next door to your brother. Isn't it exciting. You'll have to tell me all about it. But first we must show you round. Paul, will you do it or shall I?'

Paul chooses to see to the children.

'You know, we all used to come here as a family when I was a child and then when my own children were small.' Madame Arnault chats as she shows me round. 'When they grew up, we didn't come so much any more and the place got all shabby with disuse. Then, after my husband died, I really thought I'd had enough of Paris. I wanted a garden, quiet, the sea, glimpses of my own childhood. And now when my friends or the children come to see me, it's a special occasion. We have longer together than we do in the city. It's some kind of solution, I guess. To old age.'

I smile into her loneliness and exclaim over the beauties of the house. It seems larger on the inside than the outside, big generous rooms which give onto each other filled with just enough comfortable old furniture not to be empty or crowded. And all of the windows look out onto views I want to pause over. The room she shows me to is all warm oak and white walls, with a big old-fashioned bed in the centre.

'It creaks a little,' Madame Arnault chuckles, 'but you can watch the sea from here.' She throws open the windows and I hear the whoosh of the waves. 'You'll be all right?'

'Wonderful, thank you.'

I wash in the corner sink and melancholy creeps up on me. I can't chase it away. Perhaps it's just the sound of the sea. I put on a bright blue sweater and brighter white trousers to try to frighten it and laugh at myself.

Downstairs the children are having supper in the kitchen, are being fussed over by a plump dark-haired woman who is introduced by Paul as Martine. She wipes her hand on her apron before shaking mine and says something in an accent I can't immediately fathom.

'Would you like a nibble of something?' Paul translates. 'Or shall we have a walk?'

'Martine is a good cook. Better than my mother,' Marie-Françoise announces.

'Hush,' Paul chides her.

'You say it too.' Nicolas takes his sister's side.

We go out through a back door into a garden lush with rhododendrons and vast hydrangea bushes. There are pebbled paths with rose trellises and further from the house, lanes shadowed by trees. Paul is quiet as we walk, abstracted, quiet for so long that finally I say, 'You're elsewhere.'

'No. Yes,' he grins. 'I was thinking about a case. It's funny, the country always makes me think of death. Maybe it's all the vegetation. The sound of things growing. Look.' He points to a window at the top of the house. 'That's where I do a lot of my writing. Maybe that's why I'm preoccupied.' He pauses. 'And because I can't touch you.'

I shiver.

'Cold?'

I shake my head and he casts me a brooding look. 'The blue suits you. You could wear the brooch with it.'

We walk. 'I never thanked you for it. It's lovely. A memento.' My voice cracks.

He laughs gruffly. 'It would be lovelier if we had a future to match the memories.'

We hear the sound of a car in the drive and walk quickly round the house towards the front. As we do so, I try to shake off my sense of melancholy. It won't quite go. It persists while I introduce Steve and

Chuck and Pierre to Paul and his mother. It clings despite the laughter of friends.

Madame Arnault takes Pierre over. She is honoured, she tells him, to meet Guy Regnier's son. Pierre seems equally pleased to meet her and politely lets himself be led away for a tour of the house and reminiscences about our father. My New York and Paris sides are slightly trickier. Steve begins by eyeing Paul too openly and says in English, 'So you're the scoundrel who's stolen away my best partner.'

I don't think Paul has quite caught the tone, for he gives me a quick glance and then says, 'I think she came willingly. At first.'

'Lucky dog.'

'I am that.'

'Wasting her time with the law.' Steve shakes his shaggy head mournfully. 'Good thing it's not America. We already have more lawyers than the rest of the world put together.'

'We need them,' Chuck intervenes, chortles so that his elfin face looks even more impish. 'We got more crime. More wrongs to right. More rights to fight.'

Paul looks at them both and suddenly smiles his most charming smile. It's taken him a moment, but he's there now. 'Welcome to the outskirts of Douarnenez, gentlemen. And to France, birthplace of the rights of man and a few women.'

Steve bows dramatically, then drapes his arm round me. 'Best PR in New York, she was. That's public relations. We're not sure about the private relations. They're still open to reasonable doubt.'

'Stop it, Steve. You're with serious people.'

'So who wasn't being serious? Oh, and here are two more deeply serious people.' He bends to Marie-Françoise's height and puts out his hand, *'Enchanté, Mademoiselle. Je suis Steve Nichols et ça c'est mon ami, Chuck. Comment allez-vous?'* He delivers all this in such exaggerated schoolboy French that Marie-Françoise bursts out laughing.

'And I am Marie-Françoise and this is my brother, Nicolas,' she says in a perfect English mirror-image of Steve.

We all giggle.

'And I can tell we are going to be *amis*, all of us.' Steve pats Nicolas on the shoulder.

The dining room has a fireplace at either end in which Madame Arnault has arranged vast bowls of flowers. We sit at the long table over which she regally presides. Pierre is next to her and I am next to him. I worry about all the questions he is being asked about Vietnam and realise at one point that he can take care of himself better than I can. His manner is always courteous so that he manages to avoid direct answers without seeming to do so. That pleases me and I find myself drifting and thinking again about how the trials of his life have shaped him. When I come out of my day-dream everyone is suddenly arguing with great earnestness about the law.

'The reason you have so many lawyers,' Paul is saying in English to Steve, 'is that your society is based on contract. Everything is there to be argued, signed and sealed. And claimed against, when the contract is broken. Here, we have contracts, yes, but behind them a whole weight of, how shall I say it, woolly tradition, customs, that many of us understand without having to put contracts to. Because we were way back then mostly the same people. But in America, you were all new. You had to write things down, so all the different peoples with their different customs could understand each other.'

'And now we understand each other even less because we have so many rules that no one knows which ones he or she or it, not to mention hyphen American this and hyphen American that, is breaking or needing to put right,' Steve grunts. 'So we have to have lawyers everywhere to work them out. And we pretend they're heroes.' He slaps his forehead with a thud.

Paul smiles but looks perplexed and I have to translate, which isn't easy since I think only Chuck and I will know what Steve is on about in whatever language.

But Paul has read his newspapers. 'Oh, you mean because of all the insult laws.'

Chuck laughs. 'We're a delicate, sensitive people. Peoples.'

'And litigious. Good for my profession, but maybe not so good for the society as a whole. Perhaps we could compare it in one way with what has happened in Italy. When politics fail, people look to the courts for justice.'

'Checks and balances.'

'And when the judges fail?' I ask.

'We go right back to the beginning.'

'Or bang bang. We shoot each other.'

'We have done too much of that,' Pierre suddenly intervenes.

'On that merry note, I think we could do with some dessert.' Madame Arnault rises and for a moment I think we have upset her. I follow her into the kitchen. She has tears in her eyes but she wipes them calmly. 'Thank you for bringing them all,' she says. 'It's just like when my husband was here. All noise and commotion.' She gives me a tranquil smile.

Morning dawns clear and bright and we brave the chill to clamber down to the beach while the tide is right. There are little rock pools and stretches of fine sand and the gulls' call is shrill and high above the noise of the waves. My bathing suit, unworn for too long, is too white and too skimpy, and I feel shy as I lift off my sweatshirt in front of my brother.

'Your sister is a very beautiful woman.' Paul is watching me.

'It runs in the family,' Steve chuckles and I think Pierre will be insulted, but he simply smiles and goes off to kick a ball round with Nicolas. 'Nice guy, your brother. Told him he should come to New York and visit the enemy's jungle so we could compare guerilla tactics, and he didn't blink. Just said, "Yes, one day."'

'He's a diplomat.'

Steve and I lie side by side in the sun while Paul and Chuck go beachcombing with Marie-Françoise and her ever-present Rabelais. 'So 'fess up,' Steve says after a moment. 'What's between you and this Maître Arnault?'

'Nothing.'

'Hey, I haven't been your private relations adviser for all these years without being able to tell something from nothing. If he looked at me the way he looks at you, I'd chuck Chuck in a twinkle. Well, for a day or two.'

'Triangle,' I say after a moment.

'Again?'

'Not again. I'm not having any more.' I turn over and hide my face in my arms.

'And you know his mother, so you must know his wife?'

'My oldest friend.'

Steve whistles. 'Ever thought of becoming gay? It's a much simpler, cleaner life.'

'What? So I could have an affair with his wife?'

'That's hardly what I meant. Is she nice?'

'She's my friend.'

'And he's your enemy? Funny kind of enemy. We're gonna end up by having to take you back to New York.'

I throw sand at him and race into the water. It is icy. As icy as a long, slow punishment. I bound through the surf until it is deep enough to plunge and then strike through cold. Eventually my limbs grow used to it. One can grow used to a lot of things.

In the afternoon we pile into two cars and head out for a walk the children particularly love. The woods are deep and shady and fern-strewn and the steep ridges appear from nowhere, as surprising as the glimmer of the distant lake. Paul walks in front with Pierre. Steve and Chuck are on either side of Madame Arnault and her occasional bursts of laughter remind me how stupid my worries were that she would be shocked by them. On the contrary. Over lunch they seemed to have become fast friends, have extracted from her the story of every bit of furniture and bric-a-brac in the house, not to mention details of her wardrobe over the seventy years of her largely Parisian life.

The children and I make up the rear. I am teaching them a song I used particularly to love as a child, probably because I thought it was naughty and the rhymes made me laugh. They make them laugh too.

> *'Qui a eu cette idée folle*
> *Un jour d'inventer l'école?*
> *C'est ce sacré Charlemagne*
> *Sacré Char-le-magne'*
> (Who was that benighted fool
> Who had the idea of inventing school?
> It was blasted Charlemagne
> Blasted Charlemagne)

I am strangely happy with the children. Maybe it's because it keeps me safe from their father's eyes which I've been avoiding all day. At one point I find myself thinking that if I had married Robinson way back then I would now have at least a couple of my own, and I wallow a little in the sentimentality of that and then come out the other side to find Paul beside me and the groupings of our walk all changed. I glance at him and think that if I had stayed with Robinson I would never have known him. I would have been unhappy not to have known him. Though perhaps it would have been better. And then I stop thinking, because he is speaking to me.

'I hope you don't mind, but I've invited Pierre to the office to meet René. He needs advice on international business contracts. And whatever we may have said about contracts last night and their clumsiness for dealing with the finer points of life, we don't want the Vietnamese losing their coastline to sharp practitioners.'

'Why should I mind?'

Paul laughs. 'You're so protective of him. I've been watching you. You're afraid he might break. Or that we might shatter him.'

I consider this. 'He doesn't know his way round our particular by-ways. And he's had a hard life.'

'Yes.' He doesn't say anything for a moment, then he adds, 'Sometimes that puts one's feet firmly on the ground. And one walks very well. While the protectors end up constructing prisons which no one, not even they, want to stumble round in.'

I don't know what he is talking about, so I say, 'Thank you for being concerned about Pierre.'

'You spend all your time thanking me,' he mutters, 'and none of it being with me.'

After a leisurely breakfast the following morning, Steve and Chuck announce that they're going to head off and start a winding journey back to Paris, so they can take in some more sights. Pierre says he would like to go with them. I am tempted to go too rather than take the train back, but Madame Arnault restrains me.

'Oh no, Maria. It's too soon. You can't all run off and leave me at once. I've got enough food in the house to feed the French army. And I was hoping you might stay at least another day or two.'

I make a demurring sound, but she rushes on. 'And Paul is staying until Tuesday. It would be nicer for you to go back with him. No point checking into the office when the Maître isn't there.' She stops herself. 'Unless you have other pressing engagements, of course.'

Before I can answer, Paul comes into the room and she puts the matter to him. 'She works for you, doesn't she? Tell her there's no rush to get back,' she laughs girlishly.

Paul hesitates for a moment. 'If there's nothing in particular waiting for you in Paris, Maria, it would be nice if you stayed. We could even work here, if you feel like it.'

'I haven't brought my computer.'

'I have.'

'So it's settled.' Madame Arnault is all smiles. 'And now we can take the children down to the beach. It might not be so fine after lunch.'

She comes to the beach with us this time, managing the steep path with casual dexterity. I sit with her while Paul goes off crab-hunting with the children. I watch her putting cream on her legs, her arms, her face. I note that her toenails beneath the trim sandals are beautifully manicured, her hair neatly gathered in a black velvet ribbon at the base of her long neck. She is one of those women who treats her body like a small private business in which the investment is largely but not wholly hers. There is no particular narcissism, only a matter-of-fact distance. If the paint is fresh, the articles nicely laid out, trade will be good and that will be better all round. It's a workable compromise between too passionate an identification with the firm and slovenly carelessness. And it seems to have served her well into age.

She is talking to me now, talking a great deal as old ladies so often do. I don't know whether it's a result of loneliness or too many years spent politely listening to husbands and hoarding chatter. I hope she doesn't regret her confidences when she stops to notice them. She is telling me about her youngest son, whose address she has given to Steve. He lives in California and he's like them, has Paul told me? Yes. And she worries about him, but what can one do? There is so little one seems to be able to do about anything.

'Oh, look.' She gestures into the distance. 'There's Danielle.'

I see a dark, long-haired woman, nicely rounded, with her arms round Paul. He is bending familiarly to kiss her.

'I always hoped Paul would marry Danielle. They've known each other since they were children. Her parents have the place round the corner and she's an investigating magistrate. Still, he didn't. Married Beatrice instead.' She casts me a searching look. 'Don't get me wrong. It's not that I have anything against Beatrice. I know you're her particular friend. It's just that she hasn't made Paul very happy. And he's my favourite, grows more like his father all the time. But I'm babbling and you'll begin to think I'm a demented old woman,' she laughs. 'It's just that I feel I've known you forever. Like a daughter. Maybe because I knew Guy. Off you go now. You'll be wanting a swim. Or go and meet Danielle. She's a treasure.'

I opt for the swim. I'm not ready for any treasures. Nor do I know what to do with all the information I've just been given. I walk for a bit in the opposite direction, towards the boulders, dunk my feet in the shallow pools between them, stroll back, letting my toes make gooey imprints in wet sand. I see an old man with turned-up trousers ahead of me and I think of my last catastrophic trip to the seashore and my heart starts to beat wildly and so loudly that for a few moments I am utterly unaware of a presence at my side. It is a man with curling dark hair and a matted chest and he is saying the usual silly things men say to women walking alone on the beach. I bark at him, 'Leave me alone', more forcefully than is necessary and then Paul is beside me and he says, 'Made a new friend?' in that flat way of his and I say, 'I'm always making new friends', and I run into the water and plunge and wish the sea would wash me away and deliver me to a place where memories didn't live.

When I emerge from under a wave, Paul is swimming beside me, his strokes matched to mine. I try to outdistance him, but I can't and we swim side by side for a while until my breath runs out and the tide washes us up in shallows far from the beach and he pulls me up onto a boulder. We lie there resting, the sun on our faces, and when I open my eyes he is looking at me so intently that for the first time in weeks I meet his gaze. He pulls a strand of hair softly away from my face and that melancholy floods through me and I know I'm going to cry, so I turn away to stare out to sea.

'Not quite the one I'd had in mind for us,' he murmurs. 'But the sea nonetheless.'

'I don't think the sea likes me any more,' I say. I tell him then about the old man in Martha's Vineyard and my intuition about Sandro. I don't put it very well, but he folds his arm round me and holds me close and lets me cry and when I stop he says, 'I'm glad you've decided to stay, Maria. Even if it's hard.'

We sit for a little while longer listening to the waves. Then he says we had better get back even though he doesn't want to, because Nicolas will start to worry, he always worries when Paul stays out in the water too long.

'Why?' I ask him.

He shrugs. 'I'm not sure. He had a bit of a bad experience as a child. Maybe it's that.'

'What experience?'

'Oh, nothing.' He waves it away. 'He swallowed too much water when no one was looking. I'll tell you another time.'

And I know he won't tell me because it has to do with Beatrice and he doesn't want to name her because I'll start defending her or maybe he just doesn't want to name her. But when we get back to the beach and I see Nicolas standing there, all skinny legs and arms and looking out to sea, I wave to him and ask him whether he wants to come in with me.

He shakes his head. 'Not now.'

'Tomorrow, then. And I'll show you all my life-saving tricks. You can save me. It's a snap.'

When he nods and gives me his crooked smile, I feel like a saint and a conniving creep all at once.

Later that afternoon clouds gather and burst with an overwhelming suddenness. Martine lights a fire and we gather in the living room and listen to thunderclaps and watch fat drops of rain plop onto shiny leaves. The felt-tips come out and the books, and when everyone is settled Paul says he is going up to his study and asks me if I'd like to come and inspect it.

I follow him up two flights of stairs and along a corridor where the ceilings are lower and he opens the door to a large-beamed room which is all nooks and arches like a little world of its own. There are books ceiling-high and windows giving out onto an expanse of stormy sea. There is a vast desk, a table, a green divan, some easy chairs, a collection of drawings and pastels on the walls and, tucked away behind an arch, a tiny fridge and a coffee maker.

He laughs as he looks at me. 'Like it? This is why I come here so often, even on short weekends when I can. It's my hideaway.'

'What are you hiding from?'

'At the moment myself mostly. Don't like what I see when I find it.' He makes a face, then grins. 'You've got freckles.'

I rub my nose and make a face back.

'If you like, tomorrow, you can work in here with me. Or there's a smaller version down the hall.'

'Beatrice's room?'

He looks away, shakes his head. 'I've told you. Beatrice never comes here. Hasn't in years and years. But since you don't believe what I say about Beatrice, let's just leave that to one side.' He walks quickly to the door and gestures me through, but I can't let it go.

'She doesn't come here because your mother doesn't like her.'

'That too. My mother with all her virtues is a terrible old bourgeoise and isn't very keen on alliances with people whose parents she can't name. They've both tried in their own ways, I guess. Let's leave it now, shall we?'

He ushers me out of the door and into another room, smaller and less lived-in, but with the same view. He looks sad now. I've taken the pleasure of it away from him and he's rubbing his forehead the way he did in my apartment that day. I touch his shoulder and he studies me for a moment, then covers my hand with his.

'Nice room,' I say. 'It's altogether nice here. Nice for the children. They're freer.'

'Yes.' He smiles so that his whole face lights up. 'Nice for the children.'

We work then, discuss his penultimate chapter which is on parricide, the most serious crime in the code books, tantamount to treason. The law of the father may not be what it once was, but the crime still carries its mythic weight, its sense that the natural order of things has been overturned – even more so when the parricide is a daughter. Lizzie Borden and her axe, the infamous Violette Nozière. I tell him that I have found some extraordinary recent cases in the US.

'But you may not want to risk going so far afield.'

He looks at me seriously, considers. Then he says, 'The only risk I want at the moment, Maria, is you.'

I stare at him and melancholy creeps over me again, rests like a thick mantle over my shoulders. I think to myself that I have never felt less dangerous in my life.

⚖ 33

Monday morning dawns chill and with too much breeze. At breakfast
Paul suggests we reverse the order of the day and leave beach or walks
to the afternoon. He doesn't look well. He looks as if he hasn't slept
all night. I hope it isn't my doing, but from the way he avoids my
eyes I suspect it might be.

Madame Arnault suggests she take the children off to a friend's farm
some miles away. They can have lunch there and we can be free to
work. We wave them off and then Paul says to me abruptly that he
wants to write and if I feel like working he has left some things on
the desk of the small study. There's a thermos flask of coffee in the
kitchen for me ready to go up.

I shouldn't be, I know, but frankly I'm miffed, and I take a coat off
the peg in the hall and stomp round the grounds until my feet are so
muddy I think I might as well go in and be a good employee and earn
my hours.

There is a brown folder on my desk. It is tatty and looks old, as if
Paul had dug it out of some dusty back shelf just to keep me out
of his way. Inside the folder there is a stack of handwritten sheets,
unpaginated. Nor is the writing particularly easy to decipher. Only
when I have turned a few pages randomly does it come to me that the
writing is Paul's and that these must be notes towards one of his own
cases. He had told me that the book wouldn't include any of these,
but perhaps he has changed his mind. Or perhaps he's just keeping
me busy.

I start to read again with new determination, a sheet at my side to
scribble queries on. I haven't had access to many lawyers' personal
notes before and the going isn't easy. It takes me a good while to work
out what the case is about and that the pages are sequential, going
through the period of the magistrate's and police investigation up to
the trial itself. There are so many leaps and lapses that at one point I
almost give up in frustration. Nor do there seem to be any names.

Only initials, and even these aren't clear, since A could just as easily stand for accused as P does for prosecution. But I don't like giving up, particularly when Paul has set the challenge, so I reconstruct as best as I can, drowning myself with coffee as I go.

It seems the case concerns a double charge of arson and manslaughter. The accused are two girls, sisters. One is a minor who is being tried in a juvenile court. Paul is defending the elder sister. The investigating magistrate and the prosecution would have it that the girls set fire to their home on the outskirts of a village, far enough from a town so that help could not instantly arrive, deliberately choosing a moment when their father was asleep, inebriated on the downstairs divan. The actual cause of death is asphyxiation.

The material evidence is all arguable: the presence of paraffin in the garden shed, which didn't catch fire since it was at some distance from the house; the presence there of paraffin-soaked rope, the remains of a piece of which was found in the house not far from the father's body; the presence on the father's wrists and ankles of contusions which could have been caused by the tying of rope but for which the forensic evidence isn't definitive.

The motive is the prosecution's strong card. After much questioning, the younger girl, who is fourteen, has admitted that the father had begun to abuse her. She also claimed that he had been violating her sister systematically, at least since their mother's death. The elder sister had on various occasions tried to protect the younger by interposing herself. The younger declares emphatically that she is glad the father (who is in effect a long-time stepfather) is dead, but she is equally emphatic that they themselves had nothing to do with it and were lucky to emerge from the fire alive.

The elder makes no accusations against the father. She is altogether more silent than her younger sister. The only thing she repeats over and over is that the flames were very hot, the smoke thick, and they are lucky to be alive. She mourns the family dog who has vanished. He was the one who liked to chew rope and it is possibly his rope that the police found near the father's body. About the father she only says that he drank too much. The problem is that at the time of the fire the doctor's report showed her to be some four months pregnant. She herself makes no allusion to the pregnancy.

I am so immersed in the reconstruction of this case that I

do not hear the knock at the door until Nicolas pokes his head in.

'Mémère says Papa is a terrible host and you're to come down straight away for some late lunch.' He grins at me.

I look at my watch and realise it is almost two, and I follow him reluctantly downstairs. Madame Arnault is busily chastising Paul while she and Martine heap the table with pâtés and cheese and bread and salad. Meanwhile Paul is desultorily laying place mats and settings.

'Papa was too silly to remember lunch,' Marie-Françoise announces to me as if this were his greatest achievement to date.

'If you treat your employees like this, you'll have a strike on your hands,' Madame Arnault adds for good measure.

'Sorry.' Paul glances up at me, but his attempt at a smile doesn't quite work. 'I was writing.'

'Those notes you've given me,' I decide to add my complaints to the rest, 'they're barely readable. But what a case! What I don't understand . . .'

'Not now, Maria.' It is almost a growl and only then do I notice he is looking at the children with something like panic.

'Of course.'

While Paul and I eat we listen to the tale of Rabelais's misadventures among the chickens, and then despite the fact that I would rather go back up to the study, Madame Arnault insists that we must all have at least an hour's walk. Otherwise what are we in the country for?

Paul brings out the wellies and we trudge along a cloud-swept strand and can barely hear ourselves for the wind and the crashing of the waves. Not that there would be much to hear. Paul has retreated into silence and Nicolas, who walks beside me, is never very talkative. Only Marie-Françoise lets out the occasional shriek as she picks up a particularly uninspiring shell. For all that, the drama of sky and sea is exhilarating and at one point as I brush against Paul and he gives me one of those lingering looks and touches my hand, I think perhaps I have misinterpreted his mood. He is simply concentrating, and not concentrating on me. It is a humbling realisation.

When we get back, I decline tea and games and race to the study. The case grips me again. I have come to a section where Paul is making notes for the defence. He argues that all the evidence of arson is circumstantial. On the other hand, the wiring in the house was ancient and the place itself something of a tip. The summer was unusually dry.

The father smoked, and in his inebriated state could easily have started a conflagration. The divan he was found on was made of highly flammable foam. Then too witnesses abound on the father's bad character, particularly after the mother's death some three years before, though some also attest that he was responsible for driving the poor woman to an early grave. Conversely, though the girls weren't particularly loved in the village, the reports are good. The elder in particular often helped out with childminding in the neighbouring town and not a word was spoken against her – except for one mother who objected to the fact that she prayed with the children too often in an utterly unconventional way.

There are then some sketchy sentences about Paul's client and how he can possibly coach her to appear at her best in court. He writes that she is beautiful in a wholly untypical way. She is very quiet, not like someone in a state of shock, but with an inner serenity. There is almost a saintliness about her, a particular beauty of the gaze. It is as if she only sees inwardly.

I don't know why, but I stop as I read this. There is an uncanny sensation in my spine. My skin tingles uncomfortably. I read the passage again three times and try to still my apprehension, then hurry on.

Paul is uncertain about how best to use the accused. She is soft-spoken and that will impress the jury, together with her manner. He doesn't want to emphasise her pregnancy since that will play into the prosecution's description of motive; on the other hand, juries have a soft spot for pregnant women and it would do the accused good to have the fact of her pregnancy made obvious to her in court. At the moment she refuses to acknowledge the notion.

I am just going back to the description of the accused again since I still have this sensation in my spine when Marie-Françoise comes into the room without knocking. She announces that dinner will be in twenty minutes and I may want to change because we have guests. She adds happily that she and Nicolas are going to eat with us. I nod at her and quickly skim through the remaining pages of the folder. It is right at the bottom of the second-to-last page that I notice a strange single paragraph. 'The accused says I am to contact a teacher called Françoise as a character witness but she won't or can't give me a family name; nor name a school. The village school has no Françoise and the Françoise in the nearest town school has never met the accused.'

I sit very still and feel the tingle in my spine explode into panic.

For a few moments I cannot move. Then I get up slowly, like a sleep-walker, and knock on Paul's door. There is no answer. He has already gone downstairs. I dress without knowing what I am putting on, brush my hair too hard, forget then remember to dab on some lipstick.

Downstairs there are too many people and too much noise. I look for Paul. He is sitting in the far corner with a dark-haired woman. I walk towards him slowly, seek out his eyes. He looks at me and I hear him mumble, 'Will you excuse me for a moment?' Then he is beside me, ushering me to the other side of the room, through an alcove.

I stare at him and I can't find the words.

'So you understand,' he says.

I shake my head. I don't understand anything.

'You do. I can see it.' He grasps my arm briefly. He looks anxious and elated all at once.

'We have to talk.' My voice is a croak.

'Later, we'll have lots of time later.'

I don't know quite how I get through that dinner. There is an old man at my side, a retired colonel or something, who talks ceaselessly and irritatingly about the impossibility of sending troops into Rwanda. Paul on my left is largely silent. The woman, Danielle, the one from the beach, is opposite him and keeps making fetching eyes and provoking him into speech. I wonder if she knows. I look round the table and wonder who does know. Madame Arnault, slimly majestic in a deep red gown? The children, who are on their best behaviour? No, not the children. But the others, the plump, elderly woman who must be the colonel's wife and whom Madame Arnault talks to like an old friend? Danielle's husband, for there must be a husband somewhere, since there is a dark-eyed girl at the table who I think I've been told is her daughter? No wonder Beatrice doesn't want to come here. My heart beats for Beatrice. Beatrice who lived with fear, with suspicion. Beatrice who needed my mother, but wouldn't name her. Why? Was my mother already dead? Had she tried herself to reach her and had no reply and assumed my mother wanted nothing to do with her?

I don't understand anything. Anything. I glance at Paul and feel his hand on my knee and I try to chew the food on my plate.

We are walking in the grounds. Pebbles crunch under our feet and the moon is high, lighting up passing clouds, casting shadows on trees and shrubs. And his face. He hasn't said anything yet except, 'Yes.

Beatrice.' He gripped my hand then and he still grips it and I realise as we walk that it isn't easy for him to talk and that to talk is to betray, a far greater betrayal than going to bed with me. I'm not sure why he should feel that, except perhaps that Beatrice hasn't told me herself. A fire is terrible. A death is terrible. But surely there cannot be any blame.

I suddenly remember Sandro and my sense of guilt for his death, even without the ordeal of a trial. And then I realise that I don't even know the outcome of this trial and that must be my first question to him. I am loath to be the one to break the silence but I do.

'And the outcome?'

He jumps a little as if my voice were wholly unexpected. 'Oh, that was fine. There was enough reasonable doubt. And I imagine the jury felt the accused had suffered enough; had in any case already spent three months behind bars.'

'The accused?'

'Beatrice.' He has difficulty saying her name. 'And her sister. Separately.'

He is silent again and I want to prod him. I also want to see his face, not these shadows. 'Will you tell me about it?' I ask softly. 'In your own words. The notes were so sketchy.'

'I'll try. It's just that it's all so unclear now. It's as if there's a film over those years.'

'Shall we go in? Up to your study? I want to be able to see you.'

We sit opposite each other in armchairs and sip the claret he has insisted on pouring out. He lights a cigarette, blows the smoke up to the ceiling, shifts uncomfortably in his seat.

'I think I'll have to tell you about myself first. It's the only way in. And it's my story too.' He laughs in self-mockery.

'I was young then. My ideals were as big as my pocket-book was small. I had been practising for two, maybe three years. I had moved away from Paris, so that I wouldn't be in the shadow of my father. Or have my life made too easy. I went to Clermont Ferrand, the depths of France. I took all kinds of cases, any that came my way, from the city, from the surrounding area. My clients were largely poor. Ordinary people who had been kicked out of their apartments when rent was in arrears; kids from rough backgrounds who got mixed up in robbery or drugs; illegal immigrants, prostitutes. I spent more time in prison in a month in those days than I do now in six. I would talk endlessly to the accused, get to know their families, try to see things the investigators had missed or at least see them differently. I never failed to go to a session with a magistrate. I read dossiers assiduously.' He looks up at me. Irony plays over his features. 'You get the picture. Lawyer on horseback, sword blazing. I was going to change the world by defending the little man's rights. And woman's.'

He pauses, waits for me to say something, but I don't speak and he goes on.

'The arson and manslaughter case was a big one for me. Important. There was enough evidence on the other side for it to be a real challenge, but I felt I could win – win over the investigating magistrate whom I knew a little, as well as the jury.' His voice drops to a whisper. 'And in the process of it all, I fell in love with Beatrice. She had been through so much, endured so much. The psychiatrist's report made that clear. Her stepfather had abused her for years, while her mother was alive as well. Beatrice had shielded her, taken her place in a way. Not that she ever spoke to me about it. Beatrice was largely silent. She just kept very still, her hands folded in front of her like a schoolgirl. And she looked at me with those eyes or maybe it wasn't even at me, and I thought, "I can save her, I can help her. I can make up to her for what she's suffered." Delusions of omnipotence, you see. I thought I could embody justice, make it work concretely, give her life, liberty, happiness.'

He gets up and starts to pace, stares out of the window into darkness. 'No, to be fair to myself and to her, it wasn't altogether like that. Beatrice was simply so much more substantial than any of the young women I had known up until then – fellow students, coy, pretty Parisians. Beatrice had felt things deeply.

'So when the trial was over and Beatrice had nowhere to go, I told her I had a spare room and if she liked she could come and stay there. She came. I imagine she thought she was coming as a housekeeper, for she would clean and tidy the apartment, cook for me . . . And then she confessed – we were speaking more by then – that what she wanted most in the world was to get through her *baccalauréat*. She had had to stop her studies, she didn't tell me why but I could guess so I didn't pry. We got all the books she needed and she started to work every day, dutifully, seriously.

'She must have been seven or eight months pregnant by then and she still wouldn't acknowledge the pregnancy. At least to me. She wore loose shirts, would never put her hands on her stomach the way pregnant women do, never spoke about the future life of the child, probably never imagined it would be born. I tried to talk to her therapist about this – for she was seeing someone, the court had recommended it, and I wasn't that madly omnipotent – but he told me with wonderfully bland professionalism that it was frankly none of my business.

'It occurred to me that, given how proper Beatrice seemed to be about everything else, she would acknowledge the child's existence only once she had a husband. So I offered myself. Oh, it was no great sacrifice. I wanted to live with her. I couldn't imagine not coming home and seeing that steady serene smile of hers. I remember it distinctly. I had just been to the prison to visit a client and on the way home I picked up a large bunch of marguerites and I handed them to Beatrice and sat her down on the sofa, took her hand and said, just like in the penny romances, "Beatrice, will you marry me?" And she looked at me and looked at me and smiled and said, "Yes".

'We didn't wait very long. I didn't think we had much time to lose. From somewhere she bought herself one of those loose Indian white cotton dresses and she plaited her hair up on top of her head so that she looked like a Dutch farm girl and we went to the Mairie and got married. It couldn't have been more than three weeks later that the child was born.'

'The child?' I croak.

'Yes.' He looks at me oddly.

'Which child?'

'Haven't you guessed? Nicolas. Poor, dear Nicolas.'

I stare at him for a long time. And then, I don't quite know why, I reach over and take his hand and hold it. We sit there quietly for a few minutes, until he asks, 'More?'

I nod.

'My mother arrived just after the birth. She had been cheated of a wedding, she said, and she wouldn't be cheated of her first grandchild. She came and she reorganised the apartment and made Beatrice's room into a nursery complete with blue-and-white cot and musical mobiles and brightly coloured friezes.'

'And she didn't know that Nicolas wasn't your son?'

Paul shakes his head. 'Not until later. My father tumbled to it. He liked to keep track of my doings and someone had mentioned to him

I'd been involved in this case – it had made the local papers – and he worked it out. Told my mother, of course, who immediately confronted me. And I couldn't lie to them so I just told them that it would be best all round if they didn't make much of it. And they didn't. They're sensible people. But they were hardly pleased.' He chuckles, then stops himself. 'No one else knows. Not amongst our friends. Not Nicolas.'

I swallow hard. 'Go on.'

'The rest is more difficult. We'd better keep it for another time.' He gets up edgily, stretches. 'It's after one.'

'No.' I shake my head. 'Now, please. We won't be able to sleep in any case.'

He laughs sharply. 'I think I'd rather not sleep than speak about it.' He is standing by the window again, looking out as if there were something to be seen and I come up to him and put my arms around him and kiss him. He doesn't altogether kiss me back, but he holds me.

'Please,' I murmur.

He shrugs. 'Okay, but I have a terrible feeling that you'll despise me by the end of it. I don't emerge as a hero.'

I laugh, though it doesn't come out right. 'I can't despise you. I've tried and it hasn't worked.'

He gives me a lop-sided smile and starts to talk again, tersely, with something that isn't quite bitterness. Maybe it's a veiled disappointment.

'After the birth, Beatrice was different. It was hard to put my finger on it. She still smiled at me in that beautiful way, but it was as if too much of her energy went into denying the things she couldn't bring herself to see. The doctors said it was a variety of post-natal depression and that it would pass. And she was still seeing the therapist. The difficulty was that she couldn't bring herself to acknowledge Nicolas's presence, even though he was there now in full flesh and lung. Even when she held him, for she did sometimes, it was as if he wasn't there, not really. And she would let him cry for too long, forget to sterilise his bottles or change him. I quickly found a woman to look after him, a granny, who was happy to stay with him late – until I got home. Meanwhile Beatrice went off to a special college and in the spring passed her Bac. She was very happy with that and I felt it was going to make the difference.

'There was another difference to make, of course.'

He looks away from me and I think I know what's coming and I'm not sure I want to know.

'Beatrice and I shared a bedroom now. There was only one left in the apartment. We would lie in bed together at night and I would hold her in my arms. But if I made any gesture – well, you know what I mean – fear would come into her eyes, her body would stiffen. She didn't run, or move, or scream, or tell me to leave her alone; she just lay there in a state of panic. Expecting a repetition of whatever it was that had happened to her with her stepfather. And of course, whatever desire I might have felt, shrivelled.' He laughs a laugh full of pain.

'It wasn't as if I had expected it would be easy. Easy was with other people and I was with Beatrice. I had read enough psychology texts at university to know that these things took time. But the reality of that physical panic hurt. It was as if I wasn't myself, as if she couldn't see me for who I was, as if all the kindness, the gentleness that passed between us – and that was the tenor of our twosome – was nothing, simply didn't exist or existed only in a separate space.' He laughs again. 'Needless to say, I took to sleeping on the sofa in the living room. The blazing sword was getting a little tarnished. But we had time. I still loved her. Still believed it could work. I had hardly married her for bed, after all. There'd been quite enough bedding before, which had proved only temporarily interesting.'

'It occurred to me sometime in that first year of Nicolas's life that it would be a good thing for all of us if we were to move to Paris. Beatrice would be further from the site of her unhappiness. People still occasionally commented on her history. And I needed to earn more money to keep the family adequately. So I found a *cabinet* that would have me – my father's name didn't harm things, but I wasn't such a terrible lawyer either. We waited out the first year of Beatrice's teacher training course and moved.'

'The move did Beatrice good. She started coming out of herself, joining student groups, committees. She's always been good at those, finds them easier than individuals. And I was happy too. There were more friends, some lucrative clients to help finance the less lucrative ones, challenges at work. We got on well, there were no rows. We were all right. Except for poor Nicolas.'

'Beatrice still couldn't see him. She would look at him and look straight through him. It was a little better when he started to speak.

She would answer him then, sometimes at least. But she never touched him if she could help it. I began to realise that at some level he was the embodiment for her of everything that had come before and she wanted nothing to do with him. He didn't exist for her as a separate person. I tried to talk to her about it, but it always ended up as a conversation about practicalities, minders, schools.'

Paul stops abruptly. 'That's enough, Maria. You can imagine the rest.'

'I don't want to imagine it. I want you to tell me.'

'Not now,' he smiles a little sadly. 'Another time, perhaps.'

He looks so tired that I haven't the heart to press him. 'Tomorrow,' I murmur. 'Please. I . . .'

He stretches his hand out to me and I take it, find myself tugged into his lap. I relax into him, feel that stirring between us.

'I haven't spoken about all of this to anyone before, Maria,' he admits. 'It's not easy. Even to tell it to myself.'

'Why are you telling me?'

'You know why I'm telling you. Because I want you to know I don't lie, I want you to trust me. And I'm gambling.'

He kisses me and I think I know a lot of things. I know I am kissing him to make up for Beatrice. I am kissing him for Nicolas and for the pain. I am kissing him because I like kissing him, perhaps too much. But I don't really know what he's gambling on. Sometimes kisses aren't quite enough.

⚖ 34

It is late afternoon and we are sitting in the train again, making our way back to Paris this time, just the two of us.

The morning was bright and warm and when I saw Nicolas I wanted to put my arms around him and cry, so I asked him if he was ready for his life-saving lesson and a little reluctantly he agreed. He can swim. It's just the waves he doesn't like. But the sea was relatively calm and we paddled out to where it was calmest and I put my arms through his and around his neck, told him to pretend he was floating in the bath and I would tug him. He closed his eyes and relaxed after a while and I pulled him along and when a wave came over us and he started to thrash I just kept on swimming and when it had passed he relaxed again and eventually gave me his awkward smile. Then I asked him whether he'd like to try it on me and he did, a little fearfully, and I laughed and told him he musn't let go or I'd drown. And he didn't let go, not even after a wave immersed us. He tugged me back to shore and I told him another few tugs like that and he'd get a medal and I kissed him on the cheek and he blushed terribly and then threatened Marie-Françoise that he was going to practise on her. And then Paul said once he had done that, he could try a really big fish like himself and we all laughed.

We are still joking, Paul and I, neither of us certain whether we want to confront heavier matters, yet both knowing that at some point we must. I can't really think of anything but that, so finally I say, 'Now. Take me up to the present.'

He doesn't pretend not to know what I'm talking about. Instead he says, 'Can I put my arm round your shoulder?'

'If you're discreet.' I'm still joking.

'Have I ever been anything else?' he mumbles, and pulls me closer to him. 'What do you think comes next?' he asks.

'The making of Marie-Françoise.' I am blithe.

'Despite your occasional flashes of fatalism, Maria, you're a determined optimist. That must be another thing I like about you.' His laugh is too harsh. 'But we'll start with Nicolas, because of this morning, because of what you did. It was important.' He squeezes my shoulder. 'Though it's not an episode I like to recall.

'Remember you said to me that Beatrice didn't come to Brittany because of my mother? Well, that's only part of the reason. The other reason has to do with Nicolas. It was when he was almost three, I guess. We were on the beach, the three of us, and I went off for a swim, leaving Beatrice with him on the shore. I looked back after a while and I saw a small crowd gathered round where I had left them. I was suddenly afraid and I swam back as quickly as I could. Nicolas was stretched out on the ground and a man was pumping his chest. He was all right after a moment. He opened his eyes and cried, but he was all right. Everyone started to tell me at once what had happened and I still don't really know except that Nicolas must have gone a little too deep and been tumbled by a wave and then another and another until a boy noticed and dragged him back.

'Beatrice was standing away from the crowd and I went up to her with Nicolas under my arm and she looked at him and then at me with an expression I can't describe and said, "Too bad", in a cold little unfamiliar voice. And I hit her then, slapped her across the face. The only time I ever have.'

He stops. His face is contorted.

'But she probably only meant too bad it had happened,' I say softly.

'I know. That's what I thought too the next day. But at the time . . . her face . . . I don't know.' He looks into the distance. 'Anyhow, all that was just to say thank you for Nicolas today.'

'Go on,' I murmur.

'Don't really know where to go. She never came back up to Brittany after that. It was an unspoken agreement. And I think it was around that time that I realised I'd stopped loving her, had given up hope or at least my sense of omnipotence. That I could somehow provide reparation for the past. Maybe they were the same.'

'You still weren't sleeping together.'

He shakes his head. 'We had separate rooms now and I stopped trying.'

'Why didn't you split up?'

'It never occurred to me. I guess I felt responsible for her. She didn't really have friends of her own. And we got on fairly well in a day-to-day way. We'd chat about this and that, her teaching mostly, I think she'd started by then, and her committees. Occasionally we had people over. We led structured and fairly separate lives. I was working hard. She was working hard. I had a friend then. A woman.' He glances at me. 'I don't know if Beatrice realised. But I don't think it would have mattered to her. She preferred me not to try.'

'How do you know?' I am suddenly angry for Beatrice. I move away from him.

'I know,' he grunts. 'She's not you, Maria.'

I glare at him and he says, 'All right, this is how I know.' He has his bitter tone now, all cynicism and malevolent irony directed mostly at himself. 'When Nicolas was about five I got this sudden notion in my head that his unhappiness – for he was unhappy, too quiet, withdrawn, sometimes I thought even a little slow – would be solved if he had a sibling, someone smaller than him to love and to hate, to tumble around with. So I put it to Beatrice, stupid really, but that's how I did it. The bane of the French rationalist education. I said to her that I knew she didn't like going to bed with me, probably because of all the ghastly things that had happened to her in her own home, but I really thought it would be a good idea if we had a child together, for Nicolas's sake, for our own too. She looked at me with that gentle smile of hers and didn't say anything, so I took the smile for agreement.'

I must look at him dubiously for he laughs and mutters, 'No, don't worry. I didn't take out my tarnished tool on the spot and overpower her. I started to woo her. I would bring her little presents, stroke her, proffer kisses. We'd go out for dinner. We even went dancing once, though that wasn't an all-out success. Beatrice had never been dancing. Anyhow, I told her all the things men tell women, you know them by rote, and one night I went to her room and tried to kiss her properly. The fear was in her eyes and the stiffness. I pretended not to notice. I turned out the lights and I started to stroke her and she started to thrash and I went as limp as a wet dishcloth.' He pauses. 'And that, my lady of much experience, is the entire story of Beatrice and my love life.'

I don't like his tone and I want to argue, so I start to say, 'But Beatrice told me . . .' and I stop and wonder exactly what Beatrice told me.

'Told you what? That we enjoyed nightly sexual bliss?' he laughs harshly. 'Good for her. I don't think I'd like to have been her talking to you and saying anything different.'

'But she said . . .'

'Fine. Believe her. But if you think men go around casually making up stories about their limp dicks to beautiful women just for the hell of it, then you have less intelligence than I've always given you credit for.'

We sit in sullen silence for a few minutes and I try to reconstruct my conversation with Beatrice. I remember her separate room in their apartment, the fluffy, maidenly feel of it, and I say, 'Maybe there's someone else.'

He gives me a startled look. 'You mean Beatrice has someone else? I don't think so,' he murmurs. 'But if she did, I'd be supremely happy.' He pauses reflectively. 'I care for her, you know. It's not that I don't care for her. She's come a long way.'

'I know you care for her. I've seen you together. You forget.'

'I don't forget.' He looks at me and seems to be about to say something then changes his mind. Instead, he muses for a moment, 'She has been paying a lot of attention to herself of late, but I thought that was to do with you. Maybe . . . No, I don't think so.'

I shrug. We are quiet again. Countryside speeds by, villages. He puts his hand on my arm. 'I'm sorry. I don't like this part of my life.'

I nod. 'And Marie-Françoise?'

'We decided to adopt. I think we both did. I don't know any more. But she's a nice little soul.'

'And Beatrice is better with her?'

'Yes. She doesn't quite warm to her, but she doesn't mind her. She treats her like one of her schoolchildren, a little stern, a little distant. But fine. Maybe it's just that she has no models from her own childhood about how one is with children.' He frowns.

'What?'

'Nothing.'

'Does Marie-Françoise know?'

'That she's adopted? I told her, in a manner of speaking, when she was about five. Because of Nicolas really. I had told him. I didn't want him to have strange ideas about where babies came from. I told him and then later her that we had chosen an extra-special sister for him from an agency that found homes for babies that didn't have any.'

He must think that I am being critical for he adds hastily, 'And it has been good for him. He's come out of himself a little and they get on. You've seen.'

He starts rubbing his temples in that way he's had of late and I say softly, 'There's more, isn't there?'

'No. It would be pointless.'

I wait and then say, 'You know I think Marie-Françoise is named for both my mother and me.'

'Beatrice chose the name. I thought it would make her happy to. And I know, found out on my birthday.'

'And you know that the Françoise, the teacher in the case notes, is probably my mother? It was 1979, wasn't it? The fire, the trial.'

He nods.

'My mother died the year before. I remember, when we went to visit her grave together, Beatrice was very keen to get the precise date. Now I know why. I guess she must have written to my mother and thought she had given her up. I didn't leave any forwarding address when I went to the States.'

'You're good at getting up and going, aren't you?' Paul surveys me reflectively.

'Not as good as I used to be, I suspect. Or I'd probably have gone by now.' I laugh and he grips my arm tightly.

We are nearing Paris. The massed ranks of suburban apartments are at our window and the train slows.

'Will you come out to dinner with me, Maria? Beatrice isn't there and I really don't know what to do with myself after all this.' He smiles. 'That's a plea.'

I squeeze his hand. 'Better not. I want to be by myself a little. Think.'

'Think about what?'

'You. Beatrice. Me.'

'You can think with me.'

'We can share a taxi.' I smile. 'Same address.'

I go home and stand in the shower and think. I think about Beatrice and how awful it must be to be in her body and be afraid when a man comes into the room. I think about her lying in bed at night and being afraid and waiting for Paul to come home and being afraid again. I think about her broken leg in childhood and her bruises and think how much she has made of herself despite it all and how Paul must have helped even in the less obvious ways. I think conversely what a beast I was to her and how I tried to steal my mother back from her and how I inadvertently all but stole her husband. Then I think of Nicolas and I say to myself that I must stop making Beatrice into a saintly victim, for she too has done harm, like the rest of us. And I think of Paul and I think that it hasn't exactly all been roses for him either. And I wonder why he has bothered to tell me about his limp dick and I laugh. Then I wonder about it more seriously and think that it is an awfully long way to go just to prove to me that he wasn't lying about his relations with Beatrice. And then I have this prickling sensation in my spine again and I realise that there are pieces of the story that are still missing.

After that I go and sit on the sofa and sip water and I see the light on opposite. He is pacing. I can see his silhouette clearly and I think how handsome he is and how he has given me his confidence, gambled on me, and in a sense I've betrayed him again, taken his pain lightly. Which is something he never did to me. Perhaps once, on his birthday. And I still don't understand why that once. But never otherwise. And he didn't leave me to stew in my misery and say, thanks for that bit of your life, chap, I'm going home to think it over. And I find the telephone in my hand and I'm ringing him and I say, 'Is a lady allowed to change her mind?'

We go to the Brasserie Lipp on the St-Germain, because it's close and because it's big enough to be private in. He's carrying a big canvas bag and I wonder for a moment whether he's made arrangements to go and sleep elsewhere tonight because he doesn't want to be alone with his dredged up memories. And because I'm like that, the thought crosses my mind that there might be another other woman and I don't like that thought, so I rub it out.

We sit and we eat salad and lamb and gratin potatoes and drink a good bottle of Bordeaux. I'm feeling shy again, perhaps because of that bag under the table, or because I know too much. But I don't quite know enough, so I ask him, after my first sip of wine, 'And Beatrice's sister? What happened to her?'

'She went into care. It was strange, that. Beatrice never wanted to see her after the case was over. I used to ask her from time to time, and she would just say, no, it's better not. I went to visit her a few times while we still lived in Clermont Ferrand. She was a sad child, furtive. Not at all like Beatrice. Perhaps they didn't have the same father. I never worked it out. Beatrice wouldn't talk. And then after we went to Paris, I wrote to her occasionally. Then I lost track. Did you ever meet her?'

'No. I never went to Beatrice's house. Well, not into it.' I flush as I remember the time Rachel and I secretly followed her home and I don't tell him that we thought her mother was a prostitute. Instead I ask, 'And her brother?'

'I didn't know she had one.'

'I think she did.'

'Well, he must have left home by the time I met her. You can ask her.'

I shake my head, too vigorously. 'If you say she doesn't want to remember, it's better not.'

'She remembers you and your mother very well though. Tell me about it.'

I tell him, a little hesitantly to begin with, but then it begins to flow and I find I'm telling him the things I don't altogether reminisce about accurately with Beatrice, because I'm ashamed of my little-girl treachery, of my jealousy too. I laugh when I finish, 'So you see, I was a bitch, even then. And my mother preferred her. My mother's better daughter, I think of her as. And if I had been a little less of a horror, maybe none of it would ever have happened.'

'Don't be ridiculous.' Paul is stern. 'All children are cruel from time to time. You should hear Marie-Françoise going on about her closest friends. But your mother and Beatrice . . . She found love there. That explains a lot. That explains . . .' he stops suddenly.

'Go on.'

He shakes his head.

'Why not?'

'There are some things I can't tell even you with the lights on.'

'So when can you tell me?'

'When I'm holding you in my arms.'

He isn't laughing and I swallow hard.

'But I haven't decided yet whether I'm going to be in your arms again,' I mumble. 'I haven't decided which is the worst form of betrayal.'

'That's too bad. Because I'm going to leave Beatrice. Not in the

330

lurch. We'll arrange it. Maybe you can decide then, come and live with me.'

He is looking at me with utter seriousness.

'You can't do that,' I say.

'Why not? She's learned to walk now. Maybe she'll learn to fly. And as I've thought about it, I've realised that I've protected her for too long. Protection is a form of prison, too, remember? We talked about that. Beatrice will be glad to get out of it. I probably remind her of all the things I was trying to save her from. I know too much about her.' He laughs abruptly. 'I don't know why it's taken me so long to realise it.'

'My fault,' I mutter. I'm not listening. 'My fault again.' I clench my fists and reach for his pack of cigarettes.

'I can't say you haven't been part of the process. You've reminded me what it can be like to be with someone you can talk to and play with and hold. And love. And the children. I'd forgotten what it was like to be, well, just ordinary with children.' He's using his lawyerly matter-of-fact tone, but his gaze lingers on me. 'Not your fault though. Just a little speeding up, perhaps. I was getting there in any case. Or I might not have allowed you in with such a thump. It's too bad you had to be Beatrice's friend.'

'And what about the children?'

He shrugs. 'I'll take them. They may be better off without her. You've made me realise that too. And she'll be relieved to be shed of them.'

'How do you know?'

'I think I know her rather better than you. I've lived with her for fourteen years.'

He is sharp and I look away and murmur, 'Poor Beatrice.'

'I think I give her more credit than you do. Shall we go? I'm not enjoying this. And I've got a heavy day tomorrow.'

'Where are you going?'

'What do you mean, where am I going?'

'With that bag.'

He grimaces. 'I thought when the evening started that you might invite me home. I brought you some law books. First-year courses. Stale from my library.'

Paul gestures for the waiter and I sit there and feel like crying and I think that he's probably right, that he does know Beatrice better than I do. What do I know about her at all except what I've wanted to know? Through a French window darkly. Needed to know, too. Like an anchor from the past to tie myself to, so that I wouldn't drift away into even more troubled waters than the ones I was already in.

We walk slowly up the Boulevard, not touching. There are animated couples all around us and the homeless late-night beggars. I empty my change purse. I need the blessing. I put my arm through his then, and he lets it sit there stiffly and I feel stupidly forlorn. We turn into the Rue des Sts-Pères and pass the Hôtel du Pas de Calais and I stop.

'If they have a room, will you stay with me?' I say. I feel like I did when I was a little girl and I tossed coins in the air, half-believing that the magic of heads or tails could make up my mind for me. And then cheating when I didn't like the result.

He looks at me and laughs. 'A gamble?'

I nod.

He laughs some more. 'Careful. I'm suddenly feeling lucky.'

⚖ 35

We both got lucky.

The trouble is when we're in bed together like this I can't remember why we're not always there. The other trouble is that I'm distinctly in love with him and that doesn't do much for the clarity of one's thinking. His hands and lips and that other part of him which I have the luck not to render limp tell me it's the same for him. So we love each other and we don't talk much and we fall asleep holding each other.

And somewhere in that sleep I have a dream. It is a ghastly dream. I am very hot, too hot, and I realise there's a fire around me, flames everywhere, and I can't breathe. I can't seem to move either and I look up and I see Beatrice and there is a strange, scary expression on her face. I scream, 'No, Beatrice, no', and she laughs and says, 'Too bad', and walks away and I'm still screaming.

'Shhh.' Paul is holding me, stroking my hair. 'You've been dreaming.'

I switch on the bedside lamp and I look at him, then look away.

'You called out "Beatrice",' he says softly.

'Yes.' I swallow some water, empty the glass, want more.

'Do you remember why?'

I shudder and tell him, tell him quickly.

'It's the case notes, the trial, everything we've talked about.'

'But in the dream she did it. I had her do it, set the fire, I mean.' I pause. 'Did you ever think she did it, the two of them, the sisters?'

He looks away, stares at the blank screen of the tiny television set perched in the corner of the room. 'Not at the time,' he murmurs. 'Not during the trial.'

'But later?' I press him. 'Come on, you can't hold back now.'

He is pensive. 'But if I tell you, Maria, I don't know how you'll face Beatrice.'

'I don't know how I'm going to face her anyway. One thing at a time.'

He studies me, then puts his arm around me and holds me very close. 'She said something once,' he confesses, 'when Marie-Françoise was about four. Marie-Françoise was lying on my bed. It was after her bath and she was all pink and shiny and naked and we were having a tickle and she was squealing and shrieking and laughing the way children do. In the midst of it I heard this sound, like a hiss, from the door, and I looked up and there was Beatrice. Her face was contorted in a way I didn't recognise and she said in a cold little flat voice, full of hatred, "She'll do it too, you'll see. Just like me. Burn you down." Then she walked away.'

I try to digest this, ask, 'What did you do then?'

He shivers. 'I didn't do anything. I got Marie-Françoise into her pyjamas and put her to bed. Beatrice had gone up to her study at the top of the house and she didn't come down again that evening. And the next day, she was as she always is, quiet and smiling, and I began to think I'd imagined what I heard or hope I'd imagined it. But this little fear stayed with me. I don't like to leave her alone with the children for too long. That's been the worst of it in a way. I can't trust her with them.'

'And you never confronted her? Asked her?'

'What's the point? There's not about to be a retrial. And the children . . .'

'But you think the sisters did it?'

'You've read the notes. They could as easily have as not. They hated him enough. With reason.'

'And you don't think they should be punished?'

He studies me. 'I'd forgotten how keen you are on punishment. It's because you haven't visited as many prisons as I have.' He laughs, then stops abruptly. 'Even if the sisters had done it, it's not the kind of crime you repeat. It's utterly specific. And maybe Beatrice's life has punished her enough. It can't be very nice living with that history. Or in her body. But if you're asking me the lawyer, I'll tell you that public recognition of a crime is important. And in a crime like this case, a light sentence. Time to recognise and work out the guilt. And then one starts again.'

I think about this. 'That's when you started to work on the book, isn't it? The one on women murderers?'

He nods, squeezes my shoulder.

We are quiet for a moment and then I ask him, because it's been in my thoughts for some time. 'You changed your mind about me, didn't you? About us. The night of your birthday party you said it wasn't possible, you closed the door in my face.'

'I didn't want to. You must know that. It was just . . . well, Beatrice and I had had a row.' His voice is suddenly raw. 'And since we don't often have rows, it was, shall we say, dramatic. And I wasn't thinking straight, didn't start to think straight again for weeks. It wasn't long before the guests started to arrive. My mother had taken the children out for a snack and we were alone. Beatrice came into my room. She rarely does that, and she started to talk about you. She told me how you were her closest, oldest friend, how much you meant to her; how you admired her and thought she was good and how she admired you; how much your mother had meant to her, had been the only person in her childhood to treat her like a human being.

'Then I said I thought you were wonderful too and how well we worked together. Maybe she didn't like the way I emphasised it, for she grew visibly tenser. She said that the reason you were so wonderful was that you hadn't had a father. And then I made my second mistake. I said not all fathers were like her father and she mustn't generalise. Then she exploded. No, that's wrong. She got that look on her face, the one I can't describe, all cold heat and hostility, and she said that if I ever mentioned any of that to you, if I ever so much as breathed a word, if she smelled anything funny between us, she would do something terrible, truly terrible. And that I knew what that meant, didn't I? I knew her.

'Then she walked off before I could say anything. I think I was shaking. I remember not being able to tie a knot in my tie. When the kids came back, I asked my mother whether she would stay with Nicolas until we were all at table. I was scared for him I guess, because that's how I'd interpreted Beatrice's threat. And then everyone started to arrive and I wasn't thinking straight. I don't even know what I said to you. What I recall is panicking when Beatrice came in and you were talking to Monsieur Tran. I thought if she heard the word "father", she'd misinterpret. Anyhow, it was a nightmare, continued to be. Though Beatrice seemed quite happy, always telling me how she was doing this and that with you. And again I got that odd feeling, as if I'd imagined the whole thing.'

He turns to me now, seeks out my eyes, strokes me softly. 'And then there I was, trapped between the two of you like a blundering bear. I tried not to see you and it was worse than when you stayed on and on in England. You were right there across the street and I saw you with that man and I thought, I'm mad, I'm going to lose her. What am I doing? So I told myself I'd talk to you and we'd work something out, somehow. And then you threw it all back in my face and I was in the trap again. You too, I know.'

He pauses, waits for me to say something, but I don't and he goes on. 'Then I woke up. Suddenly. On the way to Brittany, it was. We were playing cards and you did something, touched Marie-Françoise. It was so ordinary. So natural, easy. And it came to me that I'd been living in a prison all these years. One I'd helped to construct for myself. Out of honour, habit, fear, I don't know. And I'd put the children in it too. And probably Beatrice. And I thought it's time to turn the key in the lock and come out. I had to make the leap and trust you.'

'So here we are,' I say.

'Here we are.'

'And now?'

'Now I'm going to love you so well that you won't be able to do without me.'

He does. Over the next weeks he does. It's a dazzling sort of existence, the kind that makes you pinch yourself every once in a while to make sure you're not dreaming, and then you know in any case that you probably are.

We don't go into each other's homes. It's not prearranged or anything, we just don't do it. It's a kind of game. Or a holiday. A time away from life. I used to be good at it and I seem to have found the capacity again. We meet for dinner or a movie or leave the office together late after work and then we stay in a hotel, randomly chosen, depending on where we are. One night, we overlook the Notre Dame from the back where the buttresses float majestically into the river. On another we find ourselves in the midst of the Ile St-Louis. We visit my childhood home in the Marais and stay in a tiny place at the corner of the Rue des Lions-St-Paul. We are like strangers in our own city and we make ourselves strange to each other, so that we can find each other all over again.

One night, because I know I'm about to get a cheque from Grant, I don my best glad rags and invite him to the Crillon and we laugh in a huge bed in the midst of gilded eighteenth-century splendour.

Paul says to me, 'It's going to be very dull living together after this.'

'I haven't said I would yet,' I murmur. 'I have to see Beatrice first.'

We haven't spoken about her since the night I had that dream and neither of us says anything for a few minutes.

Then he says, 'I've started to look for a new apartment. If you like, you can help me. I want the arrangements to be in place by the time the children start school.'

'And Beatrice?' I say in a small voice.

He meets my eyes. 'I've tried to reach her at her hotel but she either doesn't get or doesn't answer my messages.'

I don't say anything else. I don't really want the holiday to end.

One evening, just before they're about to leave Paris, we take Steve and Chuck out for dinner. We all talk and giggle too much and afterwards, as we're walking along the quais and Steve is at my side, he says, 'The triangle's resolved itself, I see. You've killed off the wife.'

'Steve!' I gasp.

'Sorry. Just kidding.'

'She's more likely to kill me off, anyway.'

''Cause her husband looks so happy. Transformed since I saw him up in Brittany. Clark become Superman. Gotta hand it to you, kid.' He chuckles ruefully. 'And here I'd put my money on having you back in New York by the fall.'

'Your filly may still come in. I'm thinking about it.'

'You don't look as if you've been doing much thinking.'

The following evening I go to a concert with Pierre. I watch him surreptitiously as we listen to a Bach concerto and afterwards, when we're home together having a late meal, I watch him some more. He's a stranger really, even though he is my brother, but because he is my brother I take my courage in hand and I say to him, 'Pierre, would you be horrified if I were to tell you that I was in love with Paul? And he with me,' I finish dismally.

He looks at me with what I think is incomprehension, a little sadly perhaps. Then he puts his arm over my shoulder in that way he's started to do and he says, 'Little sister, love never horrifies me. Only its opposite.'

Later he asks me when I am going to come and visit him in Vietnam and meet his wife and my niece and nephew. The words 'niece' and

337

'nephew' make me smile and I tell him, 'As soon as you're back and settled and you invite me.'

He nods and I think he's pleased.

Vesna comes round the next day for a French lesson with Jasha and his guitar. The school has closed down for the summer but we thought we'd carry on, if a little erratically. Jasha plays me two French songs he's learned and she looks on proudly.

After we have had our lesson, she announces to me in English and in her deep-throated, deadpan voice, 'I have met a man. A little old, perhaps. But he is kind. Funny, no?' she grins, twisting her long brown-gold hair round her fingers. 'He is a bit like you. He doesn't expect me to be good always, like the others, and say thank you every time I breathe.'

I smile at this characterisation of myself.

She smiles too, then whispers comically, 'And he thinks I am beautiful.'

'You are,' I say.

'What? With my skinny legs and face and my hundred wrinkles? I look like a dried-up old paprika.' She bursts into gleeful laughter. 'Jasha, your mother is an old paprika, right?'

We laugh some more and hug each other and then she says I must come and eat in her restaurant tonight, because there is a new cook and he will only be good for a week before he gets lazy.

I take Paul. The restaurant is behind the Bastille which is still not an area I like to come to, but I hold on tightly to his arm as we cross the spoke of the wheel on which my mother was killed. Then I tell him about it and he kisses my nose and says, 'Poor little Maria,' and just as we go into the restaurant, he adds, 'I'll lend you mine.'

Vesna treats us like visiting royalty, bringing us dishes so heaped we cannot finish them. At one point she puts her arm around me and whispers dramatically, 'So this is what you have been hiding?'

I don't answer and she turns to Paul, puts her hand on her hip and says in her not altogether perfect French, 'I hope you are very good to her. Maria is my especial friend.'

She sounds like a tough barmaid issuing a challenge and Paul laughs and says he tries very, very hard, but he will try even harder.

When we go, he kisses her on the cheek and in the street, he tells me he likes her very much and asks me what her status is in the country and whether she needs help with papers. I tell him shamefully that I don't know, but that I will find out.

We walk on a little, then he turns to me and says, 'I know it's a little late, Maria; but this report came in today from England. I'd really like to go through it with you. Would you mind if we went back to the office for a bit? It's easier to work there than in a hotel room.'

I startle myself and ask, 'Wouldn't it be simpler to go back to my place?'

He looks at me as if he hasn't heard me properly and then he kisses me right there in the midst of the Bastille.

I hope my mother doesn't mind.

It is the next day that the postcard comes from Beatrice. I stare at the picture for a long time, not daring to turn it over. The picture shows swirling surf and rocky tree-clad cliffs and very blue skies above a caption saying 'Ile de la Réunion'. I don't know why she has chosen to go there. Perhaps it's simply the furthest place from France where you can still speak French.

Finally, holding my breath, I turn the card over.

Beatrice writes:

> Dear, dear Maria, I am so happy. I feel so free, as free as you. Maybe I'm becoming a little bit like you. No cares, no children, no committees, no husband!!! It's bliss. You are my teacher. Just like your mother. I may stay an extra week. Your friend, Beatrice.

I examine the handwriting on the card carefully to make sure this is really from Beatrice. I know it is, yet I can't quite believe it. The Beatrice who has taken up residency in my mind, the Beatrice of Paul's narrative, is not this person. I put the card away carefully in a drawer. I do not tell Paul about it. Maybe because it is so obviously directed at me and it would be a further betrayal. Maybe because it would confirm him too quickly in his notion that Beatrice would be happier outside the prison they have inadvertently constructed.

But I do fly up to Brittany with him. I wasn't going to but somehow after Beatrice's card, I feel more entitled to my holiday time. And he wants me so much to come. I told him if he was going to talk to the children, I really shouldn't be there, and he looked at me with a per-plexed air and said he didn't see why, but that in any case he wasn't going to talk to them now. He wanted to wait until he had longer with them. And in all fairness, he wants to speak to Beatrice first, and he still hasn't been able to reach her.

'She'll be back next week in any event,' he says to me. 'And then we'll sort everything out.' When I flinch he puts his arm round me and reassures me and tells me he knows everything will be fine.

So we go to Brittany and we play with the children and we pack them up for their respective camps. At night Paul steals into my room and when I plead familial modesty, he laughs and tell me his mother is a woman of the world and the children never wake at night and we'll be a lot quieter than the weather.

And when he comes into me to the sound of the sea, I am very happy.

⚖ 36

Beatrice does not come back when she is expected. Paul frets and I mention as casually as I can that I had a card from her and she said she might stay an extra week.

'Why didn't you tell me?' he asks.

I flush and mumble that I thought I had double-crossed Beatrice enough.

'Did she say something I shouldn't know?'

Sometimes I think Paul should have been an American lawyer. He enjoys cross-examination.

'Woman talk. And that she was having a good time.'

'That's nice,' he replies and I know he wants to ask me more but then changes his mind.

He is on holiday from the office now and he writes every day, working from home. He printed out the first chapters for me and the title page and I gasped a little when I saw it because it has my name on it under his.

'That's not right,' I tell him. 'I haven't written anything.'

'Yes, you have. This book is more than the words on the page. Think of all those hours. Anyhow, it will help in your chosen career.' He winks at me.

'It's still not right. It's not accurate.'

'Okay,' he growls, takes a pen and crosses out the 'and' between our names and replaces it with a 'with'.

'Better?' he laughs.

'A little better.' I laugh too.

By the following week, we're not laughing. Beatrice has still not come back and by the week after that we're seriously worried. Paul rings the hotel she was staying at to find that she's checked out and there's no forwarding address. He rings the airline only to be told that no, they have no record of her changing her flight.

I say we will have to go to the police and he is not certain about this, because he thinks if Beatrice is all right, she will be terrified to have the police inquiring after her. He faxes a lawyer's office on the island and asks them to make discreet inquiries about any accidents or hospitalisations. We wait. We are both nervous.

Paul jokes and says, 'I really haven't done away with her, you know. I only love you to distraction, not to madness.' The joke doesn't quite work and he tells me he has found an apartment and he wants me to see it and I say I want to see Beatrice first. He tells me if she isn't back in another week, and we've had no news, he is going to fly out there.

I sit and look out of my window onto the house opposite and I think of Beatrice. My eyes wander across the empty windows and up to the attic room and I wonder what Beatrice is doing. And then the memory comes back to me of that couple locked in an embrace, that couple I thought was Beatrice and her husband all those months back. I think of Beatrice's postcard and I feel my lips curling into a smile.

I know you're going to think I made this up so that I could be happy, have Paul and keep him daily too. And that Beatrice is really sitting up there in her attic room, flinging poisoned darts at me. But it isn't like that.

I had a letter from her on the day Paul was set to fly off to the island. Here it is. She really wrote it. And there was no return address.

My dear, dear Maria,

I have become just like you. Really I have and it's wonderful. I didn't want to tell you before, because I didn't quite know how to, but I'm not coming back. I don't ever want to come back. I'm in love, you see. Funny. I met him at a teacher's conference in Paris during the winter, just after we found each other, you and I. I think you gave me the courage for him. He stayed for a while and we got to know each other a little. Now we know each other more. He's a lot younger than me and I think I prefer that. You remember you said, 'It depends.' He's very, very sweet and we're happy together. Like that. Like you. He loves your dress, though I haven't told him it's yours.

He's from here and so we want to stay here. I feel so free here. I feel I can do anything, become anyone.

You'll tell Paul for me, won't you? He won't mind. He doesn't get angry, not very often anyhow. And he'll explain it to the children. They won't miss me. I know they won't. I'm not really very good with them. Paul is better at all that than I am. I just pretended. And you'll look in on them from time to time. I would like that. Would like to think of you with them.

Thank you. Thank you for everything. Thank you for coming back and showing me. I don't think I quite knew how to be a woman before.

Your friend always,
Beatrice

I show the letter to Paul and now I dig out the postcard too and he reads them both. When he looks up at me his eyes are very blue and dreamy and he hugs me and says, 'She's learned to fly. She'd learned to walk and now she's learned to fly.'

And there's our happy ending. Except in the soft morning light, we rarely walk off arm-in-arm into a golden distance. Unless we have the children with us, that is. And the past is still there. I see it every day in Nicolas. But in any event, as I've lived all this through, I've learned it's better not to try to eradicate it, despite its weight and miseries. Otherwise it leaps out to confront you when you're least ready with an even more frightening face.

We live in an apartment overlooking the Luxembourg Gardens. I'm very happy that there's no house opposite. I've stopped looking into other people's windows.

When we moved in there and the children arrived, Marie-Françoise asked me, 'Do you think Maman hates us? Is that why she left?'

'No,' I said. 'I think she just wanted to live something different.'

Marie-Françoise nodded wisely. But she looked a little sad. 'I hope she's all right,' she said.

'Do you miss her very much?' I asked.

She thought about this and said, 'I'm not sure. I'm happy, I think. And I like you.' She curled up to me then. 'But it's strange.' She was quiet for a while, then she lowered her voice and said in a very grown-up way, 'I think Papa's happier though.'

'Let's hope he stays like that,' I laughed.

'Oh, he's not difficult to please,' she reassured me. 'All you have to do is tickle him under the chin. Like this.' And she showed me.

I've tried it and it seems to work. But I have a whole new set of worries now which I didn't have before. I sometimes worry when I see women eyeing my altogether too attractive partner in a particular way. I worry when Nicolas is home late or when I'm late getting home from my classes. Ordinary, everyday worries.

But most of all I worry about Beatrice. I worry about her having become me. She is so alone. And what if her past comes tumbling in on her or if her man leaves her?

I worry too that one day she will come walking through the door and demand back what is hers. I want her to know that it wasn't a theft, more of an exchange. That's fair, isn't it? The law allows exchanges. We just walked through each other's windows and into our dreams of each other, a little blindly perhaps, but then seeing is always partial.

So this book is really for Beatrice. To tell her how we came to change places and fill up the bits in us that were lacking. Maybe that's all we ever wanted.